# The King's Marauder

## Also by Dewey Lambdin

*The King's Coat*

*The French Admiral*

*The King's Commission*

*The King's Privateer*

*The Gun Ketch*

*H.M.S. Cockerel*

*A King's Commander*

*Jester's Fortune*

*King's Captain*

*Sea of Grey*

*Havoc's Sword*

*The Captain's Vengeance*

*A King's Trade*

*Troubled Waters*

*The Baltic Gambit*

*King, Ship, and Sword*

*The Invasion Year*

*Reefs and Shoals*

*Hostile Shores*

# The King's Marauder

*An Alan Lewrie Naval Adventure*

Dewey Lambdin

THOMAS DUNNE BOOKS
ST. MARTIN'S PRESS
NEW YORK

This is a work of fiction. All of the characters, organizations, and events portrayed in this novel are either products of the author's imagination or are used fictitiously.

THOMAS DUNNE BOOKS.
An imprint of St. Martin's Press.



www.thomasdunnebooks.com
www.stmartins.com



The Library of Congress Cataloging-in-Publication Data is available upon request

ISBN 978-1-250-03005-4 (hardcover)
ISBN 978-1-250-03004-7 (e-book)

St. Martin's Press books may be purchased for educational, business, or promotional use. For information on bulk purchases, please contact Macmillan Corporate and Premium Sales Department at 1-800-221-7945, extension 5442, or write specialmarkets@macmillan.com.

First Edition: February 2014

10 9 8 7 6 5 4 3 2 1

*To the memory of the HMS* Bounty,

*which was lost in Hurricane Sandy off*

*Cape Hatteras, the Graveyard of the Atlantic.*

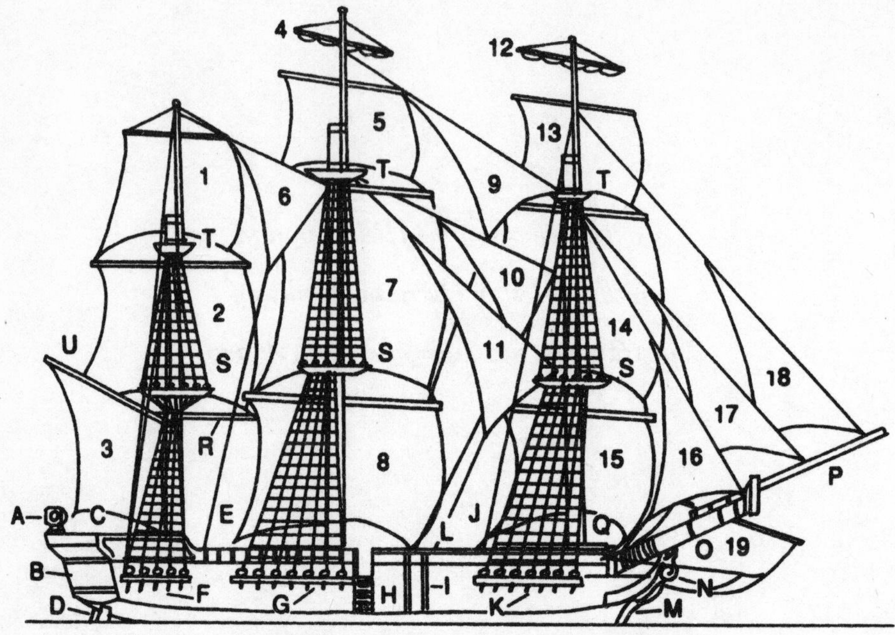


Full-Rigged Ship: Starboard (right) side view

1. Mizen Topgallant
2. Mizen Topsail
3. Spanker
4. Main Royal
5. Main Topgallant
6. Mizen T'gallant Staysail
7. Main Topsail
8. Main Course
9. Main T'gallant Staysail
10. Middle Staysail
11. Main Topmast Staysail
12. Fore Royal
13. Fore Topgallant
14. Fore Topsail
15. Fore Course
16. Fore Topmast Staysail
17. Inner Jib
18. Outer Flying Jib
19. Spritsail

A. Taffrail & Lanterns
B. Stern & Quarter-galleries
C. Poop Deck/Great Cabins Under
D. Rudder & Transom Post
E. Quarterdeck
F. Mizen Chains & Stays
G. Main Chains & Stays
H. Boarding Battens/Entry Port
I. Cargo Loading Skids
J. Shrouds & Ratlines
K. Fore Chains & Stays
L. Waist
M. Gripe & Cutwater
N. Figurehead & Beakhead Rails
O. Bow Sprit
P. Jib Boom
Q. Foc's'le & Anchor Cat-heads
R. Cro'jack Yard (no sail fitted)
S. Top Platforms
T. Cross-Trees
U. Spanker Gaff

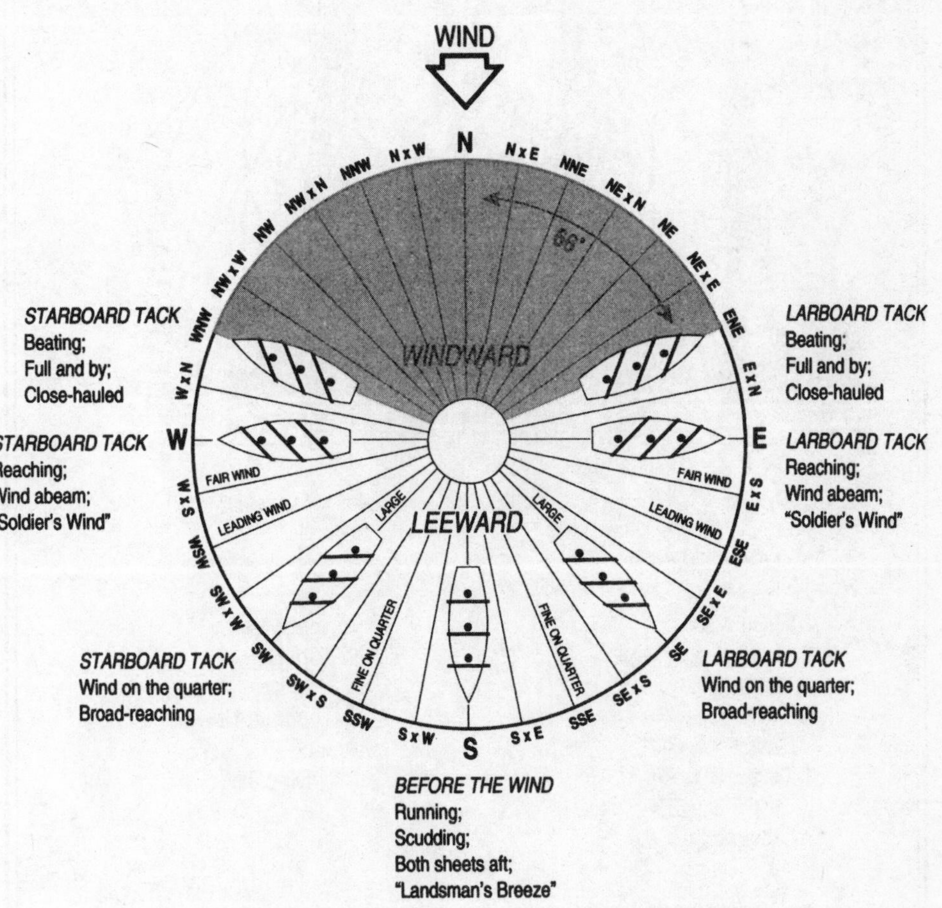


*POINTS OF SAIL AND 32-POINT WIND-ROSE*

ANDALUSIA
N
Mi.
20
40
CÓRDOBA
SEVILLA
Huelva
La Rabida
GRANADA
Palomares
Garrucha
Mojacar
Sierra Alhamilla
Sierra Nevada
Sierra de Almijara
Órjiva
Almeria
Sanlúcar de Barrameda
MÁLAGA
Almuñécar
Motril
Adra
El Ejido
Aguadulce
Roquetas de Mar
Almerimar
Salobreña
Cabo de Gata
Costa de Almeria
Serrania de Ronda
Benalmádena
Cádiz
Puerto Banús
Fuengirola
Marbella
Estepona
Sierra Bermeja
Costa del Sol
San Roque
Cape Trafalgar
La Lina de la Concepcion
Algeciras
Gibraltar
Tarifa
Strait of Gibraltar
Ceuta
NORTH ATLANTIC OCEAN
MEDITERRANEAN SEA

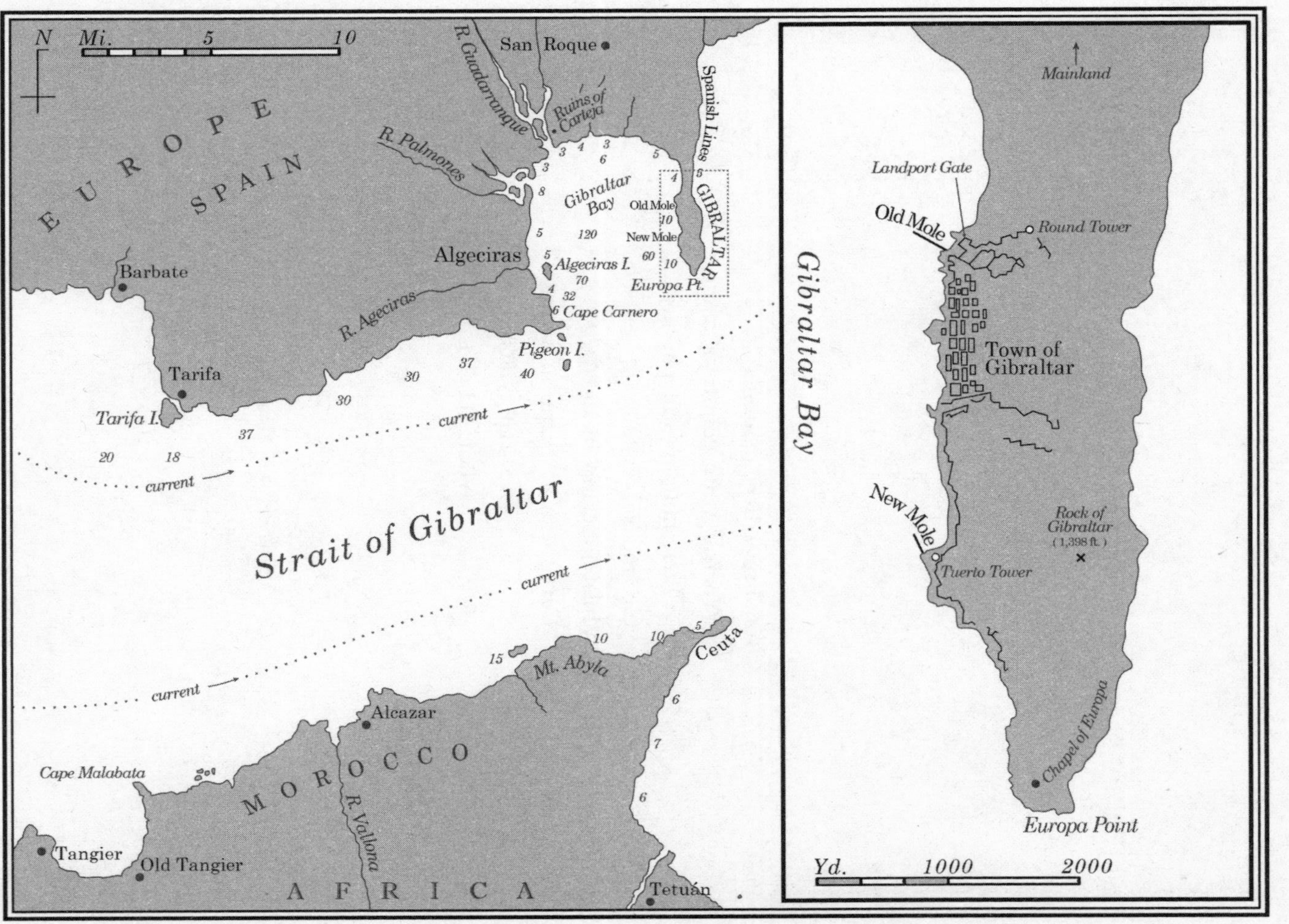
N
Mi. 5 10
E U R O P E
SPAIN
San Roque
R. Guadarranque
Ruins of Carteja
R. Palmones
Spanish Lines
GIBRALTAR
Gibraltar Bay
Old Mole
New Mole
Europa Pt.
Algeciras
Algeciras I.
Cape Carnero
Pigeon I.
R. Ageciras
Barbate
Tarifa
Tarifa I.
current
Strait of Gibraltar
Ceuta
Mt. Abyla
Alcazar
MOROCCO
R. Vallona
Cape Malabata
Tangier
Old Tangier
A F R I C A
Tetuán
Gibraltar Bay
Mainland
Landport Gate
Round Tower
Town of Gibraltar
Rock of Gibraltar (1,398 ft.)
Tuerto Tower
Chapel of Europa
Europa Point
Yd. 1000 2000

You brave heroic minds
  Worthy your country's name,
    That honour still pursue;
  Go and subdue!
Whilst loitering hinds
  Lurk here at home in shame.

"To THE VIRGINIAN VOYAGE"
MICHAEL DRAYTON (1563-1631)

# PROLOGUE

A wet sheet and a flowing sea,
A wind that follows fast
And fills the white and rustling sail
And bends the gallant mast;
And bends the gallant mast, my boys,
While like the eagle free
Away the good ship flies, and leaves
Old England on the lee.

"A Wet Sheet and Flowing Sea"
Alan Cunningham (1784-1842)

# CHAPTER ONE

After a few months at his father's estate in Anglesgreen, in the North Downs of Surrey, the bustle and clatter, the crowded business of London and its teeming throngs seemed loud and alien to Captain Alan Lewrie, RN. Oh, he'd come up to the city very briefly in January for his quarterly appearance before the Councillour of The Cheque to collect his half-pay, but then had just as quickly coached back to rusticity, and further healing. This time, though, London seemed more promising, more challenging, and Lewrie was prepared for a longer stay, to lay siege, as it were, at Admiralty right through the budding spring of 1807 for as long as necessary 'til he'd gotten himself a new active commission.

Pettus, his manservant, and former cabin steward aboard his last ship, the 38-gunned Fifth Rate *Reliant* frigate, had no such concern for the long term, though, and was sliding from one side of the front coach seat to the other to peer out the windows at all of the hubub, as eagerly as some "Country-Put" who'd spent his entire life in one wee village. Pettus did so so energetically that Lewrie had half a mind to chide him to sit still. Thankfully, their coach came at last to the corner of Duke Street and Wigmore Street, and their pre-arranged lodgings at the Madeira Club. A letter in request, one quick reply, and Lewrie and his man had been assured room for as long as he wished; it was a certitude, for Lewrie's father, Sir Hugo St. George Willoughby, was one of the founding investors in the club, and Lewrie was considered a legacy, and at a much-reduced rate, to boot!

"At last," Lewrie said with a sigh after their long and slow trip up from Anglesgreen to Guildford, then to the city, on winter-muddied and rutted roads, a trip which had seemed twice as long as usual, with twice the usual traffic. "I'm badly in need of a jaunt to the 'Jakes', and a mug o' somethin' warm!"

By calendar it might be April of 1807, but the winter had been harsh and had lingered. Even with a greatcoat on, and a wool blanket over his lap and legs, the day had started raw and showed little sign of improvement. At least it was not raining, Lewrie could conjure, though the skies were iron grey with quick-scudding low clouds.

The club's doorman scuttled down from the raised entry stoop to fold down the coach's metal steps and open the door, doffing his hat as Lewrie tossed aside the blanket and stepped down to the kerb.

"So good to see you, again, Captain Lewrie," the flunky said.

"Good t'be back, aye," Lewrie replied. "You'll see to my traps and all? Good. Come on, Pettus, let's go in and get warm!"

There was a new clerk behind the entry hall desk and its many letter slots and outerwear racks, who looked up from his paperwork as the doors opened, admitting a quick breath of nippy damp wind, and a gentleman new to him.

"Captain Alan Lewrie," Lewrie said, naming himself as he took off his hat and gloves, "I believe ye have rooms reserved for me and my man?"

"Ehm . . . let me see . . . yes, we do, sir," the clerk perked up after looking over his lists quickly. "On the third storey, facing the street, sir, but with a fireplace that draws very well."

"Topping!" Lewrie heartily exclaimed, clapping his gloves on the palm of his opposite hand, before Pettus helped him remove his greatcoat.

The new clerk wondered whether this Captain Lewrie was Army or Navy, for there was no outward sign since he was garbed in civilian suitings; he wondered, too, if the fellow had had a long bout of fever, for the man's black coat, figured cream waistcoat, and buff trousers seemed loose on his frame. Beyond that, the clerk beheld a gentleman who looked to be in his mid-fourties, about nine inches above five feet tall, a gentleman who wore his own hair instead of a wig, hair that was slightly curly, mid-brown, brushed back at the temples and over his ears in waves, joined with longer new-styled sideburns, and aha! As this Captain Lewrie turned to speak to his manservant, the clerk espied a wee sprig of a queue at the nape of his neck, bound in black ribbon; so he must be a Navy officer!

This Lewrie seemed a merry sort, with bright grey-blue eyes, merry enough to make the clerk smile a bit broader than his usual wont bestowed upon club members—'til he spotted a faint vertical scar on the man's left cheek. Perhaps, the clerk thought, this Captain Lewrie was not *always* quite so merry, and was a fighting man to be reckoned with!

"We shall see your luggage sent up to your room, sir, and lay a good fire," the clerk promised. He handed over a large key with an oval brass tab.

"I'll leave you t'that, Pettus," Lewrie said, "and once I've re-discovered the 'necessary', I'll be in the Common Rooms."

There was a good fire ablaze in the Common Rooms, too, when Lewrie entered it, and he went to it to rub his cold hands before its warmth, even turn his backside to it and lift the tails of his coat.

"Damned raw day," someone comfortably ensconced in one of the leather wing-back chairs by the fire commented. "Why, good Captain Lewrie!" older Mister Giles, a man of substance in the leather goods trade, exclaimed. "Well met, sir! Up from the country at last, hah! I say, Showalter, Captain Lewrie's back!"

A younger fellow on the opposite side of the fireplace dropped his masking newspaper and rose to his feet with a smile to offer his hand. "Grand to see you, again, sir. Bless me, but do I note that you no longer have need of your walking stick? Capital!"

Showalter had at long last won himself a seat in the House of Commons, a couple of years back, and was quick to inform Lewrie with some glee that he'd just been re-elected by an even greater majority on the hustings. Lewrie recalled that Showalter had spoken of being married with children long before, but still lodged at the Madeira Club when Parliament was in session, leaving wife and children back in his home borough.

"It took a bit of doing, but I finally got strong enough to do without, thankee," Lewrie informed him, looking about for a seat close to the fire. One of the club's waiters in breeches, a livery-striped waistcoat, and white apron, came over at once, dragging another leather wing-back chair for him, and taking his order for a wee pot of very hot tea, with a dollop of rum.

"Healed up and fit enough to seek a new ship, are you, sir?" Mr. Giles good-naturedly asked. "Well, that's grand. Can't allow a fellow such as yourself to be idle and out of the game for too long."

"My thoughts exactly, Mister Giles," Lewrie agreed as his tea was quickly fetched to him. "What's been acting in London in my absence? Anything good at the theatres?"

"Well, I'm not all that much a patron of the stage," Showalter told him, "not like our former member, Major Baird, haw!" he added, pulling a face. Before he had finally found a suitable wife, Major Baird had haunted Covent Garden and Drury Lane, in search of covert, upright, and oral sex from the orange-selling theatre girls. "I favor the symphony, myself, and I heard a good'un two nights ago. That Austrian fellow, Beethoven? He named it the *Eroica*. It plays through the month . . ."

"Dedicated to the Corsican Ogre, Napoleon Bonaparte," Giles grumbled, working his mouth in distaste, "damn his eyes."

"*Re*-dedicated to Admiral Nelson, as the programme declared when I attended," Showalter corrected. "And rightly so."

"Amen," Lewrie agreed, thinking that he would take it in.

"And, Baird's still a member, though he don't come by half as much as before," Giles supplied. "A man needs good company and a fine meal every now and then, finer than what his own household can offer, I'd expect. Get away from wife and kiddies?"

"Pilkington is still with us," Showalter told Lewrie. "Still as much a Cassandra as ever. Gloom, doom, and the ruin of trade."

"Perhaps not a *true* Cassandra, sir," Giles quibbled. "Mind, she was always *right* in her dire predictions, quite unlike Pilkington."

"The Berlin Decrees have Pilkington nigh-wailing and wringing his hands," Showalter said with a laugh.

*Mustive missed somethin' in the papers,* Lewrie thought; *What the Devil are the Berlin Decrees? Should I admit my ignorance?*

"I recall readin' *something* of 'em in the papers," Lewrie carefully said with a dismissive shrug. "After Christmas, I think?"

"Yes, after Napoleon finished off the Prussians," Mr. Giles said, nodding in agreement. "The Ogre said he'd make economic war as well as the regular sort against us. Now he's taken most of Europe and set up his so-called Confederation of the Rhine, he decreed that every port under his control will deny any British goods, and forbid anyone in Europe to have truck with us, cutting us off from any and all of *their* goods."

"Yes, and any neutral ship that's put into any of our ports to be inspected for contraband, he'll seize," Showalter huffily stuck in. "The nerve of the man! If the Americans, for example, obey our Orders In Council and call in Great Britain first, they'll be banned to land their goods in Europe. If they sail direct for the Continent, despite us, *our* Navy can seize them, so God only knows what the neutrals will do. Caught 'twixt the Devil and the Deep Blue Sea, what? I *did* hear that the Americans might just embargo all European trade altogether!"

"Tosh!" Lewrie exclaimed. "Sharp-practised Yankee merchants to just give up *trade?* That's inconceivable."

*So* that's *what it's all about*, he assured himself.

"It'll never work, you know," Mr. Giles pooh-poohed. "There's Portugal, there's still the great trade with Russia, with us getting all her hides and timber, Sweden and her iron ore, there's our goods going to the United States, and so many ports still open to us in the Mediterranean . . . and, our avid and able smugglers."

"And the Danes," Showalter reminded them.

"Why, the leather trade's never been better!" Mr. Giles boasted. "Austria, the Russians, as they rebuild their armies, their orders for boots, shoes, and soldiers' accoutrements have never been higher. Do mark my words, sirs . . . Napoleon's much-vaunted Continental System is more-like to result in the utter economic strangulation of France!"

"And, pray God, sir, all Napoleon's allies," Showalter gravely said with a firm affirmative nod of his head.

"Wool's high, too," Mr. Giles ruminated, looking sage and content. "Mister Meacham . . . you haven't met him yet, Lewrie, he's new to us, from the Midlands . . . was in town a month ago to contract with agents for foreign buyers of his goods, and was positively *exultant* with the results! So much so that he contemplated opening an entire newer and larger mill, due to the great demand."

"Almost every member I've spoken to here with any ties to the manufacturing or export trade still seems to be doing extremely well," Showalter contributed with a grin. "That's not to say that it'll last, but for now, Bonaparte's edict is toothless. And, as Mister Giles believes, it'll hurt the French much more than us. We've the whole *world* for our market, our colonial possessions aside, with the largest fleet of merchantmen, and the

Royal Navy to protect them. And what do the French have? Blockade, laid-up ships, grass growing on the piers, and grinding poverty."

The Madeira Club had been founded by Sir Hugo St. George Willoughby, Sir Malcom Shockley, and four or five other gentlemen, most of them in trade. Sir Malcom and Lewrie's father could have joined one of the more esteemed gentlemen's clubs like Boodle's, Almack's—well, in Sir Hugo's case, that might've been a stretch since he had been tainted with the tarbrush of a rogue ever since the Hell-Fire Club had been exposed—but it had been Sir Malcom's, and the bulk of the original founders', idea that there must be a place where sober and industrious men who'd made themselves, and made large piles of money in trade and manufacturing, could commingle, lodge comfortably when in London, dine extremely, well, and enjoy a fine wine cellar. Such men might be bags wealthier than the members of the prestigious gentlemen's clubs, but they were in *Trade,* did not own great country estates, had not attended Oxford or Cambridge, and did not live on their rents and the produce of their lands. It was good odds they would be rejected if they tried to apply.

Lewrie couldn't have cared less whether they were secret Druids. The Madeira Club offered clean, comfortable rooms, good meals, and a *very* extensive selection of wines—they even managed to stock some of his favourite aged American corn whisky!—and he would be the last person to denigrate someone else because he was not titled or one of the great, landed Squirearchy. His own knighthood and baronetcy was a bitter joke to him, already, awarded more, he suspected, for political ends to drum up patriotism during the run-up to the re-start of the war with France in 1803. Besides, it had cost the life of his wife, Caroline, shot down on a beach near Calais, a shot meant for him, as they had fled Paris during the Peace of Amiens.

Commercial sorts the bulk of the members might be, but most of them were decent company, during the rare times when Lewrie was not at sea and back in London. The only thing that irked him was the demand for proper decorum and quiet in the wee hours. He could *never* bring a woman up to his rooms on the sly, and riotous hoo-rawing, loud music and song, and flung rolls at meals were right out, too! The club members liked to go to bed early, sleep soundly, and rise too damned early for Lewrie's likes, but . . .

The tall clock in the entry hall chimed half-past five, seemingly a signal to conjure the arrival of several more members, some of them new to

Lewrie, and younger than he. There was a great bustle to doff hats, cloaks, and greatcoats, then rush to the fireplace for a warm-up of hands and backsides. Tea, coffee, and brandy were called for, and swiftly delivered. Lewrie was introduced to the new ones, striving to retain all their names, and was greeted by some of the longer-timed members he'd met before. The newer members, after thawing out, drifted to the tables and seating arrangements in other parts of the Common Rooms.

"Nice-enough fellows," Mr. Giles allowed in a hushed voice to Lewrie, leaning over towards him. "But, most don't lodge here, thank the Lord. Our new'uns are a bit too boisterous for me. The club's changing, perhaps not for the better. Why, next thing you know, we will have women dined in!"

"Ahem," someone said in a low voice, coughing into his fist. "Captain Lewrie?" It was the manager, Hoyle.

"Aye, Mister Hoyle?" Lewrie replied, swivelling about.

"My apologies, sir, about your assignment of rooms. The clerk is new, and did not know of your, ehm . . . infirmity," Hoyle muttered, all but wringing his hands. "I will see that you're moved to a lower storey . . ."

"Not a bit of it, Mister Hoyle!" Lewrie said with a laugh. "I am not the man I was when last I came, in January. I'm fit as a fiddle, and even danced the hours away at the last country ball, so the third storey's just fine for me. No reason for my man, Pettus, to be shifting my things round."

"Really, sir?" Hoyle said, eyebrows up in surprise. "Why, that is wonderful . . . good news, indeed. My congratulations, sir! Do you need anything, though, just let us know."

"Thankee, Hoyle, and I shall," Lewrie assured him.

Mr. Giles levered himself up from his chair after Hoyle left.

"Save my seat for me, will you, gentlemen? I will return, anon. And, does the waiter come round in my absence, I'd admire a brandy. I think it's late enough in the day to indulge. Sun's under the yardarm, hey, Captain Lewrie?"

"Somewhere in the world, aye, Mister Giles," Lewrie agreed.

"In cold weather, he's a permanent fixture by the hearth, is our Mister Giles," Showalter wryly whispered as the older fellow departed. "And, none too keen on some of the newer members. Why, half of them are *junior* partners in their concerns, not owners. An attorney or three, fellows from the 'Change, even some serving officers. Poor Giles is sure they'll steal his seat if he's not careful!"

"Sounds as if things might become more lively round here than in the past?" Lewrie speculated.

"Only partially," Showalter seemed to mourn, "and that only 'til bedtime for the oldsters. After that, it's funereal, more's the pity. At least, the mood's brighter at mealtimes, and the victuals are still excellent!"

# CHAPTER TWO

"Will there be anything else tonight, sir?" Pettus asked after he'd tugged Lewrie's top-boots off, hung up his suitings, waist-coat and shirt, and handed him a thick robe.

"Don't think so, Pettus, no," Lewrie told him. "I think that I have all that I'll need 'til morning."

His best-dress Navy uniform was hung up on a rack in a corner, brushed and sponged for his appearance at Admiralty, the coat with the star of the Order of The Bath attached, the blue sash that went with it freshly pressed wrinkle-free, as was his neck-stock and shirt. Snowy white duck breeches awaited the morning, as did a pair of gold-tasseled Hessian boots, newly daubed and brushed. There was a carafe of water with a clean glass atop, for rinsing sleep from his mouth and brushing his teeth with tooth powder. His "housewife" kit for shaving was laid out by the wash-hand stand, and a half-pint glass bottle of whisky stood on the nightstand. The chamberpot was clean and empty, so far, and in all, he was set for the night.

"Six in the morning, sir?" Pettus asked.

"Aye, six, and have a good night, Pettus," Lewrie bade him.

Once alone, Lewrie poured himself some whisky and went to the chair by the fire, taking along a candelabra so he could at last read one of the London papers, abandoned in the Common Rooms after supper.

The supper, well! As toothsome as his personal cook, Yeovill, prepared his meals, the club's cooks could give him a run for his money. There had been breaded flounder, sliced turkey with red currant sauce, and prime rib of beef for the main courses, with lashings of green peas, beans, hot-house asparagus, and potatoes, both mashed and *au gratin*, with sweet figgy-dowdy to finish it off, then port or sherry, nuts and sweet bisquits to cap it all off.

Showalter had been right; the company at-table *had* been most lively, witty, and amusing, more so than Lewrie could recall from his earlier stays. Nobody had broken into song, but they could have!

Of course, after supper, a good part of the diners had left to return to their regular lodgings or go about the town to seek their further amusements, or pleasures, and but for a few hold-outs in the Common Rooms, the club had gone quiet once more, with most of the members who lodged off to bed at an early hour. After a brandy by the fire, Lewrie had toddled off, too.

Even with the four candles and the light of the fire reflected off the brass back plate, reading the paper was hard going. He gave it up and went to bed, doffing his robe and quickly sliding under the thick covers, snuffing all but one candle to savour his whisky.

Lewrie did, before pulling up the blankets and coverlet, raise his right leg and look once more at his thigh, grimacing again at the ragged, round, and dis-coloured puckered scar from a lucky long-range shot by a Spanish sailor, made even worse by the rough and un-gentle ministrations of his Ship's Surgeon, Mr. Mainwaring, as he'd probed deep for the bullet, the patches of cotton duck from his breeches, his silk shirt-tails, and his muslin underdrawers with long pincers gouging remorselessly for the very last thread.

That wound was not the only one he'd suffered in his twenty-seven years in the Navy, but by God, it had been the most painful, a shrieking agony that seemed to last as long as the pangs of Hell! Even the thought of it made him shiver. He'd come to from a fever and laudanum-laced stupor to find himself in constant, throbbing pain, bound up in baby swaddles, fouling himself, and helpless, unable to crawl out of his hanging bed-cot and make it to his quarter-gallery, for an embarrassing fortnight. When he did manage to move without the pain immobilising him, it had taken Pettus and his cabin-servant, Jessop, to support him for a fortnight more.

*At least I could wipe mine own arse!* he thought.

When he could put slop trousers or breeches on, and attend to ship's business once more, there had first been a crutch to aid him, with a watchful Pettus or Jessop at his elbow, still. Graduating to a walking stick had felt like marvellous progress, but . . . he had had need of it from their break in passage at St. Helena all the way to England, through decommissioning *Reliant*, reporting to Admiralty, and going home to Anglesgreen, and his father's house. At least Sir Hugo had patterned his house after a rambling Hindoo *bungalow* so there were no stairs to manage!

He'd gone on half-pay a *cripple*, a weak-legged shambler with a dubious future. Even mounting or dis-mounting a horse, or taking a morning ride at only a walk, not a trot, was a fearsome chore, and could cause a dull and deep ache! For a time, Lewrie had dreaded that not only would he never be called to service again, there was a good chance that he would be doomed to be only *half* a full man!

*Thank God*, again, *for Will Cony*, he grimly thought.

Over the years since first settling in Anglesgreen near his in-laws in 1789 to live upon a rented farm, whenever Lewrie had returned, whether from London or the sea, his first stop had always been the Old Ploughman public house. In the early days, when old Mr. Beakman had owned it, the Old Ploughman looked and felt smoky, grimy, and ancient, as it indeed was, the interior dim and low-ceilinged, the plastered walls and overhead beams dark with hundreds of years of hearth smoke.

Its customers were mostly the common folk of the village, with small farmers, cottagers, and day labourers thrown in. The finer Red Swan Inn, a larger and airier red brick building which sat at the far Western end of the long, grassy-green common which ran along the narrow river that bisected Anglesgreen, had always been the best establishment but it had not been for Lewrie. The richer Squirearchy gathered there, including Sir Romney Embleton, the largest landowner around and magistrate, and his spiteful son Harry, who had "had his cap set" for Caroline Chiswick, who had married Lewrie instead, just before taking on his first, command of little HMS *Alacrity* in 1786. They had returned three years later with one child born and another on the way, making Harry grind his teeth anew.

No, Lewrie would never be welcome in the Red Swan, even now that Harry had managed to find a woman who would put up with him and had a family of his own!

A few years back, Lewrie's long-time manservant, cabin-steward, and Cox'n, Will Cony, had come back to Anglesgreen with carefully saved prize money, with a foot shot off to end his own Navy service, and he and his wife, Maggie, had bought the Old Ploughman from Beakman, and had turned it into a much cleaner, brighter tavern, where Lewrie would always be welcome.

And such was the case when his coach rattled to a stop on the gravelled turn-out, bearing Lewrie, Pettus, Jessop, and Yeovill, with a second dray waggon following with Liam Desmond and Patrick Furfy aboard, which bore all his cabin furnishings and personal goods.

"Captain Lewrie, sir!" a fit and good-looking young fellow in a publican's blue apron called out once he had come out to see what the noise was about. The lad looked like a younger version of Will Cony, but Lewrie couldn't recall his name, right off. There were three boys born to the Conys, and Lewrie's sons had played with them, no matter what his in-laws and Uncle Phineas Chiswick thought of it.

"Little Will, sir!" the lad prompted, beaming fit to bust.

"Good Lord, the spittin' image of your dad at his age!" Lewrie exclaimed as he carefully levered himself off the bench seat into the doorway of the coach. "Where *do* the years go? 'Little', my eye!"

"Father! Captain Lewrie's come home!" Little Will shouted over his shoulder towards the half-opened doors. "Come quick!"

Lewrie put his good left leg on the first of the folding metal coach steps, clung to the door to place his sore right one on it, then slowly descended, wincing when he put weight upon his bad leg. Once on the ground, his stout walking stick eased the pressure. Just at that moment, Will Cony came out, began to smile a welcome, but froze, and got a worried look oh his face.

"Dear God, sir, but what've the bastard Frogs done t'ya!" Will gasped, coming close as if to give him a shoulder to lean on. "Let's git ya in outta the cold, and sit ya down with a mug o' warm ale."

"Wasn't the Frogs, Will, but the Dons, this time," Lewrie said. "And aye, a good chair and a pint of your best'd be more than welcome. Ale for all. Summon the coachee and the waggon driver, Pettus, and I expect they're in need, too."

*Christ, we could make a passable pair o' drummers!* Lewrie imagined as they went inside. Will Cony's artificial "board foot" boot shuffled and thumped with each step, right alongside the matching tap of Lewrie's cane almost made a *rubato* rhythm!

He shed his hat and greatcoat and took ease in a sturdy wooden chair at a table near one of the fireplaces, letting out a wee sigh of relief from pain. A moment later, though, and Lewrie was struggling to rise as Maggie Cony and the other two Cony sons came bustling out from the kitchens. "La, don't ye be gettin' up, Cap'm Lewrie!" Maggie cried. "Lord, but it's good t'see ye back, hurt or no. Ye remember Thomas and Anthony, little Tony? Well, none of 'em so little now. Ye'll be suppin' with us here?"

"I sent word ahead to my father's place that we'd be arriving, so I expect his house staff's layin' on something, but thankee for the offer, Maggie," Lewrie explained. "I wouldn't want them to put themselves out for nothing. Now I'm ashore on half-pay, you'll be seein' more than enough o' me, for mid-day dinners, and t'read the papers."

"A pint o' the fall ale, sir," the fetching brunette waitress Lewrie recalled from three years before said, bustling to the table with a tray of filled mugs. "An' may I be so bold as t'welcome ye back, sir," she added, with a smile and a brief curtsy.

"Thankee, uh . . ." Lewrie replied, stuck for another name.

"Why, ye recall Abigail, Cap'm," Will Cony said, laughing out loud. "She started with us a bit afore ya got *Reliant* and went away. Don't know what we'd do without 'er."

"Ye could pay me more, am I that good, Mister Cony," Abigail teased before turning away to see to the others at the table.

"So, ya paid her off, at last, sir," Will Cony said, "an' what o' th' local lads I rounded up for ya?"

Lewrie could reassure him that of the twenty volunteers that Will had recruited from Anglesgreen and the farms around, all but two of them were alive and well, though by now surely parcelled out to other ships in need of crew whilst *Reliant* went into the graving docks to be substantially rebuilt. It was the way of the Navy, as Will Cony ruefully knew.

"Hated t'give 'em up," Lewrie admitted. "The local lads might have come aboard as raw Landsmen, but they made fine topmen and Ordinary Seamen by the end. All of 'em a parcel better than the dregs from the County Quotas. Even worse than what the 'Press dragged in for us, in the old days, Will. My word, that is a damned fine ale, as good as you've ever brewed!" Lewrie told him, after a first, deep taste.

"Aye, we've had a couple o' good years," Cony modestly boasted, "fine barley, fine rye, and splendid hops, and folk hereabout tell me even the Red Swan can't match us. But . . ." he went on, sighing, "nowadays, folk're callin' for city-brewed ale, beers, porters, an' stouts, and there's chapmen in all the time, floggin' waggonloads o' kegs, an' tryin' t'sign me up t'one brand, exclusive. Puttin' th' squeeze on us somethin' fierce. Fine for a big town with lots o' taverns, but here?"

"*I'd* drink yer ale th' whole day long, Mister Cony, an' even say no t'Guinness!" Patrick Furfy hooted from his table.

Lewrie had no time to tell Cony of his adventures, nor how he had been wounded, promising that he would be back in another day, once he'd gotten settled at his father's estate.

"It may be I'll become a *permanent* fixture," Lewrie said with a grimace, tapping his right thigh. "The Navy may not have me anymore."

"Well, it ain't like the Dons shot it *off*, sir!" Cony exclaimed. "Or, yer 'saw-bones' shortened ya. A few months in the country'll do wonders for ya, we'll see t'that. Maggie's cookin'll put some meat on yer bones, an' we'll have ya dancin' by spring. Look at me, sir, with my foot shot off. I *walked* meself t'rights, an' now I'm as spry as a *pup*, an' wot *I* could do, *you* can do, s'truth. I'm yer man fer that!"

"I may take you up on that, Will," Lewrie promised, though not putting too much hope in the offer. "As for now, though, we'd better be gettin' on to my father's place before dark. What's the reckoning?" he said, reaching for his coin purse, and the new-fangled paper currency.

"You settle in, and come on back down, when yer up to it, Cap'm Lewrie, and we'll see to ya," Cony offered again.

# CHAPTER THREE

The Old Ploughman just might be the only place in Anglesgreen where Lewrie felt true comfort. He certainly did not feel at ease at his father's house. Of only one storey or not, Sir Hugo St. George Willoughby had built *Dun Roman* to ramble all over the gently sloped hilltop, incorporating the ancient ruin of a stone watchtower into it, with a Hindoo-style covered gallery across the front of the central section, English weather be-damned, a gravelled roundabout drive in front of that, with a Mediterranean-styled fountain, replete with three very lasciviously carved water-bearing nymphs in the centre, all surrounded by terra cotta planters and flowering shrubs, in season.

*Just how much loot* did *the old fart fetch back from India?* he was forced to wonder; *And where did he develop such good taste? And then he just* had *t'name it so lamely!*

"Done Roaming", which was the real meaning upon which the pun of *Dun Roman* was based, was more fitting on a weekender tradesman's cottage in Islington, for God's sake! Oh, it had been grand when Lewrie had first seen it, ages ago, and once inside, it had gotten made over over the years into a marvel. Spacious entry foyer, first salon to the right, library-office-study to the left; formal dining room aft of that, smaller *en famille* breakfasting room off that, then the entertaining hall astern of all those, big enough for a game of tennis, and the rare ball. There were two wings, with four bed-chambers in each, with his father's the largest. One could use a guide to find one's way about, making Lewrie feel as if he was but temporarily residing at a sumptuous hotel!

The house staff was new to him, too, as much as he and his entourage was to them, so everyone felt wary and on guard, from the cool and dignified butler, Mayo, his wife the housekeeper, the footmen and maids, maids of all work, the stout old cook, Mrs. Furlough, who looked on Yeovill as a threat to her job security, right down to the coachman and grooms and the wee young scullery maid!

Lewrie had a set of rooms dedicated as his, with some of his old settee furniture, writing desk, and books and bookcases from the time that he and his late wife, Caroline, had rented a farm and had run up a pleasant house when they'd come back to Anglesgreen from the Bahamas in 1789 . . . painfully, Sir Hugo had hung Caroline's portrait in there, the one done in '86 when she'd been a new and happy bride.

At least he had Pettus as someone familiar to do for him, and Jessop, when he wasn't hanging round the barns and stables, gawking and full of a thousand questions, since he'd never been on a working farm before, having been dredged up on the streets of Portsmouth. As for Desmond and Furfy, they'd been to Anglesgreen before, and after a few days of loafing, had pitched in with the farm work, what little there was with winter coming on, assisting the estate manager and the grooms, exercising the saddle horses and teaching Jessop to ride.

Chalky, Lewrie's mostly-white cat, and Bisquit, the former ship's dog, had a myriad of rooms, wardrobes, cabinets, and corners to explore in the house, though the youngest footman had to be assigned to keep an eye on the dog so the polished wood floors and expensive carpets didn't get soiled.

Poor Bisquit. As *Reliant* was de-commissioned, draughts of sailors were paid off and re-assigned to other ships, leaving Bisquit without his long-time playmates and those who would sneak him treats. No one could think what to do with him. The Midshipmens' mess which had snuck him aboard as their pet in the beginning certainly could not take him to their new ships, and neither could the Commission Officers; any new captain of theirs might have Bisquit thrown ashore to fend for himself! Even the Standing Officers who remained with the ship 'til she was at last scrapped could not keep him; their wives and children would be living aboard with them 'til *Reliant* was out of the yards and re-commissioned and would eventually have to place the dog's fate in the hands of the frigate's new captain. At least Lewrie had a farm, or, technically, he had access to his *father's* estate, where Bisquit could thrive, and, should Lewrie ever gain a new ship and an active commission, the dog might remain, so he had decided to fetch Bisquit along, with a stout leather leash tied to his collar should Bisquit get too distracted and lope off on the journey to get hopelessly lost.

Except for the Old Ploughman, Anglesgreen wasn't all that welcoming, either. His late wife's family had never been all that high on Lewrie from the beginning. His brother in-law Governour Chiswick, once a panther-lean young man, was now pretty much the model for that caricature character John Bull, sure of his opinions, quick to speak them, loud, and as stout and round as an overfed steer. Their uncle, Phineas Chiswick, who had grudgingly taken them in as refugees after the American Revolution, penniless refugees at that, was now in his dotage, a whinnying, drooling, wheelchair-bound wreck with no surviving male heir, so it would be Governour who would inherit everything, and Governour had been managing in his place for so long that he'd become ever *more* sure that his way was best for everyone, and looked on Lewrie as an un-wanted interloper.

Lewrie might have found an ally in his other brother in-law, Burgess Chiswick, but Burgess was now a Major in a regiment of Foot, and only rarely down to Anglesgreen, and his own estate and house, which just happened to be the one that Lewrie and Caroline had rented and built, the farm and house that Uncle Phineas had sold right out from under him after Caroline had died. Burgess had married, and his new father-in-law, Mr. Robert Trencher, had purchased it for a wedding present, making Uncle Phineas Chiswick a pile of "tin"!

Perhaps the most distressing of all was the reception that Lewrie got from his own daugther, Charlotte. Ever her mother's child, she had once been the dearest little angel, sweet and adorable—even if he'd never gotten the hang of raising a girl; boys were much easier for Lewrie to understand—who'd adored her father. Once!

That had changed once Caroline began to get scurrilous letters intimating that Lewrie was an unfaithful cad, naming names, citing salacious intimate details, and turning Caroline into a suspicious, bitter harridan, even suspecting and raging at their completely innocent ward, Sophie de Maubeuge.

Sophie? Never. The rest, unfortunately, was too damned true, revealed in spite by a former lover, Theoni Kavares Connor, with whom Lewrie had fathered a child, which fact had taken him some time to discover. Charlotte had been the only child at home to soak up her mother's anger. Already turned against him, Caroline's murder as they had fled France was the final straw, Lewrie's fault alone, and *damn* Harry Embleton and Governour Chiswick for convincing Charlotte that that was true!

A day or two of retiring early and sleeping late to catch up on years of missed rest, hours in the library with books new to him, and tentative walks outdoors, checking up on his favourite saddle horse, Anson, but unsure if he was ready to try riding, yet, Lewrie *had* to call upon her at Governour's house, where Charlotte had lodged since he had been called back to service in the Spring of 1803. He clambered, painfully, into a one-horse carriage and let the unfamiliar coachman, Waddey, bear him over.

Governour's sweet but meek wife, Millicent, came dashing from the parlour as their butler announced his arrival, and rushed to give him a hug, crying, "You poor man! We are so relieved to see you alive. When we got your letter saying that your ship would be paying off and you would be coming home, so *cruelly* wounded, I've been half beside myself with worry! So many earnest prayers have we lifted to Heaven for your healing."

"For which I thankee kindly, Millicent," Lewrie replied, giving her a warm hug back. "The healing's coming, slowly. Perhaps a spell in the country'll do for the rest. Is Governour in?"

"He's been called away to speak with Sir Romney and some others at the Red Swan," Millicent told him with a toss of her head. "Local politics, to prepare for the next by-election to keep Harry in office."

That was a slap in the face; Lewrie had sent a note round that set the date and time of his coming.

"And Charlotte?" he further asked.

"She's in the parlour," Millicent said. "Come in and see her."

Lewrie stumped his way to the wide double doors and stepped through. For a second, his heart jumped as if he'd seen the ghost of his late wife, for Charlotte, now fifteen, was eerily the very image of Caroline as she had been at eighteen when first he had met her in her family's poor lodgings in Wilmington, North Carolina, just before the evacuation of Loyalists had begun.

Charlotte was primly seated in a wing-back chair near the tall windows, a teacup and saucer beside her, and that pestiferous little lap dog of hers balanced on the chair's arm. At its first sight of him, it picked up where it had left off years before, wiggling as if ready to attack, and barking shrilly. Charlotte's gaze was level and neutral, and she made no attempt to rise and give him even the barest greeting. Her only reaction was a slow, indrawn breath.

"Hallo, Charlotte . . . back from the wars, at last," Lewrie said, starting to walk towards her with a tentative grin on his phyz.

"Yes, you are, as *anyone* may evidently see," Charlotte replied in an arch drawl suitable to some fatuous ass who had just announced a blinding glimpse of the obvious.

"Oh, sit you down in the other chair, Alan, and have some tea," Millicent prompted, going to Charlotte's chair to scoop up the noisy dog and shoo it towards the entry hall. It came right back to defend its mistress, making fake lunges at Lewrie's boots, to the point that Millicent dumped it in the hall and shut the doors on it, at least muting the growls and yaps.

He stayed a little more than an hour, and a testy one it was.

Yes, Charlotte had gotten his letters, but left it to Governour to inform him of her progress. Yes, she had heard from her younger brother, Hugh, and of his doings aboard HMS *Pegasus,* and the battle of Trafalgar. Yes, she also had gotten letters from her older brother, Sewallis, also a Midshipman aboard the Third Rate HMS *Aeneas*. *Most* pointedly, she recalled Sewallis's description of being in Portsmouth the same time as Lewrie, and dining with him . . . and his *new* woman!

"The lady is Miss Lydia Stangbourne, the sister of Percy, Viscount Stangbourne," Lewrie explained, "both of whom I met the day that I was knighted and made baronet, at Saint James's Palace."

"Yes, Sewallis *said* that you had begun associating with the better sort," Charlotte had simpered, "though he also said that there are rumours that she is a divorcé? And, in his opinion, nowhere *near* as pretty as our mother was," she'd concluded with a sniff.

No, he hadn't forced Sewallis to go to sea, that had been the lad's own idea, and of his own doing behind everyone's backs, he had to explain for the umpteenth time. And no, he was not getting ready to replace Caroline with another, either!

Of his recent exploits, taking part in the re-capture of the Dutch colony at Cape Town, and his jaunts ashore with the Army, and hunting, then the foolish expedition over to Buenos Aires and the Plate River Estuary, Charlotte was dismissive.

"The papers say that Commodore Popham and General Beresford were both captured, and the entire army lost, and both are to be tried for it," Charlotte said with a *moue*. "A ludicrous endeavour, but one suitable to you, one must suppose," she'd scathingly said, all the while smiling nigh wickedly.

"Charlotte!" Millicent weakly chid her. "Your own father!"

"No matter, Millicent, no matter," Lewrie had said, surrendering any hope of ever thawing his relationship with his daughter. She had, absent her mother, become a product of Governour's biting tutelage, a pupil of his bile. Charlotte had been given a decent education in all the social graces. Lewrie was sure that she excelled at music, grace of carriage, and the housewifery skills necessary for her to become the mistress of some fine house. Earlier on, Governour had written to express how well-tutored and well-read she was. It was just too bad that her lessons in graciousness in speech towards all had been wasted!

*God help the poor bastard who takes* her *for a wife, if he don't toe her line to a Tee!* Lewrie concluded.

"I think I'll be going," Lewrie had announced at last.

"Oh, must you, Alan?" Millicent had fretted.

"So soon? Must you *really?*" Charlotte had echoed with sarcastic feigned sweetness, then pointedly looked away, tending to her teacup.

"Charlotte!" from Millicent, again. "Stay a while longer, Alan, do. Governour is sure to be home, soon."

"I'll run into him, surely. In the village, at church?" Lewrie had said with a shrug. "*Adieu*, my dear."

"*Adieu*," Charlotte had responded with a very brief sweet smile.

*A* proper *father'd break out in tears,* Lewrie told himself on the coachride back to his father's house; *But all* I *want t'do is give the little bitch the thrashin' of her life! She wants t'be Governour's brat, let* him *have her, and* without *my money t'support her arrogant, snippy airs! Let* Governour *pay for all her gowns and bonnets, and the food she eats, and I'll save myself fifty pounds a year, and keep the money I'd planned for her dowry in the Three Percents!*

He wasn't welcome in Anglesgreen, could not think of a single house where people would be glad to greet him. He *could* have camped himself and his people at his father's house in London, but that would not have lasted a week; the old bastard would've run them all off at gunpoint! It would have cost him some, but he *could* have forseen the consequences and rented a small country place just outside London, up the Hampstead Road, or even out to the East in Islington.

"Best, I heal up and go away," he muttered to himself, massaging his achy thigh. "Get started on whatever it takes, straightaway."

Will Cony had overcome *his* maiming. He'd offered to aid Lewrie to overcome his, too. *Why not?* He nodded his head, agreeing with himself, as he determined to ride if he could, coach if he must, down to the Old Ploughman and take Will Cony up on his offer, the very next morning!

# CHAPTER FOUR

"Ow," Lewrie said with a wince, muffling himself to appear stoic and manly. "Bloody stupid damned beast!" he added, reining what *had* been his favourite riding mount to a halt, and steeling himself for a dismount. He coaxed Anson over to the mounting block, slipped his right boot from the off-side stirrup, took a deep breath, and swung over and down, with the reins and his stout walking stick in his left hand. "Uhh!" he grunted as his right leg took his weight.

The Old Ploughman's "daisy kicker" lad took the reins for him and led the horse away to the hitch-rails, leaving Lewrie atop the old wooden mounting block that was usually used only by ladies, trying to decide which leg he'd trust for the first step down. He chose the left one, switched the walking stick to his right hand to support him, set his left boot on the ground, and felt the thigh muscles of his right leg quiver in weakness.

"Christ, this'll never work," he muttered, slowly turning round.

"Tcha, Cap'm Lewrie, you're doin' better," Will Cony said as he swung his substantial bulk from the saddle of his own horse and came to join him. "We haven't been at it a fortnight, and ya made the better part of a mile, this mornin', afore ya had t'saddle up. I'll lay ya a shillin' ya make th' whole mile, t'morra."

Saddling up! Anson wasn't as tall as a blooded hunter or thoroughbred, but getting astride each morning could almost look comical to any passersby. The well-gravelled lane down from *Dun Roman* was a slight slope, but even turning his horse athwart the lane with Lewrie on the uphill side for an inch more advantage was a dread, trusting his right leg long enough to get his left boot in the stirrup, after hiking that better part of a mile, and feeling his wounded leg begin to quiver and ache. This daily exercise was as exhausting as several miles of march following General Sir David Baird's army last January when the Dutch Cape Colony had been re-conquered; Blaauwberg Bay to the Salt River in one day, with a battle included!

Maggie Cony felt it her duty to fatten him up. As soon as he sat down at a table near the fireplace, out came a plate of scrambled eggs, crispy strips of bacon, potato hash, thick slices of toast, with a bowl of butter and a pot of red currant jelly close by, and a cup of scalding hot coffee, which would be refilled several times. Some days it would be pork chops, a smoke-cured ham steak, or a chunk of roast beef instead of bacon. At least Lewrie's aches and pains got rewarded!

Will Cony did a tour of the large room to see that all of his other customers were being taken care of, then fetched himself a mug of hot tea from the kitchen in back, and came to join Lewrie.

"How's he doin', Mister Cony?" Abigail, the brunette waitress, asked as she came to refill Lewrie's cup.

"Nigh a mile t'day, Abigail, nigh onta a mile," Cony boasted.

"That's grand, it is!" Abigail cheerily said. "By Christmas, I wager you'll be runnin' fast as your horses, Captain Lewrie. Do you wish more cream?"

"Aye, thankee," Lewrie agreed.

"I always wondered," the girl breezed on after fetching more cream, "why your father called his house *Dun Roman*."

Lewrie chuckled, then explained the "Done Roaming" pun, which made Abigail groan. "The old tower, well . . . before the Romans came, ancient Britons built wooden hilltop forts, and they called 'em *duns*, and some folk think the tower was a Roman watchtower, but it's too far from the Guildford, Chiddingfold, or Petersfield roads to do 'em any good. Most-like, it was some Norman lord who planned t'run him up a castle and tower, and went broke before he could finish it."

"That, or our people ran th' French bastard off," Cony hooted.

"The church, Saint George's, came later, maybe in the 1500s," Lewrie speculated. "The tower? *Maybe* five hundred years before that."

"*That* old? Lordy!" Abigail exclaimed in surprise.

"And, if ya'd seen th' tavern afore me an' Maggie re-did it, you'da known that the Old Ploughman's nigh older than the church!" Will Cony said with a laugh. "It ain't called th' *Old* Ploughman fer nought."

"As old as me coffee, Abigail!" an elderly follow cried out, raising a laugh, and the girl went to his table to begin joshing with him and his mates.

"Ya been doin' th' sword-play ev'ry day, too, Cap'm Lewrie?" Cony asked as he stirred some of the fresh cream into his tea.

"In the afternoons, after a *good* long rest," Lewrie told him, scoffing his attempts. "Heavy Navy cutlasses, against Desmond or Furfy, for about a half-hour. All I can manage, yet," he said with a shrug. "Yeovill, Pettus, and Jessop have taken up the drill, too. Bored, I expect. Since my father keeps such a large staff, even when he's not here, there's little for them t'do, and Yeovill can't even get within *smellin'* distance of the kitchens, 'less Mistress Furlough'll take a meat chopper to him. It's a damned pity, 'cause she's only a passable cook. Roast, fry, boil, repeat if necessary, hah! Takin' breakfast here's the best meal I see.

"Then, I'll have t'saddle up that fractious damned horse, and trot back uphill," Lewrie gravelled between bites. "Like today, Anson has been ridden so little since I sent him up to Father's stables that he just *won't* go at a walk. Trot, lope, canter . . . ouch!"

"Speakin' o' ancient Britons, sir," Cony slyly said, "ya ever hear of an ambler? They were very popular, back when yer tower and th' church, and th' village were young. Ya don't see 'em much anymore . . . but, there's a smallholder a few miles from here who still breeds 'em, an' sells one, now an' again."

"What's an ambler?" Lewrie asked, perplexed.

"Why, it's a horse, sir!" Cony said with a grin. "They're stout an' cobby, sorta shaggy-lookin', with big hooves like a Clydesdale, an' just as plumy-hairy round th' fetlocks, but they're not over eleven or twelve hands at the withers, and as gentle as baa-lambs. Best of all, they've got a peculiar gait like no other horse. They *pace* at a fast walk . . . how they got their name . . . and can go for hours an' hours, an' th' rider might as well be sittin' in a rockin' chair for all ya'd know, steady as a rock.

"Now, it may be ol' Mister Doaks'd rent ya one for a few weeks, just 'til yer strong enough t'manage yer own horse," Cony suggested. "What say I ride over this afternoon an' speak with him, sir, and if I can strike a deal, I'll bring one up t'th' house t'morra mornin' for you t'try."

"We could try one out, aye," Lewrie agreed after a ponder. "Do ye think a pound note'd suit him?"

"Bring ya change *back*, Cap'm Lewrie," Cony promised.

"'Tis good I *didn't* bet ya a shillin', sir, for I'da lost," Cony said as they stopped by a gnarled old oak tree. "That's a full mile ya done this mornin', an' Maggie's sureta throw in a beef steak t'reward ya! Want t'go a bit more?"

"A furlong more, maybe . . . to the stile yonder," Lewrie decided.

"Yer on, sir!" Cony quickly agreed and they paced off once more, leading their mounts. They made that furlong to the stile, then drew to another stop, with Lewrie panting a little. He reached down to massage his right leg which still felt weak, but this morning, at least, it did not ache quite as loudly as the day before. He led "Peterkin" round alee and contemplated the brute.

The rented ambler *was* a shaggy thing, with hair almost as long as Scottish red cattle, its coat mottled grey with long white mane and tail. Its back was broader than an average saddle horse, so his usual saddle would not suit, and for two shillings more Cony had rented this older-style saddle with a prominent horn, a taller and wider cantle at the rear, and broader stirrup straps. He had tried out mounting up at the house's stables, still using the mounting block, adjusting the length of the stirrups to fit him, but now . . .

"Ye goin' t'cooperate, Peterkin?" Lewrie asked it.

The ambler swivelled its head round to look at him and gently whickered, but stood stolid and still, with no tittups.

"Right, then," Lewrie said, steeling himself for sudden pain, and reaching up for the saddle horn. He lifted his left leg and got the toe of his boot in the stirrup and levered himself up and over, and winced . . . but not as badly as before. He clucked and kneed the horse into a walk, then a trot, then a lope, then . . . the ambler began its "amble", as if cantering or galloping were lost arts. "My God!" Lewrie hooted, "it's goin' like a Cambridge coach!"

Cony had to set his horse at a lope to keep up with him, and the last three-quarters of a mile to Anglesgreen went by in a twinkling! Then, after his breakfast, though still using the mounting block, he set Peterkin to his mile-eating pace right off, and it really was a very smooth, jounceless ride up the rising lanes to home, the smoothest of his life.

"I think I love this thing!" Lewrie crowed as he drew rein at the house, and everyone, even Pettus, who was not much of a horseman, wanted to try the ambler out.

Will Cony couldn't ride up to accompany him every morning, but Desmond, Furfy, or Sir Hugo's hired groom, Fowlie, could go along with him on his morning hikes. Fowlie usually rode, leading the ambler as far as Lewrie could walk, then rode with him the rest of the way, but Desmond or Furfy usually led their own mounts to walk alongside him. Both were extremely fond of their own breakfasts at the Old Ploughman, and the chance to flirt with Abigail, Patrick Furfy got tongue-tied and blushed, but Desmond, with a true and merry gift of gab, did the best with her, making the girl's eyes sparkle and laugh out loud.

"And that's how Will and Maggie got together," Lewrie cautioned, "flirtin'. Ye ready for marriage, Desmond?"

"Well, I s'pose a man could do worse, sor," his Cox'n said with a wince at the mention of the word. "Marryin', though . . . Gawd! Who'd have a poor sailor f'r a husband?"

"Maggie Cony," Lewrie teased.

Each morning, Lewrie forced himself to go a furlong more than the day before, and in the afternoons, after a fortnight, he added a walk about the property, down to the stables and barns, the paddocks and pens, and out to the edges of the cleared land round the house. Bisquit was his company on those strolls, eager for new scents, and a thrown stick . . . even if the dog did sometimes confuse Lewrie's walking stick for a toy a time or two, tugging at it to encourage their game. Bisquit would also get distracted by the squirrels or rabbits, but he was, in the main, a good dog and always loped back to Lewrie's side when called.

What to do with the hours between the trip to the village and the stroll, though? Lewrie had all his personal weapons, and in his father's office-library there were enough firearms to field a dozen soldiers, so he added shooting competitions near the foot of the hill to the South, down near the rill, with a rise beyond that as a back-stop. Muskets, fusils, fowling pieces, Hindoo Moghul *jezzails*, blunderbusses, and all sorts of pistols were tried out, and even Jessop and Pettus and Yeovill became passable marksmen.

He *could* have gone hunting in the woodlots, had there been any game worth shooting. He was no longer a Chiswick tenant, denied fish or game which all belonged to the landlord. He was the son of a freeholder on his father's acres. Furfy, though, quickly found the rabbit warrens and snared a few each week, and Jessop got rather good at potting squirrels with a fusil musket.

When it rained or snowed, though, Lewrie had little to occupy his time. He would read by a crackling fire, with Bisquit drowsing by Lewrie's chair, or across his feet, and Chalky, his cat, nodding close to the grate, or spraddled cross one arm of his chair, always with one wary eye out for the dog's doings.

On one of his strolls down to the stables, he saw the junior groom hefting gallon pails of water in each hand, and lifting them up and out to show Fowlie how strong he was, and Lewrie got two of them and filled them with rocks, increasing the weight until he could hold them out and pump them over his head, or swing them back and forth, and found that when he crossed heavy naval cutlasses with Desmond or Furfy, his blade felt no heavier than a butterknife. Needless to say, his footwork at cutlass drill still was lacking.

Harvest festivals, church ales, and supper dances came round, and Lewrie did get invited to some, even Sir Romney Embleton's and at Governour's house a time or two, but he still had need of his walking stick and did not dance, still had need of Peterkin the ambler horse, hot, steamed towels to wrap, round his thigh, and willow bark teas at least twice a day.

The village's surgeon-apothecary hired by Sir Romney Embleton, Mr. Archer, came to cheek up on him every now and then, and he had offered laudanum to ease Lewrie's aches, but Lewrie declined. By November, the aches were not all that bad, and only came when he over-extended himself.

Christmas came and went, and Lewrie had Fowlie return the ambler to his owner, Mr. Doaks. He could manage Anson, again! With more exercise, the horse had become more biddable to go at a walk, and when he was put to the trot or canter, it didn't hurt at all.

At long last, one morning a few weeks before Easter, Lewrie led Anson all the way to the village, on his own feet without need of his walking stick, with Bisquit frisking along with him.

"Good mornin', Will . . . Maggie," he said as he and the dog breezed in. "Good mornin', all."

"Mornin' to ya, sir!" Cony chirpily greeted him. "We've some fine ham f'r yer breakfast this mornin'. And, I reckon yer dog'll be wantin' a slice'r two, as well."

"Here, Will," Lewrie said, handing him the walking stick. "I've no more need of it. Ye can hang it over the fire, or use it for kindlin'. I hiked all the way, today," he boasted. "Oh, I'll ride back, but only 'cause it's perishin' cold this morning," he added after he'd taken a seat at his usual table.

"Huzzah, sir!" Will Cony crowed. "I *told* ya walkin' it away'z th' cure for ya. Wot Mister Archer'd call 'thera' . . . good for ya! Ya ready t'go up to London an' Admiralty, soon'z the weather breaks, I'd expect?"

"The first dry day we get, aye!" Lewrie assured him. "Hey, pup! Want some fried ham? Yes? Ah, you're a good 'un!"

# CHAPTER FIVE

"Good luck, sir," Pettus said as he helped Lewrie into his boat cloak and handed him his hat in the Madeira Club's anteroom.

"Not much'll come of this first visit," Lewrie told him, shrugging off too-high hopes. "All I can manage will be t'let 'em know I'm still alive, healed up, and available. I'll probably be back before mid-day. But thankee for the good wishes, anyway."

It was another breezy and nippy morning, and Lewrie had the club porter whistle up a one-horse hack. He *could* walk all the way, but damned if he would!

Lewrie alit and paid off the coachee in front of the arches of the curtain wall at Admiralty, then hitched a deep breath, squared his shoulders, and walked into the courtyard. It looked to be the typical busy morning, for the courtyard was full of slowly pacing officers and hopeful Midshipmen, and the tea cart was doing a thriving business, in sticky buns and sausages, handing out mis-matched mugs and cups as fast as they could be filled.

"Top o' th' mornin', sir," a grizzled old tiler rasped at him as he approached the doors. "Though I wouldn't get me 'opes up too 'igh, Cap'm. 'Less ye come at their biddin', ye'll 'ave a long wait, an' there's 'underds in there waitin'."

"Morning to you, too," Lewrie said with a faint smile of remembrance. For as long as he could recall, the tilers at the Admiralty were a surly, nigh-insulting lot, former Bosuns or Bosun's Mates who had become unmaimed Greenwich Pensioners, and old fellows who took great joy in bossing officers about. He was *almost* back in service!

Lewrie checked his hat and gloves and boat cloak with the porters, and faced the infamous Waiting Room, which was elbow-to-elbow full, with nary an empty chair to be seen. With so many warm bodies there, the Waiting Room gave off its own particular heat, and smells faintly tinted with salt, tar, and sweat. It must have rained sometime in the wee hours, for Lewrie could also discern the odour of wet wool. Damned if it all smelled . . . nautical!

He plastered a calm smile on his face to show confidence, and slowly paced the room 'til he spotted one of the First Secretary's, Mr. William Marsden's, clerks.

"Good morning, sir," Lewrie said, trying to recall if this one was the "Happy-Making" clerk or the one who dealt with the disappointed. "Captain Sir Alan Lewrie. I wonder if you might see this letter to the Secretary for me, informing him of my availability?"

"Of course, sir," the clerk agreed, then broke away to go up the stairs to the offices above.

Right after his hike all the way to the village on foot, Lewrie had penned a letter to Mr. Marsden, saying that he would be coming up to London, in hopes of an interview. This letter would tell Marsden that he was in town and . . . waiting.

He managed to find a seat after a minute or two, thanks to one very young Lieutenant who thought it a good idea to surrender his to a senior officer who just *might* be taking command of a ship in active commission, and in need of his skills. He even gave up his copy of the *Tatler*!

The magazine proved handy. No matter how long he'd been in the Navy, no matter how many officers he'd served with, there never was a *one* of them in the Waiting Room that he knew in the slightest when he was there. Lewrie determined that he would sit and read 'til the mid-day rush for dinner, then depart with the throng and go back to the Madeira Club for an afternoon nap.

*I might skip tomorrow*, Lewrie thought as he turned pages; *Else I look as desperate as those gammers over yonder.*

Though he did not know their names, there were some familiar faces in the Waiting Room. The two "gammers" were Lieutenants in their mid-to-late fourties, salty "tarpaulin men" who still sported queues as long as marling spikes at the napes of their necks, who haunted the place on a daily basis. And, damned if there wasn't the very same Midshipman who was rumoured to have been calling every day going on three whole years! No-hopers, all, men with no "interest" or patronage who most-like had no income beyond their half-pay, even some Post-Captains and one Rear-Admiral were there this morning, burned permanently brown and as creased as old parchment by long years of previous sea-duty, but now, for one reason or another, un-employable.

*One half-day, every* other *day,* Lewrie told himself; *I swear I can smell* that *stink, too, and I don't want it on me!*

There was an older Post-Captain in a frayed and worn uniform, with ecru woolen stockings instead of white silk or cotton, who suddenly began to cough as if he would hock up half a lung. The old fellow plucked a handkerchief from a side pocket of his coat and put it over his mouth as he began to gargle phlegm and wheeze for his breath.

*Perhaps a half a day, once a* week*!* Lewrie amended to himself as officers to either side of the old fellow began to lean away, or head for the courtyard tea cart or the "jakes" as the liquid-sounding hacking went on and on, and the old Post-Captain went red in the face.

"Perhaps, sir . . ." a Lieutenant nearby suggested, helping him to his feet to steer him outside for fresher, clearer air.

"That don't sound good," a Commander with his single epaulet on his left shoulder muttered to the officers hear him. "Consumption, or Pleurosy, most-like. Anybody know him?"

"Lots of Consumption 'board my last ship," a Lieutenant commented with a wry expression. "Winters in the North Sea, and all our hands cooped up below, with no ventilation, our Surgeon said did it. I'd put my money on Pleurosy, though. The poor fellow don't look as if he's been at sea in ages."

"A bad winter in a boardinghouse, aye," the Commander agreed.

Lewrie went back to his magazine, but, after another hour or so, he had to abandon his seat for a trip to the "necessary", then went out to the courtyard for hot tea, picking up his hat and boat cloak on the way. He pulled out his pocket watch as he stood in the queue, finding that it was nigh eleven in the morning.

*An hour more, and I'm un-moorin',* he told himself as he turned to idly look about the courtyard.

"Good Lord, sir . . . Captain Lewrie?" someone called out.

"Hey? Mister Westcott? Well, just damn my eyes!" Lewrie cried in response as he spotted his former First Officer from HMS *Reliant,* and broke out in a broad grin, leaving the queue to go shake hands. "What the Devil are you doin' here, Geoffrey? I thought you were t'go aboard a new frigate."

"Bad luck, that, sir," Lieutenant Westcott said with a rueful expression. " 'Twas to be the *Weymouth* frigate, a thirty-two, coming in to pay off and refit, from Halifax. Onliest trouble was, she never turned up. After loafing about for two months, Admiralty decided she had foundered somewhere in the North Atlantic and gone down with all hands, without a trace. The hands we'd gathered went off to the receiving ships, and the rest of us were left to twiddle our thumbs."

"After I wrote Admiralty reccommending you?" Lewrie said with a dis-believing scowl. "I told 'em you'd be best employed commandin' a ship of your own, even advance ye to Commander."

"And for that I'm heartily grateful, sir," Westcott said, beaming one of his quick, tooth-baring grins that some people found fierce and off-putting, "but, it doesn't seem to signify with the Navy so far."

*I wonder if that has anything t'do with our bein' part o' Home Popham's idiotic invasion o' Buenos Aires last year,* Lewrie considered; *Did we all get tarred with the same brush?*

"Well, if it's any comfort, I've been twiddlin' my thumbs down at Anglesgreen all winter, myself," Lewrie told him.

"Oh, you don't . . !" Westcott said, looking him over. "Where's your crutch, or cane?" he exclaimed with joy.

"No more need of either!" Lewrie boasted, even essaying a dance step or two to show off, causing them both to laugh, and explaining his winter regimen. "You're goin' in to announce yourself?" Lewrie asked. "I'm for tea, myself, then I'll be right in."

"No rush, in my case, sir," Lt. Westcott said with a despondent shrug. "I'll join you for tea. Christ, anything's better than sitting in there all afternoon. I can sometimes conjure that the Waiting Room is the ante-room to Hades . . . and just as warm!"

They got their tea, with sugar and a dollop of cream that the vendor swore was "fresh-ish" that morning, and wandered a few feet off to sip and savour the warmth on their hands round their mugs.

"You've stayed nearby t'Whitehall, in London all winter?" Lewrie idly asked, fearing that Westcott was over-extended for funds.

"Cross the river in Southwark, sir," Westcott said with another rueful shrug. "Number Nine, Mitre Road. It's been all quite snug and comfortable, and quite reasonable, too. Some of our prize-money came due, from our fight off the Chandeleurs . . . in 1803, at *long* last, hah! And, my father sends me twenty-five pounds *per annum,* so the half-pay on top of all that has kept me well-fed and entertained.

"And, there's the landlady," Westcott smugly added, flashing a grin. "A rather delightful widow in her early thirties."

"A snug berth . . . as it were, Geoffrey?" Lewrie posed with one brow up. For as long as they had served together, Lt. Westcott had been known as a man simply mad for "quim", able to discover a willing wench in the middle of a jungle, or upon a desert island. He was, in point of fact, so libidinous that he put Lewrie in the shade!

In answer, Westcott only cocked his brows and beamed.

"And, dare I ask, sir, if you and Mistress Stangbourne are still on friendly terms?" Westcott went on, between sips of tea.

"A sore subject, Geoffrey," Lewrie told him with a frown, and a wince. " 'Least said, soonest mended', and all that."

"Oh! I'm sorry, sir," Westcott said, looking abashed.

"So am I," Lewrie sadly agreed. "I'll tell you of it, sometime. Here, now! How'd you like a fine supper with me at the Madeira Club, where I'm lodging? Dine you in, let you sample the best of its wine cellar, and put you up for the night?"

"Sounds delightful, sir!" Lt. Westcott perked up.

"Mind, the lodgers retire damned early, but, we could find some amusement after . . . the theatres, perhaps?" Lewrie suggested.

"I could give my man, Mumphrey, a night off," Westcott happily mused. "You remember Mumphrey, sir? One of the wardroom servants from the *Reliant* frigate? Landsman who served a quarterdeck carronade?"

"Vaguely," Lewrie replied, thinking that Geoffrey Westcott was better-off than he'd realised, if he could afford to pay a manservant to do for him, even on half-pay.

Both men swilled down the last slurps of their tea and returned the mugs to the cart vendor.

"Well, I must go in and do my weekly begging, sir," Westcott said with a faint laugh.

"As do I," Lewrie said, as well. "I'd only planned t'stay 'til mid-day, then go find dinner. D'ye intend to bide all day?"

"I had planned to, aye, sir, but all I really need to do is to announce my presence, remind the clerks where I lodge, and that I'm still available, so . . ." Westcott said, ending with a shrug.

"Aye, let's sit and plead 'til noon, then find a good ordinary or chop-house," Lewrie offered. "My treat. Damme, Mister Westcott . . . no matter our circumstances at present, it is damned good t'see you, again!"

They turned and walked to the doors together. The tiler looked up and began his spiel.

"H'its damned crowded in there, Lieutenant, an' there's a mob o' others already waitin', so, 'less ye've been sent for . . ." he rasped.

"Heard it! Heard it!" Westcott hooted back with a grin.

# CHAPTER SIX

"Anything for me?" Lewrie asked the club servant behind the anteroom desk as he shrugged off his hat and boat cloak.

"Ehm . . . yes, sir," the desk clerk perkily replied. "A letter from a solicitor, a Mister Mountjoy?"

"Excellent," Lewrie said, breaking the wax seal and unfolding the note on his way to the Common Rooms for a warm-up in front of the fireplace. "Ah hah!"

Mr. Matthew Mountjoy, his long-time solicitor and prize agent, wrote to inform Lewrie that he had just received a tidy sum from Admiralty Prize-Court, and that he had deposited it all at Coutts' Bank for him. Even with all four ships of Captain Blanding's small squadron "in sight" when they had fought and taken the four French warships off the Chandeleur Islands off the mouth of the Mississippi and Spanish Louisiana, in 1803, cutting each British ship's share to a fourth of the total sum, Lewrie's traditional "two-eighths" was still an impressive sum, and it had been *Reliant* alone that had run down and taken the other 74-gun ship which had been sailing *en flute* as a trooper, so her value, less the value of the removed guns, was another welcome amount!

*Five hundred pounds to Coutts', and the rest into the Three Percents,*

Lewrie determined, smiling in delight as he re-folded the letter and stuck it into a coat pocket. Tomorrow, he would call on Mountjoy, visit the bank, make the transfer to the Funds, then take out enough for a shopping trip. Once warmed, he summoned a club waiter and ordered a brandy. Some enterprising smuggler along the coast must have good connexions, for the club had obtained several ankers of French brandy.

The Three Percents, though; the thought of them brought the painful memory of his last conversation with Lydia Stangbourne's brother, Percy, Viscount Stangbourne, at their vast house outside Reading.

"If Lydia is determined never to marry, Percy," he had pleaded, "me, or anyone else, then she must be provided for. Perhaps you could set aside money in the Funds, in her name . . . some in a solid bank, too, so she'll have independent means, the rest of her life."

"Before I gamble it away, hey, Alan?" Percy had tried to tease, which effort had fallen flat. Percy's new bride, Eudoxia Durschenko, had kerbed his penchant for gambling deep, fearing for the security of herself and her first child-to-be.

"Her two-thousand-pound dowry is her own, too," Lewrie had stated.

"Christ!" he muttered, shaking his head, shaking off the memory, and brooded near the warm fire, slowly sipping his drink, putting off any thought of dressing in civilian clothes for the symphony that evening, or much of anything else.

Lewrie had written Lydia as soon as he had completed *Reliant*'s decommissioning and had gone up to London to turn all the paperwork over to Admiralty, telling her of his possibly-crippling wound, and that he would go to Anglesgreen to heal up, if possible. Lydia had written back, promising to coach down, but he had asked her not to, in fear that seeing him in his current condition might make her think the less of him, and, once he had realised how *he* was received by his daughter and in-laws, allowing Lydia to face that same sort of reception was the last thing he'd wish for her.

Finally, round Christmas, he had given in to her continued invitations and had coached up to Reading for the holidays with what few suitable presents he had been able to purchase in the new shops in the town.

Foxbrush, the Stangbournes' country estate, put any great house Lewrie had ever seen to shame. It was immense, a late-Palladian pile of three storeys, as long as a First Rate ship of the line and as deep, less the inset centre courtyard and carriage entry and broad steps to the front doors, as a frigate. It was spiked with over a dozen chimneys, all fuming in promise of warmth.

Flunkeys in blue-and-white Stangbourne livery had rushed down to Lewrie's coach to fold down the metal steps, open the door, and hand him down, then gathered his dunnage from the coach's boot.

The family descended the long flight of stairs more sedately, with Lydia in the lead, and Percy tending his pregnant wife, Eudoxia. Lurking astern of them was Eudoxia's father, Arslan Artimovich Durschenko, the evil-looking one-eyed former lion tamer from Daniel Wigmore's circus/menagerie/theatrical troupe, in which Eudoxia had once belonged as a trick shooter with muskets, pistols, and re-curved bow, and trick rider and *ingenue* actress. Her father wore his usual scowl of disappointment to A, clap eyes on Lewrie, and B, see that he was still alive! In his new role as Percy's horse master and chief trainer to Viscount Stangbourne's personally-raised cavalry regiment, the old bastard was looking particularly prosperous.

"Oh, God, you!" Lydia had cried, clinging to Lewrie, and almost sending him tumbling. "I am so glad you are finally, actually, here!"

"It's been too damned long, aye!" Lewrie had breathed into her hair, leaned back to peer long and deep into her emerald-green eyes, then had given her another long and close embrace.

It had all *started* so jolly, at least.

There was his leg and his walking stick; there were those long and broad stone stairs, and once his set of rooms was ready, after a hot punch in the *small* salon (which was as big as his father's grand ballroom!) there were the several flights and landings to the upper storey where he could un-pack, and rest before having to come back *down* for supper. That first meal, and the breakfast the next morning, had been just the intimate family circle. From there on, though, it was a constant round of holiday suppers, at Foxbrush, or at the houses of Stangbourne neighbours.

There were dances, in which he could not participate without going arse-over-tit. There were strolls about the property, shortened for his benefit, and morning or afternoon rides with Lewrie on an unfamiliar horse that was as spirited as his own, Anson, back home. And, there were steeplechases or cub hunts, in which he did not take a part at all, seeing them off from the bottom of those detested stone stairs, then returning to the interior of the great house to drink, read, and sulk whilst everyone else trotted off in a clatter to follow the hounds to gay "ta-ta-ras".

Percy arranged shooting parties, even though he was a bit leery of *women* taking part, and it didn't help that Eudoxia would insist on going along in her "condition", then proving to be the most accurate of them all, with Lewrie second-best and Lydia sometimes out-shooting him.

The best of all was the late evenings after supper, when Lewrie could retire to his rooms, and, once the house was quiet with all but the scullery maids in the kitchens retired for the night, Lydia would make her stealthy way to his bed.

Lame Lewrie might have been, but at least his "wedding tackle" still worked!

"I still do not understand why you did not wish me to come down to see you," Lydia had purred, snugly tucked into his arms with her head on his shoulder, and her hair the colour of old honey spilled on his chest. "One might imagine you would be ashamed of me, Alan."

"Ashamed o' *me!*" Lewrie had laughed off. "You think me a cripple now, you should've seen how lame I was a few months ago. My old Cox'n and the lads've worked me daily, and I'm still not my old self."

"Well, in *some* things you are," Lydia had purred, stretching like a cat against him. "You were afraid that if I'd seen you then, I would have thought the less of you?"

"Yes," he had confessed. "If the bullet had hit me an inch or so off where it did, I'd be a peg-leg, not fit for anyone, or anything else. Can you imagine how useless and idle I would've been, then?"

"But, you are not, and do you continue on with your exercises, or whatever you've been doing, you will be completely whole by Spring," Lydia had encouraged, then had gone sombre. "Then the Navy will have you, again, and you will be off to God knows where for several *more* years. I cannot bear the thought of that."

"I'm sorry, Lydia dear, but the Navy's what I do, all that I know how to do by now, and . . . it's the only thing I'm *good* at. I'd be bored to drunken tears, else," he had gloomed. "If the war ever ends . . . which I can't even imagine . . . well, my prospects'd put me in a permanent sulk. Half-pay, and lots o' readin'? Hah! Not kind to women who take up with sailors, but . . ."

"No, it is not," Lydia had whispered, with a hitch of breath.

"Besides," Lewrie had gone on, "Anglesgreen's a dull place, and *you'd've* been bored after a couple of days. Most of the local folks're 'chaw-bacon', even the prominent ones, like Sir Romney Embleton. His son, Harry, hates me worse than the Devil hates Holy Water!"

He had told her how Harry had plans to marry Caroline back in the long ago, before Lewrie had won her heart, describing how badly Harry had taken it, and how Caroline had lashed him with her reins and made his "bung spout claret" when the hunting hounds had treed Lewrie's old cat, Pitt, and Harry had tried to drive the cat down to be savaged.

"Then there's the in-laws, and my daughter, Charlotte," Lewrie had said with a huge sigh. "I wanted t'spare ye that," telling Lydia how *he'd* been greeted, and his dread for how they would welcome her as the "new woman", Caroline's replacement, and the foul rumours of how it had been Lewrie's fault that Caroline had died.

Lydia Stangbourne had not thought of herself as a beauty when she was a child, and still didn't accept the fact that she'd grown to be handsome and fetching. Her first exposure during a London Season when she was eighteen had been a cruel disappointment. Even with £500 for her "dot", other girls with less dowry had out-shone her, so much so that she'd refused her mother's pressure to try again 'til several years later, with £2,000. She'd been mobbed by greedy young swains eager for her *per annum*, not her. Revolted, she'd played arch, aloof, and cynically scornful, which had made the greediest *praise* her for her "modernity"!

When she finally did marry, she'd been deluded by a beast in human form, from whom she'd fled after a few months and had the family solicitor apply to their Member in the House of Commons to file a Bill of Divorcement, resulting in over two years of charges and counter charges gushingly reprinted in all the papers before Parliament had granted her her freedom. All of that had turned her into a Scandalous Woman, not fit for Genteel or Respectable Company.

If Lydia had been cool and guarded with her emotions before, those early years did not hold a candle to how sensitive she was now to even the slightest rejection, insult, guarded snicker, or cutty-eyed glance! Lydia comported herself icily aloof in public settings, only revealing her true and easy self with family or a small circle of girlhood friends.

Lewrie had noted that of the five close female friends Lydia had, the ones to whom he had been introduced over the holidays, all but one of them was nowhere near what one could call pretty or fetching. They were matrons, by then, chick-a-biddies with broods of children and complacent husbands of looks less than handsome. Monied they might be, high in the local landed gentry and Squirearchy, but none of them were what Lewrie could call scintillating company; they were comfortable for Lydia, safe, sure, and ever accepting.

"It all sounds so bleak," Lydia had said with a long sigh. "Your daughter and in-laws . . . your son, Sewallis, when I met him in Portsmouth . . ."

"Charlotte said he'd written her, after," Lewrie had said.

"Then I can only imagine *what* he wrote of me," Lydia had said with a toss of her head, "for he did not act in the *least* approving of me. Lord, what a *small* world to which we are reduced!"

"Well, we'll always have Reading," Lewrie had quipped.

"Your family dis-approving, most of England looking down their noses at me? What sort of life could it be, did the war end, and you were ashore for good?" Lydia had dejectedly sighed. "Even if we did decide to make our relationship more . . . permanent, there would be no change. With no welcome from your family, it would be even worse!"

"We . . . we just tell 'em all t'sod off, go to the Devil and shake themselves, Lydia," Lewrie had replied. Admittedly, his use of the word "we" was so fraught with dread that he did stumble over it. A fond and passionate relationship when he was back from the sea was one thing; a *permanent* arrangement was something altogether else! Oh, he was fond of her, missed her when he was gone . . . but marriage for a second time?

"I sometimes wonder whether life would be so much easier did I stay in the country, at Foxbrush, and limit my world to Reading and Henley," Lydia had gloomed. "I am so at ease here, and dread going to London, or anywhere else, lately."

"A long way from the coast, though, Portsmouth or Sheerness, or wherever I put in," Lewrie reminded her.

"When you *rarely* return," she had said back, nigh snippily.

"But, I'm here now," Lewrie had teased.

Fierce and passionate lovemaking had seemed to cheer her up.

From that night on, though, Lewrie had sensed a subtle change, a distancing from him, as if she thought it better for her to forsake him than to continue hoping that circumstances would change for the better in future.

Christmas Eve, Christmas Day, then Boxing Day brought more temporary house guests. There were grand suppers, music, and carols sung, with Lewrie tootling on his humble penny-whistle to the great amusement of the others, and on Christmas Eve, gifts were exchanged. She did not come to his rooms, fearful of exposure by the many guests.

Lewrie had brought a satin baby gown for the expectant Eudoxia, found in the drygoods shop in Anglesgreen, and for Percy a twelve-bottle case of Madeira port that Will Cony had ordered down from London. For Lydia, he'd found an iridescent dark green wool-and-silk–woven shawl, which had made Eudoxia laugh, clap her hands, and jape that the shawl might be the equivalent to the "paper of pins" from the old rhyme in sign of a plighting of troth! Lydia made the proper noises in gracious delight, but it had irked Lewrie a trifle that she was not all that enthusiastic, and he had caught her a few minutes later, seated apart and fingering the shawl, looking very pensive.

And Lewrie had found it odd that his holiday gift was not from Lydia alone, but from her brother Percy, as well, though it was a splendid one; a double-locked and double-barrelled fowling piece with the barrels aligned over-under along the same line of sight. It was set in a glossy walnut chequered stock, and chased with silver inlay and intricate engravings.

"A Wallace!" Percy had crowed. "I discovered it when we passed through London from the coast, and the arrangement of the barrels made such perfect sense that I got one for myself, as well, ha ha!"

"My God, it's magnificent, Percy!" Lewrie had exclaimed, awed and stunned by its beauty, its perfection, and how much a custom fowler must have cost. He'd felt like a miser in comparison, but a new firearm had always given him immense delight.

"I can't wait t'try it out," he had declared. "Thankee, Lydia, Percy, and Eudoxia, I must also add. Such a crack shot must've had a say in buying it. Christ, you've made me stupefied!"

The Stangbourne estates consisted of thousands of acres spread all over the county, where deer and game birds could be found. Percy swore that they would go fowling after church services on Christmas Day, and he made good on his promise, resulting in such a bag that the Christmas-night supper and the servants' Boxing Day supper prominently featured roast pheasant and massive pigeon pies.

It would have been wonderful to stay on a few more days, lounging about and feeding off Stangbourne largesse, but Lewrie had to get back to Anglesgreen, and his regimen. It was well that he did leave, for the last night had been the very worst.

Lydia had wanted to stroll in the decorative gardens behind the great house, bleak as they were in mid-Winter, and as cold and snowy as were the prospects. Wrapped up warmly, she and Lewrie went anyway, for the fresh air, and to work off a hearty dinner.

"You must go tomorrow," Lydia had begun, sounding glum.

"Fear I must," he'd told her, equally depressed.

"And, you won't be back 'til late in the Spring," she'd added.

"Have t'get fit and back to normal, after all," he'd agreed.

"Before you come back here, you will surely go up to London to seek employment with Admiralty, first," Lydia had reasoned. "If you *do* fully restore yourself, of course?"

"Well, it's what I do for a living, so yes, I'd go to London, first," Lewrie had told her, feeling the first disturbing twinges under his heart, sure that there was a shoe to be dropped on him. He'd looked towards her, but her face was set, half-hidden under the cowl of a greatcoat, with her arms crossed inside a fur muff that she held clenched to her middle. "We could meet there, spend a few weeks, perhaps . . ."

"No," Lydia had whispered, shaking her head. She had tried to glance at him, but lowered her gaze to the toes of her shoes. "I told you that I do not find London comfortable for me, any longer. Nor do I wish to sneak about from Willis's Rooms, to a spare bed-chamber in Grosvenor Street, to a . . . a *bagnio* taken by the hour . . . any more than I wish to expose myself to the gawkers and snooty gossipers. I cannot, and I will not, play a part-time paramour. My heart . . . !"

He had reached out to embrace her, but she had stepped clear, and she finally looked him in the eye, her expression as bleak as the winter-sere gardens.

"I have loved you dearly, Alan," she had confessed, "but there can be no 'we', and I cannot continue loving a man who is never *here*. The long separations are more than I can bear, and our few days together are so short and fleeting that they feel more like a brief waking dream, too flimsy to snatch back after rising."

"But, Lydia, dear . . . !" he'd protested, his heart sinking into his stomach in shock, "I thought we were both happy with . . . !"

"You, perhaps, Alan," she'd chillingly accused, not in anger but in sadness, "but men are so easily pleased, are they not, when things are going their way? *Making* love is so much easier than giving one's heart in love completely."

"You think I don't love you, Lydia?" Lewrie had objected.

"I am sure that you do, Alan," Lydia had said with a sad smile, "in your own fashion. That is the hardest part to bear. I hope that you will always think of me fondly, as I will of you, but . . . I cannot continue this way, of us being not one thing but not quite another, and . . ."

"Then, marry me!" Lewrie had blurted out. "Let's wed, today!"

*Christ! What'd I just say?* he had thought.

That had made her weep, at long last.

"I have not had much luck with married life, Alan," Lydia had said, lifting a mittened hand from her muff to wipe her eyes, with a rueful laugh. "I told you once, before you went off to the Bahamas, that I feared the risk to my heart too much to marry you, or anyone. And, remember what you told me, the night after we met at the palace, when you were knighted? In the Cocoa-Tree, I think it was . . . when I complained of being labelled a scandalous hussy, being pursued by men such as Georgey Hare, and dreading to be re-enslaved and ruled by a man?"

"I told you to forget it all, and enjoy your life," Lewrie had recalled, vividly, and sorrowfully. "But . . ."

"Thank you for the offer, Alan, but I believe that I will follow that advice, and live my life," Lydia had told him, reaching out to stroke his cheek in gratitude for his gesture. "I find it safer to be me, alone, with no more pretensions to so-called wedded bliss. Or, a pleasureable but sordid continuing *amour*, the sort expected of a woman as scandalous as me," she'd said with another scoffing snort and a toss of her head.

"What's next, a nunnery?" Lewrie had gawped, which had made her laugh out loud, crinkling her nose which Lewrie had always found to be endearing when she did so.

"Percy and Eudoxia will have many children, I fully expect," she had said, "and I hope to be a doting aunt, as I am godmother to my old friends' children. Life here in the country will be fulfilling, and comfortable."

"And safe," Lewrie had added, slumping in defeat.

"And safe," Lydia had agreed. "Now. If you do not mind, Alan, I wish to go down to the stables, by myself, for a while. There is a mare that's due her first foal, and a new litter of pups I'd like to look in on. I'll see you at supper." Then Lydia had walked away, a firm and industrious stride to her pace, leaving him stunned beyond belief.

He had stayed at Foxbrush a few hours more, discussing the matter with Eudoxia and Percy, who were as thunder-struck as he was, and pleading that if she was determined to live life her own way she would have the means to do so. Then Lewrie and Pettus had departed, taking lodgings in Reading for the night, rising early, and coaching back to Anglesgreen the next morning.

"Ah, Captain Lewrie!" Mr. Giles chummily barked as he entered the Common Rooms, making a bee-line for the fireplace and rubbing his cold hands. "Been to Admiralty, I see. How did it go?"

"Early days, sir," Lewrie said, coming out of his dour reverie to find that his brandy glass was empty, perhaps had been for some time. "As uncomfortable as the Waiting Rooms are, I think I'll only pop in once a week, and wait for a letter to come."

"Quite right!" Giles declared with a firm nod. "Appearing anxious doesn't work well in business, either. Gives the other fellow the upper hand, what?"

"Seen Showalter, yet, Mister Giles?" Lewrie asked, getting to his feet.

"Not yet, but he'll be along, unless there's a call for a division in Commons this afternoon," Giles said, smiling almost angelically as he flipped the tails of his coat up and put his bottom close to the fireplace's heat. "Aahh!"

"I thought to ask him where that symphony he liked was playing," Lewrie said. "Perhaps the desk clerk knows, if Showalter's runnin' late. I'll go change into *mufti*."

"Lord, one hears so much more Hindoo slang hereabouts, these days," Giles carped. "So many younger folk coming back *nabobs*, simply stiff with grand earnings. Must be a way to sell the Hindoos proper shoes . . . now there'd be a killing! Sandals . . . hah!"

"See you at supper, Mister Giles," Lewrie said, departing for the stairs. He trooped up slowly, not due to any infirmity, but lost in gloomy thoughts which had arisen now and then since he'd departed Reading, and the Stangbourne estate.

*What a hellish waste of a good woman,* Lewrie ruefully thought; *Givin' up on London, and all her symphonies, plays, and such? Samuel Johnson said a body who's tired o' London is tired o'* life! *No more love, no more pleasure, ever again? It's like she's been got at by Hannah More, or the bloody Baptists! It'll be soup kitchens in the stews, and good works, next.*

He had to question himself, though, on whether he had ever truly loved her in the permanent, 'til death did them part, sense. At best, he could confess to a powerful fondness, and dammit all . . . Lydia had never looked more lovely than she did when she rejected him! More desirable, more fetching . . . than if she had said yes to his proposal.

*She* rejected *me!* he gloomed.

# CHAPTER SEVEN

The next fortnight passed most lazily for Lewrie, with rounds of shopping for a few new articles of uniform, and some additions to his civilian clothing, and social calls on people he knew and liked, some he knew but slightly distrusted, such as one of his old school chums who'd been expelled with him, Clotworthy Chute, his father at last, and people whom he thought might be useful, such as Peter Rushton's brother, Harold, who held a position under the Secretary of State at War. One never could tell when Harold might give Admiralty a nudge.

His old steward, Aspinall, had made enough money off his books to buy into the publishing house which put them out, was now happily married, and was still keeping his mother and his sister, Rose, in a snug house of their own, retired from domestic service, and Lewrie had spent a pleasant afternoon with them.

He looked up the maker of his Christmas fowling piece, and his gunsmith shop, and ended up purchasing a brace of long-barrelled pistols in the same over-under configuration.

And, there were the music halls, the galleries which displayed new paintings and sculpture. He didn't need to buy any, but looking was a good way to kill an afternoon. There were plays and farces in Covent Garden and

Drury Lane theatres, and the public gardens where he could idly ogle young women after a supper on the town. He could hire a saddle horse and go cantering round St. James's Park and Hyde Park on the rainless mornings. He could walk from one end of the Strand to the other, to keep his leg fit, and peer into the bow-window shop displays. And, after that fortnight, Lewrie was surprised to discover that the city's delights were beginning to pall, as if *he* was growing tired of London, perhaps even tired of *life?*

He still made his weekly visits to Admiralty, and ran into Lt. Geoffrey Westcott a time or two, who had decided that a once-a-week call was to his advantage, too, which allowed them to have a decent dinner together before going their separate ways for another week.

"Off to Admiralty this morning, are you, sir?" Hoyle, the club manager, cheerfully asked as Lewrie got himself fitted out with his hat and boat cloak in the ante-room.

"If it's Wednesday I must be, Mister Hoyle," Lewrie japed back.

"All success to you, sir," Hoyle rejoined. "Now, don't forget that Mister Ludlow will be hosting card night this evening, with hot punch and sing-alongs."

"Hmm, rather racy for the Madeira Club, ain't it?" Lewrie asked with a brow up.

"To end at eleven, sir," Hoyle said, "*sharp,* for the benefit of the older members, of course. It improves the attendance at the supper, and the sale of spirits," he added with a sly look.

"Next ye know, we'll be gamblin' and lettin' ladies in," Lewrie speculated. "The new Cocoa-Tree, perhaps?"

"This club, sir?" Hoyle scoffed. "We'll never be that woolly. Lewis, summon transport for Captain Lewrie, would you?"

*Might be a nice way t'end the day,* Lewrie thought as he alit from a hired one-horse coach and paid the driver; *Pity I don't have my penny-whistle with me. A few shillings fluttered on cards, take on some hot punch, and sleep in late, tomorrow. God knows, I've nothing* better *to do!*

He suffered the cheery abuse from the tiler, chequed his hat and cloak, and looked up one of Secretary Marsden's clerk to make his presence known, then searched the Waiting Room for Westcott.

"Here, sir," Westcott said, waving him over. "I've managed to save you a seat, and today's *Gazette*."

"Mornin', Geoffrey," Lewrie said, sitting down. "And how are you, today?"

"Main-well, all considered, sir," Westcott said with a pleased look and a brief flash of a toothy grin. "Topping, in point of fact."

"One of our members, Ludlow . . . recall meeting him?" Lewrie said. "Doesn't *make* things, but he's big on the 'Change in the trade of leather goods, is hosting a card and punch party at my club this evening, and the supper will feature several game pies and a saddle of venison. Interested?"

"Oh, that sounds tempting, sir, but I fear I must beg off. I have other plans," Westcott said with a grimace of disappointment to miss such a feast.

"Your landlady?" Lewrie teased.

"Ehm, no sir, not tonight," Westcott cautiously admitted with a sly grin. "There's a very fetching young seamstress I met when having some new shirts run up. *Most* . . . promising."

"Just remember the Saturday mess toast, Geoffrey," Lewrie cautioned. "Sweethearts and . . . landladies . . . may they never meet."

"One in Southwark, t'other in the Borough," Westcott quipped with a wink. "I've already read this half of the paper. Want it?"

They passed the next two hours comparing news stories and palavering their opinions, good or bad, on what they'd read. They went out for tea and some fresh air in the courtyard, then returned.

"Captain Sir Alan Lewrie?" one of Marsden's clerks called out. "Is Captain Lewrie present?"

"I'm here!" Lewrie cried back, chiding himself for sounding too eager, and shooting to his feet as if stung.

"The First Secretary wishes to see you now, sir," the clerk said.

"Wish me luck, Mister Westcott. We may be onto something good," Lewrie muttered, then went to the bottom of the stairs to follow the clerk. The clerk opened the door to Marsden's office and ushered him in.

"Good morning, sir," Lewrie said to the First Secretary.

"Ah, good morning to you, Sir Alan," Marsden said back, looking haggard and worn. He had been in the job seemingly forever, and the years had taken a toll. "Do sit, sir."

"Thankee, sir," Lewrie replied, plopping himself down.

"Ahh, hmm," Marsden said with a long sigh. "I note that you are no longer employing a walking stick, Sir Alan?"

"Over the winter, sir, I've worked my way to complete health," Lewrie told him. "I could dance a jig if you need proof of it."

"No, no, that will not be necessary," Mr. Marsden said with a brief chuckle. "I will take your word for it. It is well that you are fit and ready to return to service."

"Avid t'do so, sir!" Lewrie assured him.

Marsden leaned back in his chair and laced his fingers over his chest in thought.

"Gad, what a disreputable business," Marsden began. "Might you have read anything anent HMS *Sapphire*, Sir Alan?"

"No, sir," Lewrie had to tell him, trying to recall the ship's name, and what sort she might be. *Must be a* new *frigate*, he thought.

"She had just come out of the Chatham dockyards and a complete re-fit, and has only been back in commission for a little over seven months," the Admiralty's First Secretary began to explain, "and is at present anchored in the Great Nore to re-victual. Unfortunately . . ."

Mr. Marsden sat back forward to slump over his desk and worked his mouth as if he had just bit into something vile.

"In retrospect, her Captain, and her First Officer, turned out to be exceedingly poor choices," he went on after a long sigh. "Both men are well qualified and highly experienced, but . . . they just would not, or could not, rub together. Perhaps it was some *contretemps* from their pasts, something personal, perhaps their families were at loggerheads, there's no knowing, but . . . they have gone and shot one another in a duel!"

"Shot?" Lewrie exclaimed. He'd served under several superior officers whom he would have *gladly* shot or strangled, but only in his fantasies. "Her First Lieutenant challenged his own Captain to a duel? That's a court-martial offence . . . like the leader of the Nore Mutiny, Parker, once challenged Captain Riou. A hangin' offence if his Captain died."

"No, 'twas the other way round," Mr. Marsden sadly imparted. "*Sapphire*'s Captain was so wroth with her First Officer that *he* issued the challenge. He could have preferred charges for gross insubordination, or let the fellow ask for a transfer, but no. I name no names, but both gentlemen are known for being rash, intemperate men, of the strictest discipline and the touchiest senses of honour."

"So, who swings for murder, then, sir?" Lewrie asked. "Duels ain't kindly looked upon, any longer."

It used to be that just any old place would do, a barn, an open field, or glade in a grove of trees, even the public gardens in London. Nowadays, though, gentlemen with especially hot grievances would have to coach to Scotland or Wales, sail to Ireland or someplace on the Continent so they could cross swords or blaze at each other, and avoid a criminal charge. "Respectability" had reared its ugly head, again!

"Neither!" Marsden scoffed. "The bloody damned fools only managed to *wound* each other, sufficient to put them flat on their backs for several weeks . . . depending upon whether sepsis sets in, and once on their feet, both shall face courts-martial, and the ends of their respective careers, do I have anything to say about it. And I do, so long as I hold this office.

"So, Captain Lewrie," Marsden said, peering closely at him. "I have a ship in need of a Captain, and you are in need of a ship and an active commission. Will you take her on?"

"Aye, I will, sir," Lewrie quickly assured him.

"Her Second Lieutenant is more than capable and *could* be advanced, and you may find that one of *Sapphire*'s Midshipmen could be made an Acting-Lieutenant for the nonce," Mr. Marsden said, more jovially and making notes on a scrap of paper.

"Might I ask the date of her Second Officer's commission, sir?" Lewrie enquired.

"Ehm . . . Lieutenant Harcourt is, ah . . . why?" Marsden paused in his search for that information.

"Might I put forward a man of my own choosing, sir? I know it is only granted to very senior officers, but . . ."

"Such an honour I believe your excellent previous service would allow, sir," Mr. Marsden cautiously seemed to agree, "but, is the said officer immediately available, or might his transfer from his current posting cause too much delay . . . ?" He lifted his hands and shoulders in perplexity.

"My choice, Mister Marsden, would be my former First Lieutenant from my last ship, *Reliant,* Mister Geoffrey Westcott," Lewrie told him. "We've worked very well together, the last three years and more. And, as for his availability, he's seated belowstairs in the Waiting Room seekin' an appointment this very instant!"

"Oh, well!" the First Secretary exclaimed, perking up considerably. "That would be capital. If you vouch for his good qualitites, then that is good enough for me, and the Navy."

"I did recommend him as more than due a command of his own, sir, but . . . bird in hand, all that?" Lewrie said with a smile.

"So, your Lieutenant Westcott would be amenable? Excellent!" Mr. Marsden said, beaming. "How soon might you imagine you could go aboard and take charge of her, sir?"

"Hmm . . . all my shipboard furnishings, and some men from my retinue are at my father's country house down in Surrey, sir. I can get a letter off to them today, but I have no idea how long it will take them t'pack up and arrive at the Nore. Is there any urgency in getting *Sapphire* back to sea, sir?" Lewrie asked.

"Well, under these despicable circumstances, no," Mr. Marsden said after a long moment with his head laid over to one side in deep thought. "She has not yet received fresh sailing orders. Most of her time in commission has been spent in three-month cruises in the North Sea and the Baltic approaches, but that could change. I expect that are you able to go aboard and read yourself in within the next fortnight, that might be sufficient. In the meantime, I will send orders down to Sheerness to announce the arrival of a new Captain and First Officer, and for her Second, Harcourt, to continue victualling, and keeping her crew exercised, 'til you arrive."

"That'd be grand, sir!" Lewrie crowed, a tad too loud and eager.

"I will send your orders and active commission documents round your lodgings within a day or so," Marsden told him, much relieved to have his problems solved. "Once in receipt, drop a note of hand by to pay for the fees."

*There goes better than fifty pounds!* Lewrie thought. Just like the first time he'd been made "Post" and appointed into the *Proteus* frigate back in 1797, he'd always had the droll idea that the quickest way to command of a ship would be to turn up at Admiralty with a full purse, and throw money at someone! The patents of his knighthood and baronetcy had cost a gruesomely high sum, too! Every honour bestowed by HM Government had a high price, one way or another.

"Thank you, Mister Marsden," Lewrie said, preparing to rise and depart. "I've spent too long on the 'beach', as has Westcott. Should I send him up straightaway, or have him wait 'til your calendar is . . . ?"

"Oh, send him up," Marsden said, with a genial chuckle. "Saves a stamp, or a messenger's time hunting up his lodgings. And I thank you, Sir Alan. It's damned good of you to take on *Sapphire,* though you've proved yourself a most accomplished frigate captain, and had a long run in that class. Seniority demands, though, that men move up and on, sooner or later."

"Hey, sir?" Lewrie asked, wondering what Marsden was maundering about. *Onward and upward, mine arse!* he thought.

"Why, *Sapphire*'s a Fourth Rate, of the *Antelope* group. Quite modern, really," Marsden said in gleeful praise, "re-fitted with iron knees, and metal fresh-water tanks. Last of her class built in 1792."

"A two-decker fifty-gunner?" Lewrie replied, trying *very* hard not to start kicking furniture.

*I've been had, by Christ!* he fumed to himself; *Is it too late t'beg off? Start limpin', again?*

"I did not mention that? How remiss of me," Marsden said with genuine regret. "Been on the job too long, I suppose. Can't say that I won't miss the office, but one does get older, and it is about time for a younger man to take my place of the First Lord's, Lord Mulgrave's, and the Prime Minister's, choice."

"Oh, surely not, sir!" Lewrie exclaimed, feigning distress to hear that. "Won't be the same with you gone."

"Oh, tosh, Sir Alan," Marsden pooh-poohed, "I only fear that it will be. I've found that Admiralty grinds on in the same old way, century to century, ha ha! Again, sir, thank you for taking on *Sapphire*, and I wish you all success in your new command."

"Thank you, sir, and good day," Lewrie replied, shaking the old fellow by the hand, then heading out.

*She's a ship, an active commission, and full pay*, Lewrie forced himself to think; *Plaster "gladsome" on yer phyz, ye gullible clown, and look* pleased *with her! Even if she does turn out t'be Tom Turdman's barge at Dung Wharf!*

He trotted down the stairs to the ground level and the crowd in the Waiting Room, looked towards Lt. Westcott, and smiled broader.

"Good news, sir?" Westcott asked, rising to come meet him.

"For both of us, Mister Westcott," Lewrie told him, putting the best face on it. "*We* have a ship! *Sapphire*, badly in need of both a Captain *and* a First Officer. I requested you, and we are both now employed!"

"That's tremendous, sir! Just grand!" Westcott loudly declared; loud enough to set many sets of teeth on edge among the un-employed.

"The First Secretary wants t'see you for a few minutes," Lewrie told him. "After your meeting, I'll be in the courtyard, havin' a tea. Mind," Lewrie continued, in a softer voice as he walked with Westcott to the foot of the stairs, "she ain't a frigate. She's a fifty-gunner, lyin' at the Nore."

Westcott made a faint *moue* of disappointment, but cheered up a second later, drolly saying, "The First Officer in a Fourth Rate gets a shilling or two more a day than the First in a Fifth Rate, even so. How did she come to need a First and a Captain both, sir?"

"I'll tell ye over dinner," Lewrie promised. "That'll be something for you and your new girl to celebrate tonight, hey?"

"The idea of my sailing away *might* prove . . . useful, aye, sir!" Westcott said with a laugh and a wink. "Melts many a girlish heart. And . . . other things."

"I'll have t'get a note to Pettus, Yeovill, Desmond, and Furfy, with a note of hand, for them t'pack up instanter," Lewrie deliberated, thinking of all he still would need to purchase in London while awaiting their arrival. "It'll take me the better part of ten days to a fortnight before I can read myself in."

"As soon as I receive my commission documents, sir, I can coach down to the Nore and lay the ground for your arrival," Westcott offered. "I don't have all your encumbrances, and could set out Monday."

"If you can tear yourself away from all your passionate leave-takin's that early, I'd be deeply in your debt, Geoffrey," Lewrie said in gratitude. "Aye, that'd work out best."

"Once I've seen the First Secretary, is there any reason for us to linger in this 'Pit of Despair', sir?" Westcott japed.

"Christ, no!" Lewrie hooted. "I've a favourite eatery over in Savoy Street, off the Strand, a truly *grand* place. When you are done with Mister Marsden, we'll whistle up a coach and celebrate!"

"Be right with you, then, sir," Westcott heartily agreed. "See you in the courtyard, then we'll hoist sail and get out of here!"

# BOOK ONE

Britons, you stay too long;
  Quickly aboard bestow you,
    And with a merry gale
  Swell your stretch'd sail
With vows as strong
  As the winds that blow you.

"TO THE VIRGINIAN VOYAGE"
MICHAEL DRAYTON (1563-1631)

# CHAPTER EIGHT

*She's a ship, an active commission, and earns me full pay again,* Lewrie had to remind himself as his hired boat approached HMS *Sapphire*, moored at least two miles from shore in the Great Nore at Sheerness.

She was 154 feet on the range of the deck and 130 feet along her waterline, just a few feet longer than his last Fifth Rate frigate, but she was so damned *tall* with that upper deck stacked atop the lower one!

The hired boat was bound on a course to pass before *Sapphire*'s bows, veer to the right in a large circle, and come alongside her starboard entry-port, but Lewrie looked aft to the tillerman and expressed a wish to cross under her stern, instead, so he could give her a good look-over before boarding.

"She's a clean'un, she is, sir," a younger boatman who handled the sheets of the boat's lugs'l commented. "Shiny'z a new penny."

"Aye, she is," Lewrie grudgingly had to agree.

*Sapphire*'s hull was painted black, sometime recently, at that, for the gloss had not yet faded. Her two rows of gun-ports showed a pair of buff-coloured paint bands, what was coming to be known as the "Nelson Chequer", and her waterline at full load sported a thin red boot stripe just above the inch or two of her coppering that was exposed. White-painted cap-rails topped her bulwarks and trimmed her beakhead rails.

*Sapphire*'s figurehead was the usual crowned lion carved for any ship not named for some hero from the classics; a male lion done in tan paint, with a bushy mane streaked with brown and black highlights, red-tongued and white-fanged, with only its crown gilded. The lion's front paws held a bright blue faceted ball against its upper chest, a gemstone that some shore artist had flicked with streaks of silver and white in an attempt to make it appear to shine. It looked fierce enough, but for its odd blue eyes!

Several of the ship's boats were floating astern in a gaggle, bridled together and bound to a tow rope, to soak their planking lest the wood dried out and allowed leaks. There was a wee 18-foot cutter or gig, a 25-foot cutter, a 29-foot launch, and a 32-foot pinnace, all painted white with bright blue gunn'ls.

The hired boat had to circle wide to clear those ship's boats, giving Lewrie a long look at her stern, which was not as ornate as he had expected. There were white dolphins and griffins along the upper scroll board in bas-relief against black, above what would be his stern gallery, which gallery sported close-set white railings and spiralled column posts. Below the gallery were the several windows of the wardroom right-aft on the upper gun deck, then a bright blue horizontal band below that, on which was mounted the ship's name in raised block letters, painted white and gilt.

*Somebody has a deep purse,* Lewrie thought; *or had.*

Post-Captains with enough "tin" could afford to have gilt paint applied, figureheads custom made, and improve the lavishness of their ship's carving work. It appeared that *Sapphire*'s recently departed Captain had been one of those men.

"Boat ahoy!" someone shouted from the quarterdeck.

"Aye aye!" the tillerman shouted back, holding up four fingers to denote that his passenger was a Post-Captain.

The lugs'l halliard and jib sheet were loosed and the sails handed, as the hired boat drifted up to the main channels and chains at the foot of the boarding battens and man-ropes. Lewrie stood and tucked his everyday hanger behind his left leg so he would not get tangled up with it as the younger boatman hooked onto the channels with a long hooked gaff, bringing the boat to a stop.

Lewrie teetered atop the hired boat's gunn'ls, grasped one of the man-ropes, stepped up with his right foot to the main channel, and swung up with his left foot to the first step of the battens, noting with gratitude that the steps had been painted then strewn liberally with gritty sand before the paint had dried, improving his traction.

At rest, *Sapphire*'s lower-deck gun-ports were about five feet above her waterline, and they were all opened for ventilation, with some of them filled with curious faces as he passed the pair closest to the battens. Once above those, the ship's tumblehome increased, making his ascent less steep.

*All the exercise is payin' off,* he thought as his head rose level with the lip of the entry-port; he hadn't even begun to suck wind! And there were the half-spatterdashed boots of Marines, in view, the buckled shoes of sailors peeking out from the bottoms of long, loose "pusser's slops" trousers, and the trill of bosun's calls in welcome.

Lewrie placed his first foot on the lip of the entry-port and made a final jerk upon the man-ropes to come aboard with a characteristic hop and stamp. Sure that he was in-board with no risk of going arse-over-tit backwards, he doffed his hat to the flag, quarterdeck, and his waiting officers.

"Welcome aboard, sir," Lt. Westcott said, doffing his own hat along with the others.

"Thankee, Mister Westcott . . . gentlemen," Lewrie replied with a grin trying to break out on his face, despite the traditional formality of taking command. "If you do not mind, I will read myself in, first, before we make our first acquaintance."

He went to the forward quarterdeck rail and iron hammock rack stanchions, 'twixt the two square companionways let into the deck to allow rigging to pass through, pulled his commission document from inside his waistcoat, where it would stay dry despite foul weather, and not be lost overboard in the climb up the battens, folded it open, and began to read loud enough for all to hear.

"By the Commissioners for executing the Office of Lord High Admiral of Great Britain and Ireland and all of his Majesty's Plantations, et cetera . . . to Captain Sir Alan Lewrie, Baronet, hereby appointed Captain of His Majesty's Ship, the *Sapphire* . . ."

He paused to look up and forward into the waist and the sail-tending gangways to either beam down the upper deck.

*Jesus Christ, but there's a* slew *of 'em!* he thought, awed by the hundreds of people in the crew, nigh twice as many as he had had aboard *Reliant*! Sailors, boys, and Marines, all gawking at him!

"By virtue of the Power and Authority to us given, we do hereby constitute and appoint you Captain of His Majesty's Ship, *Sapphire,* willing and requiring you forthwith to go on board and take upon you the Charge and Command of Captain in her accordingly. Strictly charging all the Officers and Company belonging to the said Ship subordinate to you to behave themselves jointly and severally in their Respective Employments with all due Respect and Obedience unto you their said Captain, and you likewise . . ." he continued, right through to the date of his commission, and the year of the King's reign.

He folded that precious document up, again, and stuck it in a side pocket of his uniform coat, then leaned his palms on the railing.

"Just about ten years ago to the month, here at the Nore, I was made Post into my first command, the *Proteus* frigate," he told his new crew, now that they were all officially his, "and I have been fortunate to command several frigates over the years. *Sapphire* is my first two-decker. She is new to me, as you are, as well . . . just as I am new to you. It may take me twice as long to get to know you all by face and name than I did the men of my last ship, the *Reliant* frigate, so I ask for your indulgence on that head.

"*Sapphire* may not be as swift and dashing as a frigate, but we . . . you and me together . . . ." he continued, "will still find ways to toe up against our King's enemies and bash them to kindling and send Frenchmen, Spaniards, and Dutchmen, and all who side with Bonaparte, to the eternal fires of Hell! I am not one to tolerate boredom for long, and have always found a way to hear my guns roar in earnest, as I trust you all wish, as well. So, let's be at it, and ready our ship for great deeds to come!"

He turned and nodded to Lt. Westcott, who stepped forward to bellow dismissal of the hands, then walked over to his waiting officers and Mids. "If you'll do the honours, Mister Westcott?" he asked.

There was the ship's Second Lieutenant, Arnold Harcourt, a man in his mid-thirties with dark hair and eyes, and a lean and weathered face. The Third Lieutenant, Edward Elmes, was younger, leaner, and blond. *Sapphire*'s Sailing Master was a rough-hewn Cornishman, George Yelland, with a great hooked beak of a nose. There were two Marine officers, First Lieutenant John Keane, a ruddy-faced fellow in his late twenties with ginger hair, and Second Lieutenant Richard Roe, a slip of a lad not quite nineteen with brown hair and blue eyes, who looked to be as new to the sea as a fresh-baked loaf, a right "Merry Andrew" with a possible impish streak, a counterbalance to Keane's severe nature.

There were a whole ten Midshipmen, led by a burly fellow in his late twenties named Hillhouse, whom the First Secretary had thought to make Acting-Lieutenant before Lewrie had offered up Westcott. He did look salty enough. Behind him were Britton and Leverett, two more men with poor connexions most-like, for they were in their mid-twenties and still had not gained their Lieutenancies. Below them were the usual sort of Mids in their late teens, Kibworth, Carey, Spears, Harvey, and Griffin, then two lads in their early teens, Ward and Fywell.

*Sapphire*'s Purser and his clerk, the "Jack In The Bread Room", Mister Joseph Cadrick, and Irby, Lewrie decided to keep a chary eye on, for though butter would not melt in their mouths on the first introductions, Lewrie sensed a "fly" streak.

The Surgeon was a thin and scholarly-looking man named Andrew Snelling who looked as if a stiff breeze would carry his skeletal frame away. The Surgeon's Mates, Phelps and Twomey, in their middle twenties, cheerfully admitted that they were medical students who were too poor at present to attend physicians' colleges, but were happy to serve alongside Snelling, who seemed to know everything medicinal, or surgical, they assured him.

The Bosun and his two mates, Matthew Terrell, and Nobbs and Plunkett, seemed solid and competent fellows, from Terrell's early fourties to the mid-thirties, with years of experience at sea, as did the Master Gunner, Dick Boling; his Mate, Haddock; and the Yeoman of the Powder, Weaver.

Lewrie would get round to the Cook, Carpenter, Cooper and Armourer, Sailmaker, and their Mates later. His goods were coming aboard.

Pettus and Jessop, Desmond and Furfy, Yeovill and his Captain's clerk, James Faulkes, had gained the deck during the introductions, and were beginning to direct his chests and crates, his furniture and personal stores up from the hired boats and aft into the great cabins. A pair of slatted crates were slung up and over the bulwarks, one containing Lewrie's cat, Chalky, mewing and growling in fear, and the other containing Bisquit, *Reliant*'s old ship's dog.

"Well, hallo, Bisquit!" Lt. Westcott cried in delight to see him as the crate was lowered to the quarterdeck. "Still with us, are you? There's a good boy, yes!"

"I'd thought t'leave him on my father's farm," Lewrie explained, "but, when the waggons were loaded, he kept hoppin' on and wouldn't be left behind. When they trotted off, he ran after 'em all the way down to the village, and the lads took pity on him. He just wouldn't let himself be abandoned by everyone he knew. No, you wouldn't, would ye, Bisquit," Lewrie cooed, kneeling down by his crate. "You are a headstrong little beast, yes, you are. God help ye, you're a sea-goin' Navy dog."

Lewrie was rewarded with excited yips, whines, and a bark of two, and lots of tail wags to implore to be freed from his crate that instant. Lewrie un-did the latch and let him out, then stood up as Bisquit dashed to say hello to Westcott, run round the quarterdeck to sniff, then dashed up a ladderway to the vast expanse of the poop for more exploring. Lewrie stood up and caught Pettus's eye.

"I'd much admire did you hunt up the Carpenter, Pettus, and see to the construction of a sand-box for Chalky, and the proper width of my hangin' bed-cot," Lewrie bade him. "We'll have a shelter for Bisquit fashioned under one of the poop deck ladderways, later."

"Yes, sir. See to it, directly," Pettus promised. "We'll have your office and day cabin set up in a few minutes more, and the dining coach and bed space ready by the end of the Forenoon."

"Excellent!" Lewrie congratulated him, then turned to Westcott. "What do you make of her so far, Mister Westcott?"

"The ship is fully found and in very good material condition, sir," Westcott told him. "She's short of at least ten Able Seamen and about a dozen men rated Ordinary, but her officers and mates have run many of her Landsmen through catch-up instruction over the last nine months she's been in commission . . . her former Captain's idea, that . . . so a good many of them can hand, reef, and steer. They know their way round a bit better than most ship's companies."

"Well, that's a partial relief, at least," Lewrie commented. "How many Quota Men, and gaol scrapings? Many troublemakers?"

"The other Lieutenants and Mids have filled me in on the hands they're leery of, sir," Lt. Westcott continued. "You'll find their names in her former Captain's punishment book . . . often."

"A happy ship, is she, Mister Westcott?" Lewrie asked.

"On that head, sir . . . ?" Westcott said in a low voice, casting his eyes up and aft towards the poop deck. "Perhaps we might go see what Bisquit's up to?"

They went up the starboard ladderway to the poop deck for more privacy, and strolled to the flag lockers where they could sit and converse with no one else listening in.

"I feel like I'm sittin' on the roof of a mansion!" Lewrie had to exclaim first, "or, halfway up the main mast shrouds."

"The poop *is* rather high above the water, aye, sir," Westcott agreed with a brief chuckle. "A happy ship? I don't believe I could say that, sir. I've only been aboard a week, so I haven't gotten the people's feelings completely sorted out, but I can say that she's of two minds. Maybe three . . . those who miss Captain Insley and thought him a proper officer . . . those who sided with Lieutenant Gable, her First . . . and the bulk of her hands who don't give a damn either way."

"Christ, sounds like Bligh and Christian aboard the *Bounty*," Lewrie said, leaning back against the taffrails.

"Captain Insley was a very formal and strict officer," Westcott imparted in a mutter, no matter the lack of people within earshot. "A no-nonsense disciplinarian, to boot, and I gather that he was a man who held most people in a very top-lofty low regard. Cold, aloof, and with a quick and cutting wit sharp enough to smart."

"Rubbed a lot o' people the wrong way, I take it?" Lewrie said.

"Especially the former First Officer, Lieutenant Gable," Westcott said, nodding. "Years ago, Insley was a junior Lieutenant aboard the old *Bellona*, and Gable was one of her new-come Mids, just starting to learn the ropes . . . Insley demeaned everything he and the 'younkers' did, had them all kissing the gunner's daughter for every failure or shortcoming, with Gable his favourite target. Admiralty wasn't to know . . ." Westcott said with a shrug and a grimace. "Healthy and long-serving officers of good experience, names on a list, and slots to be filled? That's all the questions to be answered."

*Like me and* . . . Lewrie thought, *well, a lot of people!*

"So, when Insley saw Gable, all he saw was the ignorant, cunny-thumbed Midshipman he once was," Lewrie decided, "and all Gable saw was his old tormenter? *Bound* t'be an explosion, sooner or later."

"Lieutenant Gable, I gather, saw *himself* as the protector of *Sapphire*'s people from Insley's ruthless discipline and punishments," Westcott added, "*and* as Insley's former victim. He spoke freely of it in the wardroom. Robin Hood? A knight-errant seeking the Holy Grail? On a godly mission, to him, no doubt. Lieutenant Harcourt sneered at his . . . quest, and told me that Gable was a molly-coddling 'Popularity Dick' who let the hands get away with murder. Lieutenant Elmes did allow that Insley was a *tad* too strict, but that's as far as he'd go to express any opinion. Caught in the middle.

"You'll see what I mean when you look through Captain Insley's Order Book," Westcott told Lewrie. "I brought a copy of yours from *Reliant*, but I haven't put it into use, yet."

"We'll go over my old one and make alterations to account for a much larger ship and crew," Lewrie said. "Aye, I will look the old one over, and see if any of Insley's standing instructions are of any use to us. Did Insley have any other admirers?"

"Harcourt; the senior Mid, Mister Hillhouse; the senior Marine officer, Keane; and the ship's Master At Arms, of course," Westcott told him, "two or three of the older Mids, too, Britton and Leverett. Most of the other Mids seem sorry that Gable's gone."

"We'll have t'keep a close watch on them, and bring 'em round to 'firm but fair,' " Lewrie determined, "and, keep a close eye on the hands, as well. As soon as a somewhat more lenient rule is established, they'll be sure t'test us, the 'sea-lawyers', gaol sweepin's, and the sky-larkers."

"Sure as Fate, sir," Westcott agreed with a grin, "but, we'll handle them, the same way we whipped *Reliant*'s people into shape."

"I count on you gettin' that done, Geoffrey," Lewrie assured him. "That's why I was so eager t'have you as my First, again."

"Won't let you down, sir," Westcott promised.

Bisquit, bored with trotting round the poop deck and marking his territory with a squirt or two, came to lay his head on Westcott's knee and nuzzle for attention.

"There's a rabbit pelt in his crate," Lewrie said as he rose to his feet, "and some other of his toys. I think I'll go below and see what my cabins are like. You two . . . amuse yourselves for a bit."

"I think I shall, sir!" Westcott agreed, getting to his feet, as well. "The dignity of my office be-damned."

# CHAPTER NINE

"God, I could play tennis in here!" Lewrie muttered under his breath as he entered his great-cabins, which were divided into a dining coach to larboard, a very large bed-space to starboard, then the day cabin aft of those which spanned from beam to beam and ended at the quarter-galleries, the transom settees, and the door to his outdoor stern gallery beyond. The partitions which delineated the compartments were thin wood, not canvas stretched over light deal frames, painted a pale beige with white mouldings, and double doors led from the day-cabin to the bed-space and dining coach on the forward walls. He had to share his quarters with four of the quarterdeck 6-pounder guns, but otherwise he had *bags* of room for his wine-cabinet, desk and chair, his round brass Hindoo tray table on its low platform, and his settee and chairs set up on the starboard side.

"There's so much space, sir, we've put your wash-hand stand in the bed-space, along with your chests," Pettus told him as he fidgetted with the angle of the collapsible chairs round the tray table.

"Mus' be plannin' on shippin' 'is woman aboard," Lewrie heard from the bed-space, where the Ship's Carpenter and his Mate were hanging up his suspended bed-cot.

"Nah, 'e just likes t'sprawl-like," he heard Jessop comment. "But 'e's a terror wif 'em ashore, an' th' First Off'cer, too. Been a widower some years, now, th' Cap'm 'as."

"A glass of something, sir?" Pettus said, over-loudly to warn them that Lewrie was in ear-shot.

"Aye, Pettus, I would," Lewrie replied, equally loudly, and winking at his cabin-steward. Nervous coughs came from the bed-space. The Carpenter and his Mate gathered up their tools and slunk out into the day-cabin, where Lewrie introduced himself, learning that their names were Acfield and Stover, and thanking them for their trouble.

He got a glass of rhenish and went out on his wide and deep stern gallery to savour some fresh air. Pettus had already opened the upper halves of the transom sash windows for ventilation, and to make sure that Chalky would not get out of the cabins that way, but the cat was hellish-quick to dash out the door with him, then leap to the top railing of the gallery's barrier, and Lewrie just as quickly grabbed him by the scruff of his neck before he tumbled overside.

"Bad place for you, Chalky . . . *bad!*" Lewrie chid him. "It's not wide enough for you." He sat the cat down on the deck.

*I've already lost one cat, and damned if I'll lose another!* he thought, determining that his stern walk might be an attractive perk but one that he might not be able to enjoy all that much without keeping a wary eye out for Chalky and his antics. Before the cat could jump back up there, he herded it inside and shut the door and went to the settee.

"Take your flummery, sir?" Pettus asked.

"Aye, Pettus, let's get me back into everyday rig," Lewrie agreed, shedding his best-dress uniform coat which bore his two medals and the star of his knighthood, then the sash which lay over his waist-coat. "I've done all my 'impressing' I'm going t'do, today. We're going t'have t'watch that damned door to the stern gallery, 'less the damned cat gets out, hops onto the railing, and goes overboard."

"We'll see to it, sir," Pettus promised. "Ehm . . . I had a wee chat with Mumphrey, Mister Westcott's man? Seems there was a bit of a scramble when Mister Westcott came aboard last week. The Second Officer, Mister Harcourt, had already moved himself into the First Lieutenant's cabin, and Midshipman Hillhouse had shifted his traps to the wardroom. When Mister Westcott turned up, both of them had quite a come-down."

"Indeed?" Lewrie coolly sniffed.

"Mumphrey says there's a cabin off the wardroom just for your secretary, and there's a day office for him, too, to larboard of the helm, so I expect Mister Faulkes will feel right regal for a change. On the starboard side of the helm, there's a sea cabin for the Sailing Master, just forward of your bed-space. I hope the fellow doesn't snore too loudly."

"If he does, we'll scrounge up some spare blankets to hang on the forrud bulkhead," Lewrie chuckled, "or if the hands at the helm take to singin' in the middle of the night."

The double wheel and the compass binnacle cabinet were just a few feet beyond the doors to his great-cabins, sandwiched between the day office and sea cabin, and sheltered under the poop deck; a very handy arrangement.

"Mumphrey also told me there's a fairly big spare cabin on the starboard side of the wardroom, right aft, sir," Pettus chattered on, "where a Captain would go, if this ship carried a Commodore, who gets these cabins."

"God forbid!" Lewrie hooted. "I haven't even gotten comfortable in here, yet! Hmm . . . I fear Faulkes will have t'be disappointed. If the Master's sea cabin is so close to the helm, that day office would make a grand chart room, with my slant-top desk and chart racks where Mister Yelland, the watch officers, and I can roll 'em out flat and do our plots. Faulkes already has his own desk over yonder," Lewrie said, nodding his head towards the larboard corner of the day-cabin, close to the door to his quarter gallery.

"Ehm . . . Mister Westcott left the former Captain's ledgers and books for you, sir," Pettus went on. "I put them on your desk."

"No rest for the lazy," Lewrie said with a sigh. "You'd best brew me up a pot of coffee, Pettus. They'll be boresome-dry going."

He *had* to read all of them, closely; there was too much risk of being docked in his pay, else. HMS *Sapphire*'s voluminous inventories of items put aboard by the various Boards of Admiralty, her guns, her shot and powder, boats, sails and spare sailcloth, galley implements and pots, lanthorns, small arms, sand glasses, rations, her miles of ropes and cables for both standing and running rigging, had been signed for by her former captain, and every niggling replacement item had had to be documented. Normally, Lewrie would consult with the previous commanding officer to balance the books and account for losses or wear, but that was now impossible. The ship was his, as were all the thousands of "things" listed in her ledgers that he would one day have to account for, to the least jot and tittle, and be charged for if things went adrift.

*No wonder some captains prefer t'go down with their ships,* he thought in wry humour; *They couldn't afford* t'replace *'em even if they were as rich as the Walpoles!*

Add to that careful perusing, there were the muster books and the assignments given to each hand for every evolution, the stacks of loose papers showing expenses and requisitions from the Sheerness Dockyards which had not yet been entered into the proper ledgers, and Captain Insley's Order Book and punishment book. He would be at it long past suppertime. What Lewrie really wished to do was prowl the ship from bilges to the weather decks, bow to stern, but that would have to be put off to another day.

Lewrie determined that he would dine Westcott in for a working supper, and would keep his clerk, Faulkes, past his suppertime, too. Westcott had been aboard a week longer than he, and would know by now enough to get him past the paperwork. As for Faulkes, well . . .

*So much for him bein' an idler with "All Night In"!* Lewrie told himself with a wee snicker as he opened the first book in the pile.

The fifty private Marines of *Sapphire*'s complement traditionally were berthed forward of the officers' wardroom on the upper gun deck; mutiny was not an un-heard-of occurrence. Lewrie's Cox'n, Liam Desmond, led the bulk of the Captain's retinue to a spare mess-table just forward of the Marines, now they were done with setting up the great-cabins, in search of their own berth spaces. They set their sea-chests round the table to sit on, and hung up their sea-bags along the thick and stout hull between a pair of gun-ports. Bisquit accompanied them out of curiosity to see where his friends were going.

"Diff'rnt than *Reliant,*" Patrick Furfy commented, looking round at the rows of 12-pounders, and the seeming hundreds of sailors idling at the other mess tables. "They ain't room t'swing a cat."

"Could be worse, Pat," Desmond said, chuckling. "We could be on the lower gun deck, with nary a breath o' fresh air."

"'At's Crawley's table," an older sailor told them.

"Who's he?" James Yeovill, the Captain's cook, asked.

"'E's th' Cox'n," the older fellow said with a sour look, "an' 'is boat crew berth there."

"I'm Liam Desmond, Cap'm *Lewrie's* Cox'n," Desmond told him. "Me mate and stroke-oar, Pat Furfy, there . . . Cap'm's cook, Yeovill, and them there's Pettus an' Jessop. Th' Cap'm's men."

"Been with him f'r ages an' amen," Furfy vowed.

"It's still Crawley's mess table, I tells ye," the older hand growled.

"What, all f'r him alone, sure?" a younger man scoffed aloud. "Crawley an' Cap'm Insley's people're ashore t'tend him in th' hospital, an' most o' them'll come back aboard'z plain Landsmen an' Ord'nary Seamen . . . if they come back at all. Michael Deavers, I am, an' I *was* in Cap'm Insley's boat crew, but . . ." he said with an iffy shrug.

"Then I reckon ye still will be," Desmond told him.

"Maybe Cap'm Insley'll keep his cook and servants on after he's faced a court," Deavers went on, "but, th' rest of 'em belongs t'th' Navy, no matter the come-down."

"With him long, ye say," another sailor nearby asked, taking a cold pipe from his mouth. "What sorta officer is Cap'm Lewrie?"

"He's a scraper, arrah," Furfy boasted, warming to the subject. "We been in more fights than we've had hot suppers."

"Much of a hope f'r that in *this* ship!" another sailor griped. "All we've done is convoy work inta th' Baltic an' back f'r months on end, an' nary a shot've we fired."

"Cap'm Lewrie'll find us some action," Yeovill spoke up, "he always does, sooner or later."

" 'E come aboard all tarted up, wif star an' sash, an' medals," the older hand sneered. "Born to it, wos 'e? Silver spoon in 'is mouth an' all?"

"*Won* 'em!" Furfy barked. "We were with him at Camperdown and Copenhagen, an' he was at Cape Saint Vincent afore that. He got his knighthood f'r defeatin' a French squadron off Louisiana back in '03, so he earned it, fair an' square."

"Tartar, is he?" a younger sailor asked. "A hard flogger?"

"Firm but fair," Desmond assured him. "The Cap'm ain't much of a flogger, but ya give him good cause an' he'll have ya at th' gratings."

"*Proteus, Savage, Thermopylae,* and *Reliant,*" Furfy added with a grin, "none o' th' Cap'm's ships did much floggin' at all."

The younger sailor looked relieved, then began to smile when Bisquit, sensing a kind soul, trotted to him and began to nuzzle his hands for petting.

" 'At's Bisquit, he is," Jessop said.

"Cap'm's dog?" the sour older hand asked.

"The *ship's* dog aboard *Reliant,*" Pettus told him. "Our Mids rescued him from the flagship at Nassau. *Mersey*'s Mids brought him aboard, but *her* Captain and officers had purebred hunting dogs, and threatened t'drown Bisquit in a sack if they snuck him back aboard again. When *Reliant* paid off, no one else could take him, so Cap'm Lewrie took him on. But, he's still pretty-much the ship's dog."

"He's a fine'un, no error," the younger sailor crooned, "ain't ya, boy? Aye, ya are! Want a piece o' hardtack?"

"Th' onliest beast who'd appreciate it, hah!" Furfy laughed. "Bisquit's th' only one who *likes* somethin' that hard t'chew!"

"An' yer beef bones, wif a shred o' meat on 'em," Jessop said. "Ye'll not have t'heave 'em out th' gun-ports wif Bisquit aboard."

"Well, now we're situated, I suppose we should get back aft, Jessop," Pettus announced.

"Aye, and I need to go forward and meet the Ship's Cook, and set my goods up in the galley," Yeovill said, getting to his feet, cautiously. The overhead did not quite allow standing head room.

"Oh, ye'll just *love* ol' Tanner!" the older sailor said with another sneer. "Th' one-legged bastard's been tryin' *t'poison* us since we been in commission! I swear 'e pisses in th' cauldrons just f'r spite! 'E's a damned sour man, 'e is."

"And you ain't?" Deavers teased.

"Damn yer eyes, Deavers," the older fellow snapped. "Ye wish a change o' mess, yer welcome to it."

"Aye, I think I do," Deavers decided of a sudden. "I see ya have but five for an eight-man mess, Cox'n Desmond, and if ya say I'm t'stay on in th' Cap'm's boat crew, I might as well shift my traps to yours, an' tell the First Officer of it. How about you, Harper?" he asked the younger sailor.

"Be fine with me, Michael," Harper agreed.

"Then, when Crawley an' his lot come back aboard, if they do, *you* can have 'em, Thompson," Deavers said to the older hand. "You'll all get along'z thick as thieves, hah hah."

"Better mess-mates 'an th' likes o' *you!*" Thompson shot back.

Bisquit left off gnawing on his chunk of ship's bisquit as his old friends departed, looking anxious 'til Deavers and Harper shifted their chests and sea-bags to Desmond's table, then settled back down on his belly to crack the bone-hard treat. And, by the time he'd eaten the last crumb, the dog found that he had won two new friends who would ruffle his fur, let him lay his head on their thighs, and tease him.

# CHAPTER TEN

"I'm beginnin' t'think that a two-decker fifty's not the *worst* ship to have, Mister Westcott," Lewrie said about a week later, after he had prowled his new command from the cable tiers to the fighting tops. "I'm especially impressed with the iron water tanks, and those iron knees."

"Well, we still have to pump from the tanks to fill the scuttle-butts so the hands can use the dippers when they need a sip or two," Lt. Westcott said as they emerged from the upper gun deck to the weather deck and fresh air. After a time, all ships developed a permanent stink that could not be eradicated, no matter how often the bilges were pumped out, the interiors scrubbed with vinegar, or smoked with burning faggots of tobacco leaf. Salt-meat ration kegs reeked, after years in cask, fat slush skimmed from the cauldrons when those meats were boiled had its own odour, and was liberally slathered on running rigging to keep it supple. Add to that the ordure from the animals in the forecastle manger, damp wool and soured bedding, the hundreds of sailors who went un-washed for days on end, and their pea-soup farts, and un-warned civilian visitors could end up stunned and gagging.

"Those knees, sir," Westcott went on. "With so many warships ordered round '92 and '93, and so many merchant ships being built, to replace losses, the Chatham yards had them forged by way of an experiment, and the class designer, Mister Hounslow, thought them a grand idea. They make her much stiffer, less prone to work her timbers in a heavy seaway. In point of fact, I heard that there is new talk of building ships with complete iron frames, with the hull planking to be bolted on, later. I asked the other watch officers and the Bosun how she held up in the North Sea and the Baltic and they were very happy with her . . . in that regard, at least."

"What *didn't* they like, then?" Lewrie asked.

"She'll go, sir . . . ponderously," Westcott said with a laugh. "She'll set her shoulder and sail stiff, but I doubt if we'll ever see her make much more than nine or ten knots, and that in a whole gale with the stuns'ls rigged, and all to the royals."

"Well, maybe we can *plod* at the French," Lewrie joshed.

"When we do come to grips, at least we have the artillery for a smashing good blow," Westcott pointed out, "though, her former Captain only excerised with the great guns once a week, and was a pinch-penny when it came to expending shot and powder at live-firing, sir. We're changing that, and once we get to sea, I'd like live-firing once each week."

"You and I, both, Mister Westcott," Lewrie heartily agreed with that plan. From his earliest days, he had been in love with the roar and stink of the guns, from the puniest 2-pounder swivel guns to the 18-pounders of his last commands. He had ordered gun drill held three times in the week he'd been aboard, and could not wait to be out of harbour where he could see his lower-deck 24-pounders, upper-deck 12-pounders, and all those 24-pounder carronades be lit off.

"Boat ahoy!" Midshipman Harvey called out from the quarterdeck, attracting Lewrie's and Westcott's attention.

"Mail and messages for *Sapphire*!" a thin wail came back.

"Keep some fingers crossed, Mister Westcott," Lewrie said as he eagerly scampered up the ladderway to the quarterdeck. "If it ain't your tailor's bills, or your landlady's love letters, we might have *orders!*"

Once upon the quarterdeck, Lewrie spotted an eight-oared cutter beetling cross the Great Nore's light chops bound for his ship's starboard side. The oarsmen and Cox'n were sailors in Navy rig, and a Midshipman sat in the stern sheets with a large white canvas sack slung cross his chest. It looked very promising and it was all that Lewrie could do to disguise a nigh-boyish sense of anticipation.

It seemed to take ages for the cutter to bump alongside the ship and for the Midshipman to make his way up the battens to the entry-port and to the quarterdeck.

"Good morning, all," the newcomer gaily announced himself to the Midshipmen of the watch, as if he did not see a Post-Captain on deck.

"Something for me?" Lewrie snapped, stepping forward.

"Your pardons, sir," the Mid said with a gulp. "Orders and mail for *Sapphire*, sir. If you would be so good as to sign for them, sir?"

Lewrie quickly scribbled his name on a chit with the new Mid's stub of a pencil, then took possession of the canvas sack. From that first hail and reply, idle hands and off-watch men had perked up their ears and drifted aft nearer the quarterdeck in curiosity and longing to hear from wives, girlfriends, and family.

Lewrie would have liked to dig into the sack that instant and snatch out his own correspondence, but that would be appearing too eager. He nodded to the cutter's Mid and turned to go aft into his cabins to sort things out, calling aloud for word to be passed for his clerk, Faulkes. Once ensconsed in privacy, though, he opened the sack and dumped the contents on his desk. "Aha!" he cheered to see a thick packet addressed, to him from Admiralty, thickly sealed with blue wax and bound in ribbon. "And pray God, not the Baltic!" he added softly.

The sudden pile of letters, and the crinkly sound of heavy official bond paper being folded open, attracted Chalky like the sudden appearance of a flock of gulls in the cabins, and he sprang atop the desk to scatter and strew them to the deck, slipping and sliding on the letters that remained, unsure of which of those on the deck he'd pounce upon first. Chalky let out a puzzled *Mrr!*, then a louder *Meow!* and dove off the desk to plow into a shallow pile like a boy hurling himself into a mound of autumn leaves.

"Ha . . . 'provide escort for troop ships now lying at the Nore'," he read. "Oh, shit . . . 'four ships named in the margin to Gibraltar to re-enforce the garrison, then report your ship to Lieutenant-General Sir Hew Dalrymple, Gov.-Gen'l of Gibraltar, and RN Commissioner of Dockyards, as available for duty, notwithstanding other duties which you will find in a separate correspondence marked "Most Secret And Confidential" you may be asked to perform from time to time' . . . what the Devil?"

He rooted round the loose letters on the desk but could not find anything with that mark, or the more usual "Captain's Eyes Only". Faulkes entered the cabins and stopped short at the sight of the mess.

"Ah, Faulkes!" Lewrie brightened, "do sort through all that lot on the deck, will you? There's one official meant for me, but Chalky's got it at the moment."

"Ehm, yes, sir," Faulkes said, kneeling to gather up as many as he could to sort through them. "This must be it, sir. . . . *ow!* It's not yours. Let go the ribbons, Chalky." He got back to his feet and handed the letter to Lewrie, then knelt again to begin piling the rest into proper order, sorting official correspondence into one pile, personal letters into another, and Lewrie's other mail into a third.

"Carry on, Faulkes," Lewrie said, rising and going to his dining coach for a bit more privacy, for this folded-over, wax-sealed letter was from the Foreign Office, and it was not only marked "Most Secret And Confidential" but "Captain's Eyes Only", as well. There was only one branch of His Majesty's Foreign Office that had ever sent Lewrie a scrap of correspondence; Secret Branch, old Zachariah Twigg's set of spies, secret agents, forgers, and associated cut-throats and assassins, and a most unofficial battalion of strong-arm muscle.

"Mine arse on a band-box," he muttered to himself as he closed the double doors of the dining-coach, sat himself down at the table, and placed the letter before him. He stared at it for a long moment, and even found himself wiping his hands on his trouser legs in dread, for nothing good had ever come of his association with that crowd.

Off and on since 1784, Lewrie had been roped into several nefarious and neck-or-nothing Secret Branch schemes or covert actions; in the Far East between the wars, in the Mediterranean when he'd had the *Jester* sloop, during Britain's involvement with the bloody ex-slave rebellion on Saint Domingue, now Haiti, even posing as a civilian merchant marine mate in search of work up the Mississippi, to hunt down Creole pirates in Spanish-held New Orleans. He had been Twigg's gun-dog, a none-too-bright but useful tool, and frankly, had always felt a most *disposable* asset if Twigg had felt that necessary. God, but they were a ruthless, faithless lot!

Zachariah Twigg was long-retired, perhaps had even joined the Great Majority by now, but his cheerfully devious protégé-henchman, James Peel, was still in play. " 'Tis Peel, sir . . . James Peel'." The last he'd seen of Peel was late in 1804, after Lewrie's secret experiments with catamaran torpedoes had proved a bust. Peel had come to cozen him into writing a letter of forgiveness to one of those Creole pirates, a young woman who'd shot him full in the chest once with a Girandoni air-rifle (and thank God the air-flask was spent!), Charité Angelette de Guilleri, the worst-named girl he'd ever met, who had taken part in hunting him and his wife, Caroline, down after they'd been warned to flee Paris in 1802. That beautiful, beguiling, but dangerous bitch had been in the party that had shot Caroline in the back and killed her, and she'd wanted his forgiveness?

Oh, but the Emperor Napoleon had sold Charité's beloved New Orleans and all of Louisiana to the Americans, turning her against him and France, and she was *so* well-placed in Paris, welcome in the salons of the elite, in the beds of Napoleon's ministers, generals, and naval officials, and it *was* for King and Country, after all, for her to be a British spy, and all it would take was a letter from Lewrie to turn her to England's advantage. And *damn* James Peel for asking that of him! Damn Secret Branch, too, for imagining him *useful*, again!

At long last, he tugged at the red ribbons and broke the red wax seals, unfolded the letter, took a deep, cautioning breath, and began to read. "Oh. Well, maybe that won't be so bad," Lewrie whispered after he'd given it a close reading. It *was* from Peel, who was now a senior agent; it was even chatty! Peel related that he had become too well-known on the Continent for covert work and had been promoted to plan and supervise others, from London.

There was rising un-rest and dis-content among the Spanish public, Peel explained, and their alliance with France, and Napoleon, had so far been a naval, military, and economic disaster. Millions in gold and silver had gone to France, part of her navy had been turned over to the French, and meats and grains which could have gone to the nourishment of Spaniards was now trundled over the Pyrenees to feed Napoleon Bonaparte's armies, and people, and that at a poor rate of return. The Spanish Prime Minister, Godoy, and his elite circle of Francophiles were almost slavish in their admiration and emulation of the French, which was engendering a rising restlestness among the poor, the middle classes, and the titled to declare Godoy and his circle as traitors, anti-Catholic, anti-Church, anti-God, and anti-Spanish.

*"We at Foreign Office put a flea in Admiralty's ear to make better Use of you, Alan, both as a man familiar with, admittedly, our brand of Skullduggery, and as a active Officer better suited to Combat than*

*onerous convoy Duties in Baltic backwaters. At Gibraltar you will be pleased, I am certain, to find that our senior Agent in charge of Correspondence with those Spaniards in positions of Influence disenchanted with the French and their own Government, and their Recruitment, is one well known to you, to wit, your old clerk, Mr. Thomas Mountjoy. Once at Gibraltar, do please make yourself and your Ship available to him for the Landing and Retrieval of Agents and Messengers working for him to sway the Spanish to renounce their Alliance with France, and if Alliance with Great Britian will not suit, at the least it may be possible to turn them Neutral . . ."*

"Boat-work, at night, hmm," Lewrie mused aloud. "Maybe."

Lewrie made a face after a second more thought. *Sapphire* had a serious drawback if Peel and his superiors in their snug London offices thought to use her, and him; his new ship drew around 18 and one half feet forrud, and nearly 20 feet right aft when properly loaded, so any agent landed on a hostile shore in the dead of night would face a very long row to the beach. *Sapphire* would have to fetch-to *miles* out to sea, where the waters were deep enough, keeping at least two safe fathoms of water 'twixt her keel and the seabed.

Lewrie folded the "Eyes Only" letter back together, rose, and went to the day-cabin. He scooped the Admiralty orders up and locked both in a drawer of his desk, then went out onto his stern gallery to look down at *Sapphire*'s boats which idled below and astern.

*Maybe fetched-to miles out might work*, Lewrie mused; *And we use the thirty-two-foot pinnace t'land our agents. Have t'paint it a dull grey, though, else it stands out at night like a white swan.*

Lewrie imagined that they would have to fetch-to or anchor so far out that no one ashore could spot them in the dark, even did they look hard for them, but . . . he found another problem; if an agent had to be *recovered*, could he get *Sapphire* close enough to spot the lamp or hooded lanthorn signal, then take long, dangerous hours to send in the pinnace and get the man off?

"Need a cutter, or a sloop," Lewrie muttered. "Sorry, Peel, I ain't your man this time."

He went back in, closing the door to the gallery behind him so the cat didn't get out, and went to his desk to write Peel at once to point out the big, two-decked flaw in Secret Branch's plan.

"I've all the mail sorted, sir," Faulkes, his clerk, told him. "All yours is on the brass table. The rim keeps Chalky from scattering it, d'ye see."

"Very good, Faulkes," Lewrie said, looking up with a grin. "Do you deliver the officers' letters to the wardroom, then place all the rest in the chart space 'til Seven Bells of the Forenoon, when you can distribute the hands' letters from home."

"Aye, sir," Faulkes replied. He had a slight drinking problem, Faulkes did, but he'd kept it in check, so far. Delivering mail from home to sailors in the middle of the first daily rum issue would keep him from seeking "sippers" from the others.

"When you drop off the officers' letters, pass word for Mister Westcott to attend me," Lewrie added. He smiled at Faulkes's departing back, knowing that the news of *Sapphire*'s orders to Gibraltar would be spread throughout the ship within a half-hour. What passed aft in the wardroom or great-cabins never could stay secret for long. Oh, Faulkes would slyly answer sailors' queries with something like, "It won't be the Baltic, again"; he knew better than to blurt out accurate details, even if he'd glimpsed at the orders. The summons for Lt. Westcott was icing on the cake, a sure sign that the ship would be sailing soon.

To where, though? He'd keep that quiet a little longer!

# CHAPTER ELEVEN

The next few days were spent lading everything from powder and shot to salt-meat casks to spare sand glasses. Lewrie spent a little time ashore in Sheerness seeing to his personal needs, but took time to make himself known to the Agent Afloat from the Navy Transport Board in charge of the four merchant vessels he would escort, and the four civilian shipmasters. Lewrie also called upon Lieutenant-Colonel Fry, commanding officer of the Kent Fusilier Regiment, which idled, and drilled to a point of madness, in shared barracks with the local garrison troops protecting Sheerness and the mouths of the Thames and Medway Rivers.

"Now, there's a forlorn hope for you, Captain Lewrie," Lieutenant-Colonel Fry groused in his borrowed temporary quarters. "Any foe that's ever tried to sail up the rivers had no trouble at all at doing so, and even the Tilbury Forts barely slowed them down. The garrison here knows it, and is barely manageable . . . drill upon drill, corporal punishment with the lash by the dozens . . . and now *my* men are shoved alongside the local no-hopers, arsehole to elbow, and ruining them! I cannot wait to get them aboard their ships and away to sea before they turn mutinous. More whisky, sir?" Fry asked, waving a hand at a tray that bore a decanter of Scottish whisky.

"Oh, just a touch, sir," Lewrie allowed. Colonel Fry's batman poured them both generous refills. Lewrie considered that he might have to develop a taste for the Scottish version, for it was getting harder to find his favourite aged American corn whisky.

"Things might not be a whit better at Gibraltar, either," Fry gloomed on, lolling his head back on the wing chair in which he sat, as if weary of it all. Colonel Fry was a long, lean, and spare fellow in his early fourties, dark-haired, dark-eyed, and looked as if he was forever in need of a touch-up shave. He seemed to be *born* glum.

"Why so, sir?" Lewrie asked, to be polite, hiding a wince over the smokiness of the whisky.

"Lord, my early days," Colonel Fry mused, almost wistfully, "I was posted to Gibraltar a couple of times, and it was all so very neat and orderly, just the finest sort of military efficiency and good behaviour. Church parade, guard mount, close-order drill and musketry twice a week, everything polished, all kits in top condition, and the social rounds delightful, well . . . then came the war in '93."

"Messy business," Lewrie commented.

"Old Eliot was a good governor, and so was General O'Hara, even if he was getting on in years," Fry went on, "but, the rotation of men got all muddled. The garrison became temporary duty for regiments who were shuttled in and out, and came back reduced by sickness and battle, and ready to get blind drunk and stay that way, and O'Hara lost control before he died.

"Then came General His Royal Highness Prince Edward, the Duke of Kent, five years ago, in 1802," Colonel Fry spat. "Ever hear of him, sir? Ever hear of how the King himself had to relieve him from command of his own royal regiment for cruelty? The mutiny he caused when he commanded our forces in Canada?"

"Must not have made the papers," Lewrie said with a brow up in astonishment.

"The Duke of Kent took over command of Gibraltar to replace old O'Hara, and had the post for a year," Fry told him, sitting up at last as he warmed to his topic. "Damned if he didn't cause *another* mutiny! Two parades a day, wake the garrison at three thirty in summer, five thirty in winter, 'square-bashing' for hours on end, working parties to shift supplies from one warehouse to another just to keep the men busy, drinkless curfews after Tatoo, confined to barracks . . . well, who *wouldn't* mutiny after a time, I ask you?"

"Is it still that way?" Lewrie asked, fearful that allowing his crew shore liberty at Gibraltar would corrupt them, too.

"To a certain extent, Captain Lewrie," Colonel Fry said, pulling a face as he reached for the whisky decanter to serve himself. "Drink still flows like water, and there are pubs on every corner, though the troops no longer get issued eight pence every day after being released from duties. Lieutenant General Sir Hew Dalrymple has been Governor since 1806, and I've had letters from officers serving under him there that conditions are much improved, but still . . . rowdy. Dalrymple's called 'the Dowager'," Fry said with a faint grin of amusement. "He's been a soldier since 1763, but only saw action in Flanders, and that was a disaster . . . not his fault, though. Put it all down to the Duke of York."

"Christ, I was *born* in 1763!" Lewrie said, snickering.

"Scylla and Charibdis . . . rock and a hard place," Fry jested, "and Gibraltar being 'the Rock', haw! My soldiers will either be bored to tears here, or debauched there, but at least they'll not have any opportunity to desert where they're going. Assuming that we can get going *soon,* Captain Lewrie, hey?"

"The Agent Afloat assures me that your troops could go aboard the transports by the end of the week, sir," Lewrie informed Colonel Fry. "The only thing that's wanting is a second warship to assist my ship. We'll be crossin' the Bay of Biscay, trailin' our colours down the coast of France, and *Sapphire* may have the guns to protect your men, but not the agility, or the speed. I wrote Admiralty as soon as I got my orders, but haven't heard, yet. Are we forced to wait much longer after your troops are aboard, then there would have to be some re-victualling, delaying us further. Then, there's the wind and the weather to contend with, of course."

"Hmm, it may be best did we get onto the transports as soon as possible," Fry decided after a long moment of thought. "The men can't desert from ships anchored far out, and even at anchor, they'll have a chance to get a *semblance* of their 'sea legs', hey? Goddamn Napoleon."

"Hey?" Lewrie asked, puzzled by Fry's curse.

"The regiment's war-raised, right after the war began again in 1803," Fry explained, "All eager volunteers and independent companies of Kent Yeomanry. So long as Bonaparte threatened us with that huge invasion fleet and army cross the Channel, my troops were up for anything, but, once that danger passed, we all thought that we'd go back to the reserves. The Fusiliers are only a single-battalion regiment, d'ye see. Now, if we were off to a field army in the Mediterranean, with General Fox, say, on Sicily, with a shot at battle, that's one thing, but *garrison* duty, well! That makes us feel, soldiers and officers alike, that that's all we're good for, and that's hurt morale."

"My tars feel much the same, sir," Lewrie commiserated, "with nothing but Baltic convoy duty 'til now. A friend of mine's cavalry regiment, much like your regiment, feels the same, I expect."

"Which'un?" Fry asked.

"Stangbourne's Light Dragoons," Lewrie told him.

"Why, I know of them!" Fry said, perking, up. "We were brigaded with them for a time. Viscount Stangbourne's done a fine job raising, equipping, and training them . . . though I don't know how he maintains them, the way he gambles. *Lovely* fiancé, if a bit *outré*. Circuses and the stage? His sister, too, though she struck me as very cool and distant. Hellish-attractive, though, in her own way."

"Aye, she is," Lewrie agreed, feeling a sudden icy stir in his innards at the mention of her name. "Let's say that, by the morning of Friday, round eight, your troops and my boats, and the boats from the transports, will be at the docks, ready to begin embarking."

"Capital, Captain Lewrie!" Fry rejoiced. "Simply capital!"

"Weather depending, again," Lewrie cautioned after tossing his glass of whisky back to "heel-taps", and preparing to depart. "A rain, no matter, but if there's strong winds and a heavy chop in the Great Nore, we'll have to delay. Can't drown half your lot in home waters, hey?"

"As your Transport Board agent says, one hundred and fifty men and officers per transport," Colonel Fry agreed, "plus the sixty dependents that won the draw.

"Horse Guards only allows sixty wives of a regiment bound for overseas duty," Fry explained, "and their children, if any. The rest . . . after they draw straws tonight, there will be a lot of wailing in the barracks. What makes it worse is that we're a war-raised single-battalion regiment, with no home barracks in one town, so the others will get scattered over half the county. Oh, well."

"Horses?" Lewrie asked, gathering his hat from a side-table, worried that he would have to arrange barges for them at the last minute.

"We will all be on 'Shank's Ponys', Captain Lewrie. Officers' mounts will be left behind," Fry told him rather gloomily. "There's no place to stable or exercise them on Gibraltar, or ride much, either."

Lewrie could recall horses at Gibraltar from his earlier stops there, though not very many; the property of very senior officers and their ladies. Gibraltar was a gigantic fortress with very little flat land, and very steep, windswept hills.

"Well, I shall be going," Lewrie said, rising. "See you at the docks on Friday morning."

Lewrie took a hired lugger back to *Sapphire,* enjoying a lively dash out into the Great Nore on a fine breeze. His boat came alongside, nuzzling behind a large dockyard barge that was loading crates and kegs up the cargo skids ahead of the starboard entry-port. He paid his fare to the boatman, then went up the battens to the upper deck to the usual welcoming side-party and bosuns' calls.

"Anything new, Mister Westcott?" Lewrie asked the First Lieutenant. "No disasters?"

"There's a letter from Admiralty that came aboard in your absence, sir," Lt. Westcott told him. "It's in your cabins. And, Mister Harcourt asked me if you would consider putting the ship out of discipline for a day or two before we sail."

"Wasn't she out of discipline after she came in from the Baltic just before the duel?" Lewrie asked, pulling a quizzical face.

"She was, sir," Westcott told him.

"Well, with any luck at all, we'll be sailing by Saturday or Sunday, so that's out," Lewrie decided. "The hands'll be issued their quarterly pay just before, and I'll not have 'em robbed by the jobbers, pimps, and whores. The crew will have to wait for shore liberty at Gibraltar, which'll suit 'em much better than a carouse aboard. Carry on, sir," Lewrie said, doffing his hat and heading for his cabins.

"Cool tea, sir?" Pettus asked after he'd taken Lewrie's sword and hat.

"Aye," Lewrie said, peeling off his best-dress uniform coat so it could be hung up on a peg out of Chalky's reach. There was indeed a letter on his desk, sealed with blue ribbons and red wax. He sat, broke the seal, and laid it open. "Aha!"

The cat was in his lap at once, rubbing his head against the white waistcoat, upon which he could do little damage. Lewrie stroked him and patted his side into his chest as he read.

"Good Christ . . . Ralph Knolles!" he exclaimed.

"Who, sir?" Pettus asked as he brought a tall glass of cool tea with lemon juice and sugar.

"My First Officer in the *Jester* sloop, *ages* ago, Pettus," Lewrie happily explained. "He's made 'Post' and commands a twenty-four-gunned Sixth Rate, the *Comus*. She's at Great Yarmouth, and will be coming to join us t'help escort the transports to Gibraltar! Just damn my eyes . . . Knolles, a Post-Captain, hah! A hellish-fine fellow!"

*Even if an old twenty-four is a* tad *weak*, Lewrie thought; *Nine-pounders, some carronades . . . no match for a big French frigate . . . or a* pair *of 'em*.

He had heard the French ventured out in pairs or in threes, these days; only their swift privateers hunted alone, after Trafalgar.

"We're t'have company, Chalky," Lewrie muttered to his cat, and jounced him as he rubbed his fur. "He's a grand fellow, is Knolles, and he was fond o' your old mate, Toulon."

*At least he pretended t'be*, Lewrie thought, grinning.

Chalky thought the jouncing and petting perhaps a tad too vigorous; he mewed and wiggled, then jumped down to dash off a few feet and began to groom himself back to proper order.

"Yeovill says to tell you that he's a fresh-caught sole for the mid-day meal, sir," Pettus informed him, "and for your supper tonight, he's whipping up a cheesy pot pie with lumps of dungeness crab meat. Might there be any need to open a red wine for either, sir?"

"No, Pettus," Lewrie said with a happy shake of his head. "The whites'll do hellish-fine."

"And, the Carpenter, Mister Acfield, hung your screen door so Chalky won't get out on the stern gallery," Pettus added, jerking his head aft.

Lewrie rose and went to inspect it. There was now a second door, hinged on the outside, laced with tautly-strung twine in a mesh, stout enough to resist Chalky's claws and keep him in while allowing fresh air to enter the cabins. Lewrie opened it and stepped out onto his stern gallery, closed it, and latched the metal ring-and-arm hook to secure it. He thought it a quite knacky innovation.

Lewrie looked round the anchorage, so full of ships waiting for a slant of wind, or orders, before sailing. *Sapphire* had swung at her moorings so that the four dowdy transports which he would escort were all inshore of his ship, trotted out in a ragged line, and all flying the mercantile Red Ensign. He looked up to take note of the Blue Ensign that flew on *Sapphire*'s aft staff, and an idea came to him, one that made him begin to smile broadly.

*It might cost me a few pounds, but . . .* he thought; *I'm going t'have t'do some shopping, ashore.*

# CHAPTER TWELVE

The Kent Fusiliers were embarked aboard their transports by Friday evening, allotted their small dog-box cabins which would contain at least eight soldiers (which they would tear down for fresh air and sleep on pallets on the deck or any-old-how before the week was out) and getting used to their scant messes for their meals.

Saturday would have been a suitable day for sailing, for there was a good wind out of the Nor'east, but for the lack of their other escort. *Comus* came into the Great Nore on Sunday, a bit before Noon, and dropped anchor about one cable off from *Sapphire* and the transport ships, after sending a cutter under sail to hunt for them. *Sapphire* made her number, then *Comus*'s number, then hoisted Captain Repair On Board. Lewrie waited impatiently by the starboard entry-port to greet the frigate's captain. A gig shot out from *Comus*, being rowed at some speed. As it neared, Lewrie was almost on his tiptoes 'til at last, *there* he was!

Captain Ralph Knolles was newly-minted, for he wore a single fringed gilt epaulet on his right shoulder, the sign of a Post-Captain of less than three years' seniority. Back when he'd first come aboard as HMS *Jester*'s First Lieutenant, Knolles had been twenty-five, fourteen years before. He was about thirty-nine now, but before he began the long scramble up

*Sapphire*'s boarding battens, Knolles looked up with a grin on his face, spotted Lewrie, and waved broadly.

A minute later and he was on the quarterdeck, doffing his hat with proper gravity, and stifling that grin 'til Lewrie stepped up to offer his hand. "Damn my eyes, but it's good t'see ye!" Lewrie said. "*Captain* Knolles, indeed!"

"Damned good to see you, too, sir," Knolles replied, shaking his hand with enthusiasm. "It's been far too long."

Lewrie quickly introduced his own officers, then invited him to go aft to his great-cabins. "I hope you're hungry, for my cook's laid on some fine lamb chops *and* bacon-wrapped quail."

"Sounds toothsome, sir, lead on," Knolles gladly agreed.

Knolles's face was more weathered and lined, but he was still lean and well-built; a captain's table had not yet thickened him. His blond brows were bushier, and his unruly mane of blond hair was just as dense as it had been . . . and, after handing over his sword and hat to Pettus, he swiped it back into place with both hands, a gesture that had never changed.

"Aspinall?" Knolles asked about Lewrie's old cabin-steward.

"He's written several books, and is a partner in a publishing house in London," Lewrie told him, also filling him in on Will Cony's new career as a publican, and of Matthew Andrews's death long ago.

"Pardons if it pains you, sir, but allow me to express my sympathy anent the loss of your wife," Knolles hesitantly said. "She was a fine lady, and damn the French for murdering her."

"Thankee, Knolles," Lewrie soberly replied. "Damn them, indeed. Now, when did you make 'Post'?" he added, deflecting the subject.

"Just last June, sir," Knolles said, turning gladsome, again. "I was First Officer in a Third Rate just before the Peace of Amiens, rose to Commander in 1803 when the war began again, and . . . poof!"

"Well-earned, too," Lewrie declared. "Ever marry, yourself . . . now you can afford to?" he teased as Pettus fetched them wine.

"Two years ago, sir," Knolles said, brightening. "We came back from Halifax for a hull cleaning, I got home leave, and Dinah was visiting the family of my childhood friends. Again, just poof, quick as a wink, and we wed! May I ask if you re-married, sir?"

"No," Lewrie said with a sad shake of his head. "With both my sons at sea, and my daughter living with my in-laws, there didn't seem a need for a wife, or a step-mother to them. And besides, I doubt if I'd ever discover anyone else who'd measure up to Caroline."

*Lydia would have,* he bitterly thought; *If she'd had the courage.*

"And your lovely French ward, sir? Mistress Sophie?" Knolles asked.

"Married to another of my First Officers, living in Kent, and the mother of at least two children, by now," Lewrie told him. "She's become thoroughly English. Ehm . . . I hope you don't mind turning our dinner into a working meal, and talking 'shop', but the Fusiliers are already aboard their transports, and if this morning's wind holds, we could be out to sea by the end of tomorrow's Forenoon."

"But of course, sir," Knolles seconded. "As I recall, we did some of our best planning over supper!"

"Good man," Lewrie praised. "My clerk's done up a copy of my signals, both night and day, and my rough plan of action should some bloody French frigates turn up. I see that you sail under the Red Ensign, independent. *Sapphire* was under a Rear-Admiral of The Blue when I took her over, but . . . have you a Blue'un aboard?"

"Of course, sir," Knolles said; every ship in the Royal Navy carried all variants of the Union Flag, along with the flags of every seafaring nation, for courtesy or for subterfuge.

"Should we encounter the enemy on our way, I'll pretend to be a Commodore," Lewrie said, beginning a sly smile, "I was one for a bit in the Bahamas, so I'd admire did you fly the Blue Ensign, as will the transports, just in case the Frogs try to take us on. With any luck, they'll take us for a squadron of frigates and shy off."

"Hah!" Knolles chortled. "As sly and sneaky as ever, sir!"

"Sly, me?" Lewrie countered. "Nobody ever called *me* clever . . . fortunate, or plain dumb luck's been more like it."

"Your reputed good *cess,* aye," Knolles said. "That was uncanny, the time we stumbled into the Glorious First of June battle, lost that volunteer lad, Joseph or Josephs? And all those seals showed up when we buried him over the side. *Selkies* and ancient Celtic sea gods?"

"The morning we stumbled into our meeting with the Serbian pirates in the Adriatic in that thick sunrise fog, and there were seals there t'warn us?" Lewrie reminisced. "We should've trusted them for a warnin' that the Serbs'd play both ends against the middle."

Chalky decided that the new interloper in his great-cabins was harmless, for he padded over from the padded transom settee and joined them in the starboard-side seating area, leaping into Lewrie's lap to glare at Knolles.

"Still the 'Ram-Cat' I see, sir," Knolles said with a chuckle.

"Chalky's a present from the American Navy in the West Indies, back in '98," Lewrie told him, stroking the cat which laid down upon his thigh as if guarding his master from the stranger. "Toulon passed over last year in the South Atlantic, just before we landed at Cape Town, under Popham."

"Gad, you were part of that South American disaster?" Knolles said with a commiserating groan. "My sympathies, sir. I don't know if our government knows *how* to give it up for a bad hand. Still, you had Toulon for a good, long time, and once I got my first command, I found that having a pet aboard eases the loneliness. I've an utterly useless terrier . . . he won't even hunt rats, if you can believe it. But, he's a comfort, is Tyge. Damned loud at times, though."

Lewrie's cook, Yeovill, had entered minutes before and had laid out the serving dishes in the dining-coach. He came out and announced that their dinner was ready.

Over their meal, Lewrie explained how he had come to command a two-decker, expressing distress that it seemed his frigate days were behind him, at least temporarily. He had no idea of *Sapphire*'s sailing qualities except for her officers' reports, had yet to conduct any live-fire drills, and worried that his new ship might prove to be an ugly duckling that *never* grew beautiful, or loveable.

"Our voyage may take longer than normal," Lewrie said over the quail course, as the red wine that had accompanied the lamb chops was replaced by a smuggled French pinot gris. "I'd desire do we get at least five hundred miles West'rd of the French coast before hauling off Sutherly, well clear of most privateers and prowling frigates. I may have yoked you to a pig in a poke, if this barge can only *wallow* at the foe, and your *Comus* only has nine-pounders."

"She sails extremely well, sir," Knolles assured him with some pride, "fast and weatherly, and can go about like a witch. My people are very well-drilled, by now, and, taking a page from you, sir, I've made sure that my gunners can load and fire as steady as a metronome, and are hellish-accurate within a cable. I've two twenty-four-pounder carronades and six eighteen-pounders, as well, so I do believe that I can deal with your typical Frog privateer or *corvette,* perhaps even hold my own against a smaller frigate."

"I'm much relieved t'hear it," Lewrie told him. "Let's say we place you at the head of the convoy, about two miles ahead and another two or three miles alee, on 'sentry-go'. I'll bring up the rear with *Sapphire*, and place the four transports in a single line-ahead column ahead of me."

"Hmm," Knolles mused, sampling the white wine as if he judged its taste instead of Lewrie's idea. He nodded as if satisfied. "Do you wish us to look like a naval squadron, sir; perhaps it might be best did you place your two-decker in the middle of the column, with two transports ahead and t'other two astern of you, a very loose two cables or so between ships?"

"That might work, if the French are daunted by the sight of us, but . . ." Lewrie puzzled, his own glass held halfway to his mouth. He frowned, took a sip, then got a cocky look. "Look here, Knolles. If the French are in force, or persist despite how *dangerous* we appear, I wonder how confident they'd feel did we all haul our wind and go on a bow-and-quarter line right at 'em? If they thought they were facing five frigates and a two-decker?"

"Oh, I don't know, sir," Captain Knolles said, furrowing his brow. "If we did, once they got within a mile or so of us, they'd see through the ruse, and realise that the transports were harmless. In that case, we'd have to signal the transports to run, close-hauled to the Westerlies, and within range to be chased down and captured."

"*We'd* still be there, t'protect 'em as they run," Lewrie pointed out. "Do we encounter three or more Frogs sailin' together, we would be up to our necks in the quag, anyway, but if it's only two, or one big'un, we'd daunt 'em in the first place, or meet 'em on equal footing in the second."

"Good God, though, sir!" Knolles almost goggled in amazement, raking the fingers of his left hand through his hair, "how do we get four civilian merchant masters to sail in an orderly column and maintain proper separation in the first place, much less convince them to play-act as warships? Do they sail into battle, they'd be as helpless as kittens! What are their burthens?"

"One's three hundred tons, the other three are of three hundred and fifty tons," Lewrie told him, calling that up from memory.

"That's only fifteen men and some ship's boys aboard one, and only a couple more hands in the other three, sir," Knolles pointed out. "I suppose they're armed, after a fashion . . . but with what? Four- or six-pounders, and some swivels? And, I very much doubt if their masters have pulled the tompions or cast off the lashings on those guns in the last year, except to look for rust."

"There are soldiers aboard all four," Lewrie said whimsically. "Perhaps Colonel Fry can be convinced that they're only *really* big muskets, and man them on their own?"

"Oh now, sir!" Knolles countered, then broke out laughing.

"Only a thought," Lewrie said, shrugging and waving a hand in the air. "Let's get out to the fifteenth Longitude, ever further from France, form 'em all in column, and *if* we're approached by the enemy, we'll hoist the Blue Ensign and trust that Shakespeare was right . . . that 'the play's the thing'. How do you like the quail?"

"Quite savoury, indeed!" Knolles said, uttering a little moan of appreciation. "What does your cook do to make it so flavourful?"

"I fear that's Yeovill's secret spices and sauces," Lewrie said with a sly grin, "and it's rare that he tells *me* how he does it, but I wouldn't trade the man for a keg of gold."

"Mmumm!" Knolles agreed, then dabbed his mouth with his napkin and took a sip of wine. "If we do get out to the fifteenth Longitude, sir, I'd serve no purpose standing alee. Perhaps I should place *Comus* no more than one mile ahead of the column."

"Aye, that makes sense," Lewrie agreed. "Now, if the French *don't* come from the East, but are discovered ahead of us, that'd be another matter . . . or, from windward. Do they appear North of us, it will be a long stern-chase, and we can wheel out of line and interpose our ships 'twixt the French and the transports, who can escape South as fast as their little legs'll carry them."

"You wouldn't wheel us *all* about and challenge them, would you, sir?" Knolles asked with one brow up.

"Might depend on the odds, hey?" Lewrie joshed.

They spent the better part of the next hour enjoying their meal, right through the berry and cream cobbler, port, and sweet bisquits, sketching plans against every contingency. By the time Pettus poured them coffee, and Jessop cleared the table, they had filled two sheets of paper with their thoughts.

"Now, the only thing left is to introduce you to the masters of our transports, Knolles, and convince them that daring, and *fraud*, is their best bet," Lewrie concluded. "I bought them Blue Ensigns, just in case."

"I rather thought you already had, sir," Knolles said, grinning.

"Shall we go, then? We'll take my launch," Lewrie offered.

On the quarterdeck, waiting for Lewrie's boat crew to bring the launch round from astern, Bisquit came frisking up, whining and *yowing* for attention. Lewrie dug into his coat pocket for a strip of Indian-style *pemmican,* which made the dog blissful.

"What do you feed your Tyge, Captain Knolles?" Lewrie asked.

"Table scraps, cook extra, sir," Knolles told him.

"Before we sail, have your Purser go ashore to Rutledge's," Lewrie suggested. "He has preserved, dried meats. American-styled jerky strips, *pemmican* with grains and dried fruits pounded in, and an host of wee sausages. Bisquit here, and Chalky, thrive on 'em. And they come in handy when I feel peckish 'tween meals, too. I've laid by a couple of hundredweight."

"You think of everything, sir," Knolles said. "But then, you always did."

"I did?" Lewrie said, pulling a wry, dis-believing face. "You do me too kind, sir! Think of everything? Hah!"

# BOOK TWO

Your course securely steer,
  West and by South forth keep!
    Rocks, lee-shores, nor shoals
      When Eolus scowls
You need not fear
So absolute the deep.

"TO THE VIRGINIAN VOYAGE"
MICHAEL DRAYTON (1563-1631)

# CHAPTER THIRTEEN

Sunday's weather was foul, but the winds came fair for sailing that Monday, and Lewrie at last got his small convoy to sea, beating out into the North Sea for a time to make a wide offing from the coast before turning South, then Sou'west to stand into the Channel and its chops well clear of Dover and the Goodwin Sands.

It was not an auspicious beginning, though. The masters of the transports, already leery of Lewrie's dispositions, and loath to agree with the Navy—they were *civilians,* after all!—brought the expression about herding cats to mind, along with many a stifled curse. *Comus* led, followed in *some* sort of order by two of the transports in trail, sort of. Warships sailing in column were used to trimming and adjusting sail to maintain separation, and had large crews to perform the work. The thinly-manned transports, though, were either too slow or too quick, barging up alarmingly close to the ship ahead before taking in a reef, or too slow off the mark to spread more sail or shake out a reef, in danger of having the ship astern of them ploughing up their transoms!

"Two columns perhaps, sir?" Lt. Westcott muttered to Lewrie after *Sapphire*'s topmen and line-tenders had clewed up the main course once more. "A nice, tidy square formation?"

"Nice? Tidy? Mine arse on a band-box!" Lewrie growled, just about ready to howl in frustration. "The cunny-thumbed, clueless . . . !"

A single cable's separation didn't look as if it would work. He considered having a signal bent on to change it to two cables, allowing 1,440 feet between ships.

*One'd* think *seven hundred and twenty feet'd be all the room in the world, but . . . no!* Lewrie thought; *The cack-handed . . . bastards! And we're barely into the Channel, yet!*

"Cast of the log, sir," young Midshipman Ward reported to Westcott. "Seven and a half knots."

"Just *blisterin'* speed, by Gad," Lewrie sneered. "Even *we* are able t'rush up and trample somebody. No, Mister Westcott, I'm not yet ready t'give up. If the winds hold direction, they just might catch on how to do it by the time we're off the Lizard."

Midshipman Ward was a youngster; he couldn't help but grin, and let out a stifled titter.

"Ain't funny, lad," Westcott glumly told him.

"Sorry, sir," Ward replied, only slightly abashed, moving away.

"What's worrisome to me, sir, is what happens when the weather turns foul, and we have to go close-hauled," Westcott went on. "They just might end up weaving Westward on opposing tacks, like so many wandering chickens. And, they're civilians. They won't tack, they'll *wear* from one tack to the other, like they usually do, with so few hands aboard. *That'll* be fun to watch. In a morbid way."

"This'll turn into a smaller version of our infamous 'sugar trade' a few years ago, is that what you're sayin', Mister Westcott?" Lewrie muttered to him, groaning in sour remembrance. That had been a disaster, from Jamaica through the Florida Straits then North 'twixt the Hatteras Banks and Bermuda, especially when ships bound for ports in the United States had tried to leave the seaward side of the convoy, *through* the lee columns!

"Just keeping my fingers crossed, sir," Westcott gloomily said. "And trusting that the transports' masters are professional seafarers."

*Then God help us all*, Lewrie thought in dread.

They did begin to get the hang of it, after a few more hours, with a steady following wind, and a less-than-boisterous sea to steady all ships, making between seven or eight knots. By Two Bells of the Day Watch, one in the afternoon, Lewrie felt confident enough that he could cease trotting up and down the ladderways from the quarterdeck to a better view from the poop deck and back again over and over. He went to the forward edge of the quarterdeck and saw Yeovill coming aft from the galley with his covered brass food barge, and decided that he would go aft and eat his delayed dinner.

"I'll be aft, Mister Harcourt," he told the Second Lieutenant, who had the Day Watch.

"Very good, sir," Harcourt replied, "I have the deck."

Harcourt's reply was a formality, perhaps too much so, stiffer and cooler than Lewrie liked. During their time in port, he had had his officers and Mids in to dine, to get to know them and take their measure, and he had noticed that Lt. Harcourt had held himself in a strict reserve, as if he privately resented the arrival of a new Captain and the loss of *Sapphire*'s first one. For certain, Westcott's arrival as the new First Officer, which had kept him in his place as the Second Officer, was resented, Lewrie had surmised, and that senior Midshipman, Hillhouse . . . ! They had both been in the same group at-table one night, and Lewrie *had* noticed some enigmatic shared looks between them, as if Harcourt and Hillhouse were allied in some way.

The Third Lieutenant, Edward Elmes, seemed a decent sort, as did most of the Mids, especially the younger ones, but a couple of the older ones, like Hillhouse, Britton, and Leverett, had struck Lewrie as much of the same frame of mind as Lt. Harcourt . . . a tad sulky and disappointed.

Thankfully, Lewrie had his "spies". Pettus, Jessop, Yeovill, and Desmond and Furfy all berthed below among the common seamen, with their ears open, and he had Geoffrey Westcott in the wardroom to pick up on the mood of his officers. All were "Captain's Men", who could not pry too overtly, round whom disgruntled, larcenous, even mutinous sailors would not gripe or complain too openly, but, by just listening, the people of his entourage could glean information and pass on should it sound dangerous. Lewrie's only lack was below in the Midshipmen's mess, since he had brought no one beholden to his patronage or his "interest" aboard with him, and despised the practise of favouring young "cater-cousins" or the nepotism of placing one's own sons in one's vessel.

" 'Vast there, damn yer eyes," Lewrie snapped as Bisquit tumbled down from the poop deck, where he'd been barking and chasing after the many seagulls that wheeled and hovered out of his reach, and pressed his way past Lewrie's legs into the great-cabins. The dog dashed about and made a rapid circuit of the day cabin, sending Chalky scrambling from the comfy settee cushions to the top of the desk, in a bristled-up and spitting huff. Bisquit trotted to the edge of the desk, snuffled at the cat, dangerously within clawing distance, and wagging his bushy tail in glad greetings, before padding to the middle of the canvas deck chequer to sit down, tongue lolling as if he was late to dinner.

"Ye know ye don't belong in here," Lewrie sternly said.

Bisquit whined and did a little dance with his front paws, with a grin on his face, his stand-and-fall ears perking up.

"Got spoiled ashore, sir," Pettus said with fondness in his voice. "Allowed the run of your father's house all winter when you were healing up? Warm fires, and treats in the kitchen, and he learned to go out to do his business. Jessop and I taught him. Put him out of the cabins, sir?"

Bisquit didn't think that his case was made, for he whined some more and rolled over onto his back, wriggling back and forth to invite someone to come rub his belly.

"Oh, Hell," Lewrie gave in, kneeling down to oblige the dog, sending Bisquit into paroxyms of delight. "You bloody pest. Aye, ye are, d'ye know that?" But he said it with a coo.

Yeovill came in with his food barge.

"Now just look what you started, Yeovill," Lewrie accused with mock severity. "All your warm kitchen fires, and treats."

"Me, sir?" Yeovill gawped. "Wasn't just me, sir!" He peered about, as if looking for support from his co-conspirators. "But, ehm . . . should I put out an extra bowl, sir?"

"Aye," Lewrie said with a sigh as he got back to his feet. "A few sausages cut up, to go with his gruel."

Mondays, Wednesdays, and Fridays were "Banyan Days" when boiled salt meats were off the menu, replaced with oatmeal, cheese, bisquit, pease pudding, portable soup, butter, and beer. But, no one with a heart could begrudge Bisquit or Chalky their jerky, sausages or *pemmican*. Except for when Lewrie had supper guests, Chalky got his in a bowl at the foot of the dining table. Poor old Toulon, who had died the year before, had had his bowl there, too, but it proved to be too small for Bisquit. He got a chipped soup bowl on the deck to hold his food. After they'd eat, Chalky nervously peered down at the dog, let out a warning hiss, then did a prodigious leap far past him to bound into the starboard quarter gallery right aft and take a perch atop the stores packed in the un-used toilet. Bisquit padded about for a time before circling round on the Axminster carpet by the low, brass Hindoo tray table in front of the starboard-side settee and flopping down to take a nap.

"Spoiled, indeed," Lewrie commented to Pettus, as his steward served him a steaming-hot cup of tea with goat's milk and sugar. "Do you keep an eye on him, though, if he looks in need of . . . going."

"Yes, sir," Pettus said with a sly look. "Hear that, Jessop?"

"Aye, I do," the servant said with a much-put-upon sigh.

Try as he might to stay aft in his cabins and write letters or read, and appear calmly confident—he thought of practicing upon his penny-whistle, but that was out, for every tootle made Bisquit howl along!—there was no helping it. Lewrie went back on deck by Six Bells of the Day Watch, had his collapsible wood-and-canvas deck chair fetched to the poop deck, and spent the last hour of that watch, and the first hour of the First Dog, pretending to loll unconcernedly, or pace about *without* appearing to fret, as his little convoy made its slow way down-Channel. The following winds from the Nor'east remained steady, and the Channel, which could be a right bitch three days out of five, stayed relatively calm, with only long rollers and waves no greater than four or five feet high, in long sets.

Even in a time of war, with French merchant trade, and the trade of her allies, denied passage, the English Channel was still one of the busiest bodies of water in the known world. It was also a body of water where French and Dutch privateers preyed upon the great convoys bound out overseas, or returning with their riches. Lewrie had cautiously ordered that his charges would hug closer to England than to the middle, just in case, but then so did every other ship with a master with a lick of sense. If the enemy could not pounce upon rich prizes fresh from India or the West Indies, they'd settle for vessels from the coasting trade, or the many fishing craft, which made the waters even more crowded. Fortunately, the Nor'east wind precluded vessels bound up-Channel for the Dover Straits from making much progess close-hauled, forcing them further out from the coast to make their tacks in more-open water, and this day's traffic was mostly out-bound off the wind, so *Sapphire* and her convoy went with the flow, their own advance blunted for half the day by the stiff currents up-Channel.

Lewrie waited 'til the second rum issue of the day had been doled out, folded up his chair and bound it to the bulwarks, then went down to the quarterdeck. Lt. Elmes had the watch, and was standing by the starboard bulwarks, peering shoreward with his telescope when Lewrie appeared.

"Your pardons, sir," Elmes said, surrendering his spot to his Captain, who owned the windward side of the quarterdeck when he was up.

"No matter, Mister Elmes," Lewrie genially told him. "Is that Beachy Head yonder?"

"Aye, sir," Elmes answered with a smile. "Three points off the starboard bows, and about eleven or twelve miles off."

"A long, slow passage, so far, aye," Lewrie commented, trying to spot the first glow of the lights that marked it. He looked aloft and forward at the set of the sails and how they were drawing, to the long, gently-fluttering commissioning pendant to gauge the strength of the winds, and found that the beginning of sunset in the West was going reddish.

"Sign of a calm night," Lewrie said, rapping his knuckles on the bulwark's cap-rail for luck. "*If* the wind holds out of the Nor'east, *if* the seas don't get up, and the French keep to their side of the Channel t'night. Eleven or twelve miles, d'ye say?"

"Aye, sir," Lt. Elmes agreed.

Lewrie looked round the deck and found the Sailing Master, Mr. George Yelland, making his way up a ladderway to the quarterdeck, his coat off, and his head bare in an idle, Dog Watch casualness.

"Ah, Mister Yelland," Lewrie called out. "A lovely early evening, hey? You will be using your sea cabin tonight?"

"Thought I might, sir, just in case." Yelland told him.

"Let's take a peek in the chart space, if you don't mind, sir. I'm thinking that it may be necessary t'come a point more Westerly, so we don't get trampled by a home-bound trade in the middle of the night," Lewrie suggested. "Hug the coast a *tad* closer?"

Once in the chart space, the Captain's clerk's former office, and a small lanthorn lit, they both pored over the charts.

"Uhm . . ." Yelland mused, sucking on his teeth in thought. "We could espy Saint Catherine's Point light round midnight, aye, sir, if we alter course. With any luck at all, we *might* be in sight of Portland Bill by dawn, and about twelve or so miles off."

"At which point, we'll alter course to West by South, Half-South or

West-Sou'west, depending on wind and weather," Lewrie decided, "and clear Start Point and Prawle Point by a wider margin."

"Looks good to me, sir," Yelland agreed, tentatively making a few pencil marks on the chart.

*Christ, does he ever have a wash?* Lewrie asked himself. Their Sailing Master's body odour was almost as rank as the smells from his clothing. Lewrie dreaded spending too much time in the chart space, conferring with Yelland, in future. Not with the door shut, anyway.

He stepped back onto the quarterdeck and into the fresher air, clapped his hands in the small of his back and rocked on the balls of his boot soles, allowing himself a brief moment of feeling pleased. *Comus* out ahead had lit her taffrail lanthorns for the night, and the transports astern of her were doing the same. The column was ragged, not the beads-on-a-string perfection of a seasoned naval column, with some transports off each of *Comus*'s stern quarters, or HMS *Sapphire*'s stern quarters, but they looked to be only one cable, or a bit more, apart and managing decently enough.

*This may not be as bad a prospect as I feared,* Lewrie thought.

"Beg pardon, sir," Lt. Westcott said, coming up from the waist with a sheet of paper in his hand. "Defaulters, I'm afraid. Damned near a dozen for Captain's Mast in the morning."

That was more than they had seen in a month aboard their old ship, and in the *Reliant* frigate, most of the sailors brought up on charges had been guilty of minor or trivial misdeeds, punished with deprivations less than the use of the cat-o'-nine-tails.

"How many serious defaulters?" Lewrie asked with a gloomy sigh.

"One fist-fight, one pissing on the lower gun deck, two quarreling or showing dis-respect to a Midshipman or petty officer, one who was trying to pilfer some jam from the galley, and the rest are either drunk, or drowsing on duty, sir."

"Christ on a crutch," Lewrie gravelled. "So much for a happy ship. Gun drill, weather permitting, in the Forenoon. Live powder and shot, for a change, then I'll hold Mast after Noon Sights."

"Very good, sir," Lt. Westcott said with a rueful look, and a heavy, commiserating shrug.

*Then again, things may* not *turn out well,* Lewrie thought.

# CHAPTER FOURTEEN

The winds swung more Northerly for a day or two, allowing their column to make their way West-Sou'west, almost on a beam wind, which was grand for the soldiers cooped up in the transports to accustom them to a ship's motions, giving them their "sea legs". It was good for maintaining the proper order of sailing, too, as they stood out beyond the Lizard and into the open Atlantic. Both *Comus* and *Sapphire* wreathed themselves in spent powder smoke for at least one hour each Forenoon to bring their gun crews back up to scratch, Lewrie's hands most especially. For a warship in commission the better part of a year, her gunners were very rusty, and initially slow to run out and fire, or reload, nowhere near Lewrie's, and Westcott's, exacting standards. Westcott confided that the other officers had commented that former Captain Insley had been more than frugal with the expenditure of shot and powder, perhaps in worry that Admiralty might send him a harsh note for wasting too much of the stuff.

In the beginning, it seemed that the roars and explosions from the muzzles was so alien and terrifying a din that the guns crews were addled by it, stunned into confusion, and the proper steps of drill blasted from their heads, standing round stupefied, or fumbling like complete new-comes at their first exposure, without a clue as to how to perform the simplest task, afraid of their great charges.

It took a whole week before the 12-pounders on the upper gun deck and the 24-pounders on the lower gun deck could run in, load, run out, and fire somewhat co-ordinated broadsides. Aiming was what worried Lewrie after that. If he ordered the launch or pinnace away to tow an empty cask—on a *very* long tow-line!—it was good odds that his gunners would sink the boat! The best he could do was to fire off a 6-pounder and order a broadside fired at the feather of spray where the roundshot struck the sea, at once, and hope for the best. And that proved to be a very *ragged* second-best, with roundshot soaring off half a mile beyond, and raising splash pillars along half the length of the convoy.

Lieutenant-Colonel Fry had much better luck with his musketry, dumping empty kegs overside and having his Fusiliers volley at them in ripples of platoon fire. Of course, his soldiers were not expected to hit anything much beyond seventy-five yards!

Lewrie would have kept them at it more often, but for the wind and weather. Further out in the Atlantic, as they strove to attain at least the 15th Longitude, the winds came more and more Westerly, and at least twice a day all ships had to wear about from one tack to the other, then make long boards for at least six hours, making progress Westward on larboard tack, steering Nor'west, then wear about to sail on starboard tack to the Sou'-Sou'west to make progress Sutherly.

Some days were just too boisterous to call the hands to Quarters and cast off the bowsings and lashings, as the winds piped up and veered or backed, and the seas got up, and the decks were soaked with rain. At least it was warm rain. On those days, *Sapphire*'s crew was exercised on muskets and pistols, on cutlasses, boarding axes, and pikes. The ship's Marines, much better shots, would fire a volley to create a rough point of aim in the sea close alongside, and the sailors would shoot at it before the myriad of shot-splashes would subside.

Discipline was another matter. There were some violations that had to be met with the "cat". When holding Mast—almost every other day, it seemed—Lewrie tried to deal with the petty stuff by awarding the defaulters with deprivations; no tobacco for a week, no rum for a week, or putting men on only bread and water. Most sailors depended on those little things to make their lives the slightest bit tolerable, and being denied their grog or "chaws" usually raised groans of real pain from the condemned. Fighting, insubordination, showing dis-respect to petty officers and Mids, though, *had* to be punished to drive the point home and make the hands fearful of violating the stern discipline necessary aboard a King's Ship.

He would start with the awarding of one dozen lashes, with the defaulter bound to an upright hatch cover, shirtless, with a wide leather sash round his middle to protect the man from errant strokes that might hit the kidneys or the buttocks. The Ship's Surgeon, Snelling, would examine the man to determine if he was fit to suffer punishment. The crew would be assembled to bear witness and take heed from their shipmate's pain. The Marines would form up to one side in the waist in full-dress kit and under arms. The Sailmaker would have fashioned a red baize draw-string bag, in which a fresh-made cat-o'-nine-tails was hidden. Lewrie would read the crime committed, cite the applicable section of the Articles of War, then ordain the punishment, and tell the Bosun and his Mates to "let the cat out of the bag" to administer that required dozen.

As the days went by, though, Lewrie could note that the names of the hands who'd been lashed did not appear again, except for the hardened few, who would commit the same petty crimes and suffer the ritual once more, with two dozen lashes for a second appearance.

"Thief! Thief! Git 'im!"

Lewrie was reclined in his collapsible deck chair on the poop, reading a novel and regally above it all, when that tumult began. He put the book aside and descended to the quarterdeck.

"What's acting, Mister Harcourt?" he asked the watch officer.

"No idea, sir," Harcourt said in his usual laconic, stand-offish manner. "I expect we shall see, shortly."

*Too bad* officers *can't be flogged,* Lewrie fumed to himself; *I'm gettin' tired o' him. He's skirtin' damn' close to the line o' mute insubordination!*

"Aha, sir," Harcourt said, jutting his chin to the main hatchway as Baggett, the Master At Arms, and his Ship's Corporals, Packer and Wray, came up from the upper gun deck to the weather deck, wrestling a burly, struggling hand with them. Just behind, a horde of men boiled onto the deck, threatening to beat the man.

"Thief, sir!" Baggett exclaimed as he spotted Lewrie at the front edge of the quarterdeck. "Landsman Clegg!"

Lewrie went down a ladderway to the waist to confront the man.

"Who did he steal from, and what did he steal?" he asked.

"From me, sir . . . Deavers," the newest hand in Lewrie's boat crew spoke up, red in the face with anger. "He took my snuff box!"

"Saw him do it, sir!" Crawley, the demoted Cox'n, accused.

"Saw him *with* it, sor!" Patrick Furfy chimed in.

"Let me see it," Lewrie demanded, and Baggett fetched it out from a coat pocket. Lewrie was surprised to see a rather fine silver snuff box, ornately engraved, and with a wreathed plain oval on the top which bore the ornate initials JED. "Yours, Deavers?"

"My mother bought it for my father, James Edward Deavers, there on the top, sir," Deavers explained, still fuming and looking daggers at Clegg. "He was a corn merchant, at Staines, 'til he went smash. It's all I have of my parents."

"It's his for sure, sor," Liam Desmond spoke up. "He messes with us, sor, and he's showed us it, once, Deavers did."

"Furfy, you say you saw Clegg with the snuff box?" Lewrie asked.

"Clegg, sor, he come aft near our mess, an' knocked Deavers's sea-bag off th' peg," Furfy began to relate.

"Saw him fumble it, and reach inside, sir," Crawley interrupted.

"Only when spoken to, Crawley," Baggett warned.

"No, no, it's allowed, this once, Baggett," Lewrie said.

"Aye, sir!" Baggett replied. "All piss and gaitors" stiff.

"You saw him take it," Lewrie demanded of Crawley.

"He hung the sea-bag back up, like it was an accident, sir, but I saw a glint of metal in his hand when he did," Crawley told him.

"And you then saw him with it, Furfy?" Lewrie pressed.

"Crawley gimme a jerk o' th' head, sor, sorta cutty-eyed, so I went forrud t'follow him, an' I seen th' snuff box a'bulgin' in Clegg's pocket. I cry out, 'Hoy, what's 'at ye got in yer pocket 'at ye took from Deavers's sea-bag', an' then cried 'thief', sor," Furfy stated. " 'At woke up some o' t'other lads up forrud, an' we all took hold o' him 'til th' Master At Arms could take him, sor."

A theft belowdecks was easily done, with half the crew on deek and on watch, and the other half catching up on their sleep. It was Clegg's misfortune that the slop trousers issued by the Purser *had* no pockets, unlike officers', and were sewn on to customise them at a later date during a "Make And Mend" day; they were usually flat to the original cloth, leaving little room inside in which to cram much. Even the small, rectangular bulk of a snuff box would stand out like a 12-pounder roundshot.

"And, what d'ye have t'say for yourself, Clegg?" Lewrie turned to the suspect.

"I staggered an' knocked *somebody's* sea-bag down, sir," Clegg tried to explain, with a pleasant expression, somewhere between confident and wheedling. "But, I hung it back up an' went on forrud, an' nary a thing did I take from it, sir!"

"Then how did Deavers's snuff box turn up in your trouser pocket?" Lewrie sternly asked.

"Never *woz* in me pocket, sir!" Clegg declared. "First I know, they's all shoutin' 'thief', jumpin' me an' pinnin' me down, feelin' me all over, an' *plantin'* it on me! Y'ask me, sir, I say that *Furfy* took it, thort better of it, an' blamed *me* for it!"

"Crawley, where were you and Furfy when you saw the theft?" Lewrie asked.

"I was sittin' at my mess table, sir, 'bout three messes forward o' Deavers's, larboard side," Crawley told him, "and Furfy was just comin' down the main ladderway, aft, nowhere near his own mess."

"Yer lyin', Crawley, you an' t'other Capum's pet, th' both o' ya," Clegg snapped. "I never done it!"

"Seems pretty-much open and shut, to me," Lewrie decided with a slow nod. "Clegg, I could hold a formal Mast later today, and we could repeat the testimonies, but . . . after hearing the evidence and the charge against you, I pronounce you guilty of violating Article the Thirtieth, of Robbery."

*God, I can recite by heart by now!* Lewrie marvelled.

" 'All Robbery committed by any person in the Fleet shall be punished with Death, or otherwise, as a Court-Martial, upon Consideration of Circumstances, shall find meet,' " he recited.

Lewrie stressed "Death", which made Clegg's brutal face turn white.

"Since we can't form a proper Court with only two Post-Captains, I *can't* hang you, Clegg," Lewrie told him. "I *could* give you an hundred lashes, but as I noted in the Punishment Book when first I came aboard, you've had more than your fair share, already. You are a Quota Man. From gaol, released upon your oath to serve your King. Am I right?"

"Aye, sir," Clegg said, much subdued, and fearful of what was coming.

"Mister Terrell?" Lewrie called over his shoulder for the Bosun, sure that the ado would have drawn that worthy nearby.

"Aye, sir?" Terrell piped up in a gruff voice, with a touch of "hopeful" that his strong arm would soon be needed to administer the cat; perhaps the punishment would involve all his Mates, too, with each delivering a dozen by rotation.

"Pipe 'All Hands On Deck' to witness punishment," Lewrie bade. "Mister Hillhouse?"

"Aye, sir?" the eldest Midshipman answered up.

"Fetch yourself a cutlass!" Lewrie barked.

"Aye aye, sir!"

Lewrie returned to the forward break of the quarterdeck, clapped his hands in the small of his back, and put his stern face on as the off-watch hands came up from below. Marine First Lieutenant John Keane turned up, as did Westcott and the Third Officer, Edward Elmes.

"Mister Keane, I'd admire did you have your drummer take place atop the main hatch cover," Lewrie requested. "We are about to punish a defaulter for theft. Mister Westcott? Form the off-watch men in a gantlet, about four planks apart, facing in, right round the waist, and up atop the forecastle if you have to, to give everyone a clear shot, and room t'swing a fist."

"Aye, sir, directly," Westcott said, sounding eager.

"All hands, off hats and hark the Captain!" Lt. Harcourt called out. "Off hats and face aft!"

In an equally loud voice, Lewrie explained the crime, the brief court, and his sentence of guilty. Then, "Sapphires! Landsman Clegg is a thief, caught red-handed. There is nothing more repugnant to a ship's company than a thief. Some of you have served other ships before, and know what it is to be shipmates. Some of you new to the Navy and this ship have learned what it is to count on your shipmates, in good times, in storms and perils. But, a thief is only thinking of himself, not his mates, nor his ship. So, instead of Landsman Clegg being triced up to get five dozen lashes, I am going to leave it to you. We will form a gantlet, and he will walk through it, with a cutlass at his chest to make sure he goes slow. You may only use your fists, no loggerheads, rope-ends, or belaying pins. Are you ready, Mister Hillhouse?"

"Ready, sir!" Midshipman Hillhouse reported with a gladsome growl of anticipation.

*I suspected he'd really relish it!* Lewrie thought.

"Twice around!" Lewrie shouted. "Begin!"

Sailors never had much in the way of possessions beyond issued necessities, and usually had no money with which to purchase better things. The simplest items, a pair of good shoe buckles, a fancier clasp knife and sheath, a locket with a picture of a parent or loved one, a ring from someone dear to them, was even dearer to them than solid coin. They *would* not tolerate a thief.

The drummer began a long roll, and the Master At Arms shoved Clegg forward, while Midshipman Hillhouse paced backwards at a very slow walk, with the point of his cutlass an inch or so from Clegg's chest. Up the starboard side their felon went, pummelled and smashed from both sides of the gantlet with hard fists, and shouted curses, cringing and stumbling. There was a brief respite when Clegg was forced up the starboard ladderway to the forecastle, but as soon as his feet were on that deck, the beating began again, cross the deck, down the larboard ladderway, and down the larboard side to the break of the quarterdeck, and round once more. By the time Clegg fell to the deck face-down, he was a bloody, bruised bulk of raw meat.

"See to him, Mister Snelling," Lewrie called to the Surgeon, who had stood to one corner, appalled, throughout the punishment. "Dismiss the off-watch hands, Mister Harcourt."

"Aye, sir," the Second Officer replied, sounding more natural, almost whimsical, for once.

Lewrie went back to the poop deck and fetched his book, then came back down and went into his cabins.

"Cool tea, Pettus," he ordered, going to sprawl on the starboard-side settee to continue reading.

"Aye, sir, right away," Pettus said. "Ehm . . . that was quite a lesson, if I may say so, sir."

"You may, and I hope it was," Lewrie agreed, propping a foot on the brass tray-table.

"By the time Clegg's back to full duties," Pettus went on, "I'd expect he'll be saying 'pretty please' and 'thank you' before he dares reach for the mustard pot in his mess."

"If they'll have him, at all, Pettus," Lewrie said, grinning briefly, and quite satisfied with his decision.

# CHAPTER FIFTEEN

The convoy attained the 15th Longitude a few days later, then hauled their wind to steer Due South, with the transports managing to perform a passable semblance of Alter Course In Succession, by then. The prevalent Westerlies in the Bay of Biscay came upon them on their starboard beams, shifting only a point or so from day to day, blowing in varying strength. A beam reach was an easy point of sail, which HMS *Sapphire* seemed to enjoy, with her decks canted over only a few degrees, gently rolling to the scend of the sea.

It was time for more live-fire exercises, this time with a target. The gun crews were able to run in, load, run out, and discharge their guns right smartly, by then, with even the hands on the lower gun deck managing to get off three rounds every two minutes with the massively heavy 24-pounders.

Two cables of tow-line were spliced together, and an empty water cask was sacrificed, and painted white. Crawley, the former captain's Cox'n, chose his men, and manned the pinnace under sail, going out a full cable's distance from the ship's larboard beam, the full 240 yards, to stream the target cask astern.

"Fingers crossed, Mister Westcott," Lewrie hopefully said.

"And one's tongue on the proper side of one's mouth, too, sir," Westcott said with a laugh.

"Haven't heard o' that'un," Lewrie confessed.

"Oh, I hear it's all the go at Woolwich, these days, sir," Westcott japed, referring to the Royal Arsenal and artillery school.

"Carry on, then, Mister Westcott, and remind 'em t'aim *damned* careful," Lewrie ordered.

Muffled cries below carefully put the gunners through the many steps of gun drill; Cast Off Your Guns, Level Your Guns, Take Out Your Tompions, Run In Your Guns, Load With Cartridge, Shoot Your Guns, then Run Out Your Guns, Prime, and Point Your Guns.

"By broadside . . . on the up-roll . . . fire!"

HMS *Sapphire* shuddered, shoved a foot or so to starboard as the larboard battery went off as one, with stentorian roars and a great pall of powder smoke that only slowly drifted alee, masking the target.

"All *over* the place, sir!" Midshipman Kibworth, posted aloft in the main-mast cross-trees, shouted down.

"Overhaul your run-out tackle, and swab out your guns!" officers on both gun decks cried.

Guns were charged with fresh powder bags, shotted, then run out once more. *Sapphire* grumbled and roared again as the many carriages' truck wheels squealed, as un-told tons of artillery lumbered up to the port sills. Lewrie thought that their time was acceptable; his pocket watch had a second hand and his gun crews were close to his demanded three rounds every two minutes.

"Point your guns!" was the order, and gun-captains bent over to peer down the lengths of the cannon, fiddling with the wooden blocks, the quoins, under the breech-ends, or called for their tackle men to heave with crow levers to lift the rear ends of the guns to shift tiny increments to right or left, lifting the carriages a few inches.

"By broadside . . . fire!"

*Sapphire*'s larboard side erupted in another titanic roar, and wreathed herself in yellowish-grey powder smoke, with hot red-amber jets of discharge jabbing out, mixed with swirling clouds of sparks.

"Closer, from right to left, sir!" Kibworth shouted. "Short, or far over!"

"Overhaul your run-out tackle, and swab out your guns!"

A third broadside followed within the required two minutes, then a fourth, a fifth, and a sixth. Despite the mildness of the day, the gun crews began to work up a sweat as they fed their cannon, ran them back out, heaved upon the levers to shift traverse, heaved again to lift the breeches so the quoins could be inched in or out to elevate their barrels, then stood clear, making sure that the recoil tackles and run-out tackles would not foul—and that their feet were safe—before the next broadside roared out.

Fifteen minutes elapsed from the first broadside, and the hands were beginning to slow, much as they would in battle, for human muscle could only do so much arduous labour for only so long. They were not machines. If they were in real combat, lasting an hour or longer, the broadsides would be discharged closer to one a minute, and those would be ragged, stuttering up and down the ship's side as if "Fire At Will" had been ordered.

"*Smothered,* sir!" Midshipman Kibworth shrilled in a joyous whoop. "The target's smothered in shot splashes!"

As the smoke drifted clear and thinned, Lewrie raised his telescope to behold a long, disturbed patch of white water round the white-painted target cask, a patch which stretched at least one hundred yards from right to left, and perhaps only fifty or sixty yards in depth. Had they been firing at an enemy ship, there would have been misses to the right or left of the foe, ahead of her bows or astern of her transom, but the bulk of the heavy shot would have taken her " 'twixt wind and water", smashing into her sides.

"I think we're finally gettin' somewhere, Mister Westcott," he said, with a sly grin beginning to form upon his face. "You lads," he addressed their youngest Mids, Ward and Fywell. "Scamper down and tell the officers on the gun decks to mind their traverses."

"Aye, sir!" and they were off, as quickly as monkeys.

Two more broadsides were fired, with even more excited shouts from Midshipman Kibworth. Word had been passed to the gun crews of the "smother", and despite their weariness, the pace of serving their guns had picked up a bit. Finally . . .

"Target's *destroyed,* sir!" Kibworth screeched. "It's gone!"

Lewrie abandoned the middle of the quarterdeck and dashed to the lee side, whipping up his telescope. "Yes, by God! Yes!"

That patch of disturbed sea, churned foamy white by the impacts of all those roundshot, was about the same size in depth, but shorter from right to left, *very* much shorter, which would have smashed into an enemy warship from bow to stern, with very few misses ahead or astern. A fine mist from feathers and pillars of spray was falling.

"Secure!" Lewrie bellowed. "Cease fire!"

That welcome order was passed down from the quarterdeck to the upper gun deck, then the lower gun deck, and the ship fell silent, at long last; an eerie, ear-ringing silence in which the normal sounds of a ship on-passage, the faint groans of the hull, the piping of the wind, and the clatter of blocks, sheets, and halliards suddenly sounded alien.

"Pass the word, you lads," Lewrie said to the Mids, Fywell and Ward. "My compliments to all, and that that was damned fine shooting!"

"Quite suitable aiming," Lt. Westcott commented as he and Lewrie pulled their wax ear-plugs out. "At much longer ranges, though, we wouldn't be all that accurate."

"At much longer range, Geoffrey, neither would the French, or the Dons," Lewrie replied, with a twinkle in his eyes. "How much gunnery practice d'ye imagine *they* get? Much like their seamanship, it is all 'river discipline' in harbour, and hope they can pick it all up on their way to somewhere. I think we'd stand a good chance, better than them, at any rate, do we run a'foul of them."

"One hopes, though, that our enemies show enough courage to try us at 'close pistol-shot'," Westcott jibed.

"Hmm . . . only a Frog seventy-four would dare," Lewrie mused. "And, what are the chances of one o' them turnin' up?"

*Sapphire* slowly returned to normal routine. The gun-ports were shut, flintlock strikers removed and returned to storage, crow levers, swabs, and rammers stowed, the guns swabbed down to remove powder smut, the tompions re-inserted, and the guns run up to the port sills to be bowsed and lashed secure. Sailors gathered round the water butts on both gun decks to slake their great thirsts, then lowered their mess tables from the overheads, fetched their stools from the orlop, and took their rests.

Pettus came up from deep below, as well, with Chalky in his usual wicker cage, and Bisquit on a leash. Once in the waist, he let the dog go, and Bisquit, who was always frightened by the great dins of the guns, whined, whimpered, and dashed about to try and take assurance from one and all. When the ladderway was clear, he trotted to the quarterdeck, tail held low and tucked, to yelp, whine, and make a *Yeow* sound at Lewrie and Westcott, pressing hard up against their legs to get pets, flopping to the deck planks to get his belly rubbed, and for Lewrie's hand to find that sweet spot that made one of his hind legs twitch. After a few minutes, Lewrie stood back up and Bisquit got to his feet, too, to place his paws on Lewrie's waist-coat for a thorough head and neck rub, his tail whisking quickly, again, and erect once more.

"Mister Elmes, you have the watch?" Lewrie asked.

"Aye, sir," Elmes replied,

"I'll go aft, then," Lewrie said. "And once again, my compliments on damned good practice with the great guns."

"Aye, sir, and thank you, sir," Elmes said, greatly pleased.

"Tea, sir?" Pettus asked as Lewrie cast off his hat, coat, and sword belt. Lewrie cocked an ear to hear Six Bells of the Forenoon Watch being struck up forward at the forecastle belfry; eleven of the morning, and half an hour before the first rum issue of the day for the ship's crew.

"I b'lieve I'll have a goodly glass o' that white wine, instead," Lewrie decided, "the one that's been coolin' in the water tub."

*I think I've earned it, this morning,* he told himself as he sat down at his desk in the day-cabin and got out a sheet of paper to begin a letter to his eldest son, Sewallis, who was still aboard HMS *Aeneas* under his old friend, Benjamin Rodgers, on the Biscay blockade.

"Interesting thing, sir," Pettus prattled on as he pulled the cork from a bottle of a tasty, if smuggled, *sauvignon blanc*. "As we were coming up from the orlop."

"What's that, Pettus?" Lewrie asked, opening an ink bottle and dipping the tip of his steel-nibbed pen.

"The ship's people, sir," Pettus said. "They were in glad takings . . . happy, and pleased with themselves . . . of a job well done?"

"Aye?" Lewrie prompted, waiting for more.

"Joshing and grinning, laughing out loud?" Pettus said further as he held up a wineglass to the light from a swaying lanthorn to check for smuts. "One could almost say that they're in much the same spirits as the people in your previous ships, sir."

"Well, that'd be gratifyin'," Lewrie said. "We've had too much division over Insley, or Gable's, followers."

"Fact, sir," Pettus said, pouring a glass and stowing the wine bottle back in the cooling tub. "'Twixt your putting that Clegg to the gantlet, and their gunnery this morning, I do get the feeling that our Sapphires are won over, sir. More . . . shipmate-y?"

"Good God, is that a word?" Lewrie joshed as Pettus fetched him his wine.

"If it isn't, it should be, sir," Pettus slyly replied.

Lewrie took a first sip, finding the wine savoury. He would have begun his letter, but Chalky was over his fright, and found that he could keep his master from drinking *and* writing both, as he leapt into Lewrie's lap to sniff at the glass and demand pets . . . *now!*

# CHAPTER SIXTEEN

Out past the Lizard, then Land's End, and past Soundings, the Atlantic had become a much emptier sea, and, as *Sapphire*'s convoy had altered course South for the transit of the Bay of Biscay, the sight of other ships had become even rarer. That was not to say that they sailed in complete isolation.

Now and again, the lookouts would disturb the day's routine at the slightest hint of what might be another ship's tops'ls, t'gallants, or royals peeking over the horizon, paler wee shapes more substantial than a phantom imagined from a combination of light and shade in the colours of cloudbanks rising on the Westerly winds. From the cross-trees of the mainmast, a sharp-eyed lookout could see out to twelve miles in all directions on a good day, and a ship of decent size for an Atlantic crossing, hull down but with all the sails of her upper masts standing, could be espied another two or three miles beyond that.

While the ships of the convoy went about their drills, swabbing, sail trimming, they might look warily over their shoulders whenever a strange sail was sighted, and would remain wary 'til whoever it was had passed on on a diverging course, and slipped back below the horizon upon their own innocent occasions.

Now and then, a strange sail might take half the day to emerge over the horizon, only five or six miles off, and on a reciprocal course; neutrals, mostly, Swedish, Danish, Prussian, or Russian merchantmen making their way home from the Mediterranean or Africa. They would dip their flags and pass on, growing smaller and smaller 'til only their uppermost sails were visible, then to disappear.

All those contacts, the solid and the spurious, were of great concern to Lewrie and his officers, for clever Frenchmen could fly a false flag to delude their prey 'til the last moment. He found himself on deck with a telescope, and fingers crossed for luck, quite often, for many a cautious hour 'til he could let out a long-pent breath of relief, and turn to pleasanter things.

Worse, perhaps, were the nights when only a pair of weak taffrail lanthorns could be made out. At night, lookouts were called down from the cross-trees, and the lookouts of the Evening and the Middle Watches were posted at bow and stern, on deck, where their range of view was much reduced, which meant that those enigmatic passing ships were much closer, and their identities could not be determined.

In the first week on passage, they had seen American merchant ships, too, crossing astern, or far ahead of *Comus* in the lead of the long column. Lewrie *knew* that they were bound for France, and should be stopped and inspected for contraband. That was Orders In Council, and the list of contraband goods expanded faster than breeding rabbits, but . . . Lewrie let them pass unmolested. There were whole fleets of Royal Navy frigates and "liners" much closer to the Yankees' destinations which could fulfill that office, and he had a convoy to guard at all hazards. If he hared out of line and went after them, he'd leave the convoy on their own for a few hours, or order them all to fetch-to and idle 'til he'd boarded and inspected the suspect vessel, then get them back into order and under way, again, wasting good weather and a good wind.

Besides, he rationalised to himself, he wasn't sure that his lumbering two-decker 50 could *catch* a swift Yankee merchantman if her master felt like making the pursuit a long stern-chase! The Americans built very fast ships! Being out-footed and out-sailed would just be *too* embarassing.

More cheering and reassuring, though, were their encounters with British convoys. One day during the second week at sea, there was an East India Company "trade" of at least sixteen tall and grand Indiamen, so big that they could easily be mistaken for Third Rate ships of the line. Those merchantmen were escorted by two frigates and a 74-gunner.

Despite the war, the convoy system managed to maintain monthly departures and arrivals, spanning the East and the West Indies, North America, South America, the Mediterranean, and the Baltic. Six months or better out from Canton in China, or Calcutta or Bombay, they were in the home stretch with all their wealth assured safe docking in the Pool of London.

After a few more days of perfect isolation on an empty sea, a fresh convoy arose on the Southern horizon, one much smaller but perhaps just as rich, flying the blue-white-red horizontal-striped flags that denoted a Portugal convoy, and sure to be filled with ports and madeiras, sherries, costly liqueurs, fruit preserves and bottled citruses. This convoy passed quite close, within a mile of Lewrie's, and both groups of ships waved hats and shirts and raised lusty cheers of welcome to each other. The England-bound sailors might have cheered to see what they might have mistaken for a squadron of warships which meant additional safety for a few hours beyond their own two escorts, and the hands of *Comus, Sapphire*, and the soldiers aboard the transports surely cheered the liquid delights aboard the convoy! Whether they could drink them, or not.

HMS *Sapphire* rang to the clatters and clangs of an hundred poor Welsh tinkers all tapping away as her hands went through the steps of cutlass drill, paired off in mock melee to hone their sword-play. On the open poop deck, Lewrie was squared off against their senior Marine Lieutenant, the stern John Keane, Lewrie's short hanger versus Keane's straighter and longer smallsword, and frankly, Lt. Keane was the better swordsman, very fast and darting, with a very strong wrist. Lewrie was in his shirt with the sleeves rolled to his elbows, working up a sweat and beginning to pant at the exertion, which seemed as wearying as any real combat he had ever experienced.

Keane lunged, and Lewrie countered with a twist to bind, then stepped forward inside Keane's reach, his left arm fending off Keane's sword hand, bull-rushing him backwards and giving him a thump in the chest with the silver, lion-head hilt, then a mock slash with the flat of his blade that, had it been for real, the wickedly honed edge would have dis-emboweled the man.

"I trample on your entrails, sir!" Lewrie hooted in triumph.

"I expire, sir, thinking last thoughts of Mother," Keane said in matching jest, though he didn't look as if he approved of Lewrie's ploy, or the hardness of that thump.

"As hellish-good as you are, sir, that was the only way that I could prevail," Lewrie cheerfully admitted. "But, a boarding action, a melee, with enemy sailors tryin' t'kill ye any-old-how is not as fine as the elegance of a swordmaster's *salle*. That's why I prefer the hanger . . . I can always get inside or under my opponent's guard."

"A break for water, sir?" Lt. Keane suggested.

"Gad, yes," Lewrie heartily agreed. "I'm dry as dust."

The First Officer, Lt. Geoffrey Westcott, also in his rolled-up shirtsleeves, had been matching blades with Midshipman Leverett, and that pairing took a water break at the same time. Westcott's harshly-featured face was split in a grin as he delivered a final suggestion to Leverett, who had been schooled, like all young gentlemen of means, in the sword, but was learning that elegance and grace wouldn't stand a Chinaman's Chance if shoved nose-to-nose, elbow-to-elbow into a melee with barely enough room to employ a sword. Westcott looked as if he had handily bested the young man, with tactics as "low" as Lewrie's.

"A good morning's workout," Lewrie said after wetting his dry mouth with a first dipper from the scuttle-butt. "Pretty-much the only decent excercise an officer can get, aboard ship. Several brisk turns round the deck don't hold a candle."

"Indeed, sir," Lt. Keane agreed. "Though I have contemplated ascending the stays and ratlines to the tops, a time or two."

"Your dignity, though, sir," Midshipman Leverett jibed, as he waited his turn at the water butt. "That's an acquired skill."

"How's the leg?" Westcott asked in a barely audible whisper.

"No problem at all," Lewrie whispered back. "Not a twinge."

Lewrie had known too many older officers who had been so long at sea who were halfway lamed by the rheumatism engendered by the cold and damp, their continuing careers a perpetual misery of aches and pains, much less anyone who had been as "well-shot" as he had been. He felt damned grateful to have avoided the rheumatism, so far, and to have healed so completely. *Well, gout's another matter,* he told himself with a wee laugh.

"Sail ho!" a lookout bawled out from high aloft.

"Where away?" Lt. Harcourt, who had the watch, shouted back.

"*Three* points orf th' *larb'd* quarter!" the lookout cried.

Lewrie and Westcott, and the curious Marine Lt. Keane, drifted to the aft corner of the poop deck's larboard side, but even from that height the horizon up to the Nor'east was unbroken, a severely straight line of blue against a fair-weather azure sky.

"In the Nor'east by East, or thereabouts," Lewrie speculated. He turned and looked aloft at the long, streaming commissioning pendant which stood out fairly stiffly with its outer length fluttering to the East by South. The Bay of Biscay's prevailing Westerlys had backed a point after dawn, giving his convoy a point free of sailing on a beam reach, perhaps endowing them with another half-knot above their usual plodding pace.

*Whatever she is, she's fast,* Lewrie thought.

To a further question from Lt. Harcourt, shouted aloft with the aid of a brass speaking trumpet, the lookout gave more details about their stranger.

"I kin make our 'er *t'gallants!*" he yelled. "Nigh bows-on!"

That made Lewrie frown. Yesterday's Noon Sights had placed them just below the 40th Latitude, hundreds of miles Due West of Cape Finisterre in Spain. Any friendly ship would have made its offing long before, and would not be sailing close-hauled *out* of the Bay of Biscay, or standing out round Finisterre.

*She* could *be one of ours, leavin' the blockadin' squadrons for Gibraltar or Lisbon,* Lewrie told himself as he clapped his hands in the small of his back and rocked on the soles of his boots; *Maybe.*

"Close-hauled on, say, Sou'-Sou'west?" he commented.

"Thereabout, sir," Lt. Westcott grimly agreed.

Lewrie went to the forward edge of the poop deck to shout down to Lt. Harcourt. "Last cast of the log, Mister Harcourt?"

"Ehm . . . eight and a quarter knots, sir, half an hour ago," Lt. Harcourt informed him.

"Hmm, not all that bad," Lewrie decided, a bit surprised that *Sapphire,* and the lumbering transports, could make such a good pace.

The typical Westerlys had already backed one point to the West by North, and Lewrie thought it good odds that it might continue to back a point more by afternoon. He *could* order the convoy to alter course to the Sou'-Sou'east; sooner or later they would have to steer for the Straits of Gibraltar, anyway, and that would put that backing wind large on their starboard quarters, which was most ships' best point of sail. They might even attain nine knots if he did so, but . . . why not?

"Mister Harcourt, make General Signal to all ships," he decided. "Alter Course in Succession, South-Southeast."

"Aye aye, sir!" Harcourt crisply replied.

He turned and looked up to the Nor'east, again, but there was still no indication of that strange sail to be seen from the deck.

*Hard on the wind, is she, bows-on to us?* he schemed; *Our turn will lay us smack cross her present course, and she'll* have *t'haul her wind, sooner or later.*

He also wondered why the strange sail *was* sailing so hard on the wind; this far West of Cape Finisterre, she had bags of sea-room by now, and if she *was* friendly, and bound for Lisbon or Gibraltar, she could have hauled her wind to a beam reach long before.

"Good morning, gentlemen," Lewrie said, keeping his suspicions in check, and off his face, "thankee for the exercise, Mister Keane, and I will see you all again at Noon Sights."

He went down the ladderway to the quarterdeck, then aft into his cabins to partake in a tall glass of his cool tea to slake his thirst, and have a sponge-off, and perhaps a change of shirt. Silk, for combat, he wondered?

All officers, the Sailing Master, and all the Midshipmen under instruction turned up with their sextants to take the height of the sun to determine their position. Lewrie and Mr. Yelland both brought their Harrison chronometers, which were in satisfactory agreement as to the exact moment of Noon. As ship's boys struck Eight Bells and turned the sand glasses, they all drew the sun to the horizon and locked the angle on their instruments. Lewrie and the ship's officers made one syndicate, over by the door to the chart room, whilst the Mids huddled together over their slates to form another.

"Are we in agreement, then, gentlemen?" the Sailing Master asked. "Thirty-seven degrees, twenty minutes North, and Fourteen degrees, fourty-five minutes West? Then I will mark it so."

"And let me see what a day on this course will fetch us, assumin' the winds hold," Lewrie suggested, starting to follow Yelland into the chart room.

"Deck, there!" a lookout's shout stopped him. "It's *two* strange sail! *Three* points off th' *larb'd* quarter. *Two* sets of t'gallants an' royals!"

"Bows-on?" Lewrie bellowed back, hands cupped round his mouth.

"Aye, sir! Bows-on, an' comin' close-hauled!"

Lewrie frowned and pursed his lips, feeling all the eyes on the quarterdeck on him. It was time to portray the proper sort of Royal Navy Captain, for their sakes.

"An hour, perhaps, before their tops'ls and courses fetch above the horizon," he mused aloud, "and some goodly time before they're hull-up. Three hours, altogether, before they're anywhere in shooting range? *If* they're enemy ships. We'll let them come to us, and, when close enough, hoist our false colours. If that don't daunt 'em, then we blow the Hell out of them.

"Carry on, sirs," Lewrie told them all, "if strenuous exertion is in the offing, I think I'll take a preparatory nap."

# CHAPTER SEVENTEEN

Lewrie didn't take a nap, of course. He spent his time aft in his cabins, going over his written orders to Captain Knolles in HMS *Comus* and the transport masters, and to Colonel Fry of the Kent Fusiliers. He dined lightly, drank only cold tea instead of wine with his meal, and asked for some hot coffee round the time that he was informed that the two strange ships' courses were above the horizon.

When a Midshipman came to report that the strangers were hull-up over the horizon, he buckled on his sword belt, took a brace of pistols already cleaned, oiled, and loaded from Pettus, and prepared to go on deck.

"Clear away all, Pettus. Off ye go to the magazine, Jessop, and the best t'both o' ye," he said. "Take care o' Chalky and see to Bisquit."

"As always, sir," Pettus gravely replied.

Last of all, Lewrie unlocked his desk and fetched out the keys to the arms lockers.

"Captain's on deck!" Midshipman Britton called out.

"Mister Elmes, I give you the keys to the arms lockers," Lewrie told the officer of the watch. "Beat To Quarters, if ye will."

"Aye aye, sir! Bosun Terrell! Pipe To Quarters!" Elmes cried.

Lewrie went to the larboard bulwarks of the quarterdeck to lift a telescope and inspect their strangers. They were still hard on the wind, coming strong, and sailing abreast of each other, with about a half-mile between them. They were three-masted, flush-decked, and gave him the impression that they were not the big 38- or 40-gunned frigates he had worried about. Warships, for certain, but perhaps smaller and weaker, somewhere round the same size and weight of metal as Knolles's 24-gunned *Comus*. That would mean that they would be armed with nine-pounders, or the French equivalent of twelve-pounders.

"Good afternoon, sir," Lt. Westcott said to announce his arrival on the quarterdeck. "Did you have a good nap?"

Lewrie tossed him a quick, sly grin, for Westcott knew that it had all been a sham.

"Leftenant Keane!" Lewrie called out, instead. "Do you keep your men down out of sight 'til called for, as we discussed!"

"Very well, sir!" Keane replied.

"I'll have the gun-ports closed 'til we're ready to run out, as well, Mister Westcott," Lewrie ordered.

"Done, sir," Westcott told him.

Lewrie looked forward past the courses and jibs to determine that the two transports off *Sapphire*'s bows showed no colours, as he had set out in his written orders, and that *Comus* was flying the Blue Ensign. He went up atop the poop deck to check on the two transports following his ship's wake, and was pleased to note that they flew no colours, and were managing to maintain column and a rough one cable of separation. From that vantage, he gave the approaching ships a long inspection with his telescope, then trotted back down to the quarterdeck.

"If they're indeed French, then they're hopeful bastards. Or half-blind," Lewrie commented. "They know *Comus* is a frigate by now, but can't they see we're *not* a big transport?"

"Even if they do recognise us for a warship, perhaps they're counting on our lack of speed or manoeuvrability to cut one or two of the transports from our clumsy grasp, sir," Westcott posed, tongue-in-cheek.

"Strange sail are French!" a lookout called down. "Deck, there! I kin see the cut o' their jibs!"

"Jibs, sir?" Midshipman Fywell muttered.

"Jibs, younker," Lt. Westcott turned to instruct him. "The way sailmakers in other nations cut their cloth and saw the panels together varies, depending on what they think the best and strongest way to take strong winds. A sharp-eyed, experienced man can sometime spot the difference."

"I see, sir," Fywell said with what passed for a sage nod.

Other Mids were coming to the quarterdeck to report that the lower gun deck was at Quarters, that the upper gun deck was ready, that sail tenders, brace and sheet and halliard tenders were in their assigned places and ready for action. Once reporting, they dashed back to their stations for Quarters.

"At Quarters, and ready for action, sir," Lt. Westcott said at last, very formally doffing his hat in salute.

"Very good, sir," Lewrie replied, all his attention on the two approaching ships. They were within two miles, by then, still on the wind. The one furthest off seemed to steer for the head of Lewrie's column, as if to take on Knolles in *Comus*. The left-handed ship nearest to *Sapphire* seemed intent on sailing right up to the middle of the column. They still showed no colours.

"They couldn't be ours, could they, sir?" Lt. Westcott wondered. "Two of our sloops of war or light frigates pulling a 'Grierson'?"

A year or so before, a Commodore Grierson had come to Nassau to re-enforce Lewrie's weak squadron of sloops, brigs of war and vessels "below the Rates", keeping his identity secret 'til the very last moment, a very clumsy jest that had frightened the life out of the good residents of New Providence, and had re-dounded to no good credit.

"If it is, I'll have both captains at the gratings, and flog 'em half t'death," Lewrie vowed. "I didn't find it all that amusin' then, and damned if anyone pulls that jape on me a second time."

He had ordered his frigate, *Reliant,* and three weak and small ships, all he had in harbour, out to confront Grierson's large squadron, *knowing* it was suicide, but prepared to go game and fulfill his duty to the last.

"About a mile and a half, now, sir," Sailing Master Yelland estimated. "Ah, *there's* their damned Tricolour flags, at last. Frogs for certain."

"And we're s'posed t'be terrified," Lewrie growled.

*Damme, don't they find it odd that we* ain't *turnin' about Sou'west and runnin' for our lives?* he had to ask himself; *These must be the stupidest, or the greediest, Frenchmen in all Creation!*

"Sir, I do believe that they're not frigates, but *corvettes,*" Lt. Westcott exclaimed after a long look with his glass. "Like our old twenty-gunned sloops of war."

"And about a mile off," Mr. Yelland pointed out.

"I'd like 'em t'come nigh half a mile, first," Lewrie said in rising excitement. It appeared that the French would not be daunted by the stolidly-plodding line of ships that showed no sign of fleeing.

*Come on, come on,* Lewrie thought, beginning a slow grin; *Come see what we have for ye!*

"Ehm . . . I estimate that it is half a mile, sir," Mr. Yelland announced.

"Mister Britton?" Lewrie barked. "Hoist the Blue Ensign, and make a signal to the convoy. Number Ten!"

"Open the ports and run out, sir?" Westcott eagerly asked.

"Damned right, Mister Westcott!" Lewrie snapped. He ran up the larboard ladderway to the poop deck to see how all the other ships were obeying his orders, schemed with Ralph Knolles and pre-planned long before while still in port at the Nore.

*Step One; Hoist Blue Ensign.*
*Step Two; Brail up main course, Navy fashion.*
*Step Three; Fifty Fusiliers to form by engaged side.*
*Step Four; Copy manoeuvres of escort ahead of you.*

All four troop transports were showing the Blue Ensign, and their main courses were being brailed up, as a warship would to avoid the risk of sparks from her own gunfire setting it on fire. Soldiers in full kit were forming along the larboard bulwarks of the transports with their firearms. The Fusiliers wore shakos, not the tall, narrow-brimmed black hats of real Marines, but they gave a good impression of a frigate's Marine complement, at a half-mile's range. Good enough to fool the French.

Lewrie looked forward to see that *Sapphire*'s huge main course was brailed up out of the way, and that Lt. Keane and Lt. Roe were sending some of their men to the fighting tops, at last, and arraying the rest behind the stout bulwarks and stowed hammock racks.

And the French!

"*Got* you, you ignorant shits!" Lewrie bellowed in his best quarterdeck voice at the foe, hoping they could hear him. "Mister Westcott? Serve the nearest one a broadside!"

The right-hand *corvette,* a little further off and aiming for the head of the long column, was already hauling her wind, putting her helm hard over and beginning to wear off the wind. Her main course was still spread, so she was fast off the mark. She had not even opened her gun-ports.

The one closest to *Sapphire* had begun to take in her course, and had opened her ports, but was also beginning to turn, presenting her star-board side to Lewrie's ship.

"By broadside . . . fire!"

HMS *Sapphire* erupted, guns bellowing, great clouds of gunpowder smoke gushing out, and clouds of sparks swirling. Lewrie found that he had crossed the fingers of his right hand for luck. He knew that his gun-ners could shoot off a concentrated broadside at one cable's range, but how would they do at close to half a mile?

"Beautiful!" he shouted, clapping his hands in glee.

There were tall pillars and feathers of spray arising round the French *corvette*, great slaps from 24-pounder shot, smaller ones from the 12-pounders, huge ones from the carronades that didn't have the range and struck short, lumbering up from First Graze to still do damage when they hit the *corvette*'s outer plankings. Before his view was blocked out by the thick cloud of smoke, he even saw some roundshot slamming into her, punching star-shaped holes!

"Mister Westcott, come about to East-Sou'east!" he ordered. "Let's go after her and serve her another!"

"Aye aye, sir! Helmsmen, make her head East-Sou'east," Lieutenant Westcott repeated. "Bosun, hands to the sheets and braces, and take the wind fine on the quarter, nigh a 'soldier's wind'!"

"Mister Britton?" Lewrie shouted aft to the signals Midshipman. "Make to *Comus* . . . her number, and Pursue The Enemy More Closely."

"Aye, sir!" Britton replied, sounding right chipper.

*Sapphire* was wheeling about, altering course to pursue her own target, slowly sailing back into the thinning, drifting pall of spent gunpowder smoke from her first broadside. That was a disadvantage for her, for this close to running "both sheets aft", almost dead downwind, she could sail no faster than the wind itself, and would wreath herself with every broad-side. He could feel the motion of his ship change under his feet.

Lewrie could barely make out the right-hand French *corvette,* which had managed to complete her wear-about, crossing the eye of the winds and taking it on her larboard quarter to run as fast as her wee legs could carry her. His own, the left-hand one, was emerging from the smoke, becoming more substantial by the second. And she *had* been struck, for he could make out bashed-in scantlings, pale raw patches where heavy roundshot had shattered her oak side and bulwarks, leaving base wood clean of paint, tar, and grime. And she was close, no more than two cables off, now! She was turning away to run, but he had her.

"By broadside . . . fire!"

HMS *Sapphire* thundered and roared, long amber flames spewing from all her larboard battery, smothering herself, and any view of the *corvette* in a fresh fog of sour, reeking powder smoke.

All that Lewrie could see were the tops of her upper masts, and they *trembled*, they swirled about as if the Frenchman had struck a shoal.

"Sir! Sir!" Midshipman Britton was shouting, sounding as if he was chortling, in point of fact. "The transport astern of us is wearing in succession!"

*At least* somebody's *doin' what I asked!* Lewrie thought. With little risk to his ship, or his passengers, that transport's master was tagging along, still playing "frigate".

He turned back to see if he could spot what Knolles and *Comus* was doing, and damned if the transport astern of him was wheeling to follow his ship, too!

"There she is!" Lt. Westcott shouted, pointing out-board at the wraith-like image of the smoke-shrouded French *corvette*. "She's lost her mizen top-masts, and her spanker!"

*Looks like she's been gnawed by rats,* Lewrie thought; *It seems my gunners* can *hit something, after all.*

"Has she struck?" Lewrie could hear the Sailing Master exclaim in rising excitement. "Or is her staff just shot away?"

"She's striking!" Westcott cried as someone fetched up a white bed sheet and began to wave it vigourously aboard the *corvette*.

"Cease fire! Cease fire, there!" Lewrie bellowed. "She just struck to us! Mister Westcott? Fetch us to, as close to the prize as you may. Mister Britton? Signal the transports to fetch-to!"

Lewrie went back up to the poop deck with his glass to see what else was transpiring. Knolles in *Comus* was still pursuing the second French *corvette,* though that ship was making a rapid exit from the scene, even setting stun'sls for more speed. The two transports following Knolles seemed glued to his stern, though much slower.

As swiftly as the terrified Frenchmen were fleeing, it appeared that it would take 'til sunset before *Comus* could catch them up and bring them to action, and if those two transports fell further and further behind, they'd be left on their own, defenceless should another raider stumble across them.

*Bird in the hand,* Lewrie thought with a shrug as he closed the tubes of his glass, and went back down to the quarterdeck. He waited for a lull, when he could speak with Lt. Westcott without interfering with his orders.

"Ah, Geoffrey, would you like to take charge of our prize?" he asked in a low voice. "If Gibraltar has enough spare sailors to make up a crew, there may be a Commander's epaulet in her. She's sure to be bought in after the Prize-Court's done with her valuation."

"Trying to get shot of me, sir?" Westcott said with a mock grimace. "That cuts sore! No, sir. I'd rather stay aboard and see what you're up to, next."

"'His men would follow him anywhere . . . if only for the entertainment', d'ye mean?" Lewrie japed. He leaned closer to whisper his next question. "If not you, who d'ye recommend? Who can we best do without?"

"I'd send Harcourt, and hope it's permanent, sir," Westcott was quick to say.

"My thoughts exactly," Lewrie said with a secretive smile, and turned to the Mids assigned to the quarterdeck. "Mister Fywell, pass word for Mister Harcourt, with my compliments."

"Aye aye, sir," the lad said, doffing his hat and scampering.

Lt. Westcott saw to boats to be brought up from being towed astern, and spare hands told off to man them and form part of the prize crew. Lewrie spoke with Marine Lieutenant Keane for at least twenty of *Sapphire*'s fifty private Marines to go aboard the prize to guard her French crew, sure to be larger than normal in expectations that she would have taken prizes of her own. *Sapphire*'s tall and skeletal Surgeon, Mr. Snelling, and his Surgeon's Mates would have to go over to tend to any French dying or wounded, if the prize didn't carry a doctor of her own, or if the casualty count was too high for that one to see to by himself.

"You sent for me, sir?" Lt. Harcourt reported, doffing his hat.

"Aye, Mister Harcourt," Lewrie replied, "I wish you to take charge of the prize, and see her safely to Gibraltar. Best done in company with the rest of us, but, she's sure t'have a large crew who won't take kindly to bein' slung into a prison hulk."

"Very good, sir!" Lt. Harcourt agreed with his first sign of joy since Lewrie had come aboard.

"Take whom ye will," Lewrie offered.

"I'll have Midshipman Hillhouse, sir," Harcourt said.

*Thought ye might!* Lewrie told himself; *Birds of a feather!*

"Former Cox'n Crawley, and a few others from his old boat crew, too, sir," Harcourt added.

"I can't assure you it'll be permanent," Lewrie cautioned, "but she's French, so her captain's wine stores should make up for it."

"I'll see to my kit, if I may, sir?" Harcourt asked, eager to be off.

"Carry on, then, sir, and the very best of good luck," Lewrie told him in dismissal.

*And oh, wouldn't it be sweet if it was permanent!* he told himself, feeling whimsical; *Harcourt gone, Hillhouse, and from what I've heard from my lads belowdecks, Crawley and his pack are the hardest of holdouts from Captain Insley's days, too.*

He took another look towards *Comus* with his telescope, and it looked as if the other French *corvette* was showing Ralph Knolles a clean pair of heels.

"Mister Britton, make a signal to *Comus,*" Lewrie ordered with a sigh. "Her number, and Discontinue The Action."

"Aye, sir," Midshipman Britton replied, sounding as if all of his hopes were dashed.

*Mine, too, lad,* Lewrie thought; *Still, it's been a good day.*

# CHAPTER EIGHTEEN

HMS *Sapphire*'s convoy skirted within twelve miles of Cape Trafalgar as they entered the Straits of Gibraltar's approaches, keeping enemy Spain, and Europe, to their larboard side, close enough for the crews and passenger-soldiers to see and marvel over, near where the famous battle had been fought not quite two years before. The coast of Africa and the Barbary States appeared on their starboard side as they began the transit, and wary eyes were cast in that direction, for though the United States Navy had humbled the infamous corsairs from Tangier and other lairs, the sight of a British convoy ripe for the plucking might be too tempting for those bloodthirsty pirates who had terrorised European coasts, even in the English Channel, for hundreds of years.

The Straits of Gibraltar were thirty-six miles long, narrowing to only eight miles wide at its slimmest point. There was plenty of depth for even *Sapphire*, and, once begun, the entrance to the Mediterranean was assured, even under "bare poles", with no sails flying. The steady Eastward-running current would carry a ship through; it would be the getting out against that current that would be an arduous and slow passage.

Lewrie ordered all ships to steer within four miles of Tarifa, and the little fortified Tarifa Island, on the North shore, almost as if taunting any

Spanish gun batteries, but a safe mile beyond the range of even the biggest 42-pounder cannon. From there, the Spanish coast trended Nor'easterly, expanding the separation from shore, with all ships firmly in the grasp of the Eastward-running current, and free of the variable swirls and eddies of currents inshore.

The bucklers had been removed from the hawse holes, the thigh-thick cables fetched up from the tiers, and bent onto the best bower and second bower anchors, and to the stern kedge anchors, in preparation for coming to anchor in Gibraltar Bay, and for the unfortunate accident of Gibraltar's dangerous wind shifts which might leave them at the current's mercy and sweep them past Europa Point and past the anchorages, forcing them to struggle, perhaps even towing themselves with ships' boats, onto the Rock's Eastern shore 'til a favourable slant of wind arose that could carry them back round Europa Point and into the bay proper, off the Ole Mole or the New Mole and the ancient Tuerto Tower, or, hopefully, right off the small town itself, which would be right handy for Lewrie's shore visits.

"Should we enter 'Man O' War' fashion, sir?" Lt. Westcott asked as the heights of the Rock hove into view, and Pigeon Island appeared off their larboard bows.

"Christ, no, Mister Westcott!" Lewrie quickly objected, laughing at the suggestion. "I'm not so sure of our people's seamanship, yet. To go in 'all standing' and muff it'd be a hellish embarassment . . . not t'mention a good way t'run aground. I'll leave that to the flashy fellows."

Extremely well-drilled, and sometimes lucky captains, could go in "all standing", then reduce every stitch of sail in a twinkling and coast to a stop to drop the best bower in one smooth operation, but there was "many a slip 'tween the crouch and the leap" as the old adage said.

"There they are, Mister Snelling," Mister Yelland, the Sailing Master, pointed out to the Ship's Surgeon. "Gibraltar to the North, and the high headland of Ceuta to the South."

"The Pillars of Hercules," Mr. Snelling marvelled, "that led to Plato's fabled kingdom of Atlantis!"

"Beyond which the ancients would not go," Yelland reminded him.

"But, they must have, Mister Yelland," Snelling objected, "for how else did the Atlantic ports of Spain and Portugal, Roman Iberia and Lusitania, get their goods to the rest of the Empire? And, back in those days, were there not Roman provinces round the shoulder of North Africa, like Mauretania Tingitania? Did not Roman seafarers know of the Canaries?"

"Well, perhaps it was only the *Greeks* who feared to go beyond the Pillars, sir," Mr. Yelland replied, looking a bit nettled for the landlubber to know more than he did.

"Aye, Mister Yelland," Lewrie said, hiding his amusement. "The Romans held the Greeks in low regard, in all things. Though, no seafarers in the ancient world liked t'get too far out of sight of land."

"Did that Mister Gibbons say much of that in his *Decline and Fall of the Roman Empire*, sir?" Lt. Westcott slyly enquired, taking a moment from his strict watchfulness. He *knew* that Lewrie had found it slow going.

"Haven't gotten t'that chapter yet, Mister Westcott," Lewrie said with a *harumph* to indicate that he'd been "gotten" for fair.

"And, there is Cabreta Point, just now becoming visible past Pigeon Island, sir," Yelland pointed out.

"Do the latest charts show Spanish batteries, there, Mister Yelland?" Lewrie asked. "I'd admire to stand into the inshore variable currents as close as we can, and shave Cabreta Point, so we don't get swept right past the bay's entrance."

Yelland looked to the commissioning pendant high aloft, then to the thin clouds that crowned the heights of the Rock, squinting in thought. "I cannot recommend a closer approach to Cabreta Point than two miles, sir," he said at last, "which is very close to the usual entry to the bay."

Lewrie paced aft a few steps to the double wheel helm, and the compass binnacle cabinet under the poop, to double-check their course. He then took a long look at the chart, pinned to the traverse board. The convoy still sailed in column on East by North, with a gentle wind from out of the West-Nor'west.

"Mister Yelland, I'd admire did we alter course a point to larboard. Do you concur?" he asked.

"Hmm," that worthy silently mused for a long moment. "That puts us into the variable currents, but we'd have to abandon the main current within a few more miles, sir. And, closer to where we may safely go about North, into the bay. Aye, sir."

"Signal to all ships, Mister Carey," Lewrie called out to the signals Midshipman on the poop deck. "Alter Course In Succession, One Point To Larboard."

"Aye, sir!"

*An hour and a bit more, and I'm shot of all this shit at last,* he told himself; *If we can't make a showy entrance, then we'll make a safe one . . . and our prize can make up for "flashy"*.

He found himself crossing the fingers of his right hand, most "lubberly" with his hand in a trouser pocket. He would *not* anticipate fresh victuals, clothing, or bedding washed in fresh water for a change, nor a long stroll ashore, nor a meal and a mild drunk in one of Gibraltar Town's many taverns. To do so might jinx it, yet!

Once safely anchored by bow and stern, Lewrie had to keep mental fingers crossed against possible disaster, for the bay and the anchoring grounds were not the most secure sort of sea bottom, and Gibraltar was infamous for gales that seemed to whip up out of nowhere, sending many a ship ashore to pound themselves to pieces on the rocks. Lewrie had ordered 9-pounder guns dis-mounted and used as weights to keep the anchor cables from straining in a sudden blow, to keep the flukes of the anchors from dragging free.

He'd had sailcloth awnings rigged over the poop deck and the quarterdeck and forecastle, too, for protection from the harshness of the sun, and the rare rains. It might have been late Spring back in England, but it was already a warm Summer in these latitudes. There was no protection from the warmth, though, when he took the 25-foot cutter ashore to the town quays, wearing his best-dress uniform made of wool broadcloth, long stored away at the bottom of one of his sea-chests. That required the sash and star of his knighthood, since he would be reporting his presence to the local senior Navy officer, the Governor, Lieutenant-General Sir Hew Dalrymple, and, most likely, the spy-master Thomas Mountjoy. He also took his sack of laundry, leaving it to Pettus to find a washerwoman.

"Doesn't look like much," Lewrie commented as the cutter neared the quays. "Almost typical Spanish, or Italian."

"Seems all soldiers, sir," Pettus said, taking the view in and sounding a bit disappointed to see so many troops strolling the quayside streets, some of them Provost men on patrol. Gibraltar Town had no civilian mayor, but a Town Major.

"Some of 'em drunk'z Davy's Sow," Liam Desmond pointed out as he tweaked the tiller. "Ease stroke."

"That sounds promisin'," Patrick Furfy snickered, turning on his thwart to steal a quick peek ashore, a huge grin on his face.

"Wimmen," Desmond added, looking expectant and hopeful.

Gibraltar Town appeared a jarring, civilian appendage to the Rock, for everywhere Lewrie looked, there were row upon row of troop barracks, storehouses, and a very busy parade ground, perhaps the largest flat place available. Regimental bands were at practise in a cacophony of tunes, and soldiers "square-bashed" by companies, scattered from one end of the parade ground to the other. Not all that far off to the Northern end of Gibraltar, where the land narrowed to a long and skinny neck, were the immense fortifications. Walls with parapets on several levels, bristling with cannons of all calibres, with loopholes for musketry, the famous towers and redoubts known to all Englishmen as the Devil's Tower and the Round Tower, where British Marines, grossly out-numbered, had fought off the Spanish and the French during the War of The Spanish Succession in 1704, they all gave the impression of a titanic giant's castle. From up there came the faint crackling-twig sound of musket volleys as some regiment or other practiced live-firing. The Lines, as the fortifications were known, would be defended as stoutly should the Spanish come against them again, as they had been in 1704.

Desmond conned the cutter alongside a large floating catamaran landing stage. Starboard side oars were tossed, the new bow man, Deavers, got his gaff hooked to a bollard, and the cutter glided to a stop alongside the landing stage. Desmond whipped a light line round a second bollard near the stern, and Lewrie and Pettus prepared to dis-embark.

"You first, lad," Lewrie had to prompt his cabin-steward. He had mostly gotten used to the Navy's ways, but needed reminding that senior officers were "first in, last out".

There was a wide gangway leading to the top of the stone quay, but it was immediately swarmed by several men and women, all shouting their wares, some in broken English or heavy foreign accents, as bad as the London barkers who stood outside their masters' shops to hawk their goods.

"*Vino!* Blackstrap, two pence a pint!"

"Preeties' girl een town, all kind! Young, clean!"

"Orange, leemon, *pomegraneta,* fresh from Tetuán!"

"Scatter, you! Keep the gangway clear, there!" a Sergeant of the Provosts bellowed, waving his halberd to shoo the hawkers off.

"Two pence th' *pint,* arrah, Liam!" Furfy chortled.

"Sorry, lads, back to the ship," Lewrie told them. "I'll take a bum-boat back, later. But, there will be shore liberty!"

That mollified them, somewhat.

"I'd best ask that Sergeant if he knows a good laundry, sir," Pettus decided.

"Aye, do so," Lewrie agreed.

"Captain Lewrie!" someone called from the head of the gangway. "Hallo to you, sir!"

"Mister Mountjoy!" Lewrie replied, looking up and recognising his old clerk. "Have you come to collect me, right off?"

Lewrie shooed Pettus up the gangway, quickly following, to take Mountjoy's outstretched hand.

"Thought it best, sir," Mountjoy said. "My word, but it's good to see you, again. It's been what, six years, since I saw you off to the Baltic, at Great Yarmouth?"

"About that, aye," Lewrie said, recalling how Mountjoy had saddled him with those two Russian aristocrats to be landed as near to St. Petersburg as possible, after scouting the thickness and breadth of the winter ice in Swedish and Russian naval harbours before Admirals Sir Hyde Parker and Horatio Nelson sailed for Denmark, and the Battle of Copenhagen in 1801. The mad Tsar Paul had pressured Sweden and Denmark into his bellicose League of Armed Neutrality, ready to close the Baltic to British trade, seizing hundreds of British merchant ships and marching their crews off to Siberia. It could not be stood while England was still at war with France and her allies, resulting in a massive naval expedition to destroy the League's navies, hopefully one at a time before the ice melted.

That arrogant, skeletal sneerer, Zachariah Twigg, had been in charge of Secret Branch then, and the nobles had been sent on with a hope that they could aid the rumoured assassination plot against the Tsar. They arrived in St. Petersburg a touch too late to take part, and the youngest one had tried to have Lewrie killed, all for the affections of a Panton Street whore.

"Now, what may I help you with, sir?" Mountjoy offered.

"First off, ye can tell my man here, Pettus, where he can find a reliable laundry," Lewrie told him with a grin.

"There's a very good one that I use, quite near my residence," Mountjoy told him. "It's not too far uphill. Let us go there."

"Ehm, shouldn't I be calling upon Sir Hew Dalrymple, first?" Lewrie asked as they set off.

"I very much doubt it he can spare you the time," Mountjoy told him. "Just send round one of those new *carte de visites* with a short note. He's much too busy, of late, hunting down foreign spies and enemy agents."

"A lot of those around, are there?" Lewrie wondered aloud.

"Strong rumours, as far as I can determine," Mountjoy imparted, "but nothing solid, and no names named. Anonymous tips about French or Spanish agents scouting the defences, some dis-affected Irish officers plotting to raise a mutiny and hand the Rock over to the Spanish, and of *course,* our anomymous tipsters will have us believe that there's a cabal of Jews at the bottom of it. Pure balderdash. The worst problem are the traders who'd sell grain and foodstuffs to the Spanish, who aren't eating all that well, these days, with the government in Madrid sending so much off to support Napoleon's larders."

"It's like a *foreign* town," Pettus said, gawking as they made their way uphill along a narrow stone street lined with stone-front and stuccoed houses, shops, and lodgings, with stout wood doors set into the fronts atop narrow stone stoops, and the windows mounted high and rather small, iron-barred for security, and fitted with wood shutters inside. "There's little English about it."

"Well, it was Spanish for hundreds of years, and Moorish long before that, Mister Pettus," Mountjoy explained. "We've owned it for only a bit beyond an hundred years. You'll hear the difference, too. There are only a little over three thousand male inhabitants on the Rock, and only about eight hundred of them are British. Maybe nine hundred from neutral countries, and over sixteen hundred are registered as citizens of enemy nations!

"Add to that, there's another two thousand or so foreign traders allowed to buy and sell here, with purchased three-month passes to let them do so . . . unmolested, mind," Mountjoy went on. "You'll hear every language of Europe, with Spanish, Portuguese, and Italian predominant. I even thought I heard some Russian, the other day."

"Hmm, sounds t'me as if Dalrymple might have *cause* t'worry," Lewrie said. "I'd think that *you'd* find it worrying, in your line of work."

In answer, Mountjoy laid a finger against his lips and made a boyish "Sshh!"

⚓

Thomas Mountjoy kept lodgings on the top floor of a stout and old house, which allowed him access to a rooftop garden area with an awning rigged over it for coolness and shade. There were slat-wood chairs and settees, and Moorish-looking pottery urns for side-tables with wood tops, and a wrought-iron metal table. Most prominent was a large brass telescope mounted on a tripod.

"Should anyone wish to do me in, I'm harder to reach up here," Mountjoy said in seeming seriousness as he invited Lewrie to "take a pew" and cool off from the exertion of walking so far uphill. "There are several very stout doors to get through, first, and by then I'm awake and well-armed. When needed, I putter with all my flowers and plants, and . . . keep an eye on Spain. See my telescope?"

There were indeed lots of potted greenery, and so many blossoms that the air was sweet with their aromas. Lewrie went to the telescope and bent down to peer through it. "Aha!" he said.

Mountjoy's aerie was high-enough up the hills that he could see over the British Lines right across the wide swath of neutral ground at the narrow neck to the matching line of fortifications on the Spanish side. Mountjoy's telescope was huge, and strong, good enough to serve an astronomer, and fill its entire ocular with the moon in all its details. He could even make out Spanish sentries pacing along at the top of the Spanish works, slouching, smoking, or yawning!

"Nice view of the harbour, too," Mountjoy told him, "and what's acting on the Spanish side of the bay, at Algeciras. Quite useful, my English eccentricities, do you not think? To all casual observers I'm in the grain trade, and keep an office in the South end of town . . . where people who report to me can come and go. Sir Hew allows me and mine to do some smuggling, in a small way, which gives my men in the field good reason to travel in Spain."

"And you keep him informed on who the real smugglers are, I take it?" Lewrie asked, swivelling the telescope to seek out his ship to see what was going on there. He stood erect and looked South and could look right cross the straits to the other rocky headland, and the massive Spanish fort at Ceuta. It was more than twelve miles off, but the powerful telescope could fetch up a decent image, even so.

"When I come across one arranging a huge shipment," Mountjoy said. "If I kept up with all of them, I'd have no time for my real tasks."

"The one that Peel wants me to help with," Lewrie said. "Before I sailed, I wrote him and told him that my ship's too big and deep-draughted t'do you much good close inshore, but I never heard back. Now that I'm here, just what is it that you need from me?' And just what *is* your main task?"

"London has charged me with turning the Spanish against the French, and getting them out of the war, perhaps even gaining them as an ally," Mountjoy baldly told him.

"You're joking," Lewrie said, gawping.

"With the carrot, and the stick," Mountjoy added, looking sly again. "Sweet talk and sympathy on the one hand, and promises of free trade, and on the other hand, making the lives of everyone from here to the French border miserable, with chaos and mayhem."

"And my part is . . . ?" Lewrie posed.

"The chaos and mayhem," Mountjoy said with a chuckle.

"Hmm," Lewrie said, with a shrug. "I can *do* chaos and mayhem . . . I've been dined out on it for years. Landings and raids, I'd suppose? Bring all Spanish coasting trade to a stop?"

"Sink, take, or burn everything that floats, yes," Mountjoy agreed. "And quick cut-and-thrust raids on coastal ports and villages. Along the way, to and from, I'll also need you to drop off some of my field agents, now and again. Picking them up and fetching them back may be too much to hope for, but I have managed to put together a few ways for their reports and informations to reach me, *somewhat* timely. It would really help, though, if, upon your first venture, you could obtain for me a small coasting vessel or fishing boat."

"Steal you a boat, right," Lewrie said. "Simple enough."

"Something dowdy and un-remarkable, and easily manned by as few people as possible," Mountjoy went on. "From the times of old General O'Hara, the 'Cock of The Rock', everyone *talks* of protecting the town and the bay with gunboats and cutters, but no one has built, or bought, or followed through on the plan. When Nelson commanded the Mediterranean Fleet, he planned for twenty gunboats, but that came to nothing, either. Individual ships sailing into the bay are easy pickings for all the Spanish gunboats at Algeciras, and the mouths of the Palmones and the Guadananque Rivers. There's nothing for me to work with."

"Something that could be handled by a Midshipman and seven or eight men," Lewrie schemed. "All of whom can speak decent Spanish, I suppose? I can get you some sort of boat, but . . ."

"I've a man coming to do the talking, if it comes to it," Mountjoy promised quickly. "In the Andalusian dialect, and high Castilian to boot . . . with lisp and all!"

"Even so, it might be best did *Sapphire* see your new boat near where you wish to land or recover agents, but stay safely offshore," Lewrie told him, going to one of the chairs and sitting down on a faded green cushion. "Best that we're not seen *too* close together."

"That makes sense," Mountjoy agreed with a nod or two. "Lord, what a poor host I am! I've a very nice and light white wine. Smuggling can go both ways, what? It's a Spanish *tempra . . . tembrani* . . . well, whatever it's called, it's quite good."

Mountjoy went into the bedroom adjoining and fetched a bottle from a dim corner, where he kept a tub of water with which to cool his wine. "Now where's the bloody cork pull?" he grumbled.

Thomas Mountjoy had been an idle and direction-less young man when he'd been Lewrie's clerk, a pleasant but callow fellow whom his elder brother, Mr. Matthew Mountjoy of London—Lewrie's solicitor and prize agent—had foisted upon him when Lewrie had the *Jester* sloop. It was hard for Lewrie to picture Mountjoy in the same trade as the thoroughly dangerous Zachariah Twigg, or James Peel. Mountjoy just didn't look the part; he was the epitome of a nice, inoffencive scion from the Squirearchy, who didn't have to really *work* at anything.

He was brown-haired and brown-eyed, and his eyes and expression seemed too merry and innocent for skullduggery. He did not give off a sense of being capable of murder, or of being dangerous.

*Well, maybe that's his best asset,* Lewrie thought; *No one would suspect him of anything. Not strikingly handsome, or remember-able. Christ, is that even a word?*

"Deacon?" Mountjoy called out. "Where did I leave the cork pull?"

A well-muscled and craggy-faced man came out of an inner room, a fellow who *did* look furtive, and very dangerous, from the way that he carried himself. "Here, sir," he said, handing it over. "You left it on the side-table, from last night's supper."

"Daniel Deacon, one of my assistants, and my bodyguard when such is needed," Mountjoy said, doing the introductions.

"Much danger to you, here on the Rock?" Lewrie asked, "With so many soldiers patrolling the town, I'd expect that it's better guarded than Saint James's Palace."

"With so many foreigners here, sir, and so many traders coming and going with temporary passes, it's best to be overly cautious," Mr. Deacon said, most seriously and earnestly, not waiting for his superior to answer the question. He had a way of glaring that could be quite dis-concerting, and held himself like a taut-wound watch spring.

"Daniel's another one of James Peel's protégés," Mountjoy said, "re-cruited from Twigg's informal band of Baker Street Irregulars."

"Formerly a Sergeant in the Foot Guards," Deacon added.

"Saved my bacon once, the Irregulars did," Lewrie told Deacon. "A *damned* efficent group."

"Thank you, sir," Deacon said, with a faint hint of a smile. "I will go out and attend to that . . . other matter?"

"Make it seem casual," Mountjoy cautioned, and Deacon departed. "A little surveillance on a new-come trader," he explained to Lewrie. "Now, let's sample this wine!"

# CHAPTER NINETEEN

"First step, then," Lewrie summed up, after a convivial, but business-like, half-hour of plotting and savouring the light, fruity Spanish white wine. "I capture you a boat. A large fishing boat will do quite nicely, about fourty or fifty feet overall. She'd be large enough t'live in if the weather goes against you, and would be the sort that ventures further out to sea than the type employed by coastal Spanish fishermen."

"And, could plausibly explain her presence near any Spanish village along the coast," Mountjoy happily agreed. "Up by Almeria, we can claim to sail from Málaga, up near Cádiz on the West, we could claim to be from Cartagena . . . chasing after the herring, or something."

"Her crew would have to actually put out nets, and have a catch aboard, if they run afoul of a Spanish *garda costa*," Lewrie cautioned. "Not that there are too many of those who'd dare set out, these days, with our Navy prowling about."

"Troops to re-enforce your people," Mountjoy eagerly prompted, making a list with pencil and paper. "Garrison duty is so hellish-boresome, I'd imagine *thousands* would volunteer. Though, Sir Hew the Dowager might be loath to give up a corporal's guard."

"Perhaps you can sweet-talk him," Lewrie said, snickering.

"He's a reasonable-enough old stick," Mountjoy agreed, again.

"I've fifty private Marines, and can put another fifty sailors ashore, without harming the operation of the ship," Lewrie volunteered. "Can I lay hands on one troop transport, of decent size, she'd be able t'carry about one hundred and fifty soldiers. Any more, and they'd be arseholes to elbows. That's what, three companies? Light infantry'd be best. Perhaps fewer," he said, after further musing, "since I would have to put enough sailors aboard her t'man the boats. The average is about three hundred tons, with only fifteen merchant seamen to handle the ship.

"Get them all ashore in one go," he schemed on, "and more importantly, get them *off* all together . . . in, raise Hell, then get out as quick as dammit . . . I'd need *six* boats. Barges, or launches, with at least eight men in each to row and steer. Scrambling nets."

"Beg pardon?" Mountjoy asked, his pencil poised in mid-air.

"Use old, cast-off anti-boarding nets hung down each side of the transport by the chain platforms for all three masts," Lewrie explained. "A boat waitin' below each." Lewrie borrowed a fresh sheet of paper and snatched Mountjoy's pencil to make a quick sketch. "The soldiers'd climb down the nets into the boats, instead of going down the boarding battens and man-ropes, one at a time, which'd take for-bloody-ever, see?"

"Wouldn't they be over-loaded, and clumsy, though?" Mountjoy said with a frown. "Laden with all the usual . . . ?"

"Light infantry, like I said," Lewrie almost boyishly laid out. "There for a quick raid and retreat. They'd need their hangers, their muskets and bayonets, perhaps double the allotment of cartridges, and their canteens. Packs, blanket rolls, cooking gear . . . all that would be un-necessary. They're not on campaign, and won't make camp."

"Oh, I think I do see," Mountjoy said.

"Of course, I'd have t'do the same with *Sapphire,* t'get all my people ashore at the same time," Lewrie fretted. "The nets, and more ship's boats than I have at present. Perhaps the dockyard here can cobble me up some more launches or barges."

"The yard's very efficient," Mountjoy assured him, slyly retrieving his pencil. "When *Victory* put in after the Battle of Trafalgar, rather heavily damaged, she was set to rights and off for England within a week. I'm certain that Captain Middleton will have all the used nets and lumber to satisfy all your wants. *Our* wants, rather."

"My orders did not name anyone," Lewrie said. "I was to report to the senior naval officer present. Middleton, d'ye say? Don't know him."

"Robert Gambier Middleton," Thom Mountjoy expounded. "He has been here for about two years, now. He's the Naval Commissioner for the dockyard, the storehouses, and oversees the naval hospital. Quite a fine establishment, with one thousand beds available."

"Well, I shall go and see him, right off," Lewrie determined. "He'll have the spare hands I need, too, most-like, perhaps even the transport under his command that I can borrow."

"Ehm . . . that's all that Middleton commands, I'm afraid. Even the defence of the town and the bay are beyond his brief," Mountjoy told him. "Now, when there's some ships in to victual or repair . . ."

"What? He don't command even a rowboat?" Lewrie goggled, and not merely from the effects of the excellent Spanish wine.

"So far as I know, Captain Lewrie, there never *has* been a man in command of a squadron permanently assigned to Gibraltar. When I got here, 'bout the same time as Middleton, there was a fellow named Otway, who had the office," Thom Mountjoy had to inform him, shrugging in wonder why not. "He was *more* than happy to leave, I gathered, 'cause he was pulled both ways by the needs of the commander of the Mediterranean Fleet and the commander of the fleet blockading Cádiz, and what was left of the combined Franco-Spanish fleet after Trafalgar. But, *neither* senior officer thought he could spare warships from his command to do the job that the Army's many artillery batteries do. If a few two-deckers and frigates come in for a few days, then the senior officer among them is *temporarily* responsible."

"Mine arse on a band-box!" Lewrie exclaimed. "D'ye mean t'say so long as I'm here, *I'm* senior officer present?"

"I fear so, sir," Mountjoy told him. He *tried* to do so with a suitable amount of sympathy, but during his years aboard HMS *Jester* as Lewrie's clerk, he had always been amused by Lewrie's trademark phrase for frustration, and could not contain a grin.

"Sorry, Captain Lewrie, it's just . . ." Mountjoy apologised.

"It ain't funny," Lewrie gravelled, scowling. He flung himself back into his chair, feeling that he was deflating like a pig bladder at the end of a semaphore arm; hanging useless!

"Good God Almighty," Lewrie muttered. "It's Bermuda or the Bahamas all over again. Backwaters like those I can understand, but Gibraltar? As vital to our interests as the Rock is? Mine . . . !"

"One would suppose, sir, that His Majesty's Government, and Admiralty, imagine that the closeness of two large fleets, able to respond with more than sufficient force should they be called upon to do so, would suffice," Mountjoy said more formally, and humbly.

"Aye, I suppose," Lewrie grumbled, his head thrown back, deep in thoughts of how to salvage his position. "Hmm . . . it's not as if either the French or the Spanish are able t'put an invasion fleet together, not after Trafalgar. They can pin-prick us with those gunboats you mentioned, cut out a prize now and then, but they can't pose any real threat."

"And if Foreign Office, and Secret Branch, can manage to manipulate the Spanish into withdrawing from their alliance with France, sir, there would be no threat at all," Mountjoy pointed out.

"And how likely is that?" Lewrie asked, still in a wee pet.

"Spain's bankrupt, and has been for some time," Mountjoy told him. "Her overseas trade with her New World colonies has been cut to nothing, and all the gold, silver, and jewels they were used to getting are not available, and what they do have is syphoned off to support the French. To make things worse, there's Napoleon Bonaparte's Berlin Decrees, which is ruining *all* of Europe, and frankly, ruining France herself.

"Bonaparte's trying to shut down all trade 'twixt all of the countries he dominates, or occupies, and Great Britain," Mr. Mountjoy explained further, "and that applies to Spain, which is going even broker because of it. Only Sweden and Portugal are hold-outs, and we *have* gotten rumours that France *may* take action against Portugal sometime in the future. But, if Spain turns neutral, then all her goods and exports are open to the world, as would all the world's goods be available to Spain once more."

"Hold on a bit," Lewrie said, sitting up straighter and lifting an interrupting hand. "How the Devil are the French going to be able to take action against Portugal? They can't do it by sea, by God."

"Well, we've gotten informations from Paris that one of Bonaparte's favourites, Marshal Junot, has been ordered to assemble an army," Mountjoy said, almost furtively. "They're calling it a Corps of Observation, and that 'Boney's' Foreign Minister, Talleyrand, is in negotiations with Godoy in Madrid about marching across Spain to get the job done."

"Christ on a crutch!" Lewrie hooted in sudden glee. "And the Dons are so lick-spittle they'd abide *that?*"

"London is trusting that they will not stand such an insult to their national pride, sir," Mountjoy said with a sly and gleeful look of his own.

"We've passed that on to 'the Dowager,' and Sir Hew relayed the rumour to his counterpart t'other side of The Lines, a General Castaños, in charge of all Spanish forces surrounding Gibraltar.

"Sir Hew has forged a very respectful and amicable relationship with General Castaños since his arrival," Mountjoy added. "The enemy Castanõs might be, but his correspondence to Sir Hew has hinted that he, his officers, and men are disgusted with their Francophile government in Madrid, 'Boney's' Continental System, and Spain's alliance to the depraved, anti-Pope, anti-religious French."

"They might rebel, and take all Andalusia with 'em?" Lewrie speculated.

"*If* the French cross the border and march on Portugal, it may be that *all* Spain might," Mountjoy said, almost in a whisper.

"Ah, but how factual is your rumour?" Lewrie had to wonder.

"We have several sources in France, and in Paris itself, sir," Mountjoy warily related, "despite the lengths that the French police go to discover them, or how strictly they intercept and read all correspondence posted, or smuggled. Trust me that our source is literally speaking from 'the horse's mouth'. She . . . forget that . . . has social access to everyone who matters in Paris."

"She!" Lewrie barked, suddenly sure of the source, and despising it. "Charité de Guilleri, d'ye mean? That murderin' bitch? That blood-thirsty *whore?* She'd lie to the Angel Gabriel! *Dammit,* Mountjoy, she helped hunt me and Caroline clear cross France to assassinate us! She took part in the murder of my wife!"

"I am sorry for that, sir," Mountjoy said, sitting up stiffer, as if stung. "But, when Mister Peel spoke with you a few years ago, and you agreed to write a reply to her letter offering her forgiveness, and . . ."

"Didn't mean a bloody word of it, rest assured!" Lewrie fumed. "That was all for James Peel's use, and I was savourin' a hope that she'd be caught red-handed and got her head chopped off for spyin'!"

"The lady . . . the woman in question, sir, has proved to be a valuable asset," Mountjoy told him, all but wringing his hands, fidgetting, and pouring them both another glass of wine for something dis-tracting for him to do. "After Bonaparte sold her beloved Louisiana and her city of New Orleans to the Americans, she was quite 'turned'.

"She has found her way into the most influential *salons,* and, ehm . . . into the beds of Marshals, Generals, Admirals, and Ministers of Napoleon's regime," Mountjoy pointed out, with a cajoling brow up. "I cannot imagine a better source, and neither does London. All she has gotten to us has been the equivalent of solid gold. If she says that Junot and his army is readying itself to march against Portugal, then we must take it as gospel."

"Damn her black soul to the Seventh Level of Hell, anyway," Lewrie spat. "I *still* hope they catch her, sooner or later, and chop her head off, no matter how useful you and Peel find her!"

"Quite understandable, sir," Mountjoy said, with a solemn nod.

"So . . . if the whore's tellin' the truth, what are *we* doin'?" Lewrie asked.

"I gather that plans are afoot, sir," Mountjoy tried to assure him, even if he was in the dark as to what, specifically. "Naturally, Foreign Office has alerted the Portuguese, and Peel has written me that we may prepare a field army to re-enforce them, and to safeguard the major ports. Beyond that, though, I fear that we must await events, then react accordingly. As for me, I am to re-double my efforts, and give Sir Hew Dalrymple all aid in his dealings with the Spanish, to sway them."

"And for that, ye need a boat, right now," Lewrie gathered.

"As soon as yesterday, Captain Lewrie," Mountjoy assured him.

"Right, then," Lewrie said, with a frustrated hough of wind. He finished his wine, then rose to gather his hat and sword. "I'll be in touch. If Captain Middleton can't help us much, perhaps you and I may speak with Sir Hew Dalrymple, to see if he can lend us assistance."

"That may be a good idea, sir," Mountjoy agreed, rising to see Lewrie down to the street.

Pettus had spent his time well, arranging for the laundry to be ready the next day, then idling in the back first-level kitchens with Mountjoy's maid-of-all-work and his fat old cook. Both women saw him off with hugs and giggles.

"Treat ye well, did they, Pettus?" Lewrie asked.

"Yes, sir," Pettus told him. "They whipped me up an omelet, and offered me some decent wine. Don't know where they got the cheese, but it was right tasty, too."

"Then you must come back to retrieve my wash tomorrow," Lewrie told him with a smirk.

"Why, I suppose I must, sir!" Pettus happily agreed.

⚓

Once back aboard, Lewrie found that both the off-watch sailors, and those still with duties to perform, were spending half their time gazing ashore and joshing most expectantly. He *had* promised them that they would get shore liberty for a change, and not put the ship Out of Discipline to allow recreation, and rutting, still imprisoned within their "wooden walls".

"They seem in fine fettle, Mister Westcott," Lewrie took note, after the welcome-aboard ritual had been performed.

"Recall that they were paid just before we sailed from the Nore, sir," Lt. Westcott casually replied, "and just itching to get a shot at spending their pay on shore pleasures. Once your boat crew returned, and boasted of what they'd been offered at the quays, and so cheaply, I expect they'd dive overboard and thrash ashore, this instant."

"Whether most of 'em can't swim or not?" Lewrie posed. "What is our state, sir?"

"Securely anchored, sir, with Marine sentries posted to prevent desertion," Westcott ticked off, "firewood and water to come aboard by the start of tomorrow's Forenoon, and the needs of the Purser, Master Gunner, and Bosun in hand and relayed to the yard. Our prize, *Le Cerf,* has been officially received by the Prize-Court, and all our prisoners transferred from her to the *Guerriere* hulk. Their badly wounded have been moved to a prison ward at the naval hospital."

"Our prize crew?" Lewrie asked.

"Returned to us, sir," Westcott said, with a wee sneer. "The Prize-Court sent people aboard for a harbour watch."

*Le Cerf,* Lewrie thought; *The* Stag.

Long ago, during the final days of the Siege of Toulon, then at shore lodgings here at Gibraltar, his wee French mistress, Phoebe Aretino, had called him that . . . her powerful galloping stag! And oh, how they *had* galloped! He got tight in the crutch, remembering.

"Very well, Mister Westcott. Carry on," Lewrie said.

"Oh, there was an invitation sent aboard, sir, from Captain Knolles," Westcott added, reaching into a side pocket of his coat. "He wishes to dine with you ashore, at his expense, this evening."

"Did he name a time?" Lewrie asked, taking the note. "Ah! Six in the evening. Aye, I'll be going back ashore for that, Geoffrey. If he's off for the Mediterranean Fleet, this'd be our last reunion, for some time. Ready the wee cutter and a Mid t'carry my answer over to *Comus,* soon as I've penned it."

"Aye, sir."

Lewrie made to enter his cabins, but spotted Lt. Harcourt atop the poop deck, and looking even glummer than usual, so he called him down.

"Welcome back aboard, Mister Harcourt," Lewrie said, doffing his hat. "I am sorry that I got your hopes up for nothing. What did the officials of the Prize-Court say to you? Any chance that they'll buy her in?"

"They seemed most gleeful to take possession of her, sir," Lt. Harcourt replied, "rubbing their hands like money-jobbers, and giving me all assurances that she *would* be purchased into the Navy, but . . . not 'til next Saint Geoffrey's Day."

"That'd be the fifteenth of Never?" Lewrie japed. There was no St. Geoffrey's Day in the Church of England's *ordo.*

"They'll send what they think she's worth to Admiralty, and it will take months for that to get there and for Admiralty to decide if they can afford her," Lt. Harcourt bemoaned, "then more months to get a favourable reply, *and* the funds, then . . ."

"Then either the commander of the Mediterranean Fleet or the commander of the Cádiz blockade chooses a favourite officer from his own flagship to have her, and scrounges up a crew to come man her," Lewrie said, half-commiserating, and half-scoffing at the Navy's ways of rewarding people. "Damn 'em. That may turn out to be a blessing for you, Mister Harcourt."

"At this moment, I can't imagine how, sir," Harcourt bleakly spat.

"That *corvette,* sound as she is this moment, will spend months slowly deteriorating at anchor, with not tuppence allowed for her upkeep by a skeleton crew, sir," Lewrie told him. "Think what a nightmare you *could* be saddled with. Don't be too envious of the fool who finally gets command of her."

"Well, there is that, sir," Harcourt replied after a moment to think that over. "Bird in the hand, and all that?"

"And shore liberty for you, so you can drown your sorrows," Lewrie reminded him. "After that, *Sapphire* is charged to remain here at Gibraltar, now and again, but we will not spend much time in port. We've all Hell t'raise along the Spanish coasts. Can't tell ye much beyond that, but . . ." Lewrie said with a cryptic smile. "Once again, my apologies that you didn't get t'keep her. And for getting your hopes up. I truly am."

"Ehm . . . thank you, sir," Harcourt said, doffing his hat in salute.

Lewrie turned away and entered his great-cabins to mull over his predicament for an hour or so before it would be time to change into his best-dress shoregoing uniform, replete with that damned sash and star. His knighthood and his baronetcy, he strongly and cynically suspected, had not come for his part in the minor action off the Chandeleur Islands and the coast of what was then Spanish Louisiana, nor had he been honoured for accumulated victories; for whatever reason the French had tried to murder him, and had slain his wife. He'd been in the papers, HM Government had determined to go back to war against France, and had needed to rouse the public's angry support for it.

Even so, Captain Ralph Knolles was not to know that, and he was in all respects a decent fellow, a patriot, and the sort who would expect Lewrie to wear those things proudly.

"Cool tea, if ye would, Pettus," Lewrie bade as he stripped off his coat and hung it on the back of his desk chair in the day-cabin.

"Coming right up, sir," Pettus vowed. "Ehm . . . when I go back ashore to collect your laundry tomorrow, sir . . . might I take Jessop along with me?"

The young cabin-servant froze, pretending to continue blacking and buffing Lewrie's best pair of boots, as if shore liberty would be no concern of his, but his ears were perked, no error.

"Hmm . . . better with you t'shepherd him than tailing along with a pack o' swaggerin' sailors," Lewrie decided. "Aye, Pettus. Take him along, so you can keep him out of trouble."

"I don't never get into trouble, sir," Jessop protested, going for "meek and angelic".

"And Pettus'll make sure ye don't," Lewrie told him.

"Aye, sir," Jessop responded, sounding a bit glum to be in need of a chaperone.

*Good God, has he grown old enough* t'want *t'caterwaul and play a buck-of-the-first-head?* Lewrie wondered; *By God, I think he has! It'll be drink, whores, and a tattoo, next!*

# CHAPTER TWENTY

Once atop the quays, Lewrie took a long moment to look back at his ship, and felt satisfaction. Dockyard barges and hoys swarmed her sides, delivering firewood for the galley and fresh water to top off her tanks. Powder, roundshot, and cartridge bag cloth was going aboard to replace all that *Sapphire* had shot off in live gunnery practice and their brief action with the French *corvettes*. Kegs of salt-meats and other foodstuffs were being hauled up the loading skids, or hoisted up with the use of the main course yard.

HMS *Sapphire*'s own boats were busy, too, ferrying supplies for the officers' wardroom, and goods for the Purser's needs, and items ordered, or hoped for, by the Bosun, the Ship's Carpenter, the Surgeon, the Cooper, Mr. Scaife, and the Armourer, Mr. Turley.

A full day spent on lading and replenishing, and on the morning of the next day, the Larboard Watch, half the ship's crew, would be allowed ashore from the start of the Forenoon at 8 A.M. 'til the end of the Second Dog at 8 P.M.; the day after, the Starboard Watch would go ashore to drink and rut, dance, holler, stagger and sing, even pick fights with hands off other ships in harbour.

Hopefully, they'd report back aboard on time, the most of them, suffer their thick, woozy heads after drinking themselves silly, and not cause so much of a riot ashore that he would have to hold an all-day Captain's Mast, or "let the cat out of the bag" on too many men. Sailors, soldiers, and Provost police were an explosive mixture. He almost felt the need to keep the fingers of his right hand crossed all day, or knock wood on every passing push-cart, but . . . he had to see Secret Branch's man, Thomas Mountjoy.

That worthy had told him most casually the day before that he kept the semblance of an office where he pretended to engage in trade, but there were dozens of those, and Lewrie had not thought to enquire just where it was, so he set off in search of it, walking South along the quays into the commercial district of high-piled rented offices, warehouses, and large shops, into a teeming throng of carts and goods waggons, sweating stevedores, wares hawkers, and wheelbarrow men, all working in some urgency. The shouts and deal-making in English were rare standouts in the loud jibber-jabber of foreign tongues. The odours of fresh-sawn lumber and sawdust, kegged beers and wines, exotic oils, fruits and vegetables—both fresh and rotten—stood out among the dusty dry smells wafting from the many storehouses full of various grains, and massive piles of ground-flour sacks inside them.

"Ah, Captain Lewrie, sir," said a voice quite near his elbow, which almost made Lewrie jump. "Deacon, sir," Mountjoy's bodyguard said. "You're looking for our offices, I expect?"

"I am, aye," Lewrie replied, "and good morning to you, Mister Deacon."

"You walked right past it," Deacon said, jerking his head to indicate the general direction. "Mister Mountjoy is expecting you. If you'll follow me, sir?"

Deacon led him back North about fifty yards to an ancient pile of a quayside house of three storeys, now converted to offices. They went up to the second level, and into a rather small two-room suite overlooking the harbour. A crowded billboard by the entry, and one on the door to the suite, announced the presence of THE FALMOUTH IMPORT & EXPORT COMPANY.

"Aha! Found him, did you, Deacon?" Mountjoy said with glee. "Take a pew, Captain Lewrie. A glass of cool tea? Took a page from your book, d'ye see, especially in these climes."

The offices were cramped and stuffy, and smelled ancient. The floorboards creaked, as did his chair when Lewrie sat himself down. Both large windows were open, and the shutters swung open to relieve that stuffiness, letting in an early-morning breeze off the bay. Mr. Mountjoy was most casual, minus coat, waist-coat, and neck-stock, with his shirt-sleeves rolled to the elbows.

"Lemon slices there, from Tetuán in Morocco," Mountjoy pointed out as he poured a tall glass of cool tea. "All manner of fresh fruit comes from there, and live bullocks, goats, and sheep. Being a Muslim country, don't expect to get any pork, though. And, count yourself lucky if you don't get ordered to sail there and fetch back water and cattle. Gibraltar's always short of water, and every good rain hereabouts is counted a miraculous blessing. West Indies sugar there, in the blue and white bowl. I have to keep a lid on. The bloody ants and roaches are everywhere."

"Not to mention rats and mice from the warehouses alongside of us, sir," Deacon said, "though they only prowl the offices after we lock up for the night." He went to one of the windows to lean with his arms crossed and peer out.

"Now, Captain Lewrie!" Mountjoy said, after Lewrie had gotten his tea stirred up the way he liked it, and had had a first sip. "I am mystified by your cryptic note. 'Possible solution, Rock Soup'. What the Devil is 'Rock Soup'?"

"I dined ashore last night with Captain Ralph Knolles, from the *Comus* frigate," Lewrie began to explain, "formerly my First . . ."

"Knolles, yes!" Mountjoy exclaimed. "Haven't seen him in ages, not since *Jester* paid off, and we all went our separate ways."

"Must be goin' soft in the head," Lewrie said, all but slapping his forehead. "Of *course*, we were all in her, together."

"Solid fellow, just capital sort of man," Mountjoy praised.

"Anyway, we got to talking about how to put together a raiding force . . . left your part out of it . . . and how seemingly impossible it seems to be," Lewrie began again. "Gettin' a transport, gettin' the troops, the extra boats, the extra sailors, and he said 'Rock Soup', smilin' fit to bust. I was mystified at first, too, but . . . it's an old tale he heard as a child, how two mercenary soldiers in the Hundred Years War, or the Thirty Years War, he forgot which, were trampin' round Europe, so hungry their stomachs thought their throats'd been cut, not ha'pence between 'em, and came upon a village where the folk swore that even if they had money, there was nothing for them to buy, since so many armed bands and armies had already been there.

"Well, the two soldiers knew the villagers were lying, and had some food well-hidden, so they asked for a cauldron and firewood, and got some rocks from a creek and started boilin' 'em up, rubbin' their hands over how good the rocks'd taste," Lewrie went on. "The village folk'd never *heard* the like and gathered round to see what they were doing. After a bit, one soldier says that the rocks'd taste better with an onion or two, and one of the farmers ran off and brought 'em onions. Then it was carrots, then potatoes, then some salt, then a few marrow bones, then a chicken, then some rabbits, then pepper and herbs, and, after an hour or so, they'd tricked the village into making a feast. Out came the villagers' bowls, bread, cheese, and wine, and they *all* dug in and ate themselves gluttonous.

"In the morning, the village saw the soldiers off with bread, cheese, and full skins of wine, so they could tramp on to the next village and perform the trick all over again. See? Rock Soup!"

"We take it one item at a time," Mountjoy exclaimed, looking as if he'd clap his hands in glee. "First off . . . hmm."

"Two, maybe three companies of infantry," Lewrie suggested. "I prefer light infantry, light companies used to skirmishing. I s'pose we'd have to go hat-in-hand to Sir Hew Dalrymple for those."

"Then, when you have the troops committed, it's only natural that the next request would be to Captain Middleton, for the yards to build the boats," Mountjoy slyly added.

"And, once the boats are begun, I go prowl about to capture a decent-sized Spanish merchantman to be our transport," Lewrie said, "or we convince Sir Hew to commandeer one from the next troop convoy."

"And, if we have the troops, the boats, and the transport, we need extra sailors to *man* the boats that will carry the troops ashore and back, and supplement the transport's crew."

"We get the transport, we get the scrambling nets, *then* the extra sailors," Lewrie gleefully schemed on. "It's good odds that the naval hospital will have men healed up from their sicknesses or their wounds, with no chance to rejoin their original ships, just idling with nothing to do! Lastly, we stock the transport with all manner of rations for all, and we're off!"

"Huzzah!" Mountjoy cried. "Rock Soup, by God! Huzzah!"

"But only, sir," Deacon finally contributed, most laconically, "if Sir Hew is of a *mind* to bother the Spanish."

"Hey? What's that, Deacon?" Mountjoy scoffed. "Whyever not?"

"The gentleman may imagine that if Spain will allow a French army march across their country to invade Portugal, then they might go so far as to allow the French to march down here and try to take Gibraltar, with Spanish armies collaborating. He may imagine that it may be better to keep all his five thousand troops here, and send for re-enforcements, instead, sir."

*Damned sharp for a former Sergeant from the ranks,* Lewrie told himself; *Where* do *Twigg and Peel find 'em?*

"All we can do is ask," Lewrie said, wondering if their bright ideas might come to nothing. "See what he has in mind, get an inkling of what he's been told by London that he hasn't seen fit to share with you, so far, Mountjoy."

"Well, I suppose we should," Mountjoy grudgingly agreed, much sobered. "Yes, I'll send a note to Sir Hew requesting a meeting to introduce you, and our plans. Keep your fingers crossed that he doesn't send you off to Tetuán for fruit and water, instead. You will run my note up to the Convent, Deacon? There's a good fellow."

"The Convent?" Lewrie asked.

"It was a convent, once, when the Spanish had the Rock. Quite a good and roomy place for his headquarters," Mountjoy explained. "I think your best will be in order, Captain Lewrie . . . Sir Alan, rather. Sash and star, all that? Sir Hew will place great stock in your turnout."

"Shave and brush my teeth, too, I suppose?" Lewrie complained.

"If you'd be so kind," Mountjoy said in wry reply.

# CHAPTER TWENTY-ONE

*Hah, I wonder why they call him 'the Dowager'*, Lewrie had to wonder when introduced to Lieutenant-General Sir Hew Dalrymple in his offices the next afternoon. Mountjoy had told him that Sir Hew had been born in 1750, had purchased a commission as a Lieutenant in his teens, at thirteen, and was now only fifty-seven years old, thirteen years Lewrie's senior. Sir Hew didn't *look* like an aged dodderer, or sound like an ancient "skull full of gruel". He seemed quite lucid, in fact.

"Is not your ship a tad too large for the operations that Mister Mountjoy, here, envisions, Sir Alan?" Dalrymple asked.

"I would have preferred a frigate, Sir Hew," Lewrie told him, "but I was given command of *Sapphire* before Mister Mountjoy's superiors thought to make use of me."

"Sir Alan has been involved in several cooperative ventures in aid of Secret Branch since the 1780s, off and on, sir," Mr. Mountjoy stuck in.

"Spying?" Dalrymple said with a sniff of dis-approval.

"Not directly, sir," Lewrie had to point out. "Providing naval support and military support in *aid* of overseas . . . doings."

"An unsavoury activity, spying," Sir Hew commented, grimacing. "Knives in the back, all that? Even are the informations discovered by such doings useful. This hint of a French army preparing to conquer Portugal is disturbing, but welcome, for instance, though the means by which it was gained, well. Forewarned is forearmed. In light of this news, hmm . . . I fear I may not spare a substantial number of troops at this moment, sirs. If France can obtain Spanish permission for their march cross Spain, then they may even goad the Spanish to mount a new assault against my defences."

"As you may see in my proposal, sir, Captain Lewrie thinks that only two or three companies of light infantry would be required, along with his Marines and armed sailors," Mountjoy sweetly, and patiently, wheedled. "Perhaps the skirmishers from two or three regiments. If the Spanish and French do assault the Rock, the grenadier companies and the line companies would be more use upon the ramparts, in the forts."

"What?" Sir Hew quickly objected, not liking that one bit. "You intend to blend companies from three regiments, troops who have never served together before, officers in charge of them who come from three regimental messes, with disparate traditions, who are suddenly supposed to work together? I do not see how that combination could be even the slightest bit successful!

"And, just where in Andalusia do you intend to make your raids, sirs?" Sir Hew continued quibbling. "From Tarifa to Estepona, close to Gibraltar? Cross the bay at Algeciras? If I am in the near future in danger of a siege of Gibraltar, I would much prefer that it comes later rather than sooner, allowing time for re-enforcements to arrive. A sudden rash of pin-pricks against the Spanish in, or near, their *Campo de Gibraltar* might cause the government in Madrid to send fresh armies to General Castaños, with orders to assail us once again."

*Deacon was right, damn him,* Lewrie thought, wishing he could scowl but keeping "bland" on his phyz; *Dalrymple won't upset the apple-cart, or hurt his good relations with the Dons.*

"Had you a fleet, Sir Alan," Dalrymple said, pleasant now that his "pet" was over, "and I could lure ten thousand men from General Henry Fox on Sicily, I would much prefer having a go at the Spanish enclave at Ceuta, cross the Straits. Blockade the place so that Spanish troops in the great fortress there cannot be ferried over to Castaños, or a French expeditionary fleet could combine with the Spanish, and mount an attack on the South end of the Rock, perhaps down near the Chapel of Europa, or the Tuerto Tower defences."

Sir Hew rose and uncovered a large map which was marked with pinned-on arrows indicating where he would like to land that theoretical army, and some dots to mark the bounds of a naval blockade.

"The Sultan of Morocco might not care to have another European power supplant the Spanish, but he would most certainly relish Spain being ousted, sirs," Dalrymple said, almost smacking his lips at the prospect, and gazing almost lovingly at his map. It was a very well-done and handsome map, certainly drawn at some expense. "I have corresponded with the Sultan at Tangier, and have hinted most broadly as to that possibility. His replies are mildly encouraging."

"Uhm, sir," Mountjoy said with a squirm of discomfort. "There is a French ambassador at Tangier, and the Sultan's court is a cesspool of intrigue. Even the broadest hints, as you say, might have already been bandied about and relayed to Paris, and to Madrid to warn them that you envision seizing Ceuta."

"*French* spies, sir," Lewrie added, summing the matter up, playing on Sir Hew's distaste for the trade. "Worst of a filthy lot."

"Here now!" Mountjoy whispered from the corner of his mouth.

Dalrymple sighed longingly over his map for a bit more, oblivious to their exchange, or Lewrie's broad grin, then slowly re-covered it and came back to his desk.

"Sadly, London has only given Fox twelve thousand men, and he's none to spare, even for Gibraltar's defence," Sir Hew told them. "If I need more, they must come from England. You say that you are here to lend aid to Mister Mountjoy's doings, Sir Alan? Does that mean that your ship will spend much time in harbour?"

"No sir, sorry," Lewrie replied. "If I must act alone and use my Marines and armed landing parties, in my own boats, I'll be out at sea most of the time. Of course, I will need to see Captain Middleton for larger boats, so I can land all my men in one group, quickly."

*Rock Soup'll have t'start with boats and scramblin' nets,* he thought with a groan; *Then I get out of port soonest, and capture some sort o' boat for Mountjoy.*

"Pity, that," Sir Hew gloomed. "Gibraltar is in dire need of a permanent naval presence. One would wish that you could have Captain Middleton build boats large enough to serve as gunboats, and man them with your sailors."

"I have my orders, Sir Hew," Lewrie said.

*Mine* arse *if you'll have me!* he thought.

"And I cannot countermand them," Dalrymple said.

*Thank bloody Christ!* was Lewrie's thought.

"Unless there is a true emergency," Dalrymple posed.

"So long as the dockyard is building more boats for me, it can produce boats for you, sir," Lewrie quickly countered, "and there are sailors and gunners recovering in the naval hospital, surely, enough to form a harbour guard flotilla, even some recovering officers and Midshipmen separated from their ships and unlikely to rejoin them anytime soon, who could lead them. Does Captain Middleton have twelve-pounders or eighteen-pounders in storage; well, there you go, sir!"

"Once Captain Lewrie had found a transport for the light infantrymen, sir," Mountjoy stuck in, springing quickly to lay the ground for another of their requests which they had hoped to bring up later, "we *had* hoped to avail ourselves of those men, to man the transport and make up the boat crews."

"In your plan sent to me, Mister Mountjoy, you stated that Sir Alan has a great deal of experience with, what did you call them . . . *amphibious* raids and landings?" Dalrymple said, lifting a page from Mountjoy's proposal to squint over it. "Boat work, in other words, or word, rather? Amphib-ious?" He worked his mouth over that.

"Buenos Aires and Cape Town last year, sir," Lewrie boasted. "The Bahamas and Spanish Florida the year before, experiments in the Channel with various torpedo devices in 1804, and landings on the Spratly Islands and the Spanish Philippines in the '80s 'tween the wars and . . ."

"Escaping Yorktown after the surrender, too, sir," Mountjoy added for him. "Two or three ships' boats got out to sea for rescue, or so I heard. Captain Lewrie's work in the Far East against native pirates, sponsored by the French, was his first exposure to Secret Branch."

"Never had to cut a throat, or stab anyone in the back, sir," Lewrie could not help japing.

*I leave all that to Zachariah Twigg, Jemmy Peel, and Mountjoy,* he qualified to himself.

"But, just where did you two envision making your raids?" Sir Hew asked, still un-convinced.

"From beyond Tarifa in the West, to near Cádiz, sir," Mountjoy assured him, "and to the East, from Málaga right to the French border."

"Hmm . . . enterprising, I must say," Dalrymple commented.

"So long a stretch that the Spanish cannot concentrate to defend against us," Mountjoy schemed on, "and our choices so varied all along the coasts that our movements would be unpredictable."

"Like the Vikings, or the Barbary Corsairs, sir," Lewrie said.

"Minus the rape and pillage, of course," Mountjoy corrected.

Sir Hew Dalrymple took a long moment to think that over, pulling at his earlobes, tugging his nose, before speaking, and that hesitantly, at last. "Hmm, does the defensive situation admit of the release of two or three companies, on a *temporary* basis, mind, to add some heft to your raids . . . now and then . . . then I *may* be able to spare you a few troops, *if* you are able to obtain a suitable transport for them. Just as I cannot countermand your orders, Sir Alan, and dragoon you to become a guardian for the bay approaches, I cannot order any vessel under the Transport Board's hire to serve under your orders. If such is the case, I cannot imagine how you and Mister Mountjoy can gather all the needed elements, but . . . I wish you good fortune in the doing, and *if* you manage to put all the pieces together, then I *may* be able to aid you. I make no firm promises, but . . . ?"

He spread his hands wide and shrugged, then stood, signalling that their conference was at an end, and Lewrie and Mountjoy had to be satisfied that he hadn't given them an outright refusal.

"He didn't say no," Mountjoy said with a sigh.

"He didn't clap us on the back and cry 'sic 'em', either. Not a good way to begin," Lewrie groused as they made their way back down to the town. "At least his sherry was tasty."

"It was Spanish," Mountjoy told him. "Andalusia's famous for it, and rivals Portugal . . . when they feel like trading with us."

"Now there's incentive for successful raids," Lewrie laughed. "Haul off lashings of the stuff . . . if I can keep my sailors and Marines from drinkin' it up, first."

"You'll see Captain Middleton, next, I suppose?" Mr. Mountjoy asked, taking off his wide-brimmed straw summer hat to fan himself, for the sun was fierce, and there was scant wind from off the bay.

"Thought I would, aye," Lewrie told him.

"When Admiral Nelson had the Mediterranean Fleet, he came with a dozen extra shipwrights to improve the dockyard," Mountjoy told him.

"They were to build gunboats for the bay defence then, too, but nothing came of it. Shortage of funds, God knows why. Most of them survived the outbreak of Gibraltar Fever in 1804."

"I never heard that it was un-healthy here," Lewrie said.

"Only every now and then," Mountjoy assured him, "though when it does break out, it's as bad as the West Indies. Civilians who can do so leave town and camp out in tents on the eastern side of the Rock, high above the pestilential miasmas, where there are cooling winds. I have been told that by the time the fevers ebbed three years ago, the garrison was cut in half. Thank God it appears to affect the Spaniards, too, else they could have put together an army and marched right through the Landport Gate!"

"Well, in any case, once I've seen Captain Middleton, I'm off to sea t'get your boat," Lewrie stated, "and our transport, too, is God just. Two-masted, about fourty or fifty feet overall?"

"That would do quite nicely, though even after all my time with you aboard *Jester*, I still know little of ships and the sea," Mountjoy confessed. "A fishing boat, no matter how badly it reeks?"

"Perhaps a coastal trader, with a partial cargo of grain, and an host of rats?" Lewrie teased.

"No matter," Mountjoy said with a wee smile, "for I'll not be aboard her. No reason to be."

"You'll just sit in your cool offices, or on your shaded gallery, peekin' through your telescope and playin' the sly spy-master, instead," Lewrie teased again. "By God, but His Majesty's Government *must* be told how they're wastin' their money on idleness."

"My dear fellow, but are you sounding envious?" Mountjoy japed.

"You're Goddamned right I am!" Lewrie barked.

# CHAPTER TWENTY-TWO

"The tea tastes diff'rent," Lewrie commented after a sip or two. He held his glass up to the light of a swaying overhead lanthorn with a squinty expression. "Fruitier?"

"Ehm, that'd be a dram or two of orange juice that Yeovill put in it this morning, sir," Pettus told him. "There's a whole sack laid by in your lazarette, along with lemons and bunches of grapes, and a few pomegranates, though he isn't sure what to do with those, as yet. There are all sorts of melons, too, The Mohammedans in Morocco don't make wine with their grapes, but they sure grow a lot of fruits and such. Do you like it, sir?"

"Aye, right tasty," Lewrie agreed, recalling how he'd relished cool tea with peach or strawberry juice offered him by their British Consul in Charleston, South Carolina, a few years back.

"Mister Snelling had the Purser buy up *barrels* of lemons, too," Pettus went on as he bustled about the dining-coach. "Even if Mister Cadrick can't sell them to the hands and turn a profit. For the good of the crew's health, Mister Snelling said, for their anti-scorbutic properties."

"Anti-scarrin'?" Jessop muttered.

"Prevents scurvy, Jessop," Pettus explained, "like wine, sauerkraut, or apples."

"Had a lemon, once," Jessop said. "I'd rather have an apple."

Jessop had the loose sleeves of his shirt rolled to the elbows, proud to sport his first tattoo on his left forearm. It was a fouled anchor.

*Christ, which came first?* Lewrie asked himself; *The whores, the rum, or that? And which of his guardians lost track of him long enough t'let him have it done? I think I'll haveta have a word with Desmond and Furfy.*

He finished his tea with an appreciative smack of his lips and a dab with his napkin, then announced that he would go on deck for a stroll.

It was a beautiful mid-morning, with thin streaks of clouds overhead, a glittering blue sea dappled here and there with white caps and fleeting cat's paws. HMS *Sapphire* trundled along on a fine tops'l breeze, her motion gentle and swaying slowly from beam to beam only a few degrees, and pitching and dipping her bows as she encountered the long-set rollers.

"Good morning, sir," Lt. Elmes said with a doff of his hat as Lewrie emerged onto the quarterdeck.

"Good morning to you, sir," Lewrie replied, tapping the front of his own hat in return. "Good t'be back at sea?"

"Aye, sir," Elmes gladly agreed. "Though I doubt that our men would agree. One whole day of shore liberty has only piqued their interest."

"Grumpy, are they, Mister Elmes?" Lewrie asked.

"Not really, sir," Elmes told him with a smile. "All in all I'd say they're in fine fettle, what with the action with the French, the prospect of prize-money to come from it, and a run ashore. And more of that to come?"

"So long as we're working out of Gibraltar, aye," Lewrie said.

That promise pleased Lt. Elmes right down to his toes, for he and the rest of the wardroom had had much more free time ashore than the ship's people. Over supper the first night out at sea, the conversations round Lewrie's dining table had been rapturous and excited about exploring the many caves, touring the massive fortifications, the excellence of their meals and the wines, the abundance of fresh fruits and vegetables (some smuggled cross The Lines from Spain) and an expedition by donkey-back to the heights of the Rock, and their encounters with the filthy Barbary apes which ran wild up there. What else his officers and Midshipmen had done with the ladies of Gibraltar was anyone's guess, and none of Lewrie's business, but count on Lt. Geoffrey Westcott to smirk, wink, and grin in sign that he had managed to find himself a liaison, if no one else did. Among those hundreds and hundreds of foreigners that Mountjoy had mentioned who resided at Gibraltar, many were women; Spanish, Portuguese, and Italian, principally from Genoa, many of whom practiced their own version of "mercantile trade" with the soldiers and officers of the garrison, those merchants, and the crews of ships putting into harbour.

Lewrie had taken *Sapphire* cross the Straits to look at Ceuta, the Spanish enclave in North Africa, and take a peek at the nigh-impregnable fortress there. There had been no shipping there, but he'd found it disturbing that there were no British blockading ships present, either. He'd trailed his colours only four miles offshore, one mile beyond the maximum range of the heaviest fortress guns, then had ordered the course altered to the Nor'east to begin prowling the coast of Spain.

"Land ho!" several masthead lookouts shouted, almost as one. "Deck, there! Land ho, two points off the larboard bows!"

The Sailing Master, Mr. George Yelland, popped out of his sea cabin on the starboard side of the quarterdeck, looking disheveled and unkempt, as if he had been napping in his clothes. "Landfall, sir?"

"Mountaintops, most-like," Lewrie commented. "Let's look at the charts."

They crossed to the larboard side of the quarterdeck and went into the dedicated chart space. Yelland dry-scrubbed his face with rough-palmed hands, making a raspy sound against his unshaven cheeks, as if to rouse himself to full wakefulness, before leaning over the chart of the Spanish coast pinned to the angled tabletop. He checked their latest position from yesterday's Noon Sights, followed the pencilled line of *X*s which showed their hourly Dead Reckoning positions, and made some humming noises.

"Mountaintops, certainly, sir," Yelland opined at last. "The Andalusian coast possesses some truly magnificent ranges. From where we reckoned ourselves to be two hours ago, we are in sight of the Sierra Nevada range. Which particular mountains sighted is still moot, but . . . the shores I believe to be about eighteen miles off, and we should sight the port of Fuengirola in a while."

"No shoals reported?" Lewrie asked.

"Not unless we proceed to within a mile or two of the coast, sir," Yelland informed him, "where the soundings show six fathoms or less."

"Very good, sir," Lewrie said. "We'll stand on as we are, and see what turns up. With the coast so mountainous, and the roads tortuous-bad, as they usually are, we might stumble upon a fair amount of coasting trade. Sorry to have interrupted your nap."

"Not a nap, sir," Yelland said, stifling a yawn. "Simply resting my eyes."

Lewrie went back out onto the quarterdeck, snatched a day telescope from the binnacle cabinet rack, and went up to the poop deck for a slightly higher vantage point. There were clouds to the North and East, but if there really were mountains up there, they were only darker, still indistinct smudges that could be taken for rain clouds beneath or ahead of the rest.

There was a whine, and a pawing at his knee. Bisquit, wakened from a nap atop the aft flag lockers, had brought his newest, favourite toy, a length of old three-inch line whipped with twine to stiffen it, with a monkey's fist fashioned at either end, and made tasty with some slush from the galley. The dog could gnaw on it like a bone or shake it like a snake in mock "kills", with delighted yips and growls.

Lewrie took it from his jaws, even if it did stink like so many badgers and was greasy and wet with saliva, got the dog dancing right and left, then threw it back to the flag lockers. Bisquit chased it down, gave it a shake, and brought it back, to do it all again. That went on for a full five minutes before a lookout high atop the mizen mast cried out, "Sail ho!"

"Carry on, Mister Fywell," Lewrie said, tossing the toy to one of the youngest Midshipmen who had been practising his mathematics on a slate. "Just don't toss it overboard by accident. Bisquit'd be heartbroken."

"Where away?" Lt. Elmes shouted aloft with a speaking trumpet.

"*Two* points off the *larboard* quarter!" was the bellowed reply. "Two-masted, and hull down!"

Lewrie took his telescope aft to stand atop the flag lockers, clinging to the larboard taffrail lanthorn to steady himself. He had just the slightest hint of two wee parchment-tan ellipses on the horizon, like the upper halves of two close-set commas.

"Eight or nine miles off?" he muttered under his breath, "and how'd she get this close without the lookouts spottin' her?"

He would have to have a sharp word with his watch officers, so that sort of inattention didn't happen again! Let Westcott, Harcourt, and Elmes pass the grief along to those deserving.

His perch was rather precarious, so after a minute or so, he clambered down and depended on the shouts between Lt. Elmes and the lookouts aloft.

The strange sail was two-masted, proceeding on a mostly Easterly course, and appeared to be about eight miles astern of *Sapphire*, though almost keeping up with the much larger ship because she was on a bee-line, whilst the two-decker was angling inshore.

"Whatever she is, she appears to be coasting from either Estepona, Puerto Banús, or Marbella, on a direct course for Fuengirola or Málaga, sir," the Sailing Master said after Lewrie returned to the quarterdeck. "Blind as bats, or un-caring, for she's surely spotted us by now, sir."

"Thankee, Mister Yelland," Lewrie replied. "How far offshore d'ye reckon her to be?"

"Five or six miles, sir," Yelland guessed.

"Very well," Lewrie said, looking up and aft.

When Lewrie had taken command of *Sapphire,* she had been a part of a squadron commanded by a Rear-Admiral of The Blue, and had flown that ensign, and she had kept that colour when escorting her convoy to Gibraltar. Once there, though, Lewrie and *Sapphire* operated under Admiralty Orders as an independent ship, and now flew the Red Ensign, which stood out more distinctly at greater distances.

Bisquit's toy came bumping down the starboard ladder from the poop deck, followed by the dog a moment later. Midshipman Fywell, at the head of the ladder, looked sheepish and embarrassed.

"Mister Fywell, instruct Mister Spears to strike our colours, and hoist those of the Spanish Navy," Lewrie told him of a sudden.

"*Spanish,* sir?" Fywell gawped.

"The one with the crowned oval with all the shit in it, mind," Lewrie said with a grin. He looked aloft to the commissioning pendant to judge the direction of the winds, and made another decision.

"Mister Elmes, I wish t'close that sail, and take her if she's worth it. Alter course two points to larboard, and make her head Nor'-Nor'east."

"Nor'-Nor'east, aye, sir," Elmes replied, turning to shout directions to the brace tenders and sheetmen. That change of course and the sighting of a strange sail several minutes before drew the attention of the on-watch hands, and those off-watch who had come up from below in anticipation of the first daily rum issue at Seven Bells of the Forenoon. Chuckles and murmurs could be heard as *Sapphire*'s men contemplated even more prize money in their pockets.

"Sir," Lt. Harcourt reported himself on deck and ready for any duty, though Quarters had not been called for.

"Sir," Lt. Westcott performed the same duty a moment later. "A possible prize?"

"Perhaps," Lewrie told him.

Westcott had a quick look about, spotted the Spanish Navy Ensign flying in place of their own, and could not help chuckling.

"Should we have Carpenter Acfield fashion a crucifix and hoist it onto the face of the main tops'l, sir?" he teased.

"A crucifix?" Lt. Harcourt asked.

"Last year off the Plate Estuary, when we fought the *San Fermin* frigate, she had a big one on the front of her fore tops'l," Westcott explained. "Didn't do the Dons much good, though, for some of our bar-shot decapitated Jesus, and she burned to the waterline, poor devils."

"Now we are ze grandees of Espagna," Lewrie played along with a bad attempt at a Castilian lisp accent, "we do not do battle weez zose heretical Engleesh, we do weezout ze Holy Presence."

For the first time, Lt. Harcourt looked as if he was amused, and honestly so, instead of giving an impression of smirking.

"Deck, there!" a lookout alerted them as *Sapphire* completed her alteration of course and settled down on Nor'-Nor'east, picking up speed on a broad reach and a leading wind. "The Chase is bearing off for shore! Six points off the larboard bows!"

"Or one point ahead of abeam," Westcott grumbled.

Lewrie went to the laboard bulwarks to take another look with his telescope. Their strange sail was not quite hull-up yet, but he could determine that her two masts sported large lugsails suspended from gaff booms, with what looked to be a single jib sail up forward. The scend from one of the sea's long rollers lifted *Sapphire* a few feet, another far off lifted the stranger a few feet, and he got the impression of a sliver of hull. They were closing on her!

"If she's a Spaniard, and we're flyin' Spanish colours, then why the Devil is she tryin' to run?" he grumbled.

"General distrust, sir?" Lt. Elmes, who was within ear-shot and assumed that he was being addressed, piped up. "After three years of war, and so many ships taken by our Navy, her master must be wary of any other ship that heaves up in sight."

"No matter," Lewrie decided. "We've a much longer waterline and scads more sail. Unless she tries t'put about, into the wind, or run herself aground, I think we've a good chance of taking her."

"Hull-up, sir!" Midshipman Carey, in charge of the signalmen on the poop deck, cried, forcing Lewrie to lift his glass once more for another look at her.

*No more than five miles off, now,* he told himself, juggling the odds of interception; *And I still can't make out the coastline, which means she* can't *get into shoal water before we fetch her up. And she's slow. Wallowing!*

"Mister Elmes, beat to Quarters," he snapped at the officer of the watch. "The upper-deck guns, the bow chasers, and the larboard twelve-pounders only."

"Aye, sir!"

A Marine drummer began the long roll, petty officers began to bellow orders, and Lieutenant Westcott took over for Elmes, freeing him to go below. Harcourt departed to take charge of the upper gun deck 12-pounders, and Marine Lieutenant Keane turned up with Lt. Roe in tow, hastily chivvying their men into full kit of waist-coats and red coats and crossbelts, which were only worn when standing sentry duty or for battle when at sea.

"We've a Spanish speaker aboard?" Lewrie asked the people on the quarterdeck.

"I do, sir," Lt. Roe said.

"Should I have need to hail her, do you stand by here on the quarterdeck 'til she's struck, Mister Roe," Lewrie said to him, "then I'd admire did you go over to her with the boarding party."

"Very good, sir!" Roe replied, looking eager for any fight.

"If she strikes, Mister Westcott," Lewrie went on, "I wish my boat crew to bring the launch up from towing, and ferry the boarding party over to her."

Bisquit knew what the long roll meant, by now, and recognised the loud noises associated with battle, and the roar of the guns. He came down from the poop deck in a rush, scampered down to the waist, and disappeared down a hatchway, bound for the safety of the orlop.

Pettus came out of the great-cabins with Chalky in his wicker cage. "Strip your cabins, sir?" he asked.

"Not unless yon ship turns herself into a ship of the line, no, Pettus," Lewrie told him with a wee chuckle. "I don't see us takin' damage from the likes of her."

After a few minutes, *Sapphire* had strode up a mile closer to the stranger, which was now four points off the larboard bows, a sure sign that they were overtaking her at a good clip. A few minutes more and their Chase loomed larger, at three points off the bows, altering course more Northerly to string out the pursuit into a stern chase.

"Colours!" was the general cry on the quarterdeck as a faded Spanish merchant flag, a "gridiron" of two horizontal red stripes on a gold field, jerkily went up her stern gaff.

*At least she's declared herself,* Lewrie thought; *But she ain't slowin' down, or lookin' relieved that we're* both *Spanish.*

*Sapphire,* so the Sailing Master estimated, was within four or five miles of the coast, and the narrow band of plains and foothills were in plain sight, sprinkled with woods, pastures, and cropfields, with hamlets and villages set back from the sea easily made out from the deck. He also stated that they were within two miles of their Chase.

"We'll stand on a bit more," Lewrie announced as he rocked on the balls of his boot soles.

Three miles from shore, within a mile of the straining Spanish ship, and Lewrie decided that it was time to end the charade.

"Mister Westcott, a shot under her bows, and strike our false colours, and run up the Red Ensign!" he barked.

One of the forecastle 6-pounders barked, hurling a shot that did not *quite* deliver the traditional warning; it struck the sea short of the Spanish vessel, caromed up from First Graze, and raised a great feather of spray right along her starboard side. Charitably, it did hit her forward of amidships; more *near* her bows than under.

*Have the foc'sle Quarter Gunner tear a strip off that gun-captain's arse, too,* Lewrie added to his to-do list; *He's damaged her, he pays for the bloody repairs!*

"Ah, hmm, sir," Lt. Westcott muttered, shaking his head. "Bad show, that."

"Let's hope no one who matters is watching, then," Lewrie told him, grimacing. "Is she going to strike, or do we have to shoot her to kindling?"

The Spaniard still stood on, even bearing up more towards the coast, as if she would run herself aground rather than be taken, showing a bit more of her stern transom to them.

"The first two twelve-pounders of the larboard battery, Mister Westcott," Lewrie snapped. "Convince the bastards!"

The order was passed by Midshipman Ward, who darted down from the quarterdeck to the waist, then to the upper gun deck. Nigh one minute passed before the gun-ports were opened and the black muzzles of the 12-pounders appeared. There was another pause as gun-captains waited for the ship to roll upright and poise level, on the up-roll. The first gun erupted, followed a second later by the next, masking *Sapphire*'s bows in a cloud of rotten-egg, yellow-grey smoke.

Lewrie lifted his telescope to look for the fall of shot, and felt like whooping aloud as one tall feather of spray heaved upwards within fifty yards of the Spaniard's larboard quarter, and the second hit the sea short and skipped, punching a neat hole in her foresail.

"That's more like it, sir," Lt. Westcott said with glee as the ragged and faded Spanish flag was not simply struck, but cut clean away to flutter down into the two-master's disturbed wake. Halliards were freed, and her gaff booms sagged, as her sails were lowered in quick surrender.

"Take in sail and fetch-to near her, Mister Westcott," Lewrie ordered. "Ready the boarding party. Secure from Quarters."

Half an hour later, and both vessels were lying still near each other, bows cocked up to windward and slowly drifting on wind and currents. Marine Lieutenant Roe, with five private Marines, and a boarding party under Midshipman Britton, secured their prize and searched her, and her crew, for weapons, and her master's cabin for incriminating documents.

Lewrie paced the quarterdeck and the poop deck in mounting impatience, waiting for a report. The Spaniard *seemed* about right for Mountjoy's covert work; she was about fifty feet on the range of the deck, filthy-looking, outwardly ill-maintained, and utterly unremarkable if she was seen anywhere along the coasts of Andalusia, even if she sailed right into Málaga, Cartagena, or the Spanish naval port of Cádiz in broad daylight. But, if the lone accidental hit by a six-pound roundshot had caused damage below her waterline, or right on it, she might sink before she could be gotten back to Gibraltar, and the day's work would be for nothing.

*Even if we* do *get her back to Gibraltar, I can't declare her as a prize, so Captain Middleton can't get any money from the Prize-Court to make repairs,* Lewrie fretted; *She's completely off the books!*

"The Devil with it!" Lewrie growled, then went down to the quarterdeck. "Mister Westcott, a boat crew for the pinnace, and pass word for Bosun Terrell. I'm going over to her."

"Aye, sir."

He tried to appear calm and patient, but it was difficult as he stood by the larboard entry-port waiting for the pinnace to be towed up from astern, a boat crew assembled under former Cox'n Crawley, and the Bosun to be filled in.

"She ain't much of a prize, sir," Terrell commented, shifting his quid of tobacco from one cheek to the other. "No great loss if she goes down."

"She could be useful, even so, Mister Terrell," Lewrie told him, mystifying the Bosun even more.

Lewrie did not relish small-boat work, and it was not the preservation of the dignity of his office and rank that made every embarking and departure from ship to shore, from ship to ship, a slow and careful evolution. Alan Lewrie could not swim!

When the pinnace came alongside the Spanish prize, he felt an even more stomach-chilling *frisson* of dread, for the boat was pitching, the Spaniard was rolling, and there were no orderly boarding battens and taut man-ropes, but only a pair of man-ropes dangling free and the main-mast shroud platform for an intermediate shelf. There wasn't even an entry-port let into the bulwarks; he would have to crawl over!

He stood on the boat's gunn'ls, balancing like a squirrel on a clothesline, a hand on the shoulders of a couple of sailors, 'til he felt the boat rise, saw the prize roll to starboard, and leapt for a death-grip on one of the dangling ropes, one foot scrambling against the hull for a terrifying second before getting the other onto the shroud platform. He clung to the stays, found a foothold on one of the dead-eye blocks, and could reach up to begin scaling the skinny ratlines, hoping that they were stronger and newer than they looked.

After a few cautious feet higher, he could swing in-board with a foot atop the bulwark cap-rail, then jump down to the deck, hiding a huge sense of relief.

"Ehm . . . welcome aboard, sir," Marine Lieutenant Roe said.

"Mister Roe, Mister Britton," he replied, tapping two fingers on his hat brim. "What is her condition?"

"Filthy and reeking, sir," Roe replied, sounding chipper. "She trades out of Málaga, so far as I can make out from her papers, and is bound home . . . was, rather . . . with a general cargo of flour and un-ground grain, rice, and some sort of meal recorded as *cous cous*, whatever the Devil that is. She also carries cheese, sausages, wine, coffee beans, and sugar."

"How many prisoners?" Lewrie asked, turning to his mid-twenties Midshipman Britton.

"Her captain, cook, one mate, four hands, and a couple of boys, sir," Britton reported. "A scruffy lot."

Lewrie looked over at the Spaniards who were huddled atop the midships cargo hatch gratings, surrounded by Roe's Marines with their bayonets affixed to their muskets. At his glance, her captain and a couple of others began to gabble their distress at him, either begging or cursing for all that Lewrie could tell.

"If you'd be so kind, Mister Terrell, would you go below and see if our hit caused any major damage?" Lewrie bade.

"Aye, sir," Terrell said, though sounding as if it was a fool's errand. "You two lads, and you, Furfy, come with me to shift cargo so I can get to her planking."

Britton and Roe told Lewrie that they had found only a few weapons aboard, some clumsy pistols, some rusted cutlasses, and personal daggers and work knives. From what Lt. Roe had been able to read so far, her ship's papers were pretty straightforward, as were her cargo manifests that did not show anything other than innocent goods.

"Though, sir," Lt. Roe sagely pointed out with one brow up in a smirk, "where they *obtained* their cargo is not mentioned, and I have not found any receipts from any sellers. Whenever I asked the master which port he'd recently left, he won't give a straight answer, and starts wailing on how we've ruined him."

"Sounds like he's smuggling," Lewrie determined. "Is there a working chart in his cabins, Mister Britton?"

"I'll go look, sir," the Midshipman said, and dashed below to a cabin right-aft, before he could be chided for being remiss. A minute later and he was back and unfolding a well-used chart.

"He sailed from Tarifa, did he?" Lewrie said. "Right past the Rock, and no one noticed!"

"In the dead of night, most likely, sir," Britton supposed.

Patrick Furfy came up from the forward cargo hold bearing a few stiff paper tags. "Mister Terrell said t' show ya these, sor," Furfy announced. "They's in English is what got his curiosity up. They was tied t'grain sacks an' such."

"Mine arse on a band-box!" Lewrie exclaimed with a laugh. "The grain's from a Gibraltar merchant! I heard that there was some trade cross The Lines, but . . . ! Once back in port, we can report the bastard to General Dalrymple."

"So that makes her Good Prize, sir!" Britton gladly said.

"Uhm . . . no, not quite, Mister Britton," Lewrie had to tell him, dashing the Midshipman's hopes for a few more shillings in his pocket. Lewrie handed the chart back to Britton and took a good look around. The Spanish coast was about three miles off, by a rough estimate. The port of Fuengirola could not be much more than twelve or fifteen miles to the East. He went aft to look at the boat that was towed behind the Spaniard, which was a 20-footer fitted with a single mast and gaff boom stowed fore-and-aft along her thwarts. It floated, and did not look as if it was too leaky.

"Ya saw those tags, sir," Bosun Terrell said, coming back on deck and wiping his hands on his slop-trousers. "There's Devil's work in her. She won't sink anytime soon, sir. The ball struck above the waterline, about three foot above, and there's stove-in scantlings we can replace, if ya really mean to keep her, that is." He still wore a skeptical look. "I thought we'd *all* be eaten by her rats."

"Thankee, Mister Terrell, and I do," Lewrie said, relieved to hear that. "Desmond, see that her boat's hauled up alongside. Mister Britton, I'm going to allow the Spaniards t'go ashore. They can take their sea-bags and keep their clasp knives. We'll put a bag of bisquit and a barrico of water in her. Mister Roe, do you see her captain below to his cabins and let him pack his traps, keepin' a sharp eye that he doesn't get away with anything else incriminating. Search all that he wants to take. And let him keep his passage money."

"Aye, sir," Roe replied.

"Tell 'em I'm settin' 'em free before you go," Lewrie added.

Roe rattled off some rapid Spanish, which prompted another bout of whining, cursing, insults, and perhaps a few sincere expressions of gratitude. They crossed themselves, pulled crucifixes from under their dirty shirts to kiss, the youngest ones bobbing their heads in thanks that they would not end up in Gibraltar's prison hulk.

"Once they're gone, we'll send the Marines back aboard our ship," Lewrie told Midshipman Britton, "and fetch the Carpenter and his Mate t'cobble up her planking. Care t'take command of her and see her safe to Gibraltar, sir?"

"Me, sir?" Britton exclaimed, much surprised. "Aye, I would!"

"Good man," Lewrie said. "Go back aboard with the Marines, and pack your sea-chest. How many hands d'ye think you need to manage her? I can't spare my Cox'n and my boat crew, mind."

"Hmm, no more than eight, sir, in two watches," Britton said after a moment's thought. "I could use Crawley and his hands in the pinnace, they're all good men. If I take the pinnace back, they can gather up their chests and sea-bags, too."

"See to it, then," Lewrie told him. "I can't say how long you will be away from the ship, Mister Britton. Once in port, you will be livin' aboard this barge 'til arrangements can be made for you.

"As soon as you get to Gibraltar, you're to go ashore and see Mister Thomas Mountjoy, at the Falmouth Import and Export Company and turn the boat over to him. If I can find pencil and paper aboard, I'll write you the address of his offices."

"Not to the Prize-Court, sir?" Britton asked, confused.

"Definitely *not* to the Prize-Court, Mister Britton," Lewrie insisted. "Trust me, it's a Crown matter which requires a vessel such as this'un. The less said of it, the better."

"I *think* I see, sir. Aye, I'll see to it," Britton replied, now more curious and bemused than mystified.

"Very good, then," Lewrie told him with an encouraging smile. He turned to other matters with his Cox'n. "Desmond, did I hear Lieutenant Roe say that this wreck has sausages and coffee aboard?"

"Aye, sor, I believe he did," Liam Desmond replied, grinning at the prospect of doing a little pilfering.

"Chalky and Bisquit need sausages, so they don't run short, and I could use a sack o' coffee beans," Lewrie told him. "See if you can gather up some, and anything else ye come across that might be good."

"Might be about all that's good aboard her, sor," Furfy said, with a grimace of distaste. "Spanish beer's as sour'z horse piss, an' th' wine'z worse'un 'at cheap Blackstrap they sold us in th' town, sure, sor."

"Sampled it, have you, Furfy?" Lewrie asked in a purr.

"Uh, me, sor? Nossor, I'd never, arrah," Furfy protested, hat snatched from his head and laid on his chest to prove his innocence.

"Does anyone know what '*cous cous*' is? Anybody?" Lewrie asked.

"Ehm, permission t'speak, sir?" Ordinary Seaman Deavers spoke up. "I ate it ashore, on my liberty, sir. It's a pasta, I was told, wee fine rolled beads smaller than bird shot. They give me a bowl of it, with a stew atop, On its own, it ain't much, but with stew and gravy, it's filling, sir. Cheap, too. Said it was like A-rab oatmeal, and comes from Tangier or Tetuán."

"And used like one would rice, I see!" Lewrie said. "Thankee, Deavers. Desmond, best fetch off a large sack or two. I'm certain that Yeovill can find a way t'use it."

"Comin' right up, sor," Desmond told him with a sly grin. He had just given Desmond and Furfy a license to steal, so long as their pockets didn't come away too full!

It was late afternoon before the Spanish two-master got under way, bound West, and tacking to make headway into the wind, against the current. HMS *Sapphire* was back under full sail, too, heading out to the open sea for the night to come. Come dawn, Lewrie intended to turn Northerly, again, and haunt the Spanish coast closer to Málaga, looking for the next item on the list, a large merchantman suitable to serve as a troop transport.

"Not a bad day, all in all," Lewrie told Geoffrey Westcott on the quarterdeck.

"Aye, sir," Westcott agreed. "By the way, I've spoken with the forecastle Quarter Gunner, and he's had a word with the gun-captain of the six-pounder. Wiggins has caught enough grief from the others already, but, a chiding never hurts. He'll take more care with his aim next time."

"Good enough, sir," Lewrie said, satisfied. "One more carrot for our 'Rock Soup'."

"A beggarly way of going about things, though," Westcott said, still amused by the term.

"Since we can't be choosers, and plain begging won't get us anywhere, what's left?" Lewrie replied. "It feels . . . piratical."

"More sly than piratical, sir," Westcott softly objected.

"*Arrhh*, me hearties!" Lewrie hooted in a theatrical growl. "I will have me a sit-down on the poop deck, and admire the sunset, if there's a good'un. I do believe I've earned it!"

He barely set foot on the poop deck, greeting Bisquit with jaw rubs as the dog put his paws oh his chest, before being interrupted.

"Your pardons, sir," Midshipman Hillhouse called from the foot of the larboard ladderway. "Permission to speak, sir?"

"Aye, come up," Lewrie said, feigning openness, and once more wondering why such a "scaly fish" as Hillhouse, with years of experience at sea, had yet to pass the oral examinations for promotion to Lieutenant.

Hillhouse trotted up the ladderway, doffed his hat, and made a brief bow from the waist before speaking. "Beg pardon, sir, but I was hoping that you would consider me to take charge of the next prize we take. I am senior to Mister Britton, and the rest, after all."

"Britton was there, which is why I chose him, Mister Hillhouse," Lewrie told him, concealing his sudden irritation. "It was not a matter of seniority. If it's any comfort, Britton won't prosper from it. That barge won't be bought in, nor will she even see the Prize-Court, and he'll be back aboard as soon as we return to Gibraltar. I know you're ambitious for promotion, as are your mess-mates, but taking that shabby scow into port, then idling for weeks, is not a way to get it."

"I have no patrons, sir, no 'interest'," Hillhouse baldly confessed, seeming irked by that fact. "Beyond Captain Insley . . ."

"Were we assigned to the Mediterranean Fleet, or the blockade squadron off Cádiz, there would be enough Post-Captains to conduct an examination board. Being a Passed Midshipman'd stand you in better stead, and when we *did* take a substantial prize, especially a Spanish or French National ship, I would then consider you the senior-most to take charge of her, but . . . we sail under Admiralty Orders, separately, and for as long as that lasts, I fear you may not gain what you desire from temporary duties, Mister Hillhouse." Lewrie laid it out for him to digest. "I don't play favourites. Nor do I deny anyone their chance t'shine for personal reasons."

"I would still request to be considered, should the opportunity arise, sir," Hillhouse stubbornly said, looking like a bulldog in a pet.

"Then you will be considered, Mister Hillhouse," Lewrie promised. "Is that all, sir?"

"It is, sir, and thank you for allowing me to speak," Hillhouse said, doffing his hat once more, performing another un-necssary bow from the waist, and departed back to the quarterdeck, then the ship's waist.

*I* don't *play favourites,* Lewrie told himself; *But I can take a hellish 'down' on the likes o' you! What a beef-to-the-heel buffoon!*

Lewrie flung himself into his collapsible canvas deck chair, a frown on his face, and a sour taste in his mouth. Bisquit nudged him with his muzzle, whining for fresh attention, and Lewrie petted and stroked him 'til he sat on his haunches and laid his chest and legs in Lewrie's lap, making wee, happy whines as he laid his head down, too.

"Now who said you could get that familiar, hey, dog?" Lewrie muttered, ruffling Bisquit's head, ears, and neck fur, which brought forth a tongue-lolling grin to the dog's face.

*Insley played cater-cousin to Hillhouse, did he?* Lewrie thought; *To Lieutenant Harcourt, too? How many others, I wonder? No wonder he feels cheated. Good God, though, a man grown, twenty-five years or so, and* still *can't stand before a promotion board?*

Lewrie sincerely hoped that the coming sunset would be a spectatular one, if only to make up for the upset that Hillhouse had engendered!

# CHAPTER TWENTY-THREE

The next month at sea entire was spent close along the coast of Andalusia, chasing after anything that dared put out. *Sapphire* sailed as far East as the approaches to Cartagena, delving into the seas off Murcia. Standing in within three miles or less of major ports, some tempting three-masted ships could be seen that could have served as their transport, but they were all well-guarded by massive shore fortresses and heavy coastal artillery. Equally tempting was the chance that a well-armed cutting-out party might steal into harbour and take one by force, and sail her out in the dead of night, but, whenever they showed up, guard boats full of soldiers appeared, scuttling like cockroaches cross the mouths of those harbours, and close round the ships.

Lewrie could at least take a little comfort from the fact that those ships sat cringing at anchor, unable to carry on any trade, for fear of his ship's presence. And, in performance of the brief that Thomas Mountjoy had given him, to raise chaos and mayhem, he could also feel some satisfaction that he had terrified the Spanish by going after anything that floated, from coasting trader to fishing boats.

None were suitable to qualify as Good Prize, but they could make grand warning pyres, once overawed and forced to surrender, then taken in close to the coast by temporary prize crews, their masters and sailors freed to make their way ashore in their own boats, then set afire, by day or night. Admittedly, *Sapphire* pursued more than she caught, and many Spaniards out-ran them, but at least they ran into port to carry the tale of a merciless *Inglese* warship prowling for prey, which they only escaped by the skin of their teeth, by God's Mercy. One of their last captures, an old lateen-rigged merchantman that they ran down off Almeria, carried a crew that wailed in terror that *el diablo negro,* "the black devil", had caught them!

And Lewrie's cook, Yeovill, had finally discovered the right amount of water and *cous cous* to boil up for an edible dish!

HMS *Sapphire* stood in towards shore yet another morning, just before dawn. The lower decks had been swept, the upper decks sluiced with water and holystoned, and the wash-deck pumps had been stowed as the hands were released for breakfast. The weather had turned rough, the last two days, with strong winds and high seas that had churned and foamed greenish-white, so it was with a sense of relief that the morning presented light winds and long-set rollers not over five or six feet high.

"Near due West, and we'll make landfall a bit West of Estepona, sir," Sailing Master Yelland estimated, bent over the chart, working a pair of brass dividers over it. "About . . . six miles offshore?"

"At least 'til Noon Sights, Mister Yelland, and then we'll alter course to Sou'west, or thereabouts," Lewrie agreed, "and make our way toward the Straits, and into port."

He stifled a yawn, for he'd slept badly as the rough weather had eased, snatching less than an hour between urges to go on deck to respond to the now-and-then lurches, rolls, and louder groans from the hull. He'd only had time for one cup of coffee, too.

"Sail ho!" came an electrifying shout from the mastheads.

"Another fire, huzzah!" said some sailor on the larboard sail-tending gangway forward of the quarterdeck and the chart room laughed aloud.

Lewrie excused himself to go to his great-cabins and fetch his telescope, then trotted up to the starboard side of the poop deck for a look-see.

"One point ahead o' th' starb'd bows, hull-down!" a lookout on the foremast cross-trees shouted down. "Nigh bows-on!"

"Bound for Estepona?" Lewrie heard Lt. Harcourt speculate on the quarterdeck below him.

"She won't live long enough to make it, sir," Midshipman Leverett boasted. "We'll cut her off, if she doesn't go about and run."

Lewrie's telescope revealed what appeared to be a two-master under gaff-hung lugs'ls and a large jib, all winged out to starboard to cup the dawn's shore breeze. He looked aloft past the brailed-up main course to the commissioning pendant and how it streamed, judging the direction of the wind, and thinking that if *Sapphire* came about to Nor'west by West, he could block the two-master's course for the obvious refuge of Estepona, drive her closer inshore, or force her to go about and attempt to run away to the West, where the only safe haven might be the mouth of a minor river.

*Sapphire* was slowly bowling along under tops'ls, fore course, spanker, foretopmast stays'l and inner and outer flying jibs, making an easy six or seven knots.

"Mister Harcourt," Lewrie called down to the quarterdeck. "I will have the main course spread."

"Aye, sir!" Harcourt crisply replied, lifting a brass speaking trumpet to call for topmen to go aloft to cast off brails, and for halliards and clews to be manned.

*Yelland said true dawn'd be ten minutes past six,* Lewrie told himself, pulling out his pocket watch. He looked aft into the East, just in time for false dawn to depart, and see the first golden blush of sunrise, which painted the horizon and clouds with deep crimson; "Red sky in the morning, sailor take warning". There would be more dirty weather to come, and he hoped that they captured the stranger in good time, so he could get his ship out into deeper waters before the new bout of foul weather caught up with them.

"Hull-up, there! Deck, there, th' sail's hull-up, and bows-on, still one point off th' starb'd bows!" the foremast lookout cried.

*Not tryin' t'get away?* Lewrie thought, finding that puzzling. If her master had any sense, and there was a single pair of eyes over there, she would have hauled her wind long since.

"Damned if I don't think she is making straight for us, sir!" Lt. Harcourt called up to Lewrie from his post below, looking eager, but perplexed. "Shall we alter course, sir?"

"No, stand on as we are, Mister Harcourt," Lewrie decided. "If she's that blind, I'll oblige the fool." He closed the tubes of his telescope and descended the starboard ladderway. "I'll be aft. Keep me informed, while I have some more coffee, and a bit of breakfast."

"Aye, sir."

Once in the great-cabin's dining-coach, Pettus poured him a fresh cup of coffee. There was a plain white china creampot filled with a few fresh squirts from the nanny goat up forward in the manger, and Pettus had shaved off some sugar from the cone kept in Lewrie's locking caddy. Yeovill swept in with his food barge even as Lewrie took his first sip, apologising for the sparseness of breakfast, seeing that it was a Banyan Day and all, but he did set out a steaming bowl of oatmeal with a plop of stale butter and treacle, and a boiled egg on the side.

The Marine sentry who guarded the cabin doors stamped boots, slammed his musket butt on the deck, and bawled, "Midshipman Harvey, SAH!"

"Enter!" Lewrie called back.

"Ehm, Mister Harcourt's duty, sir, and I am to say that the strange sail is still bows-on to us, and shows no sign of fleeing us."

"My compliments to Mister Harcourt, and he is to stand on. Have the hands eat, Mister Harvey?" Lewrie asked the young Mid.

"I believe they have, sir," Harvey replied.

"The last look I had of our odd stranger, she'd didn't appear t'be much of a threat, but I'd admire did Mister Harcourt lead and prepare the six-pounders on forecastle and quarterdeck, and have the Marines turned out under arms."

"Very good, sir!"

"Bless me, Mister Harvey," Lewrie brightened, peering closely at the Midshipman's face, "but do I note that you are in need of a *shave?*"

"Ehm, yes, sir!" Harvey proudly admitted, stroking his upper lip with a finger.

"A trim of your locks might not go amiss, either, Harvey," Lewrie said. "Carry on."

"Aye, sir!"

"Ye wouldn't have one o' Chalky's wee sausages t'spare, do ye, Yeovill?" Lewrie asked, enviously eying the cat at the foot of the table with his head deep in his food bowl.

"Always, sir," Yeovill said with a twinkle in his eyes.

Happily chewing away, Lewrie returned to the quarterdeck with his telescope to look outboard at their strange, fearless oddity which was now only about two miles off, and still coming on as bold as a dog in a doublet.

"Damn my eyes, but I could *swear* she looks familiar," the First Officer, Lt. Westcott, who had come up from the wardroom, vowed. "Now where . . . ?" he wondered.

"She appears just another of the typical coasters hereabouts, Mister Westcott," Lt. Harcourt said with a shrug, "though her wish to be captured is odd."

But, by the time that both ships had closed to within one mile of each other, Lewrie had a sneaking feeling that they had seen her once before, too.

"What's that?" Harcourt barked, lifting his glass to give her another close look. "God's Teeth, there's someone waving a British Jack over yonder!"

In Lewrie's ocular, there *was* a Red Ensign being wig-wagged at them by someone amidships of her starboard rails, and other people on her decks were waving hats, coats, and shirts at them as if very glad to see them! A moment later, and the strange vessel handed her foresail and began to round up into the wind, hauling her mainsail taut and setting her jib cross-sheeted to fetch-to.

"Damned if we *haven't* seen her before," Lewrie exclaimed. "We took her a month ago. It's that same filthy old grain barge! Close her near as you may, Mister Harcourt, and prepare to fetch-to."

"Aye aye, sir!" Harcourt replied, sounding even more perplexed.

Within a quarter of an hour, both ships were cocked up into the wind, and a rowboat manned by two oarsmen and a tillerman, with two passengers aboard, was stroking for *Sapphire*'s starboard entry-port.

"Side-party to render honours, sir?" Lt. Harcourt enquired.

"They don't exactly look Navy t'me, sir," Lewrie said, looking the newcomers over. "Let's wait 'til we know who they are."

The rowboat hooked onto the mainmast channel platform and two men scrambled up the boarding battens to the open entry-port, making Lewrie wonder if King Neptune's scruffy court had come to call, for both were most oddly dressed, and looked more like itinerant Gypsies.

"*Hola, señores!*" the first aboard gaily called out, sweeping off a shapeless felt hat to make an exaggerated low bow. He wore a cracked pair of buckled shoes with no stockings, grease-stained and tar-stained slop-trousers, an equally-dirty shirt and a waist-coat made of tan leather. "*Hola, amigos!* I, Vicente Rodriguez . . . better known as John Cummings . . . greet you. I am master of the *Gallegos,* the splendid ship you seized for me!" He did so in a Spanish accent, then in an accent that put Lewrie in mind of Kent. "And you there on the quarterdeck, I assume would be the gallant Captain Lewrie? Greetings from Mister Thomas Mountjoy, who also expresses his thanks for his fine new vessel!"

"Has the circus come to town?" Lt. Westcott grumbled under his breath.

"I'd wait for the jugglers, first," Lewrie muttered back, then stepped forward to greet Rodriguez/Cummings. "Welcome aboard, sir. However you name yourself," he said, offering a hand.

"Allow me to name to you my compatriot, sir," Rodriguez/Cummings announced, turning to the other new arrival, who had held back behind the loquacious Cummings, peering about with a top-lofty air as if he was amused by it all, or found *Sapphire* a low-class pigsty. "Mister Romney Marsh, a man of so many identities that they are impossible to enumerate. Romney, this is Captain Sir Alan Lewrie, Baronet."

"Honoured t'make your acquaintance, sir," Mr. Marsh said in a clench-jawed Etonian accent, the sort that usually got right up Lewrie's nose. Marsh offered his hand, then quickly switched to a Bow Bell's Cockney, "an' 'aven't I 'eard o' you, your 'onour, sir, hah hah!"

"Mister Mountjoy sent for assistance to expand the reach of his posting, sir," Cummings elaborated. "We arrived at Gibraltar only one day after you left port."

Lewrie only half-heard that; he was still goggling at Marsh, who had just as quickly turned Spanish and was singing some song with a daft grin on his face, lisping away like the haughtiest Castilian.

*Bloody lunaticks, the both of 'em!* Lewrie thought.

"Ehm . . . shouldn't we be discussing such in private, Mister Cummings?" Lewrie asked. " 'Under the rose', all that?"

"Well, we shouldn't stay too long in company with your ship, lest watchers ashore associate *Gallegos* with the Royal Navy," Cummings said, "but, perhaps a few minutes, over a glass of something?"

"That great American, Benjamin Franklin, once wrote that 'wine is God's way of telling us that he loves us, and wishes us to be happy',"

Romney Marsh cited, turning his face angelic. "Yes, make us happy, please do, Sir Alan!"

"This way, then, gentlemen," Lewrie bade. "Mister Harcourt, we will remain fetched-to a while longer. Alert me does a strange sail turn up."

"Aye, sir," Lt. Harcourt replied, trying not to laugh at the continuing antics of the mysterious Mr. Marsh, who was practising some dance steps, and humming to himself.

"Wine, Pettus," Lewrie requested once they were all seated in the starboard-side settee area. "Tea for me."

"Oh, but the sun *is* below the yardarm, Sir Alan," Marsh said, "since it has just arisen. Ah, you have a cat! Hallo, puss. *Venir, el gato bonito!*" he crooned with his head over to one side.

Chalky would have none of it; he crouched down with his tail tucked round his front paws near the wine-cabinet.

*Someone in here's got some sense,* Lewrie amusedly thought.

"You're re-enforcing Mountjoy, you said, Mister Cummings? He said he had a man coming to command his boat, should I be able to get him one," Lewrie asked, by way of beginning, and getting their meeting over quickly, so he wouldn't have to deal with them for long.

"And, you did a splendid job of it, sir," Cummings replied as Pettus fetched a bottle and two glasses of a smuggled Spanish white. "Yes, I'm to play-act a local trader, bearing goods smuggled out of Gibraltar, which as you know, thrives despite the regulations against it. I've always played around boats, I've always had a good ear for languages, and especially for Spanish and Portuguese, and the regional dialects. Nowhere near Marsh's talents at it, but I cope. We're to enter Spanish ports all along the Andalusian, Murcian, and Catalan coasts, ostensibly to trade, but also to pick up reports from agents in place, along with tavern talk. Carry instructions from Mountjoy, that sort of thing, find answers to questions, and fill in the gaps in what we know, and don't know."

"A dangerous business," Lewrie commented as Pettus brought him a tall glass of cool tea with lemon and sugar.

"As you'd know best yourself, Sir Alan," Romney Marsh said in a secretive whisper, leaning a tad closer than Lewrie liked. "We were told of your doings up the Mississippi to Spanish New Orleans a few years ago, and how you scotched that Creole pirate business. Mister James Peel sends his regards. His fondest regards."

Marsh said that in yet another guise, this time sounding like the idlest, most affected courtier at St. James's Palace with the grandest airs. Lewrie didn't much care for simpering, either!

"Not all that dangerous, Captain Lewrie," Cummings stuck in, "for my brief doesn't require that I meet our agents face-to-face, but deal with drop-points where their reports are secreted. And Mountjoy is counting on the luxury goods we carry to make our presence welcome. I also have enough bribe money to mollify even the most-corrupt Spanish authorities. Marsh here has the more dangerous job . . ."

"Volunteered for it, gladly," Marsh said in a loud boast, "for God, King, and Country. And, for the thrill of it all."

"He's to go to Madrid, and nose about," Cummings said in awe of the mission, and Marsh's daring.

"And get back, I presume?" Lewrie dryly asked.

"Contact whom I can among the influential in Madrid who oppose the French, and the Godoy administration," Marsh preened, all but buffing his fingernails on the lapels of his waist-length leather jacket, "gather impressions of the sentiments of the common people and tradesmen, soldiers, and such. Perhaps *influence* whom I can, as well, and spread a little sedition. *Then*, get back to the coast and wait for *Señor* Rodriguez an' heez feelthy *barca* to peeck me up, *comprender?*" he said, slipping into a Spanish accent once more.

"And how may I aid you two in that?" Lewrie asked, imagining that they would have steered well clear of *Sapphire* at first sight if they didn't *need* something.

*Just like gettin' roped in by Zachariah Twigg as useful to his schemes ages ago in the Far East*, Lewrie sourly thought; *There's never an end to it! There's* always *something more!*

"You'll note, sir, that we've a large horizontal patch of new, white sailcloth in our foresail, from luff to leech," Cummings told him. "By that sign you will know us, hah hah! If we must meet I will show a very badly faded, but perfectly strong, red jib, and you can pretend to chase me out of sight of land, and any watchers. Do you encounter us along the coast, and we're anywhere near a port, I'd like you to chase after us . . . clumsily, so I can put in and escape, to the congratulations of other Spanish mariners, do you see?"

"That's all?" Lewrie asked, both puzzled and relieved.

"That's the nub of it, Captain Lewrie," Cummings said, tossing up his hands and grinning. "Now, over on the Atlantic coast, round Cádiz, we'll have to take our chances with our blockading ships, 'til Mister Mountjoy can get word to the Admiral commanding . . . Saumarez, the last I heard . . . but I'm still not sure if we'll be sent there in the near future. What's left of the Franco-Spanish combined fleet is still sulking in port, there, and the city's an armed fortress, so we have very few assets in Cádiz, and getting an agent, or agents, sneaked in is even more difficult."

"Oh, I suppose I could, if asked," Marsh slyly boasted. "What is one more priest among many, one more sandalled peasant droving his pigs to market, or a proud *hidalgo* on a fine horse?"

"Marsh can portray himself as Catholic as the Pope himself!" Cummings bragged. "He can conduct any rite, or a Mass, in Latin *and* Spanish. I've seen him do it, to practise."

"The benefits of a classical education, Cummings," Marsh said, "and a . . . dare I say, a widespread, catholic interest. Small *C* 'catholic', mind. Church of England, myself, and *damned* proud of it!"

"One never knows just who he is when he comes down to breakfast," Cummings said with a laugh. "Costumes, wigs, false beards, and mustachios . . ."

"Well, it's said that 'clothing makes the man'," Marsh airily stated. "Amateur theatrics was my chief delight at school, and with the help of Secret Branch, I've honed my skills by studying under the very best in Covent Garden and Drury Lane."

*He's daft as bats!* Lewrie thought, amazed at his smug expectations.

"Do you ever want for droll amusement when in London, Sir Alan, you must attend Pulteney Plumb's Comedic Revue in Drury Lane," Marsh imparted, leaning close once more as if touting a sure-thing long shot horse at Ascot.

Lewrie, in mid-sip of his tea, spluttered a gulp in his lap!

*He's deader than cold, boiled mutton!* Lewrie thought; *Soon as he steps ashore, the Spanish'll be askin' him if he's up for a match of cricket! Pulteney bloody Plumb, of all the . . . !*

Once he calmed himself, all he could say in reply was, "Seen it."

"Man's a genius, as is his wife," Romney Marsh praised.

Lewrie thought that perhaps James Peel hadn't told Cummings or Marsh *all* about Lewrie's past, or his association with Pulteney Plumb during the Peace of Amiens, when he'd somehow insulted Napoleon Bonaparte at a *levee* in the Tuileries Palace in Paris, and had to flee for his life to Calais, pursued by police agents and soldiers, and it had been that daft fool Plumb and his wife who had spirited Lewrie and his wife clear cross France in a variety of costumes and guises, re-living his younger days of doing the same thing for condemned French aristocrats as part of a larger secret collaboration, and naming himself the "Yellow Tansy"!

Lewrie had to grudgingly admit that Plumb *had* gotten them to the coast, where a schooner was waiting to bear them to Dover, as it had during The Terror in 1793 for the Yellow Tansy, the Ruby Begonia, or other human smugglers of that coterie. It had only been bad luck that the French had caught up with them as the schooner's boat was in the surf, just feet from showing the French a clean pair of heels.

*Less he knows, and the less said of Plumb, the better,* Lewrie thought, almost snarling his displeasure.

"You show a red jib, I chase you out to sea for a 'rondy', and if not, I pretend t'chase you. Got it," Lewrie summed up. "D'ye need chasin' today?"

"It would not hurt, I suppose," Cummings said. "We're bound to Estepona, first, then Almeria, then Málaga, where we land Marsh. The roads are better from there to Madrid."

"Not Estepona," Lewrie quickly cautioned. "Your ship's master and crew I let go free, there, and they'd have you hung for piracy as soon as they recognise her. But, let's be about it, before someone ashore sees us together." He set aside his glass of tea and rose to bring matters to a welcome close.

They saw Cummings/Rodriguez and Romney Marsh/The Multitude off without a side-party or debarking honours, though Lewrie doffed his hat from the lip of the entry-port as they scrambled down the battens to their waiting rowboat, thinking that he *might* see Cummings again, but Marsh? The odds were definitely against it. There were some people who were just too confident to live!

Oddly, when the boat was about one hundred yards off, Marsh took off his narrow-brimmed hat and waved back at *Sapphire*, shouting "*Floreat Etona!*", for some reason or another.

"We've one of his fellow Etonians aboard?" Lt. Harcourt wondered aloud. "Who, I can't imagine."

"The Captain, very briefly, before he was expelled," Westcott informed him from the corner of his mouth in an amused whisper.

"Expelled? For what?" Harcourt asked, surprised.

"You'd have to ask him," Lt. Westcott said, with a snicker.

"Perish the thought!" Harcourt said with a mock shiver.

"Mister Harcourt," Lewrie said, returning to the quarterdeck. "You may get us under way, slowly. Once their vessel is around five miles off, we will put about and pretend to chase her past Estepona."

"*Pretend*, sir?" Harcourt asked, all a'sea.

"Under-handed, secret Crown doings, sir," Lewrie sternly told him, "and pray the Good Lord keeps you at arm's length from such."

"Aye aye, sir. Get under way, then come about in chase," Lieutenant Harcourt replied, his curiosity piqued.

"*Gallegos*, that's funny," Midshipman Kibworth said to one of his mates, Midshipman Carey, in a tittery mutter.

"What's funny, Mister Kibworth?" Lewrie demanded.

"I was told that one of Columbus's ships was named the *Gallegos*, sir," Kibworth cringingly explained. "It means 'dirty whore', and to avoid embarassing Queen Isabella, they changed it to *Santa Maria*." He could not help blushing red and snickering to dare say a bad word.

"Ah, the further benefits of an education," Lewrie bemoaned. "I think that's enough slang Spanish for one day, don't you?"

"Ehm, aye aye, sir," Kibworth said, with an audible gulp.

"Carry on, Mister Harcourt," Lewrie said. "I'll be aft 'til the change of watch."

*Moppin' tea off my waist-coat,* Lewrie thought; *And airin' the stench o' spies from my cabins.*

# BOOK THREE

Be frolic then
Let cannon roar
Frighting the wide heaven.

"TO THE VIRGINIAN VOYAGE"
MICHAEL DRAYTON (1563-1631)

# CHAPTER TWENTY-FOUR

"Just where in the bloody world did ye dredge *him* up?" Lewrie asked Thomas Mountjoy a few days later as they sat in the lush bower of greenery on Mountjoy's roof gallery.

"It does take all kinds," Mountjoy said, with a sigh, "doesn't it? Personally, I don't think Mister Romney Marsh will last a week on the road to Madrid, but I had no say in it. Cummings, I requested, for I know he's good, for an amateur 'yachtsman'. People senior to me and Mister Peel pushed Marsh on me, despite Peel's misgivings."

"Dammit, Mountjoy, as soon as the Spanish arrest the fool, the authorities'll suspect everyone who doesn't shout praise for France, and start roundin' them up, too," Lewrie groused. "They'll be seein' British spies in their toilets. And what the hell's a 'yachtsman'?"

"Idle rich, and titled dilettantes who muck about in sea-going boats," Mountjoy explained. "Or race each other in small ones."

"They go t'sea for *fun?*" Lewrie gawped in amazement.

"There's some 'New Men' of industry who'd cruise the world if there wasn't a war on, in their own ships the size of trading brigs or schooners," Mountjoy went on, finding it amusing, and an example of how people wasted their new-made fortunes. As far as he and Lewrie knew, only the

King had an official Royal Yacht, which never left the Thames, and had rarely ever been used.

"Of all people t'give lessons on cloak and dagger play-acting, the Foreign Office chose Pulteney Plumb! Jesus!" Lewrie carped.

"Without Mister Twigg's cunning, now he's retired and doesn't even consult any longer," Mountjoy said with a glum shrug. "There are all *sorts* of hen-headed men in charge, who have their own ideas about fieldcraft. At least, Cummings and Marsh also brought along lashings of money for me to work with. Give London long enough, or become too desperate for results, and I expect they'll be ordering me to dress up in women's clothing, with lessons on how to flutter a fan!"

"Now there's an ugly picture!" Lewrie joshed, making a face.

He had a mental image of Thomas Mountjoy in a flounced red gown with tall hair combs, a black lace *mantilla,* with a rose in his teeth, doing the *flamenco* all the way to Madrid, and it *wasn't* pretty!

Mountjoy had been sprawled on the cushioned settee, wineglass in hand. He sat the glass down and rose to cross the gallery to his telescope, bent, and scanned the harbour.

"Lewrie," he said over his shoulder, "if all else fails, what does it cost to *hire* a ship? How does Admiralty do it, and how much might it set me back?"

"Hmm, something large enough for trooping?" Lewrie mused, feet up on a hassock and slumped into a deep padded chair. "They usually run about three hundred fifty tons, and if their bottoms are properly coppered, the Transport Board pays their owners nineteen shillings a month, maybe a full pound per ton, these days. Skin-flint owners try to get by with wood-sheathed bottoms, or no protection at all, and they go for less. But, I wouldn't recommend 'em. Copper sheathing's your man, even if they're hard t'find. Expensive, though."

"That's . . . four thousand two hundred pounds a year," Mountjoy said with a groan. "Damn! And the upkeep and pay for master and crew atop that? Damn."

"Well, Admiralty usually pays the owners and ship's husbands, the investors," Lewrie explained, idly wondering if there was enough of that light white Spanish wine left in the bottle for a top-up, or did they need to open a new one. "So the pay, rations, and necessary ship's stores come out of that, and if they get damaged, the Navy will repair them. From that sum, the master gets his passage money for unexpected expenses, and re-victualling."

"How many troops can they cram aboard a ship that big, a three hundred fifty-tonner?" Mountjoy pressed, coming back to the sitting area to take a squint at the bottle, too, and dribble a bit into both their glasses.

"The goin' rate's one soldier for every two tons, ah thankee," Lewrie told him. "Now if we only had some Swedish ice for this wine."

"No more to be had, and it isn't even high summer, yet, there's a pity," Mountjoy said, looking gloomy. "Something smaller, say, about *three* hundred tons, that'd be one hundred fifty soldiers . . . three companies? Just about what we planned for, and the lease would cost less."

"London didn't send you *that* much, did they?" Lewrie asked.

"No, they didn't," Mountjoy groused. "If you can't capture one that's suitable, and if Middleton at the yards can't contract with a ship under Transport Board authorisation, then I suppose we're stuck."

"Well, don't look longingly at me!" Lewrie said with a laugh. "I can't speak for Admiralty, either."

For a moment, Mountjoy *had* looked at Lewrie with a gleam of inspiration in his eyes, just as quickly dashed.

"I'll have another go at it, then," Lewrie promised. "Take on stores, re-victual, and give my crew a day of liberty, and I'll head out to sea, again. *El diablo negro* might find better pickings further East, nearer Cartagena, Valencia, maybe even Barcelona."

"*El diablo negro?*" Mountjoy asked.

"That's what the people in the last vessel I burned called us," Lewrie said, tossing the last of his wine to "heel-taps" and getting to his feet. "I'd best go see Captain Middleton at the dockyard, too, and see how he's coming with my boats and nets."

"Rock Soup," Mountjoy glumly mused, then got to his feet to see Lewrie down to the street. "I suppose I should go to my offices, too."

When first Lewrie spoke with Captain Robert Middleton about his boats, he had requested them to be over thirty feet long, more like his launch, or the wider-bodied 32-foot barges that he'd used in the Channel in 1804 when experimenting with "catamaran torpedoes", and which he had kept (since HM Dockyards had never officially asked for them to be returned!)

and used on raids along the coast of Spanish Florida in 1805, and to ferry Marines and sailors ashore at Cape Town and Buenos Aires the year before.

To get soldiers out of the boats and onto the beach quickly, he had wondered if there might be some way to square off the bows and make some sort of ramps, but Middleton and his shipwrights had laughed that to scorn. The sketches that Lewrie and Geoffrey Westcott, a dab-hand artist in his own right, brought which limned boats with high gunn'ls behind which the oarsmen would row through square ports, like ancient Greek or Roman ships, with ramps like gangways that could be extended over the bows, had made the shipwrights shiver in dread of even trying to build boats which could drown everyone aboard in a twinkling.

Of the six boats he'd requested, Lewrie found only two skeletons begun, their keels, stem posts, and stern posts and frames resting on baulks of scrap timber, with none of the planking started. They were, he was told, to be thirty-six feet in length, and very beamy. Middleton was of the opinion that if Lewrie could not employ them, they would make fine gunboats to protect shipping in the bay.

At least his sets of scrambling nets had been completed; other than that, Lewrie had been badly gulled, and all he could do was stomp off in high dudgeon!

All that was left for him to do ashore was to find some place to dine, sulk, and fume, and take a glass or two more than necessary aboard, even if he had to be hauled back onto *Sapphire* in a Bosun's chair!

A few streets up from the quayside, nearer to Dalrymple's headquarters in the Convent and the parade grounds, he discovered a chophouse that advertised itself with a large swinging signboard sporting a red lobster on yellow, by name of Pescador's, a two-storied establishment with a tavern and common rooms below, and a roofed and trellised upper dining room which faced the harbour and provided an airy, cool respite from the mid-day heat.

A young fellow led Lewrie upstairs to that dining room, seated him at a table for two, and referred him to a large chalkboard menu on the back wall which featured standard fare in yellow chalk and daily specials in white.

"Do you have any ale?" Lewrie asked.

"Oh, yayss, *señor*!" the young fellow assured him. "We have the deep, cool cellars, and have several favourite English ales, porters, and stouts. The owner is the retired Sergeant-Major from Chelmsford, himself, Mister Chumley, and he always say that without English beers, he would be out of business, hah hah!"

"I'll have a tall, pale Bass," Lewrie decided.

"Waiter will be right with you, *señor*!" the lad promised.

The open-sided dining room was much of a piece with Mountjoy's rooftop gallery, Lewrie thought, for it was awash in potted greenery, with hanging baskets of flowers round the outer balconies, and a cool tiled floor. White wood-slat chairs and tables with gay red tablecloths abounded, only partially filled with diners at that hour of the day; Army officers for most part, with a smattering of civilian men . . . and women.

The waiter, a swarthy fellow who looked vaguely Moorish, but who spoke in a British accent reminiscent of Lewrie's neighbours in Surrey and Anglesgreen, brought him a pint of ale and took his order for the *fritura mixta,* which he rapturously described as a combination of mussels, crab, and sardines in a wine and chili sauce, with a few slivers of anchovies, fried fish, and a grilled lobster tail, which of course came with white wheat rolls, butter, and steamed asparagus. He recommended a nice Italian white *pinot* to accompany the meal.

The establishment would have offered a fresh green salad, but for the fact that Gibraltar had very little arable land—most of the Rock was vertical!—and what could be traded, or smuggled, across The Lines from Spain could not be counted on, day-to-day.

*I think I could like this place,* Lewrie told himself. He was cooler, already, his ale was crisply refreshing, and there were women in the dining room, a rare sight for a sailor; young, pretty, merry women whose scents rivalled the flowers. He rather doubted that they were wives, though. Most of the officers he saw were Lieutenants or Captains, in their late teens to mid-twenties, and men of low rank did not marry so young.

*What was it that Burgess once said?* Lewrie tried to dredge up from memory; *Ah!* "*Lieutenants must* never *marry, Captains* could *marry, Majors* should, *and Colonels* must *marry!*"

He realised that these chirpy, cheerful young women must be the junior officers' girlfriends, or their mistresses. There were very few proper wives of senior military officers or Crown officials who'd risk voyaging to an overseas posting in time of war, who would have to leave their children at public schools, or with relatives, to spare them from foreign diseases. Hence, no respectable matrons present to demand that the "ladies of the evening" be shoved back into brothels, out of sight, out of mind, and be unable to corrupt the morals of the town, and lure their husbands' subalterns and clerks from the Right And Proper Way.

These alluring young creatures in their finery were likely hired courtesans or high-priced doxies!

*And here I sit with all my cundums stowed in my sea-chest!* he sadly throught.

As Lewrie's first course arrived, along with the Italian *pinot* cool from the deep stone cellar, another Army officer came up from the common rooms, a Captain of some infantry regiment, with a young woman on his arm. He was older than the others, in his late thirties, or so Lewrie judged, broad-shouldered, deep-chested, with reddish-gold hair and long, thick sideburns brushed forward in the latest style, down to the lobes of his ears. It appeared that the semi-tropical sun didn't agree with his complexion, for he was florid. It appeared that those younger officers didn't appeal to him, either, for he glared at them with haughty disdain, and he awarded Lewrie a similar glare as he and his companion were seated at a table for two by the balcony railings, an empty table apart from Lewrie's.

The Captain's companion, though . . . Lewrie lifted an appreciative brow as he got a good look at her. The Army Captain's back was to Lewrie, back and shoulders almost broad enough to block his view, but she seated herself facing Lewrie, with her chair close to the balustrade, so he could get a peek every now and then.

*Deliberately?* he hoped.

Compared to the junior officers' doxies, she was not a superb beauty, nor was her long, dark, almost black hair coiled and roached into an elaborate do, but was worn in a long, gathered mane, parted more to the left than the centre. On the way in, she'd worn a wide straw hat with the ribbons bound under her chin, but as soon as she sat down, she swept it off. Dark eyes, nicely arched, brows, a touch of an olive complexion, a rather fine nose, a very kissable mouth, and a firmly rounded but narrow chin . . . not beautiful, but more matter-of-factly hellish-handsome, Lewrie determined.

She didn't look happy, though, he decided; pensive was more like it. Her companion was prattling away, but her attention was on the harbour, the quayside, a hanging flower basket, or a caged bird warbling above their table. She reached up to the cage and a faint smile spread on her face. She looked down, met Lewrie's eyes, then smiled a bit broader.

"Ah, Miguel!" the Army Captain boomed to the waiter. "A cool ale, t'start with, and a white wine for the lady."

"Michael, sir," the waiter said in correction, keeping a bland look on his face, as if he'd done this many times before.

"Yes, yes, so you say," the officer said, laughing him off. "I will have the roast beef, and she will have the chicken, won't you, my dear? As you always do, what?"

"I would like . . ." she said, turning to look at the chalkboard menu on the inner wall, "the *gazpacho*, and the fried fish, this time."

"Please yourself," the Army Captain dismissively said, with a harumph of slight irritation thrown in for good measure. "You should know their entire *repertoire* by heart, by now."

"As often as we dine here, *sim*, I do," she replied, looking a tad morose. If it was a complaint, it was a weak one.

*Spanish, is she?* Lewrie asked himself; *Portuguese, or Genoan? None too pleased with him, whatever she is. A kept woman, under his "protection", most-like. Maybe she'd* like *t'kick over the traces, but can't afford to? Poor tit.*

"Simply can't fathom how anyone could relish cold soup!" the Army Captain grumped. "The Frogs with their cold potato mess . . ."

"*Vichyssoise*," she supplied, absently.

"Know what it's called," he snapped. "Had it, and I didn't think much of it. As silly a notion as tossin' fruit in a pitcher of wine. The utter ruin of a good wine, and barely makes cheap, sour wine palatable, hah!"

"The *sangria* is refreshing," she told him, sounding as if she would make a very minor rebellion, with one brow up the only sign of being vexed. "Your English punch . . ."

"Mother's Milk, m'dear!" he hooted, "and with champagne in it, the Nectar of The Gods! Can't beat a good English punch, haw haw!"

She made no reply to that assertion, but faced away and leaned her arm on the balustrade again. Lewrie studied her, now intrigued, and as she turned her face back to her keeper, Lewrie locked eyes with her for a second, tossed off an exaggerated shrug, and pulled a face. He was rewarded with a quick, furtive smile, before the waiter came with their beverages, and Lewrie's main course, on his tray.

As hungry as he was, and as tasty and toothsome his meal, Lewrie dawdled over his plate, shifting in his chair now and then to get a quick look at the young woman, and was able to share glances with her, which began as shy smiles and proceded to frank, speculative regardings. The bad part of that was haying to listen to her companion monopolise their conversation, him talking and deriding just about everything foreign, and laying out his schemes for winning the war.

Lewrie noted that the other subalterns and their girls sloped off rather quickly, instead of lingering over their drinks and flirting idly. It seemed that Captain "John Bull" had a depressing effect on them, too.

The fellow put down his first pint of ale quickly, and ordered a second, then slurped his way through a whole bottle of claret with his roast beef steak, which only made him louder and more opinionated. By the time Lewrie had finished his meal, topped off with a Spanish *flan* for something sweet, there were very few patrons in the dining room.

At last, there was nothing for it but to summon the waiter and call for his reckoning, leaving a generous tip and making sure that he called him "Michael" as he thanked him and got to his feet.

Standing and gathering up his cocked hat, Lewrie could get a better look at the young woman over the top of "John Bull", and he liked what he saw. She seemed slim, with a fine bosom, a firm and graceful neck. A wee gilt cross on a thin gilt chain glinted at the base of her throat. At his rising, she looked up, her gaze level and appraising, and he nodded a smile at her, which engendered a fleeting smile and the faintest of nods in reply, with a slow lowering of her lashes.

As Lewrie trotted down the stairs to the common rooms, then to the street, Lewrie could thank her companion for one thing, at least; the Army officer's loud voice had, in the course of his harangue, declared "Maddalena, m'dear", so Lewrie had a name, well, part of a name, to conjure with!

# CHAPTER TWENTY-FIVE

Over the next two months, HMS *Sapphire* spent all but two weeks at sea, still searching for a suitable vessel to serve as a transport. Lewrie took her West to Cape Trafalgar, near Cádiz, not above poaching if he had to in the blockade fleet's patch, with nothing to show for it. They chased many coasting vessels and sea-going fishing boats, frightened many, and caught and burned several, before returning to Gibraltar to confer with Mountjoy, who swore that he had written to Mr. Peel in London asking for more money, or some influence with the Admiralty Transport Board. So far, there was no joy in that direction.

*Sapphire* went back to her old hunting grounds, from Estepona to Valencia, pursuing, taking, and burning what they could, with equally dismal results. In mounting gloom, Lewrie even ordered the ship over to the Balearic Islands, and ravaged the fishermen and small traders of Formentara and Ibiza, and sailed several times round Mallorca and the main port of Palma. He did manage to capture a merchant brig of about 150 tons which at first seemed promising, but proved to be dangerously rotten, her bottom nigh-eaten through by ship worms and rats from the inside, and not even wood-sheathed, much less coppered. Did he send her off to the Prize-Court at Gibraltar with her shoddy load of cargo, he doubted if the meagre prize money would pay half of the Proctor's fees! Once again, her small crew was allowed to row away just off Palma by a mile or two, and she was set fire, as an example of what happened to Spaniards who dared share the sea with the Royal Navy.

Just after that, strong gales whipped up, forcing the upmost masts and yards to be struck down, the tops'ls taken in to second or third reefs, the main course brailed up, and when the seas thrashed and clashed in fury, all 1,100 tons of the ship got tossed so violently that the galley had to shut down two days' running, and several of the heavy-weather storm sails blew out and had to be replaced, with men aloft in a howling gale and a continual stinging rain.

By the time the weather moderated, and the top-masts could be hoisted back into place and the standing rigging re-mounted to secure them, Lewrie was more than ready to head back to a secure harbour.

"I'll have the twenty-five-foot cutter for my needs, Mister Westcott," Lewrie told the First Officer, turned out in his best shore-going uniform. "You can use the pinnace and the launch t'fetch water and firewood, then the Purser's fresh supplies."

"With so little expended since our last port call, I expect we can have everything needful aboard by sundown," Geoffrey Westcott said as he pulled out his watch to check the time. "And with any luck, that will include a Moroccan bullock and a couple of Spanish hogs for fresh meat, too, sir."

"Some of those heavenly cured hams that they sell across The Lines, yes!" Lewrie enthused. He looked round the deck and found his cabin-steward, Pettus, and his cook, Yeovill, turned out in their own shore-going best, Yeovill in a civilian hat, a waist-length white-taped and brass-buttoned sailor's jacket with a red waist-coat underneath, a clean pair of tailored white trousers, and good buckled shoes, with a pair of gaudy-coloured stockings peeking from the trousers' hem. He had his list, and a purse of Lewrie's passage money. Pettus was also looking very dashing and nautical, with a laundry bag at his feet. It seemed that the old laundress near Mountjoy's lodgings had an attractive daughter, so Pettus had taken extreme care with his appearance.

"Wish we had one of those, sir," Lt. Elmes, who had had the watch as they'd entered harbour, wistfully said, jutting his chin at several merchantmen lying at anchor up by the Old Mole, one of them flying the plain blue flag of the Agent Afloat from the Transport Board. A convoy had come in from England, supply ships bearing shot and powder, salt rations and foodstuffs, and at least two large ships that looked like the right size for troop transports.

"Wish away, Mister Elmes," Lewrie said, giving them a covetous leer. "Pray, cross yer fingers, spit and whirl about thrice . . . whatever works."

"Aye, sir," Elmes replied in good humour.

"Carry on, Mister Westcott, I'll be . . ." Lewrie began.

"Boat ahoy!" Midshipman Spears cried, hailing an approaching row-boat with only one oarsman aboard.

"Letter fer yer Cap'm!" the oarsman yelled back, letting go his oars for a moment to cup his hands round his mouth.

"Come alongside!" Spears shouted, then went through the opened entry-port and down the battens to the mainmast chain platform to take the letter, then scramble back up and deliver it to the quarterdeck.

"Ah, hmm," Lewrie muttered as he broke the wax seal, unfolded it, and read the quick and cryptic note. "Indeed!"

"Good news, sir?" Westcott asked.

"Could be," Lewrie said, with a sly smile. "Carry on, sir. I'll be ashore."

Mister Deacon, the bodyguard, answered the door at Mountjoy's lodgings and let Lewrie in, offering a terse "welcome back, sir" with no hint of a smile, despite the good news in Mountjoy's note.

"Mister Deacon, well met, again," Lewrie replied before going up the several flights of stairs. "There'll be a couple of my men calling, my cabin-steward, and my cook. Don't break them."

"I stand warned, sir," Deacon replied, with a tight grin.

At the top of the stairs, the heavy iron-bound oak door to the lodgings stood half-open, for a change. Lewrie stepped through, giving out a "hallo", and found Mister Thomas Mountjoy at a desk in his shirtsleeves, flipping through a sheaf of papers and a thick ledger.

"Lewrie!" Mountjoy cried, leaping to his feet and rushing over to welcome him in with a wide grin on his face. "We've done it! Well, part of it, or at least one more stop forward."

"'A large turnip added to the soup', your note said?" Lewrie asked with a brow up in query.

"An hellish-big 'turnip', yes," Mountjoy boasted. "Sir, we've gotten ourselves a ship! Come out to the rooftop gallery and have a squint at her with my telescope!"

Lewrie tossed his hat on the cushioned settee outside, rushing to the telescope. It was already fixed upon the ship in question, and all he had to do was bend down a bit and put his eye to the ocular.

"She's the *Harmony*," Mountjoy eagerly told him. "Three-masted, as you suggested, so she can load troops into all six boats at once from her chain platforms and shrouds, though she's not a trooper, but carries general cargo. She's a *touch* under two hundred fifty tons, but she was recently re-coppered, I was assured."

Mountjoy's telescope was powerful enough to show Lewrie that even still fully laden, *Harmony* had a strip of new-penny clean copper at her waterline. Her furled and brailed-up sails were as white as if they had just come from a sailmaker's loft, and her paint had been touched up recently.

"Two tons per man, that'd let us put at least one hundred and twenty-five officers and men aboard her, all told, right?" Mountjoy pressed.

"No more than ninety to one hundred," Lewrie had to tell him, still studying her. "We'll have to make room below for about fifty or more sailors to handle the boats, and the rations t'feed 'em all, too. I don't see a single gun in sight. She sails unarmed?"

Whether a merchant ship could really mount a decent defence if attacked by pirates, an enemy privateer, or a warship, given how few crewmen that cheese-paring owners and captains hired, it was Lewrie's experience that most of them carried *some* armament.

*Must count on muskets, pikes, cutlasses, and a few swivel guns,* Lewrie thought, looking for the forked iron stanchions along the tops of *Harmony*'s bulwarks in which swivel guns, usually light 2-pounders, would be set if threatened. He saw a grand total of six.

*No doubt they're stowed* far *below, and haven't been brought up in ages,* Lewrie told himself with a wry grimace; *Most-like gone completely to rust, and I doubt if there's a man in her crew who knows a damned thing about usin' 'em!*

"Well, perhaps she always sails in convoy, under escort, and her owners don't feel the need for guns," Mountjoy lamely tried to explain. "Does she really need artillery?" he asked.

"No," Lewrie said with a shrug, standing back up and turning to face him. "Not as long as she sails with us, *Sapphire* can protect her. She looks like she has swivel guns, and anything heavier, 6-pounders on wheeled carriages, would just take up deck space."

"Well, that's all fine, then," Mountjoy said, brightening over his new acquisition, and Lewrie's seeming satisfaction with her. "I've found this marvellous sparkling white wine from Portugal, it just came in. Not exactly a champagne, but it gives a fair approximation. Let's open a bottle and toast our addition to 'Rock Soup', hey? Now, where the Devil did I leave that bloody cork puller?"

The search for the requisite implement took several minutes, and it was finally found under a decorative pillow on the upholstered settee in the small salon adjacent to the outdoor gallery.

"Ah, that is spritely!" Lewrie commented after a sip, "not too sweet, either, not like a sparkling German white. Costly? I may go buy a case, if there's any left t'be had."

"I'll show you where," Mountjoy promised. "Or, as you sailors say, 'I'll give you a fair wind' to it, hah! And no, not dear at all. Nothing like what the ship's cost me. Well, Peel, and Secret Branch. *Harmony* is two hundred and thirty tons, but her owners insisted that if she's to be used in an active military role, they rounded her burthen up to two hundred and *fifty* tons . . . evidently, they love round numbers . . . and demanded *twenty-five* shillings per ton."

"Damme!" Lewrie exclaimed. "All our troopers that carried the army to Cape Town last January only cost nineteen!"

"Ah, but they never came under fire, and once empty, they were used to carry the defeated Dutch soldiers home, then went back to general work," Mountjoy carped. "Peel wrote and told me that the owners had to hire a new master for her, after the first one objected to the risk. Half her old crew cried off, too. Not that there's that many sailors aboard her, to begin with."

*Harmony*'s owners, and the Transport Board, were equal when it came to miserliness; neither would pay for more than five sailors and ship's boys for every hundred tons of burthen, which meant that she'd be handled by only ten hands, plus master and mates, cook, carpenter, sailmaker, bosun, and such, and Lewrie simply could not imagine how it was done! His whole life had been in warships in which no less than fourty sailors were crammed aboard, arseholes to elbows, even in the smallest cutters, and there were hundreds aboard most frigates, and *Sapphire,* more than enough muscle for even the hardest tasks.

*How the Devil do they even get the* anchors *up?* he wondered; *Or reef, or strike top-masts in a blow?*

"You've gone aboard her?" Lewrie asked.

"As soon as she dropped anchor," Mountjoy assured him. "I met her master, a Mister Hedgepeth, and looked her over, though she still had a full cargo aboard, waiting for the barges and stevedores, so I couldn't tell you much about her belowdecks. God, but Hedgepeth is a *dour* old twist! The only reason he took command of her was that he's to be paid ten pounds extra a month than the owners pay him, and that comes out of my budget, and I'm to be liable for any and all repairs needed, if her *paint* gets scraped in the course of our activities, and he insists he'll demand *more* in future, if the job looks more dangerous than he was first told."

Mountjoy went on to relate how he had approached the Commissoner of the dockyards, Captain Middleton, before *Harmony* had arrived, and told him that he *might* have to use Admiralty labour, lumber, and stores to repair a civilian ship. Mountjoy's reception had been more than cool; more like a winter's night at the North Pole!

"By the by, your boats are ready," Mountjoy said, pouring them a top-up as they sat a 'sprawl under the shade of a canvas awning on the gallery. "Six double-enders, he told me, thirty-six feet long and ten abeam, with room for small carronades in their bows."

"He *still* thinks he'll get 'em as gunboats, damn him," Lewrie griped. "Well, once *Harmony*'s landed the last of her cargo, he'll be busy convertin' her innards . . . at Admiralty expense. Why?" Lewrie said with a laugh at Mountjoy's expression. "Ships altered to carry soldiers need their holds partitioned, and beds built, to accommodate them. Scads of mess tables, her galley refitted t'feed at least one hundred and fifty . . . some cabins made for their officers? I suppose I'll have t'give up a Lieutenant, or a couple of senior Mids, to take charge of the crews for the boats. That'll ease the workload of her own small crew, too, when we're on-passage."

The list grew longer in his head, when he considered how much food and water must be carried in her, how many spare muskets, flints, bayonets, and cutlasses would have to be requisitioned from Captain Middleton's warehouses, and . . . sailors released from the hospital and re-assigned, with any lacks in their kits made good, or replaced entirely.

*A Purser!* Lewrie realised; *Someone t'sell 'em tobacco, keep an eye on the rum issues, replace their broken mugs and plates?*

"I fear you're going to be paying out a lot more, Mountjoy," Lewrie warned him. "Or your superiors will, to recompense the Admiralty, for all that's wanting for our little expeditions."

"Now why do I feel as if I've been set upon by a pack of bully bucks?" Mountjoy said, with a sigh.

"You'll feel like you've been cudgelled half to death, before all we need is rounded up," Lewrie hooted back, then began to tick off those needs. Mountjoy held up a hand and went to the desk to fetch a pen and paper, before allowing Lewrie to begin again. By the time it was complete, Mountjoy had to shake finger-cramp from his hand, and a fresh bottle of sparkling wine had to be opened.

"Is it possible we may be asking for a tad *too* much, I wonder?" Mountjoy said after a long, sullen silence. "What if we can't get any sailors from the hospital? Could you spare men from your ship?"

"Well, if I had to, I *could* give up fifty hands and a couple of Midshipmen," Lewrie admitted, equally gloomy. "But, there goes the men I intended t'arm and land alongside my Marines. I could send the Purser's clerk, Irby, our 'Jack In The Breadroom', t'dole out sundries and such, too."

"With about an hundred soldiers aboard, do those men need the spare weapons, then?" Mountjoy asked.

"No," Lewrie said. "I could send a chest full of pistols aboard, and cutlasses, so they can defend themselves after they land on the beaches. They'd stand by the boats, and not go inland, waiting for the soldiers to finish their tasks, and come back to be taken off."

"That solves one problem, then," Mountjoy said, "and one less request, or burden, demanded of Captain Middleton. That may mollify him a bit, once he sees the whole list. Maybe he won't scream quite so loudly. Rations, hmm."

"At least enough for three months," Lewrie stated.

"Really? How long did you intend to stay out? Just rampaging up and down the coast, Will-He, Nill-He?" Mountjoy asked.

"What d'ye mean?" Lewrie queried back.

"Now I've a way to communicate with my agents, and . . . sources, *via* Cummings and his boat," Mountjoy pointed out, "It seems to me that we could gather information about how well-defended certain objectives might be, and lay our plans accordingly. Strike the Dons where they aren't? You *might* plan one specific operation, based on the best intelligence, load the troops aboard *Harmony*, sail out and attack it, then return to port so we can plan the second.

"Now, if there were two or three tempting targets within a day or two of sailing," Mountjoy went on, perking up for the first time in an hour, "you could go after them, depending on the weather and how rough you judge the landing might be, and not be away from port for more than a fortnight, so you wouldn't have to cram too much aboard the transport at any given time, leaving more room for soldiers and your sailors."

"You learn as much as you can about Estepona, say, rough hand-drawn maps prepared by your people can be copied for my Marine officers and the officers commanding the soldiers, and we *plan* how to go about it, one target at a time? Hmm," Lewrie slowly grasped.

When he'd been a temporary Commodore in the Bahamas two years before, he knew nothing of what lay a stone's throw behind the beaches and inlets of the coast of Spanish Florida, and he *had* rampaged up and down the shore like a blind pig rooting for truffles, sure only that there would be settlements round the inlets, and that there were towns marked on his copies of old Spanish charts. Mountjoy's concept was a "horse of another feather" as his old Cox'n, Will Cony, would say. It was . . . bloody *scientific!*

"Damme, I like it, Mountjoy," Lewrie exclaimed. "I love it!"

"I've been gathering information, already," Mountjoy told him, "though I haven't requested maps from my people, yet, but will do so, as soon as Cummings returns from his present trip."

"Mountjoy, I swear you're a bloody genius!" Lewrie whooped.

"Well, if you say so," Mountjoy said, beaming.

*More time in port,* Lewrie happily contemplated; *Then short, hard jabs at the Dons. Spread chaos and mayhem, in spades!*

And when not pummelling the Spanish, there was a chance that he could dine at Pescadore's more often, where Maddalena whoever-she-was complained that her keeper always took her, and learn more about her!

# CHAPTER TWENTY-SIX

"You've done a fine job of it, Mister Mountjoy," Lewrie said after a tour of *Harmony* from bow to stern. "The 'big turnip's' ready."

"Oh yes," Mountjoy drolly replied, with a roll of his eyes. "I have Captain Middleton, and every shipwright in the dockyards, angry with me, Hedgepeth grinding his teeth and growling like a cur every time I meet with him, *Harmony*'s cook ready to jump ship if we expect him to prepare rations for nigh two hundred men, and the ship's mates cursing me for taking half their cabin space for the Army officers. If I'd ordered their women raped, and their children boiled alive, I don't think I could have done better!"

"No matter, Mountjoy," Lewrie told him, "change always bothers people, big changes irk them worse, but they'll learn to cope. Make adjustments? And, you have your maps, and intelligence."

Lewrie had taken *Sapphire* back to sea after their last meeting, and had stayed out for another month of cruising the coasts of Andalusia, doing more threatening and chasing than capturing and burning Spanish coasters and fishing boats. From Estepona to near Cartagena, there were no longer many Spanish mariners who would dare go too far out, lest *el diablo negro* got them.

In point of fact, Lewrie had to admit that he could not take all the credit. The brig-sloops and frigates of the Mediterranean Fleet were working close inshore of the provinces of Catalonia, Murcia, and the sliver of seacoast of Aragon, ranging further afield than the French naval bases of Marseilles and Toulon. *Sapphire* had run across several of them and had closed to briefly "speak" them, bantering as to who was poaching in whose territory. *Most* of it was good-natured.

And, he'd come across agent Cummings's boat a couple of times, the last encounter a meeting far out at sea at Cummings's summons of the faded red jib. He was bound for Valencia, but had garnered maps and notes on an host of possible objectives for Lewrie to rush back to Mountjoy at Gibraltar. The man's personal reports painted a grim picture of want, poverty, and unemployment among the Spanish people as the government in Madrid slavishly enforced Emperor Bonaparte's Continental System which closed all Europe to British trade and goods. He even went so far as to predict that if things did not improve for the Spanish people, there would be a rebellion, sooner or later. He had no trouble finding willing informants, and some who had asked for arms from the British.

To Lewrie's lights, Thomas Mountjoy was looking a tad haggard, but that was to be expected. He had a lot on his plate lately, what with dealing with *Harmony*'s conversion, the yards, and the stores warehouses, looking under every rug on the Rock for spies and Dalrymple's imagined rebellion, double-dealing smugglers, and sifting and sorting all the reports from his own agents to stitch together plausible and trustworthy assessments to send back to London, with only Deacon for help in the doing.

*I could've stayed in port and helped*, Lewrie thought; *But, the ship would've gone t'rot. Better him than me!*

"Now the transport's about ready, you should get some sleep," Lewrie offered to atone for his absence.

"Still too much to do," Mountjoy countered. "I'll only sleep deep when all the ingredients are in the pot, and you're off for the first raid. Oh God . . . Hedgepeth."

*Harmony*'s Master had come up on deck to take the air. He *was*, as Mountjoy had described him, a dour twist. He was long and lean, squinty-eyed, eagle-beaked, and only put in his dentures for dining, which turned his sour mouth inwards. He wore his hair, what was left of it, grey, long, and thin, and seemed to shave only once a fortnight. Hedgepeth was a proper "scaly fish", a real "tarpaulin" man, seared the texture and colour of old deer hide gloves by decades at sea. He was the best that could be hired, in truth, but by God, he was a trial!

"Cap'm Lewrie . . . *Mister* Mountjoy," he said in a deep, gravelly voice, turning the "Mister" into a speculation as to whether Mountjoy truly deserved it, touching the brim of a civilian hat.

"Captain Hedgepeth," Lewrie greeted him with a doff of his hat. "The yard's done a fine job of her, d'ye not think?"

"Only if yer damned Navy puts her back t'rights when yer done with her, Cap'm Lewrie," Hedgepeth groused, "or she'll never carry a decent cargo again. Might's well turn her into an overnight packet on the Thames, with all them bloody cabins. Ship horses, maybe, for the stalls're ready and waitin', ain't they."

"I see the scrambling nets are aboard, sir," Lewrie went on.

"For all they're worth, aye," Hedgepeth said, scratching at his whiskers. "Here now, ye puttin' an Agent from the Transport Board aboard, who'll tell me how t'scratch my own balls?"

"There will be Army officers aboard, of course, Captain, but their brief starts when they wade ashore in the surf," Lewrie tried to explain. "I'm placing fifty of my hands aboard t'man the boats and steer 'em, and two of my senior Midshipmen. Normally, it's one Mid per fifty men, but on-passage they're to take orders from you. There will be an extra cook, which I'll have to scrounge from the naval hospital, to assist yours, and my Jack In The Breadroom to stand in as a Purser. All will answer to you, sir."

"All o' that makes for one helluva crowd," Hedgepeth said, taking a moment to spit over the quarterdeck bulwarks, "lubberly Redcoats heavin' over the side, wanderin' about in everyone's way like so many stray hogs, and yer fifty sailors layin' about idle. Shit!"

"Use 'em, watch and watch, Captain Hedgepeth," Lewrie offered. "Cut your men's workload 'til they have to man the boats. *Sapphire*'s your main defence should we run into trouble at sea, but you'd have armed soldiers, well-trained sailors t'fend off boarders, and a way to use your swivel guns to best effect."

"We get into that much trouble, a Spaniard or Frog'd lay off and shoot us t'pieces 'fore they'd try t'board us," Hedgepeth sourly pointed out. "Aye, we'll play yer games, Cap'm Lewrie, though I don't think much'll come of it. *Mister* Mountjoy here's payin' the reckonin'. Ye know yer bloody boats're too heavy t'hoist aboard, even *with* all yer Redcoats and tars heavin'. I tow all six like a string o' ducklin's, I doubt I'd make four or five knots."

"Then I'll just have to reduce sail and keep close to you," Lewrie promised, trying hard not to sound impatient, but Lord, the man was surly!

"Fun t'watch, heh heh," Hedgepeth said, with an open-mouthed laugh, which was not all that pretty. "Jolly!" he suddenly bellowed in a quarter-deck voice louder than Lewrie had ever heard. "Boil me up a pot o' black coffee, Jolly, ye idle duck-fucker!"

The ship's cook, a fellow nigh as old and ugly as Hedgepeth, popped his head out of the forecastle galley, shouting, "Beans grindin' an' th' warter a'roilin', sir!" Lewrie was amazed to see that Jolly had all his arms and legs. Most Navy cooks were Greenwich Pensioners and amputees, given an easy job instead of being discharged.

"We'll take our leave, Captain," Lewrie said, doffing his hat.

"Cap'm Lewrie . . . *Mister* Mountjoy," Hedgepeth said, nodding and turning away with a twinkle in his eyes. "Heh heh heh."

Once seated aft in his 25-foot cutter, and the oarsmen making way to the quayside to drop Mountjoy off, Lewrie turned back to look at *Harmony*, and the six large boats nuzzling her hull. "She'll do, Mountjoy, she'll do main-well," Lewrie told him.

"What's next?" Mountjoy wondered.

"See the hospital, get a cook," Lewrie japed. "I'll send my man, Yeovill, t'see if there's anyone who can do a bit more than boil water."

"Troops," Mountjoy countered. "We've all the pieces in place, but for them, and without a committment from Sir Hew Dalrymple, we're in a cleft stick. Two companies, right?"

"Aye," Lewrie said. "Correct me if I'm wrong, but hasn't Peel or somebody written him to make the request already?"

"Well, he's had our written proposal for months, and our oral presentation," Mountjoy said, "and I've written him several times to keep him abreast of our progress, so the project can't slip his mind. And yes, Mister Peel wrote me to say that he had written Sir Hew *requesting* co-operation, but . . ." Mountjoy lifted his hands in seeming frustration. "Dalrymple will pay attention should he hear it from Admiralty, or Horse Guards, but a *request* from the Foreign Office's Secret Branch? I don't know."

"Aye, he's a real 'down' on cloak and dagger doin's," Lewrie agreed.

"It's low and sneaking to real gentlemen, totally without honour. Fortunate for us that *we've* learned how t'be low and sneaking."

"Well, *I* haven't had to cut any throats, *yet*," Mountjoy mildly objected. "Don't believe we *teach* that class. There is no real training, don't ye know. We just get pitched in under a senior, and do the best we can with what we've got."

"Low cunning, and crass slyness," Lewrie said, with a laugh. "I think we qualify. We should put our heads together and plan what to say that will convince Dalrymple t'give us what we want. Cover all the items, and have answers ready for anything we imagine he might ask, or differ with. Christ, write it out so even I can recite by rote. Use simple words when ye do. Just a thick-headed sailor, me."

"Lewrie, you do yourself an injustice," Mountjoy disagreed.

"Let's be as clever as Zachariah Twigg," Lewrie pressed. "If that doesn't work, we can always threaten Dalrymple's family!"

Mountjoy gawped at the absurd suggestion for a second, wondering if Lewrie was serious, then burst out in a peal of laughter that nigh doubled him over, and it took him a long minute to recover and speak again. "Right then, a planning session, all day tomorrow, at my lodgings, and we'll run it all by Deacon, he's a good head on his shoulders."

"Bring all your latest agents' and informants' reports, with their maps of possible targets, too," Lewrie suggested. "And, what about what Cummings sent you, about the insurgents who've requested arms and ammunition? *That'll* make his nose hairs quiver, I expect."

"Yes, it might, wouldn't it?" Mountjoy brightened. "Tomorrow, all day."

"Should I bring the wine?" Lewrie teased.

"I don't know," Lieutenant-General Sir Hew Dalrymple very slowly said as he tugged at an earlobe, sounding weary and dubious, once Lewrie and Mountjoy had finished their carefully prepared presentation a few days later.

*Christ, he ain't 'the Dowager'*, Lewrie thought in well-hidden exasperation; *He's more like the old maiden aunt ye only have over at Christmas!*

"I must admit that you have achieved quite a lot since first presenting your plans to me," Sir Hew went on, rewarding them with a quick, fond smile, and just as quickly gone. "And it would be a shame did your scheme not come to fruition. Yet . . ."

That word was drawn out several seconds long, fading off into a sigh. Lewrie and Mountjoy looked at each other, openly grimacing when Sir Hew looked towards the ceiling, as if seeking inspiration.

"All we need now are troops, sir," Mountjoy gently reminded.

"Two companies," Lewrie stuck in.

"And there lies the rub, sirs," Sir Hew told them, coming back from his inspection of the ceiling. "After explaining the possible ramifications of what Spain might do, given the reports of Marshal Junot's army assembling, Horse Guards in London, and General Fox on Sicily, have promised me an additional battalion or two, yet . . ."

*There's that bloody word, again!* Lewrie thought in a huff.

"And yet, sirs, I must husband all I have, and all that I may receive, to defend Gibraltar," Sir Hew Dalrymple concluded.

"Ehm, may I enquire, sir, if you thought to mention the need to include detachments for offensive operations to London, or to General Fox on Sicily?" Mountjoy asked, sounding as if he had crossed fingers, hope against desperate hope.

"Believe I did so, in passing, Mister Mountjoy," Sir Hew said, looking cross to be questioned.

"Offensive operations along the coasts may tie down a fair number of Spanish troops," Lewrie quickly said, "if we hit 'em hard and often enough, sir. They'd have to garrison every little seaside town or fishing port, re-enforce their coastal forts, batteries and semaphore towers, or *erect* batteries. That'd limit the number of troops and guns that the Spanish could muster to lay siege to Gibraltar. Go in for a penny, earn a pound in dividends!"

"Not anywhere near Gibraltar, though, sir!" Mountjoy eagerly added, taking new heart. "We'd strike further afield."

*He's lookin' at me like I'm a talkin' dog,* Lewrie thought; *An idea from the likes o' me that helps?*

"We would do nothing to ruin your fairly cordial relationship with your counterpart, General Castaños," Mountjoy slyly went on, "from which I am certain that you glean useful information upon the mood of the region. Yet, if Spain and France plan a move against you here, our raids could delay and limit his massing of forces by the Spanish, requiring the French to commit *their* troops, and their march to here would take so long that London would have more than enough time to send you all the re-enforcements you could wish, sir."

"Perhaps that would end with British armies in Spain, meeting 'Boney's' armies head-on, sir," Lewrie suggested.

"That would be promising," Sir Hew said, leaning back to fantasise for a moment. "But, landing British troops against allied Franco-Spanish armies . . ." He sighed and went gloomy again.

"Well, Sir Hew," Mountjoy said, with a grin, "it has been our aim all along to break that alliance and get Spain out of the war. Neutral if possible, able to trade with the world again, or as a British ally in the best case."

"Teeterin' on the edge, Sir Hew," Lewrie contributed, and drew a quick under-lid glare from Mountjoy who feared that Dalrymple would misinterpret on which side Spain *might* teeter.

"Nowhere near Gibraltar, or General Castaños's military region, d'ye say?" Dalrymple mused, pulling an earlobe again. "In that case, some *limited* offensive raids *might* . . ." He paused, then reached out to pluck a china bell from his desk-top and ring for an aide. A massive set of old oak doors opened, and an Army Captain entered.

"Sir Hew?" he asked with an eager-to-serve smile.

"Captain Hughes, the troop transports that arrived a few days ago," Dalrymple enquired. "Of what units do they consist?"

"One squadron of horse, sir, two regiments of foot which will go on to General Fox," Captain Hughes easily reported off the top of his head, "and several companies of replacements for various regiments." Hughes had all the regiments' numbers, and the numbers of troops at the tips of his fingers, the perfect aide.

*I* know *this bastard!* Lewrie realised; *He's that opinionated twit in the seafood chop-house with that girl t'other day!*

Up close, and face-on, Captain Hughes was the epitome of a war-like officer, beefy, strong, and wide-shouldered, with a deep voice. His red uniform coat, with gilt lace epaulets, black facings and silver and red button loops, his shirt, neck-stock, and white waist-coat and matching breeches were immaculate and exquisitely tailored. Hughes's boots were so well-blacked and buffed that they might have been made of patent leather.

*Give him a beard and put him in hides, and he'd make a damned fine Viking*, Lewrie thought; *The shitten bulldog!*

"Experienced, are they, Hughes?" Damrymple asked. "The replacements?"

"Fresh-trained and sent off from their regiments' home barracks I believe, Sir Hew," Hughes said, with a superior smirk. "Newlies."

"Two companies from the 77th, hey? Hmm," Dalrymple mused, and drummed his fingers on his desk. "Had their regiment suffered a great many casualties on campaign, I would have thought that their Colonel would have requested more from their home battalion. Perhaps whoever he is, he can soldier on without them, then. Full complement of officers with them, Hughes?"

"Two Captains, two Lieutenants, and two Ensigns, sir," Hughes rapidly ticked off. "I do not know of their experience or abilities."

"And have I made you conversant with any plans for offensive, seaborne raids along the coasts, Hughes?" Sir Hew asked further.

"I do believe that I might have come across some mention here and there in the course of sorting your correspondence, Sir Hew," Hughes hesitantly said, cocking his large head over to one side.

"Allow me to name to you, sir, Captain Sir Alan Lewrie, Baronet, and Mister Thomas Mountjoy, of the, ah . . . Foreign Office. Sirs, my aide, Captain Daniel Hughes, seconded from the 53rd Foot," Dalrymple said, rising to summon them together for the requisite handshakes. "And what did you make of such plans, Captain Hughes, given your scant familiarity with them?" Dalrymple asked him.

"They sound simply capital, Sir Hew," Hughes replied eagerly. "A topping-fine venture!"

"Good, good, then," Dalrymple said, beaming. "Glad to hear you find them so. Captain Lewrie has managed to arrange all the necessities with which to put the plans afoot, but for the troops. His complement of Marines aboard his ship will be a part of any landings alongside those two companies of the 77th."

"How many men in all would that be, Captain Hughes?" Lewrie asked him, sure that he was the sort who would have the numbers.

"Including officers, sergeants, and corporals, that would be one hundred and twelve, Captain Lewrie," Hughes quickly supplied.

"Just about right," Lewrie told him. "About as many as the transport can manage. Them, plus my fifty-six . . ."

"Under a Captain of Marines, sir?" Hughes asked, with a bit of a scowl, as if imagining that Dalrymple might place him in command of the landing party. Hughes looked most eager for a fight.

"A First Leftenant, sir," Lewrie told him.

"Hughes, as welcome as are your skills as my aide," Dalrymple said, "still I have felt your desire to command troops again. For this task, I believe I will appoint you to take charge of those two companies of the 77th, and Captain Lewrie's Marines when sent ashore on any of the raids."

"I would be *delighted* to serve, sir!" Hughes loudly declared, puffing up his thick chest in pride. "Let us be at 'em, what? Yoicks, and tally ho!"

"And, for this duty, I think advancing you to a Brevet-Majority would not go amiss, either, Hughes," Dalrymple added.

"You do me too much honour, sir!" Hughes exclaimed. "But thank you for it, all the same!"

"Agreed then, gentlemen?" Dalrymple asked them all.

"Quite," Mountjoy assured him. "My thanks to you, Sir Hew."

"With the troops, and Major Hughes's experience, I am confident we'll raise chaos and all the mayhem one could ask for," Lewrie added. "We must fill the Major in on what we intend, and begin the training for the troops as soon as we can."

"Mind, though, Captain Lewrie," Hughes cautioned, "one mustn't expect *too* much of men straight from the parade ground and the firing butts, ha ha! Takes months on campaign to make proper soldiers."

"Well, then they'll have less to un-learn," Lewrie told him in good humour. "We'll get them their sea legs, first, and their 'duck feet,' second. Where t'practice, though. Can't do it here in the harbour for all the Spanish spies and watchers over in Algeciras t'see. Perpaps down by Europa Point, or a bay on the Eastern side of the Rock."

"Bring those companies' officers in to explain what's needing, too," Mountjoy suggested. "They won't be happy with the new task."

"I'll see to turning them eager," Hughes boasted.

" 'Growl they may, but go they must', is it, sir?" Lewrie asked Hughes. "Just so they come t'see it as an adventure, not an onerous chore. Let us depart and leave Sir Hew be. He's done us handsomely, and I'm sure he has many other pressing matters on his plate. Thank you, again, Sir Hew. We will keep you apprised of our progress, and of our first choice of objective."

"And, it will be up to you, Sir Hew, to approve or object to our choices," Mountjoy added to mollify the fellow.

"Is there a spare office where we can read you in, as it were, Major Hughes?" Lewrie asked the newly-promoted officer.

"I'm sure we can find one," Hughes said, pulling an expensive-looking pocket watch from a breeches pocket. "Though, hmm. Do you wish to begin at once, this very hour, or might I attend to some other business first, sirs?"

"It is near Noon, aye," Lewrie said, consulting his own watch. "Let's say we meet back here in the Convent at one thirty?"

"Capital!" Hughes boomed. "Just topping-tine! I've a dinner companion, d'ye see, and can't wait to give her the news."

"You're married, sir?" Mountjoy asked, wondering why a sensible man would bring a wife overseas.

"Not so's you'd notice, no sir," Hughes imparted, with a wink and a smirk.

"Don't share too much," Lewrie cautioned. "Ye never know who's listening. Mum's the word with civilians."

Hughes gave him a quick scowl as if to say "will you teach my granny how to suck eggs?", but Lewrie had seen him in action once, and was none too sure that Hughes could contain himself from bragging over his brevet promotion, his new command, and how he would sail off to win the war all by himself . . . as he'd boasted that day at Pescadore's.

"One thirty, then, sirs," Hughes agreed, putting away his watch. "I will meet you here at the appointed time. Good day!"

Hughes sailed back into his anteroom office to fetch his hat, a black beaver fore-and-aft bicorne with heavy gilt tassels to either end, adorned with swept-back egret feathers, and so arced that the tips fell almost level with his nose and his shoulder blades.

"Impressive," Mountjoy said after he had departed.

"What, the man, or the hat?" Lewrie joshed.

"Well . . ." Mountjoy replied, puzzled.

"I'd not be one t'look a gift horse in the mouth, Mountjoy, but I've seen him before," Lewrie explained as they made their own way out of the headquarters building to the street, and their own dinner. "Here on

Gibraltar, the other day," he went on, describing his meal at the seafood house, and Hughes's demeanour with his girl.

"Was she fetching, sir?" Mountjoy asked, looking a tad askance.

"Aye, she definitely was," Lewrie confessed.

"Perhaps her being with him has prejudiced you against him," Mountjoy suggested. "A bit of jealousy, what?"

"I'll allow that that plays a part, but only a wee'un," Lewrie shrugged off. "Remember the old adage, 'great talkers do the least, we see'? He's a *grand* talker, is Brevet-Major Hughes. Why, I wonder, is he seconded to staff work, and not with his regiment?"

"Surplus to requirements?" Mountjoy pondered.

"Tosh!" Lewrie dismissed. "He bought himself a commission for life in the 53rd, and once in, an officer is *always* a member of that regiment 'til he's too old t'serve and he sells his rank out to the highest bidder, gets crippled or dies, or gets cashiered for conduct un-becoming, or plain stupidity. Most-like, after a few years, the others in his mess couldn't *stand* the bastard, and when Dalrymple was castin' about for an aide-de-camp, they saw their chance t'be shot of him!"

"Or, he makes General," Mountjoy pointed out. "Maybe Captain . . . Major Hughes, rather . . . has better connexions than most, and his posting is a way to give him a leg up to a substantive Majority, not a brevet rank. From his uniform and his kit, I'd imagine that he's a fellow from a wealthy family, eager for his advancement. Money, and 'interest', go hand in hand, after all."

"Perhaps," Lewrie grudgingly allowed.

"I hope you do not hold anything against him, sir," Mountjoy said in a soft voice. "Getting him, and those troops, has been as hard as pulling Sir Hew's teeth . . . if he had many left. Now we're on the cusp, I would hate for any grudges to hamper us."

*Damme, he's all but givin' me* orders*!* Lewrie thought in shock. Mountjoy had been his clueless, landlubberly, ink-stained *clerk* back in the long-ago, a *lad* more than ten years his *junior,* and it cut rough to be chided, even in the mildest way! He was a bloody civilian, for God's sake!

" 'Yes sir, no sir, two bags full'," Lewrie growled, pretending to tug at his forelock like a tenant or day-labourer. "I promise to be good, Daddy." Which drew a laugh from Mountjoy.

"I wonder where he's dining," Mountjoy said. "It is tempting to see if his girl is all that fetching."

"At Pescadore's, and she is," Lewrie told him, providing him a brief description.

"Damned good establishment," Mountjoy commented once he was done. "It might be fun to simply pop in and . . . ?"

"Temptin', aye," Lewrie said, "but . . . no. We'd best not. If Hughes thinks we're spyin' on him, it'd just ruffle his feathers."

"Well, he has some impressive feathers," Mountjoy japed.

*And an impressive woman*, Lewrie thought, half-wishing that they *could* just happen to amble in so he could get a longer, closer look at Maddalena. *Dammit, I* may *be jealous of him!*

# CHAPTER TWENTY-SEVEN

Over the next few days, Lewrie began to suspect that he had misjudged Major Hughes. He and Mountjoy had Hughes up to Mountjoy's lodgings so they could lay out the agents' reports and sketches in greater privacy than they could in a borrowed office in the Convent, and they were amazed how Hughes grasped the possibilities so quickly, and raved over the prospects. They took him out to *Harmony* to tour the troop accommodations, and Hughes was a fount of good suggestions for improvements and tweaks to make the men—his men, now—more comfortable.

On his own, Major Hughes had arranged shore billets for the men of the 77th and their officers, had arranged provisions and cooking facilities for them, and had worked them into the rotation to use the parade ground for close-order drill, and at least a weekly use of the firing range, with ammunition to boot. In all, Hughes was a paragon when it came to working out the niggling details, and carried on in a brash, burly, charge-ahead manner. He also got Lieutenant Keane and Lieutenant Roe and their Marines ashore to participate. The loudest voice on the parade ground was his as he put them through the usual "square-bashing" and mock battle manouevres, with all three companies abreast to make rushes by company, with the others covering them, and even thought to rehearse mock retreats to the "beach" once the raids would be over, either opposed by Spanish forces, or getting off without a shot being fired at them. Major Hughes was most enthusiastic. Unfortunately, that enthusiasm did not extend to the 77th's officers.

Lewrie and Mountjoy discovered that lack of enthusiasm at their first meeting, a dinner served in *Sapphire*'s great-cabins, followed by a presentation of the overall scheme, complete with large hand-drawn plans pinned to the bulkheads. Even though Lewrie had ordered his cabins scoured with vinegar, smoked with faggots of tobacco, and citronella pots set out, they all looked as if the usual stink of a warship might gag them, to start with.

The 77th Regiment of Foot was not an old or distinguished unit, and had only been raised in 1793, at the start of the War of The First Coalition, and had only taken part in one overseas expedition, and that had been the disastrous Dutch Campaign of 1798, where the British Army had been driven back to their transports by the highly-experienced French and Dutch, looking hapless, and as dangerous as so many sheep. There had been a rumour, Mountjoy learned on the sly, that the 77th would be going to the West Indies, aptly known as the "Fever Islands", where untold thousands of British soldiers had sickened and died in the annual ravages of Malaria, Yellow Jack, Cholera, or Dysentery since the first wars over their possession.

Hence, the prices for officers' commissions had plummeted like stunned seagulls and a great many of the original regimental officers' mess had sold out to seek commissions in other units, resulting in an host of new, in-experienced young men.

Captain Kimbrough, for instance, was only nineteen, and Captain Bowden was eighteen. Lieutenant Staggs was seventeen, and his counterpart in the second company was only sixteen, so young and new to their uniforms and accoutrements that their leather still squeaked! The Ensigns, Litchfield and Gilliam, who had not been invited to the first introduction meeting, were even younger!

"Now, once the transport fetches-to into the wind, or comes to anchor off the beach," Lewrie lectured, pointing to one large sheet of paper pinned to the bulkhead, "my Navy tars will haul the boats alongside, drop the scrambling nets over the side, and man the boats, here, here, and here, right under the chain platforms of *Harmony*'s shrouds to either beam. Your men will form up at the shrouds in six groups."

"Platoons," Major Hughes contributed.

"Right, platoons," Lewrie amended. "At the order to man boats, you'll see your men down into the boats, and they'll cast off and row shoreward, forming line-abreast so all six boats, along with the four from *Sapphire* which carry my Marines, arrive on the beach, or quay, or solid ground, pretty-much as one."

"We're expected to *row,* sir?" Lt. Pullen asked, sounding as if that much exertion was beneath him. He looked appalled.

"The *sailors* do the rowing, Leftenant Pullen," Hughes snapped. "Don't be an arse."

"You and your men sit on the thwarts in-board of the oarsmen," Lewrie told Pullen. "Soon, as the boats ground, the sailors'll boat their oars, and some will jump out into the surf to make sure that the boat is secure. You'll note in *this* sketch that the dockyard built them all with a square-ish bow platform. You'll leave your boats by the bow, run up to the edge of the beach . . . by platoons . . ." Lewrie said with a nod to Hughes, "and then set off towards your objective. My men will remain on the beach to guard the boats 'til you return."

"If I may, sir?" Hughes interrupted. "Your men will carry the minimum of accoutrements, musket-bayonet-hanger-haversack, with spare flints and fourty cartridges-brass priming horn-cartridge box containing fourty rounds-water bottle-firelock rag to keep out the wet, and snot rag for blowing your noses, got that? Packs and blankets will not be required, as we will only be ashore for a few hours, nor will rations beyond a bit of cheese, bisquit, or a wee sausage. It will be like a boy's first romp with a wench . . . in quick, and out quick."

Pullen and Staggs tittered and blushed.

"Hopefully, *someone* is satisfied," Marine Lieutenant Keane japed. He and his fellow officer, Lt. Roe, seemed *ages* older than the 77th's officers, who seemed total innocents in comparison.

"We're going to practice all this, starting tomorrow, weather and surf depending," Lewrie told them all. "Right after breakfast, the boats will be alongside the quay to ferry you and your troops to the transport. You'll go aboard, get assigned quarters, make up your beds, and stow away your equipment, then spend the night aboard, to get accustomed. Weather allowing, the next morning will see us out at sea, down by Europa Point or the old Chapel, or on the Eastern side in one of the bays, far from prying enemy eyes."

"And we'll keep at it 'til we can board the boats, land ashore, deploy, then return to the ship as quickly and as efficiently as is possible," Major Hughes sternly said, putting them on notice. "Speed is of the essence. Success depends upon giving the enemy as little warning as possible. A question, Captain Kimbrough?" he asked to an up-raised hand.

Kimbrough crossed his arms over his chest before speaking. "It seems to me, sir, that this ship, and the transport, can be seen a long way off, so . . . isn't getting to within a mile or so of the shore more than ample warning of our coming, and our intentions?"

"If done in broad daylight, aye, Captain Kimbrough," Lewrie told him. "We intend to close the coast in the wee hours of the night, and begin the landings before dawn . . . at first sparrow fart."

"In the *dark?*" Kimbrough gasped.

"Can't be done!" Captain Bowden said, blanching. "It'd be an hopeless muddle in the dark. The men aren't trained . . . !"

"The Navy does it all the time, let me remind you, sirs," Major Hughes gruffly countered. "Right, Captain Lewrie?"

"We do, sir," Lewrie replied. "As for fighting at night, operating in the dark, recall Lord Cornwallis's loss of his blockhouses which sealed his fate at Yorktown, taken by the Yankee Doodles in the dark. General Bonaparte took the last forts and batteries on the peninsula in a rainy night assault, which forced us to abandon Toulon. I was there to see that'un. I took a French frigate in the South Atlantic in a stormy night with half a gale blowing. Well, there was a lot of lightning," he admitted. "It *can* be done."

"But the men aren't used to . . . !" Bowden insisted.

"We'll *get* them used to it," Hughes barked, cutting him off. "That's what the rehearsals are for. God above, you sound as if you *and* your troops think that Raw Head and Bloody Bones are lurking in the night, eager to suck your souls! The men will learn their roles, and get good at them, if *you* gentlemen explain it to them with enthusiasm, and *lead* with enthusiasm. Your confidence in them, and in the method by which we strike the enemy, will make *them* confident."

That shut the young officers up, though it didn't make them appear any more eager. All slumped in their chairs, arms crossed over their chests, looking abashed and sullen, sharing queasy looks among them. Lewrie wasn't sure that that very sound advice did them much good.

The task of leading put upon them was what officers *did,* what their families had paid for them to be—leaders of men! Perhaps it was the way that Hughes had imparted his sageness was the problem; too harsh and demeaning.

"Damned slender reeds, sir . . . damned slender," Major Hughes sourly commented after the junior officers had been dismissed and sent ashore. Hughes had lingered over a last glass of wine before taking his own departure. "Christ, what a clueless pack of tom-noddies the Army is awarding commissions to these days!"

"Well, any damned fool with money can buy his way in," Lewrie said. "One'd think, though, that they knew what their chosen careers would ask of 'em. 'If ye can't take a joke, ye shouldn't o' joined'!"

"Hah!" Hughes barked with wry humour, slapping his knee. "I have seen this over the years, Captain Lewrie. Until recently, the British Army hasn't left their home barracks except for a brief annual week of road marches, encampments, and field exercises, and it's all a lark of champagne, claret cups, horse racing for young officers, and high spirits in their messes each night. Mirth, glee, songs, music, the mess silver, and comfortable beds."

"Sounds grand," Lewrie replied, "and damn my father for shovin' me into the Fleet!"

"It's much the same the rest of the year, with long spells of leave for shooting, fishing, or chasing young ladies," Hughes groused, "and once the drill for the day, the inspections once a week, is done, most young officers stroll back to the mess for drinks, leaving their men to the sergeants, and only know their troops by names in a muster book, and without their books, they wouldn't have a clue who they are. They do not *lead*, they simply *pose* in the proper *place*, by God!"

"Can't do that in the Navy," Lewrie told him, "livin' cheek by jowl with 'em for months on end, and knowin' 'em by the odour of their farts."

"*This* lot, Lord," Hughes bemoaned, more than happy for Pettus to top up his glass. "Oh, I can understand that this wasn't what they expected. They thought they'd be in the chummy comfort of the mess, with the bands playing, the colours flying, the bugle calls, and the excitement of battle on a field of honour . . . not rolling about in a ship, getting wet from the knees down, separated for who knows how long from their regiment, and asked to do the total unknown things.

"Home, hearth, and family is the regiment," Hughes mused with a note of fondness in his voice. "Recruited from the same county they grew up in, for the most part, many of the rankers childhood friends. A grand system is the way we build our Army, *quite* unlike the French *levee en masse,* which rounds up unwilling conscripts and shoves hordes of strangers together."

Lewrie would have mentioned that the Royal Navy *pressed* hordes of strangers together, but didn't think it was a good idea, even if it resulted in tightly-bound ships' companies in the end.

"I expect you will lead our young fellows to the *water,* as it were, *and* make them drink, whether they like it or not," Lewrie said in jest.

"Damned right I shall, sir!" Hughes exclaimed. "By the time I am done, they'll know their stuff and swear that they *volunteered* for the privilege!"

"I have no doubt you will, sir," Lewrie stated.

"What we're to do, you know, Captain Lewrie," Hughes said after a swig of wine, "is revolutionary, a method of attack never before attempted. Why, with a few more transports and some escorting warships, I can easily envision the landing of a whole battalion of specially-trained troops at once, overwhelming any objective, defended or not. What was it you called it in your proposal which you sent to Sir Hew . . . an *amphibious* operation? God, a fully-established Amphibious Regiment on Army List, perhaps someday an entire Amphibious Brigade! And the officers in at the beginning leading and training the additional troops to glory, honour, and promotion, hah!"

"Well, only if we make a success of it, mind," Lewrie told him.

"We shall, we shall, by God!" Hughes boasted.

*And you'll be Colonel of the regiment, or be made Brigadier, or be knighted for it?* Lewrie thought; *Damn, but he dreams ambitious!*

"Well, sir, I must take my leave," Hughes said after tossing back the last of his wine, and rising. "It's Mess Night at the headquarters, and we've a fresh bullock from Tetuán. Moroccan cattle don't make the *best* roast beef, but they'll do in a pinch, hah hah!"

"See you aboard the transport in the morning, then," Lewrie said, "though I would've thought that your last night ashore for some time would be better spent with your mysterious dining companion."

"Time enough for her, *after* a good supper," Hughes said with a wink as he clapped on his grandly feathered bicorne.

"I'll see you to the entry-port, sir," Lewrie offered, thinking that if he were in Hughes's shoes, he'd have given the roast beef supper a *wide* miss.

# CHAPTER TWENTY-EIGHT

"Mine arse on a *band-box*, the . . . !" followed a moment later by "the cretinous, cack-handed, cunny-thumbed bloody . . . *lubbers!*"

Lewrie's oldest and worst cocked hat was flung to the deck for the third time, and it wasn't even eleven in the morning, yet, but the latest attempt to dis-embark the soldiers of the 77th from *Harmony* to the boats was no better than the first three over the last five days, and Lewrie was sure that it was disappointing enough to make the Archbishop of Canterbury start kicking children!

"It might look better in the dark, sir," Lt. Westcott quipped.

"If we ever get that far, we'll drown the whole crippled lot, and start fresh!" Lewrie roared. "These people couldn't climb down off a bloody *foot-stool!*"

*It ain't even that rough a morning,* Lewrie bemoaned, watching the Redcoats swaying and clinging for dear life to the scrambling nets, and the easy pitch of the waiting boats alongside the transport. The sea was mild-enough, though there was moderate, foaming surf at the foot of the Rock, sweeping in to wet every inch of the narrow beach, and spew round the rocks. What he had estimated to only take ten to fifteen minutes had turned out to be closer to half an hour just to get them all aboard and settled, much yet to get the boats ashore.

Off *Sapphire*'s bows, his own four boats were already filled with his Marines, loafing in a rough line-abreast about a cable off, waiting for the Army to sort themselves out.

"My thanks, again, Mister Westcott," Lewrie said to his First Officer in a brief, calm moment. "The boat, ye know. How and where ye got it . . ."

"Best not enquire, sir," Westcott said, with a taut grin. "The less you know, the better."

The smallest of their boats, the 18-footer jolly boat, had disappeared, miraculously replaced one dark night by a spanking-new 25-foot cutter to match the one they had, and when the sun rose, there it was, painted white with sapphire-blue gunn'ls just like their others. Admittedly, the paint had still been *wet*, but . . . ! The jolly boat had been too small to be useful except for carrying a very few passengers ashore and back, or rowing the Bosun round right after anchoring to see that the yards were level and squared with each other. He was the only one who missed it.

"*Harmony*'s starboard-side boats are shoving off, sir," Lieutenant Harcourt pointed out. "They're clearing the ship, just afore her bows."

"Twenty-five bloody minutes, Christ!" Lewrie spat.

"Faster than before, sir," Westcott said. "That'd be Captain Kimbrough's, I believe."

Young Captain Bowden's company was only halfway loaded into the boats on the transport's larboard side. Lewrie put his telescope to one eye and could make out Bowden by *Harmony*'s mainmast stays, mouth open in rage, disgust, or impatience; at that distance it was hard to tell. Major Hughes was aft by the mizen stays, arms wind-milling in the air to urge the last few soldiers to go down the nets. He looked red in the face as the last man went over the bulwarks at last, then wind-milled his way forward to bellow at Captain Bowden.

"One boat's coming off, sir," Harcourt reported.

"Coming?" Lewrie yelped. "So is bloody *Christmas!*"

At very long last, all the boats were full and stroking shoreward in line-abreast. At least *Sapphire*'s sailors were professionals at rowing and conning the boats. They all grounded on what passed for a beach roughly about the same time, and their passengers scrambled out over the bows much more quickly, as if glad to find even a patch of solid ground on which to stand, relieved and delighted to escape boats and ships for even a few minutes.

They looked comical, even to Lewrie's frustrated eyes, huddled almost shoulder-to-shoulder at the foot of the nigh-vertical, barren cliffs, wetted to their shins as the surf rolled in, with some soldiers balancing themselves on the boulders and scree rocks that had accumulated at the cliff's base over the centuries.

"Mister Harcourt, the six-pounder, if you please," Lewrie said. "Signal the return. Then pray . . . earnestly."

After the crack of the gun, and the sight of the small cloud of sour smoke from its discharge, the soldiers filed up to claw their way back aboard the boats and take their seats on the inner parts of the thwarts, muskets jutting upwards and held between their knees. One by one, the boats were shoved off the beach, the oarsmen stroking to back-water out far enough for one bank of oars to back-water, the other to stroke forward and turn them round bows-out toward the waiting ships, right in the middle of the surf. All the boats pitched and rolled, cocking their bows or sterns high as incoming waves set them to hobby-horsing, but, after a few minutes, all were clear and on their way out, with the unbroken rollers lifting them a few feet, then dropping them between sets.

"Is the weather getting up?" Lt. Westcott speculated aloud, looking up to the commissioning pendant, the clouds, and the steepness of the wave sets.

"The surf *is* breaking a tad more boisterous, sir," Lt. Harcourt agreed.

"You can feel it," Lewrie said, leaning over the bulwarks for a look at the sea ruffling round the hull. "If we get those clumsy bastards back aboard, we'll call it a day, then stand out to sea."

"Aye, sir," Westcott replied.

Lewrie paced the quarterdeck, now and then ascending to the poop deck for a better view with his telescope, willing himself to be calm, stoic, and un-moved, but that was a hard task. The boats came alongside *Harmony* in their proper places, bowmen hooked the channels with their gaffs, one bank of oarsmen took hold of the scrambling nets to keep the boats close alongside and keep the nets somewhat taut as soldiers tentatively made their way up the transport's side to heave a leg over the bulwarks and partly roll back aboard.

"Time, Mister Elmes?" Lewrie asked from the poop deck.

"Twenty-one and one half minutes for the soldiers to get back aboard, sir," the Third Officer told him. "A bit quicker."

"That's 'cause they know the rum issue's coming as soon as they do," Lewrie scoffed.

"Perhaps we should set a rum keg on the beach next time, then, sir," Elmes joshed. "And the first boat ashore gets full measures."

"Then they'd get so drunk we'd never get them back!" Lewrie said, relieved enough to banter once again.

His own Marines had come back aboard *Sapphire* much more quickly, the boats had been tented with taut tarpaulin covers to keep out rain and sloshed-aboard seawater in rough weather, and were already being led aft for towing astern once the ship got back under way. Muskets and accoutrements were stowed away, and the Marines had removed their red coats, neck-stocks and waist-coats, only worn when standing sentry or when called to Quarters for battle.

The Sailing Master and the Midshipmen under his instruction had gathered to take Noon Sights with their sextants and slates, though it was a pointless endeavour for *Sapphire*'s officers, for once, since the ship was still fetched-to about a thousand yards offshore. Lewrie had been so intent upon watching the soldiers' return that he had missed Eight Bells ringing the change of watch.

"All hands back aboard, sir, arms and boats secured, and ready to get under way," Westcott, who was now the officer of the watch, reported. "Rum first, sir?"

"No, I want sea-room first," Lewrie decided as he slowly came back down to the quarterdeck. "Just in case."

Hundreds of sailors and Marines stood about the deck in the waist, along the gangways, joshing each other, pleased with their own exertions, and jeering at the poor showing of the men of the 77th, looking aft for word of their own rum issue.

"Bosun!" Westcott shouted, "hands to the foresheets and braces! Stations for getting under way!"

There was a collective groan at the delay, but on-watch hands sprang to their duties, and within minutes, *Sapphire* had come about, and under reduced sail, slowly clawed her way a mile or better out to sea, with *Harmony* trailing her.

"I'll be aft, Mister Westcott," Lewrie finally announced. "I think a good, long sulk is in order. I may even curse the cat!"

Once in his cabins, Lewrie shucked his coat and undid his neck-stock for comfort, pummelled his battered hat into a semblance of its former shape, and flung himself onto his settee. Chalky came dashing with his tail erect and mewing as he leapt into Lewrie's lap for some long-delayed pets, butting and stroking his cheeks on him.

"Tea, sir?" Pettus asked.

"Aye," Lewrie agreed, still a bit glum.

The muted music from the ship's fiddler and a fifer came to him, playing "Molly Dawson" at a lively beat, and there was a cheer raised as the red-painted and gilt rum keg got fetched up from below.

"Think they'll get better at it, sir?" Pettus asked as he came back with a tall tumbler of cool tea, lemoned and sugared to Lewrie's likes.

"They'd better, or I'm wastin' everybody's bloody time."

The weather did get up for the next two days' running, forcing both ships to keep well out in deeper, open waters, with lots of rain and stiff quarter-gales keening in the rigging. The cancellation of training gave Lewrie enough time to sift through every detail of his plans for teaching lubberly soldiers.

Loath as he was to admit it, he had put the cart before the horse, expecting too much too quickly. "River discipline!" he had blurted out over supper alone in his cabins, feeling much like Archimedes shouting "Eureka!" in his bath water.

Fresh-caught landsmen rounded up by the Press, new-come volunteers, were never expected to be slung aboard a warship and forced to man the guns, tend to the braces, sheets, and halliards, scale the ratlines, take on the perilous passage by the futtock shrouds to the tops, and lay out on the yards, right off. It took weeks safely anchored in port to introduce them to the rudiments before any captain would dare set sail, not just trusting to luck to make a safe passage.

Once the weather cleared, Lewrie ordered both ships back to Gibraltar, and came to anchor near the New Mole. The soldiers were sent ashore to their temporary barracks for a day and a night, fresh rations were fetched aboard *Sapphire* and *Harmony*, and both crews were allowed shore liberties before getting back to business.

Then, in the calm waters of Gibraltar Bay, the landing boats were led round to their stations, and the soldiers were ordered over the side, without muskets to impede them at first. Into the boats and sit for a while, then out of the boats and back on deck. A break for water, and they were ordered to do it all over again, several times in the first day, to the point that *Harmony*'s decks could be cleared in a quick ten minutes.

The next day the drills were done with muskets and all accoutrements, all day long less intervals for water, rum, mid-day meals, and the soldiers were only released from practice late in the afternoon, just before the second rum issue. With a steady, unmoving deck and boats that did not pitch and heave about, the soldiers' time got even better.

On the third day, the boats were manned, the nets deployed, and the soldiers scrambled down to their places, but this time, the boats rowed off to form line-abreast and stroked in to within close pistol-shot of the quays to glide in so the soldiers could exit over the bow platforms, form by platoons on the town's dockside street, then get back into the boats and return to the transport to scramble back aboard to do it all over again. Those evolutions raised a great deal of mirth and curiosity in the town, and a lot of good-natured joshing from the town Provosts, dock workers, and off-duty soldiers of the garrison, and some sharp-eyed, calculating looks from civilian men.

*Spies, agents, and informers be-damned,* Lewrie thought, shaking his head over the necessity, sure that there were several powerful telescopes on the other side of the bay at Algeciras the like of Thomas Mountjoy's, watching their every move and wondering what it was about.

There might be dozens of Spanish greengrocers and fruiterers on their way back across The Lines emulating the American rebel, Paul Revere, shouting, "The British are coming!" he imagined, and a grain merchant or three crying, "Two if by sea!"

Then, for the next two days, all sailors and soldiers were left to idle, only forming up and entering the boats after the nights had fully fallen, with all glims and lanthorns extinguished. That wasn't to prevent the Spanish seeing them practise, but to get the soldiers used to the drill as if in a moonless, overcast black night at sea.

By then, the men of the 77th could perform the evolutions just as efficiently and quickly as *Sapphire*'s Marines could, and Lewrie was at last a lot more sanguine of their chances.

It was time to see Mountjoy for a mission.

⚓

"Puerto Banús looks promising," Mountjoy decided after sifting through his latest reports and agents' sketches. "Look here, there's a battery to the left of the harbour entrance, about twenty feet higher than the town itself, on a little pimple of a rise. It's an open redan, a stone semi-circle mounting only three eighteen-pounders, or the Spanish equivalent, in weight of metal."

"That'd be about fifty gunners and officers, in all," Lewrie estimated. "I can keep them occupied with gunfire."

"About what my informer observed, yes," Mountjoy agreed. They were out on his rooftop gallery, screened by the canvas awning, and enjoying a decent breeze that cut the day's heat, bent over the iron table before the settee. "Now, there's a good, broad beach over here to the right of the harbour. Some scattered houses, as you can see, and the report is that small boats are drawn up on the shingle behind it for the night, in the outer part of the harbour. Groves of trees to the right of that, then three windmills to grind grain, and a granary further inland by about an hundred yards. Behind that is the town proper, and the houses are close together. I'm not sure if we should go much beyond the granary."

"Street fightin', in the dark, with a surprise round every corner, in every window? Aye, we'll burn the granary and the mills, and call it a good day's work. Though I'd *like* t'spike those guns," Lewrie said. "Has your informer gotten a good look at the battery?"

"Not too close, no," Mountjoy said, with a shrug. "But he did see a doorway on the backside of the rise where their powder magazine must be, sunk underneath the battery. His sketch shows a long wooden barracks a little way behind the rise, and an old stone fisherman's house off to the right of that and a little more inland, where the officers lodge, is my guess."

"Damme, I could put my Marines to that, arm the men who handle the boats to aid them, and take the place," Lewrie schemed. "There is a good beach in front of the battery, isn't there? Damme! Once we surprise the Dons and drive 'em off, loose gunpowder scattered on the guns' carriages'd set 'em alight and burn 'em up. Hell, we lay a powder train to the magazine, and it'd blow the whole thing sky-high!"

"Hmm," Mountjoy considered, frowning. "Far be it from me to tell you how to spread the requisite mayhem, but . . . might that be a tad too enterprising, right off? If they keep a good watch, and there is any sort of moonlight, they'd be ready for you."

"The most important objective is the battery," Lewrie countered. "If it's taken and destroyed, the Spanish will have to waste effort and money replacin' it . . . drawin' troops for a larger garrison, military engineers, and new artillery pieces. Stone workers to lay a stronger, bigger emplacement, hey? No, the battery's the main course, and the mills and granary are the *lagniappe,* as they said in Louisiana . . . the 'little something extra'. We land everyone against the battery, and deal with the rest after, with any opposition already eliminated."

"Well, we did promise Sir Hew we'd whittle down any possible re-enforcements sent to General Castaños," Mountjoy said with a sigh, leaning back into the settee's cushions. "I'll put Deacon to copying the sketches so all officers involved can have them. How soon might you need them?"

"No tearing hurry," Lewrie said. "I've let the soldiers ashore to their barracks for a day or two as a reward, and my own people are due shore liberty, by watches. Say, two days from now? We'll get the officers together for a briefing before we set off. And, I'm in need of fresh laundry. Ehm, you wouldn't have a second objective in mind fairly close to Puerto Banús, would you?"

"Not right offhand, no," Mountjoy promised. "I think just the one raid will suffice, for now. Babies must crawl before they learn to walk, after all. Let's get the rough edges smoothed down before we hit our stride."

"Meaning, 'Lewrie, don't make a muck of it', hey?" Lewrie asked, with a wry expression.

Mountjoy made no reply, but raised a brow and nodded.

*That's what comes of bein' thought an idiot,* Lewrie sullenly told himself as he strolled downhill from Mountjoy's lodgings to the quays; *The up-and-comin' younkers like Mountjoy think they know better than older farts like me. Get a few years on me, and they marvel if I can eat with a knife and fork! Can't even* imagine *what the puppies of the 77th make o' me. Hallo?*

He spotted Major Hughes a'stroll along the quays with a woman on his arm, his free hand gesticulating at the harbour, and, from the way his egret-plumed bicorne dipped like a hobby-horse, was happily and boisterously engaged in conversation with her, which conversation seemed to be one-sided, for the woman's hat and head did not follow his pointing.

Lewrie could only see the couple from behind, but he fancied that she was the intriguing Maddalena. Her dark hair was worn simply in a long fall at the nape of her neck, not teased, roached, or ironed into an intricate updo like most women with pretensions to style wore it, and in comparison to the usual flounces and flummery, her gown was simple, a pale yellow, high-waisted affair trimmed in white. Her up-turned sun bonnet partially masked her head to protect her complexion, tied with a yellow ribbon under her chin.

*Hmm, slimmer than I thought,* Lewrie appraised as he neared them, noting that her gown was more a sheath than a loose, bell-shaped thing, a modest muslin or linen instead of richer fabrics.

". . . and since our families are closely connected, Sir Hew was most accepting of my ideas, don't ye know, m'dear," Major Hughes boasted. "Now that I've gotten my men trained, it only awaits the go-ahead from him."

*What? Christ on a crutch!* Lewrie fumed inside; *Takin' credit for it, are you? And boastin' that loud where ye shouldn't?*

He'd gotten close enough to overhear that, along with half the dockworkers on Gibraltar, and overtook the pair as they drew to a stop to admire the transport with its waiting landing boats nuzzled alongside.

"Why, Major Hughes, is that you?" Lewrie cheerfully called out, pretending pleasant surprise. "A good mornin' to ye, sir."

"Oh, ah!" Hughes replied, turning to regard him with real surprise, his complexion flushing redder. "Ashore for the morning, are you, sir? Well met, Captain Lewrie, well met."

"And to you, sir," Lewrie said, doffing his hat.

"I was just telling Maddalena here about the training we have been doing," Hughes went on. "My pardons. Captain Lewrie, allow me to name to you Mistress Maddalena Covilhã. Maddalena, I name to you Captain Sir Alan Lewrie, Baronet, of the Royal Navy, and the Captain of the *Sapphire*, out yonder."

"Mistress Covilhã, a pleasure to make your acquaintance," he said, sweeping his hat onto his chest and making a wee "leg".

"Captain Lewrie, the delight is mine," she replied, dropping him a slow curtsy, though keeping her brown eyes on his face, in which there was, alongside a pleased curl of her lips, a glint of amusement.

"Covilhã," Lewrie said, trying on the name, "is that Spanish, Italian, or Portuguese, if I may enquire?"

"I am Portuguese, sir, from Oporto," she said with a smile and some greater animation, "though my family long ago lived in a town of our same name."

"Oporto!" Lewrie exclaimed with an easy laugh. "My father was there for several years . . . hidin' from his creditors. Never been to that city, but he said it was most pleasant. And, he adored all the wines, of course."

"But, how can a gentleman of the English aristocracy be so poor that he must seek shelter from debt, Captain?" Maddalena wondered, with a shake of her head.

"He was a Knight of The Garter, but our family was bankrupt, and never noble. He won his knighthood, as I did mine, As for bein' a Baronet, let's just say that King George the Third was havin' a bad day when he dubbed me a knight."

Maddalena pretended shock that Lewrie would speak so casually of a monarch, much less his own, though she had to stifle an outright peal of laughter.

"Really, sir!" Major Hughes chid him, appalled.

"Really, he did, sir," Lewrie gladly rejoined. "There was a long line of us t'be honoured, two or three ahead of me were dubbed Knight and Baronet, and I expect it stuck in his head, so when it came my turn, there it was. I thought it wouldn't count, but the palace flunkies told me that the Crown don't *err*," he related, drawing out "err" into a long growl that sounded more like "Grr", which set the girl tittering, and Hughes going redder in the face.

He was trying hellish-hard to please, and going for charming, witty, and amusing, and was delighted to see that his effort was working. Mistress Covilhã was giving him the same sort of speculative regard she'd shown him when he'd dined near her and Hughes at Pescadore's, a frank consideration that he might be more fun than her present companion.

"Well, we were just about to dine, Captain Lewrie, so I'm sure you will excuse us," Major Hughes said, looking a trifle irked.

"But of course, sir," Lewrie allowed.

"Perhaps Captain Lewrie might care to join us," Maddalena suggested quickly.

"Wouldn't care t'intrude," Lewrie pretended to beg off.

"Oh, but he must, Major Hughes!" Maddalena eagerly insisted, going kittenish and coy. "You are the . . . brothers in arms?"

*Major?* Lewrie scoffed to himself; *Is she in his regiment? Why not "my dear" or "darling", or* "woolly bear"*? She don't sound all that affectionate with him.*

"We work in close co-operation, yes, m'dear, Captain Lewrie to the sea-side, and me on the land, but . . ." Hughes tossed off as if it was the sketchiest of associations.

"Then between the two of you, you can tell me all about it," Maddalena sweetly said,

"Well, if you'd care to, sir," Hughes grudgingly allowed, looking as pleased with the idea as a Hindoo served a slab of roast beef.

"Well, I must confess t'feelin' peckish," Lewrie said with a shrug, as if it did not matter a whit, "but, do allow me to play host. My treat? Where did you plan to go?"

"Thought we'd dine at Pescadore's," Hughes gruffly said.

Maddalena made a face, hidden from Hughes by the side of her bonnet, and allowed her to share a wry smile with Lewrie.

"An excellent choice," Lewrie congratulated. "Let us go."

Later that afternoon, at his total ease in his cabins aboard *Sapphire,* and slowly nursing a cool glass of *sangria,* the discovery of which delighted both him and his cook, Yeovill, Lewrie reviewed their mid-day dinner with a great deal of satisfaction.

When the waiter, Michael/Miguel, had asked for their beverage choice, Lewrie had ordered a pitcher of *sangria,* claiming curiosity, and Maddalena had seconded him, leaving Hughes to his pale ale, siding with the girl to win a bit more favour, and thank God that it had proved sweetly enjoyable. For his entree, Lewrie had gone for the fried fish and cracked-open lobster, as did Maddalena as if taking her cue from him, leaving Hughes to his roast beef and potatoes.

He'd given Maddalena a culinary tour, from Canton in China to Indian fare at Calcutta, regaling them with the spiciness of the West Indies, the game meats of Cape Town, the glories of Low Country fare in the Carolinas in the United States, even the moose, elk, and cod of Halifax. Hughes, it seemed, had not travelled all that far, and could only speak glowingly of salmon, grouse, and pheasant when shooting or fishing in Scotland.

Despite a strong urge to do so, Lewrie had not boasted of his naval career, or his battles, hopefully leaving the *impression* that he'd done a *slew* of things heroic, mentioning only the battle off the Chandeleur Islands of Louisiana which had won him his knighthood in 1803. The faint scar on his cheek? A youthful idiocy when he was a Midshipman, in a pointless duel on Antigua, and he hadn't even won the girl in the end!

She had asked if he was married, or had children, and he had told her of Sewallis and Hugh, now both at sea in the Navy, and his daughter, Charlotte, back home at Anglesgreen (the less said about that sullen, spiteful wench the better!) and that his wife had died five years before, leaving the details to her imagination; leaving Maddalena with the notion that "poor, widowed Alan Lewrie" was lonely and alone, and possibly available. He told her of his cat, Chalky, who was good company at sea, and the ship's silly dog, Bisquit, and how he'd been acquired, pretending to laugh off the idea of his loneliness . . . upon that head, at least.

Did Hughes's regiment have a mascot animal, like the "Regimental Ram" of the Light Dragoons he'd escorted to Cape Town? The coat of arms and badge of the 53rd featured a gryphon, but, being mythical, were rather thin on the ground, unfortunately.

All in all, it had been a fine dinner, for Lewrie, at least. And, when Maddalena had glided off to the "necessary" leaving Hughes and himself alone, he had had the wee joy of cautioning Hughes to be careful where, and with whom, he revealed any details of what they were training for.

"Sir Hew's a bee in his bonnet about spies on every street corner already, and I dare say he may be right, with all the foreigners on Gibraltar," Lewrie had hinted, "and keepin' Mister Mountjoy up nights lookin' for 'em, when he ain't rootin' round for what he calls *agents provocateurs*. I'm sure ye can be somewhat open with Mistress Covilhã, but only in private, hey? 'Under the rose', and all that?"

Hughes had grumpily assured him that "the silly baggage" was not a spy, had no maidservant to pick up on careless statements, and did for herself, and in the end had more sense than to blab in the markets. "Women, what?" Hughes had scoffed. "We could most-like include her in the briefings, and she couldn't make heads or tails of it in the end."

*What a perfect, purblind fool is Hughes,* Lewrie thought in smug delight; *The bluff bastard doesn't see her as anything more than a convenient "socket", and doesn't know the first bloody thing about keepin' a woman fond, and it's God's own truth that she doesn't much care for him.*

It was the lot of many women in this life to make the best of their shortened circumstances, were they poor, widowed, and had no husband or kinfolk to support them, and it was the rare woman who could follow any sort of trade. The brothels and alleys were full of them, and the prettiest in domestic service were fair game for the masters and the masters' sons, which usually led to the brothels eventually.

However Maddalena had ended up on Gibraltar, she had had to settle for being a kept woman. Hughes had taken her "under his protection", as the saying went, the lucky shit, paying for her lodgings and up-keep somewhere here in the town, but was so abstemious that he didn't provide her with a cook or a single maid-of-all-work when one would be hired so cheap?

*Now, what can I make o' this?* Lewrie wondered with a sly grin on his face; *Mountjoy'd most-like warn me off t'make sure that Hughes stays agreeable, but . . . hmm!*

# CHAPTER TWENTY-NINE

"By the deep, five!" a leadsman in the forechains shouted aft. "Five fathom t'this line!"

"Close enough, I think, Mister Yelland?" Lewrie said to the Sailing Master.

"Aye, sir," Yelland agreed, sounding a tad eager to bring the ship no closer to the shore. But for a wee glim in the compass binnacle, HMS *Sapphire* showed no lights of any kind, and Yelland was deprived of a peek into the chartroom to consult the local chart. With its lanthorn unlit, and with no windows or ports, it would have been moot, anyway. All officers had committed the details of the coast to memory, along with the soundings.

"Mister Westcott, fetch her to," Lewrie ordered. "And if God's just, we should find ourselves about a half-mile off, by sunrise."

One Bell was struck up forward at the forecastle belfry as the ship was put about to cock her up into the wind, with the jibs, staysails, and spanker driving her forward and the squares'ls laid aback to retard forward motion. It was half past four in the morning, usually the time that lookouts were posted aloft instead of standing watch on deck, the time for wash-deck pumps to be rigged and swabs and holystones fetched out to scrub the decks. This pre-dawn morning, though, was time for battle. The cutters, launch, and pinnace were being led to their stations alongside both beams, and the scrambling nets were being heaved over. In the waist, *Sapphire*'s Marines shivered, yawned, and shuffled their feet as they waited to board those boats, wearing full kit, muskets, cartridge pouches, sheathed bayonets, haversacks at their left hips, and full water canteens.

"Show one light to seaward, sir?" Midshipman Kibworth asked.

"Aye," Lewrie agreed, and a small hooded lanthorn was brought up above the bulwarks and its wee door opened. Everyone on the quarterdeck peered outboard, looking for its mate, and after a long minute, there was a tiny amber glow from the transport, *Harmony*, announcing her position, and the fact that she, too, was fetched-to and ready to disembark her troops.

"Hmm, a bit further out to sea than us, sir, and further from the beach. That will make a longer row for her people," Lt. Harcourt commented.

"Captain Hedgepeth has a touchy bottom, it appears," Lt. Elmes quipped. "Afraid of being goosed?"

"The boats are alongside, now, sir, and we're ready to go any time," Marine Lieutenant Keane reported from the bottom of the starboard companionway ladder.

"Very well, Mister Keane, you may begin boarding, and the very best of good fortune go with you," Lewrie allowed.

"Thank you, sir," Keane replied, returning to his men.

There was a noisy bustle and the drum of boots on the deck as the Marines lined up at the entry-ports and the nets, as the sailors who manned the boats went over the side to lay out their oars ready to hand, and take hold of the bottoms of the nets to make the Marines' descent easier.

"Once they're gone, we've enough room to play tennis, or bowls," Midshipman Fywell muttered to Kibworth, and that was true. With over fifty of *Sapphire*'s people seconded to the transport, the boats' crews away to get the Marines ashore then stand guard over the beach, and the Marines themselves, the ship's berthings below were echoingly empty.

Lewrie groped his way to the binnacle cabinet to fetch out one of the night-glasses and returned to the bulwarks to peer shoreward. A telescope for use at night presented an image upside down and backwards in its ocular, which took some getting used to. At full extension, Lewrie could see a few lights. Two were lower in the ocular, and he took those for lanthorns or torches along the stone parapet of the battery. To the left of those, actually to the right of the battery, there was a dim light in the window of a fisherman's cottage, and one square of vertical grid. What was there?

"Bugger the bloody thing," Lewrie muttered, lowering the telescope and relying on his eyes. Behind his back, officers and watchstanders grinned.

The grid, he determined, was a wood-shuttered window with a light inside, leaking round all four corners of the badly fitted shutters. Further up the town there were a few more lights, some half-hearted attempts at street lighting, or lanthorns hung outside some taverns or lodging houses for travellers. The windmills, the granary, and the secondary objectives were indistinct black lumps on dark grey. Puerto Banús was deeply asleep, it seemed, and even the fishermen were still a'bed, else the quays and gravelly harbour shores would be lit up with dozens of glims as nets were removed from the drying racks and stowed, rowing boats hauled back into the water, and the larger offshore boats would be hoisting sails already.

"Our boats are away, sir," Lt. Westcott reported.

"Very well, Mister Westcott," Lewrie replied. "Mister Kibworth? Show two flashes from your lanthorn to *Harmony*."

"Aye aye, sir."

It took another three or four minutes before the transport made a replying signal light, announcing that her boats were also away and laying on their oars, waiting for the three-flash signal to row ashore.

Two Bells were struck; it was 5 A.M.

"We're really going to do it, by God," Lt. Elmes muttered with rising excitement. He could not yet quite make the fellow out, but Lewrie could hear his new Hessian boots, of which Lt. Elmes was especially proud, squeaking as the Third Officer rose and flexed on the balls of his feet.

They had sailed from Gibraltar three days earlier, but once at sea, another bout of squally weather and rough seas had sprung to life, forcing the ships to stand well offshore under reduced sail, with the men of the 77th Foot at the bulwarks to "cast their accounts to Neptune" as they suffered their first exposure to the way that *Harmony* rode the swells. One would have thought that their long voyage from England to Gibraltar had given them *some* sort of "sea legs", but, evidently it had not. They were as sea-sick as so many dogs.

Lewrie had delayed the attack one full day after the weather had moderated to let them recover, fearful of shoving them ashore and into combat, still crop-sick and puking from a ship still reeking of vomit.

*As long as I've been at sea, the smell'd make me shit through my teeth,*

Lewrie thought, recalling how a kindly older sailor had put it when he'd gone aboard the old *Ariadne* the first time in 1780.

"A trader told me that down at Tetuán, the Arabs say that the dawn is when one may distinguish 'twixt a black thread and a white one, sir," Lt. Westcott said in a soft voice by Lewrie's elbow.

"Makes sense, I suppose," Lewrie replied. "Have you tried it, yet?"

"Going half cross-eyed, but nothing yet, sir," Westcott japed.

Lewrie went back to the binnacle cabinet to stow away the night telescope, then bent over the compass bowl's glim to consult his watch, and found that it was twenty minutes past 5 A.M., and ten minutes to Three Bells. He stood back up and peered shoreward once more. Those large windmills could now almost be made out, a bit more distinctly.

"Three flashes, Mister Kibworth," Lewrie snapped. "Let's get our people on their way, before any sentries can spot 'em."

Both ships lay about a half-mile from shore, and it would take long minutes, perhaps a whole half-hour for them to ground and land the troops, uncomfortably close to the period of muted greyness, the arrival of false dawn, when those Arabic threads *could* be distinguished, and a watcher ashore could espy the two ships and the boats that beetle-crawled their way to the beach.

*Damme, did I leave it too late?* Lewrie fretted to himself; *Ye poxy fool, I* should've *sent the signal at Two Bells!*

Now that the operation was committed, he felt a *frisson* of dread, for, by the faint light of the stars, and a sliver of a moon that was just rising, he could make out the disturbed-water splashes from the boats' oar blades as they dug in, rose, and trailed hints of phosphoresence!

Lewrie knew that the soldiers, Marines, and sailors going ashore in the dark, their young officers also, would be feeling the same sort of icy, stomach-clenching dread of the unknown.

*I pressed for this, I planned it, arranged it, come Hell or high water, and if it don't work, or I get a lot o' people killed, it's me that takes the blame,* Lewrie fretted.

If the whole thing went smash, it would be tempting to write a report to Admiralty to try and pass the onus of failure off on to someone else; Lewrie had seen that done too many times before. To do so, though, would force him to face the fact that he wasn't clever enough, or smart enough, to manage senior command, and had spent his career in the Navy coasting by on supreme good luck!

"Christ, but command is a vicious bastard!" he whispered.

At that moment, he would much rather have been one of his Midshipmen in the landing boats, with but one simple task to perform and no responsibility beyond the gunn'ls of his boat.

*A simple task for simple bloody* me*!* he thought.

"I think I can make out . . ." Lt. Westcott intruded on his frets, "yes, I can see the oar splashes, sir. They're in close to the beach."

Lewrie looked out over the bulwarks and spotted them for himself, finding that the boats *were* closing in on the shore, but not in the hoped-for single line-abreast.

"Where the Devil are *Harmony*'s boats goin'?" he exclaimed, gripping the cap-rails. "Can't they see the bloody lights on the bloody battery? They're too far off to the left!"

There was no way of signalling them to change course, and they were too close to shore to do so, without steering right, *parallel* to the beach, before turning again to make their grounding.

*This is goin' t'turn t'shit!* he grimly told himself; *Even in this next-to-nothing surf, some are sure t'get overturned!*

If the operation failed due to that mistake, perhaps he *would* write that report to Admiralty, a blistering one!

Lewrie dashed up the ladderway to the poop deck for a slightly better view, even though false dawn had not yet greyed the skies, but by then, even the oar splashes and faint phosphoresence had vanished. He realised that for good or ill, the boats and all those men were now ashore, and there was nothing he could do about it!

Several long minutes passed with nothing happening, no blossoming of lights round the battery to indicate that the sentries had wakened and spotted the troops, then . . .

"Gunfire, huzzah!" young Midshipman Fywell cried aloud, hopping up and down in excitement.

"Still, young sir!" Lewrie heard Lt. Harcourt snap. "Bear yourself with the proper demeanour!"

Wee red and amber fireflys were twinkling ashore, quite merry to observe, rippling along in a line in what Lewrie recognised as platoon fire. Long seconds later, after the first winkings, he could hear the faintest hint of twig-crackling as many weapons were discharged.

"False dawn, at last, sir," the Sailing Master, Mr. Yelland, called up to him from the quarterdeck below. "At, ehm . . . five fourty-seven."

Black threads, white threads . . . now it was dark grey land and white surfline, dull grey windmills and stone battery, and red tunics with white crossbelts, billows of gunpowder smoke, soldiers in tall shakoes in a long two-deep line fronting the battery, and another pack going round the right of it, disappearing into the rising smoke. One of the artillery pieces fired with a roar, adding more smoke to the confusion, and a roundshot moaned far overhead of *Sapphire*'s masts.

"I don't suppose we should respond to that, hey, sir?" Westcott asked from the foot of the ladderway.

"Not without killing our troops, no," Lewrie said, grimacing. He had called his crew to Quarters, but had not issued orders to load or run out, and the only weapons from the arms chests had been given to the shore parties.

That was the only shot from the battery, though, and the next sounds that could be made out from shore sounded like thin cheers and feral shouts. That thin line of red-coated soldiers could be seen as they swarmed up the slight slope to the parapets and scrambled over it. A moment later and a small British boat jack was being waved and wig-wagged over the parapet in vigourous fashion.

"We've taken it, then," Westcott said, with a whoosh of relief.

"Thank God!" Lewrie said, with more emotion than was proper to a Navy Post-Captain. "That's the first part done," he added, returning to the correct calmness. "Now's the mills' turn, and all of the boats in harbour that we can reach. Assuming of course that there's not a garrison that's moved in since the last agent's report."

"If so, the battery was the most important part, as you said, sir," Westcott pointed out. "If they appear, we can retire in good order, with the morning's honour intact."

"Keep your fingers crossed," Lewrie cautioned. "And carry on, Geoffrey. I think I'll go below and see if there's any coffee."

Thankfully, Puerto Banús had no Spanish military presence beyond the artillerists who had manned the battery, and the rest of the morning was spent merrily destroying as much as they could. The windmills were stone towers, but the upperworks, the rooves, mill vanes, and all the gearing that drove the grist milling stones were wood, and the landing parties turned those tall towers into roaring chimneys. The large granary, pitifully low on flour or un-milled wheat in sign of the devastation which Napoleon Bonaparte's Continental System had wrought upon the Spanish people, was lined with several levels of wood storage racks, and they burned quite nicely, too, so hot a fire that the slate roof caved in and the granary shed slabs from its eaves.

The smaller fishermens' boats drawn up on the shingle for the night succumbed to boarding axes, their bottoms smashed in, then run into the slack harbour waters to sink. Wood rudders, oars, and fishing nets were gathered up to make a fine bonfire. Landing boats penetrated the inner harbour without a shot being fired, or a single Spaniard to be seen, and armed parties boarded the larger boats to tow them out to the middle of the harbour and set them alight.

Lastly, all but a few of the troops were rowed back to their transport and the small number that remained ashore dealt with the battery and its guns. The guns were spiked at the touch-holes, trunnions blown off with borrowed Spanish gunpowder, and their wooden truck-carriages set afire. The long wooden barracks and the smaller officers quarters behind the battery were set afire, and a long length of slow-match laid to the powder magazine beneath the battery.

When the last shore party was about a cable offshore, the magazine exploded, heaving stone blocks from the parapet and the thick flagstones of the battery high in the sky, flinging heavy guns aloft, and all in a great gout of flame and sickly yellow-tinged white smoke.

The boat crews and the Marines returned to *Sapphire* just in time for "Clear Decks And Up Spirits" to be piped for the rum issue, which raised a great, self-congratulating cheer. There was an even greater one when Lewrie ordered "Splice The Mainbrace!" for full measures for all hands, with no debts to be paid to "sippers and gulpers" for any favours rendered. The same signal was made to *Harmony*, with similar good cheer among the men of the 77th.

"Leftenant Keane t'see th' Cap'm, SAH!" the Marine sentry at Lewrie's cabin door shouted, stamping his boots and musket hutt.

"Enter," Lewrie called back.

"Good afternoon, sir," Lt. Keane said as he approached the day-cabin portion, where Lewrie was sprawled on his settee with Chalky in his lap.

"Good afternoon to you, Mister Keane," Lewrie said, waving a hand at one of the chairs. "Take a pew, and let me express my congratulations, again, for a fine day's work."

"Ehm, thank you, sir," Keane replied, seating himself primly, with his hat on one knee, his expression stony.

"A glass of something for you, sir?" Lewrie offered. "Wine, or might ye try my cool tea?"

"I believe I will assay your tea, sir," Keane decided. "I have not tasted it before."

"Pettus, a glass of tea for Mister Keane," Lewrie called out to his steward. "Now, why the long face, Mister Keane? You look as if ye have something serious in your mind."

"You have not begun your report to Admiralty, sir?" Keane hesitantly asked.

"Not yet, no," Lewrie told him. "I thought I'd do that once we get back to Gibraltar, and combine our part with Major Hughes's."

"Upon that head, sir . . ." Keane said, then paused as if summoning up his courage. "Things did not go quite as well ashore as it may have appeared. The Army lot . . ."

"Landed too far left of the battery, aye," Lewrie finished for him. "Even though all they had to do was row for the lanthorns on the parapet, and had to run t'get in the right place."

"Well, there is that, sir," Keane allowed, "but, once there, and in place alongside us, they just . . . stalled. There were no more than three or four sentries on watch in the battery, and the rest were asleep in the barracks. Hughes could have crept up and taken them at once, or he could have sent his companies in at a rush, and the battery would have been ours with hardly a shot fired, and the Spaniards in the barracks captured. Instead, he ordered his men to form line and load, the sentries heard him . . . I think the *town* could have . . . the sentries fired at him and his men, ran to wake the rest, and then the 77th began to volley by platoons, trading massive fire with only a few, no more than four or five, enemy soldiers, sir."

"Damme, just blazin' away at nothing?" Lewrie said, frowning. "How long did *that* go on?"

"Long enough for the Spanish to load and fire one of their guns and turn out of barracks, sir," Keane said, looking angry, appalled by poor tactics. "We did not fire on the Spanish, so I doubt if they were even aware my party was there, it was still so dark. I took my Marines round the right side of the battery, fixed bayonets, and made a charge into them after serving them a volley. We shot a few, skewered a few more, and the rest of them threw up their hands, and some dropped their weapons or gun tools and ran off. At that point, it got quiet enough that I could shout, 'take the bloody battery, charge' and the soldiers finally moved."

He spat "soldiers" like a curse.

"Good, quick thinking, Mister Keane," Lewrie said, "as I will say in my report."

"I fear that Major Hughes was none too pleased with my action, sir," Keane said, allowing himself the faintest grin. "After we rounded up the Spanish prisoners, he made it plain that it was *he* who was in command ashore, and that I should have kept my men in line with his and . . . 'what the Hell does a Marine know of infantry tactics?' was how he put it, placing a great emphasis upon the difference between a Major and a mere Leftenant."

Lewrie stroked his cat slowly, mulling that over for a minute or two whilst Keane got his tea and took a few sips.

"What Admiralty wishes to know is whether the attack was successful, Mister Keane," Lewrie finally said. "Not the tactical, or personal disputes. It may be a good idea, though, once we're back in port, to get Hughes, his company commanders, and you together for a re-hash, under the guise of what worked, and what we could do better. Just how big is a platoon, anyway, Mister Keane? How many are there?"

"Well, in our case, I'd say the same number as we have boats, sir," Keane informed him. "For the 77th, that would be about eighteen or nineteen men plus non-commissioned and one officer. As many men as can be crammed into each of their larger boats."

"So, their two Lieutenants, two Ensigns, and two senior Sergeants could command their six platoons, the Captains could oversee them, and Hughes would direct them all?" Lewrie asked.

"Lord, you speak heresy, sir!" Lt. Keane exclaimed, laughing and making a mock shiver. "The Army would *never* give such responsibility to Sergeants or Corporals, nor to boy Ensigns, either. That duty is for gentleman officers only, and experienced ones of proper rank. They drill, march, and fight in well-ordered battalions, regiments, and brigades. A light company can be sent out ahead of the line on their own, but only to skirmish for a while before returning to the left of the regimental line. They might form foraging parties in small lots, but that's about it."

"Damn!" Lewrie groused, and gave out a sigh. "My fault. When we planned the raid, I didn't stress going round the battery by companies, or the companies acting on their own."

"That could be raised during the review, sir," Keane allowed, "but you may find it hard to impart. The Army simply doesn't think that way. We might have been better off with an all-Marine force."

"If wishes were horses, we'd all ride thouroughbreds," Lewrie scoffed. "We're stuck with what we have, and lucky t've gotten them. And, it ain't as if they're a bad lot. I gather that most of their officers have gotten the hang of what we're doing, and we've taught their men new skills. Perhaps we can bring them round to a little more . . . flexibility."

"Perhaps, sir," Lt. Keane said, though he didn't sound all that hopeful. "More flexibility in their thinking and reacting to the situation is wanting."

"You mean in Major Hughes's thinking," Lewrie countered.

"Indeed, sir," Keane solemnly agreed. "If only to limit casualties."

*Sapphire*'s Marines had not suffered any hurts beyond some minor scrapes and bruises, though the 77th had had three wounded, none too seriously, or so Surgeon Mister Snelling had reported once he had returned from *Harmony.* If Major Hughes had thought to rush the battery at bayonet-point, quietly, the whole operation could have ended with no British casualties, Lewrie imagined.

Keane finished his cool tea, pronounced it a fine concoction, and took his leave, Lewrie remained on the settee, stroking Chalky, and frowning.

"We were lucky this time, cat, d'ye know that?" he muttered to his pet. "The next'un'll take a lot more planning before we set it in motion, and I'm going to ruffle even more feathers before we do."

Chalky looked up at him slit-eyed and beginning to purr.

There were Midshipmen Hillhouse and Britton to speak to as to why two experienced, well-salted young men had gone so far astray from the proper stretch of beach. There was a harder part awaiting him over how the detachment of the 77th could move more quickly if the situation warranted it. The hardest part of all, Lewrie suspected, was getting Major Hughes to explain his actions, and mend some of his ways.

"Hard-headed, blusterin' bastard," Lewrie muttered aloud.

"Mister Keane, sir?" Pettus asked as he retrieved Keane's empty glass to rinse out.

"Not him, an Army officer," Lewrie corrected him.

"Oh," Pettus said. "But aren't they all that way, sir?"

"God, let's hope not!" Lewrie said with a laugh, while thinking that Major Hughes was a harder nut to crack than most. He recalled his boasts to Maddalena that first dinner at the seafood chop-house about the proper way to win the war, and how he'd go about it if only given the chance.

*A very bloody* thick *nut, indeed,* Lewrie thought.

# CHAPTER THIRTY

"Feeling ambitious, Captain Lewrie?" Mr. Thomas Mountjoy asked him once they had gone over the results of the raid on Puerto Banús.

"Depends on what you have in mind," Lewrie replied, wondering what he was getting at. "Another raid?"

"Two, actually," Mountjoy responded, slyly grinning, "Within a day's sail of each other. Look here," he urged, fetching out a chart to spread on the marred old dining table in his lodgings. "There are semaphore towers all along the coast, in grovelling emulation of those that Bonaparte has built all over France."

"In grovelling emulation of the British semaphore system that we built, first!" Lewrie interrupted him, with a scornful hoot.

Years before Napoleon Bonaparte had come to power, Admiralty had erected long chains of signalling towers from Whitehall to every major seaport, from Falmouth to Dover, the Downs, and the Goodwin Sands and Great Yarmouth. Signal towers were really an ancient idea, mentioned in recovered Roman texts; they had used large flashing tin mirrors by day, and torches by night, and could send complex messages further and faster than the quickest despatch rider. Unless blinded by a blizzard or pea-soup fog, the wig-wagging vanes atop the Admiralty building could whirl like a dervish's arms and transmit orders to the Nore or to Portsmouth in ten minutes or less. Lewrie didn't know exactly how the code worked, or what the many positions of the vanes meant, but was smugly convinced that the semaphore system was a marvel.

The French system put up all along their coasts he'd found useful, too, it must be admitted, especially at night, when the French hung large glass oil lanthorns on the vanes, replacing the black-painted pig bladders; Lewrie had been able to determine where he was along the coast at night by spotting the first one in a seaport town, then keeping count as he sailed along. They were as good as lighthouses!

"Anyway, as I said, there's a chain of them from Málaga to Almeria, then to Cartagena, one of their main naval ports," Mountjoy went on. "If they're a French idea, then Godoy and his Francophiles simply must have them, though, from the reports I've gotten, they're nowhere near finished, and Spain's so 'skint' it'll be a wonder if they can ever afford to complete them. They've none leading inland, so far as I know . . . just along the coasts. If that coastal warning chain is broken in a few places, the Spanish would have to re-build them and give them a stronger garrison, depriving Sir Hew's friend, Castaños, of troops . . . and costing them money they don't have."

"What do your informants say of possible opposition?" Lewrie asked him, frowning.

"The towers themselves are thinly manned, just enough men to work the day, and another team for night," Mountjoy said, shrugging off worries. "Watch for signals in two directions, copy them down, and work the arms to send them on. The ones closer to Almeria might be too risky, since there's a sizable garrison there, foot, horse and all, but . . . down here at Almerimar, there's a tower right on the shore that's isolated, several miles removed from El Ejido, and even further from Berja, inland, where there sometimes are at least a company, or strong detatchment, of Spanish infantry. You could be in, burn it, and be out before a rider could summon them. Here's the sketches I've obtained, and the nature of the beaches," he said, placing them atop the chart they had been studying.

The semaphore tower, as depicted, was made of wood with ladders leading up through several open platforms to the larger one at the top where the arms, or vanes, were worked. It sat on a high spot at the back of a small bay open to the sea, with the small, sleepy fishing port of Almerimar situated on lower ground to the right of the tower, straggling up a lesser slope inland to grain fields, pastures, and orchards.

"It looks t'be an easy proposition," Lewrie cautiously allowed. "I wouldn't have t'land my troops in the full dark, this time. We're going after the town, too?"

"Let's not bother with the town, this time," Mountjoy suggested, making a face. "It's poor enough, already, and our aim is to win the Spanish over, eventually, not enflame their centuries-old hatred for us."

"I thought you *wanted* chaos and mayhem?" Lewrie said, confused. "You agreed to burning the mills and granary at Puerto Banús, and all the fishermen's boats," he pointed out.

"I did," Mountjoy admitted, "but once Dalrymple read my report, he shot me a stiff note saying that he'd have no truck with making war on civilians, and if we did not stick to destroying strictly military installations, he'd pull the troops away from us. Now, do we put the torch to Spanish *army* food supplies, that's one thing, but food stores for civilians is quite another, and completely against the pale."

"Humph," Lewrie said with a snort, and a toss of his head. "To do that, we'd have t'land in a major city, and need Hughes's fantacy of an entire brigade! Oh well. Aye, it looks as if Almerimar is possible, even in broad daylight. All the troops at the tower can do is madly wig-wag their tower's arms, callin' for help."

"Then, if they wish to keep the chain of towers up and running, they'll have to re-build it, and post at least a company of soldiers there to defend it, next time," Mountjoy cheerfully pictured. "A company to each tower, and you hold back whole regiments from marching to join General Castaños."

"You said two towers?" Lewrie prompted.

"Over here," Mountjoy said, gathering up the first set of hand-drawn sketches and pointing to another coastal town further West, to a cluster of small towns; Almuñécar, Salobreña, and Motril, close to the foothills of the Sierra de Almijara. "Might be a tougher nut, mind you. The main road to Granada, inland, joins the coast road halfway 'twixt Salobreña and Motril. Salobreña's right on the coast, with Motril higher up and inland, but with grand sea views, so my reports say."

"There's a semaphore tower there, at Salobreña?" Lewrie asked. "Anything else?"

"The semaphore tower is all that matters," Mountjoy told him, "though it will be harder to get at, since it's at the back of the town, on a higher spur, It would've made more sense to build it nearer to Motril, which is uphill, but for a ridge East of Motril that blocks the view."

"We'd have t'fight our way through a *town?*" Lewrie exclaimed. "What happened to bein' sweet to the Spanish? Ye can't trust soldiers t'not loot a little, on the sly, and if fire's exchanged, there's the risk o' civilians gettin' shot. If the government in Madrid is apin' the French, they'll have their own equivalent of Bonaparte's *Moniteur,* and play up the deaths and destruction like the Americans played up a few dead rebels as the Boston Massacre!"

"It's on the extreme outskirts of the town," Mountjoy pointed out, producing some more sketches from his field agents and informers. "Look here. Up here's the tower, about a quarter-mile inland from the beach, beyond a grove of trees, some pastureland, an orchard, and a few scattered houses, barns, and out-buildings. It's not as if you'd be chargin' through the *streets.* Sort of below the village of Motril, but out past the last of the ridge, where the sightline to the towers further East is better."

Lewrie ignored the sketches for a moment, looking closer at the chart, and finding an host of wee markers which resembled tall, skinny triangles with vees above them, all along the coast.

"Mountjoy, there are hundreds of the bloody things . . ." he said.

"Well, not hundreds, really," Mountjoy objected.

". . . about eight or ten miles apart, else they couldn't even *begin* t'read what signal they're making. I expect the expense for all the needed telescopes is horrid, even so. Why don't we just burn the one at Almerimar, and work our way West, startin' at dawn and ending by dusk?"

"You told me that it takes an hour or so just to get the men ashore, and hours more to complete the destruction as you did with the battery at Puerto Banús," Mountjoy dis-agreed. "I doubt you could hit no more than two, before the Spanish Army could respond, especially if you kept it up for several days. You might even draw warships out of Cartagena, and then where would you be? So far, the Mediterranean Fleet has kept them penned up in their ports, and, after the trouncing they took at Trafalgar, the Spanish may be loath to lose any more precious ships, but . . . a series of raids like that would *sting* them out."

"Are you *insisting* it has t'be Salobreña, Mountjoy?" Lewrie asked, all but gritting his teeth. That sense of old, of being Twigg's dim but useful gun-dog, was back, with a vengeance.

"Given what little information I've been able to glean, these two objectives are the only ones about which I know the most," Mountjoy grimly told him, shaking his head sadly. "Unless there are troops on the march, of which I would also know nothing, these two have no garrisons, no batteries, and the closest garrison would be at Órjiva, and that's about ten miles inland, and they're all infantry, so they'd take hours to hear of your presence in the first case, and even more hours to march down, arriving long after you've sailed, in the second."

"Well . . ." Lewrie temporised, not caring for the prospects in the least, but feeling that he had no choice but to go along with it.

A fortnight at sea, weather permitting, just to burn one insignificant semaphore tower, then return to Gibraltar, would be a waste of everyone's time and efforts.

"Very well, then," he growled in surrender. "We'll strike both, beginning with Almerimar. It's the easiest, and quickest, and the one with the least risk of opposition. Just to keep the landing parties in trim, I'll close the coast a bit later in the morning, just round pre-dawn, so we can see where we're going, land them at the first of the sunrise, and get them off round mid-morning.

"I s'pose the tower works round the clock?" Lewrie asked, leaning on the table with both hands. "Pig bladders for day signalling, and some sort of oil lanthorns at night? Good, then there'll be more than enough oil for the burning, and I'll only have to send a keg or two of gunpowder ashore t'help that along. Then . . ."

He studied the chart more closely, considering that the tower at Almerimar would be sending an urgent message as soon as *Sapphire* and *Harmony* were spotted closing the coast, to Roquetas de Mar to the East, to Adra in the West, with word of the raid sent as far as Salobrena and thence to Málaga.

"Then, Salobreña?" Mountjoy prompted.

"A diversion," Lewrie finally explained. "Once the troops are back aboard, I'll cruise Easterly and let the tower at Roquetas de Mar have a good, long look at us, perhaps stand as far as the Cabo de Gata, before turning out to sea. Let the Dons think I'm bound up the coast towards Cartagena, Alicante, or Valencia, instead. We'll double back and go at Salobreña last, and land the troops in the full dark."

"They'd be better at that, by then, is your thinking?" Mountjoy assumed, nodding quite cheerfully now that Lewrie had given in. "We have more of that good Spanish white, the *tempranilla,* and I've got a plate of some fresh cheese and good cured ham. D'ye think we need the mustard pot, too?"

"I'm a sailor, and we're both British," Lewrie said with a grin. "Of course, we need a dab of mustard."

They went out to the rooftop gallery with the wine and a plate of cheese and cold cuts. Lewrie sat down and began to study the drawings of Salobreña, considering it the harder nut to crack, and the one that most worried him.

"You, ehm . . . mentioned some minor problems with the last raid? Some . . . worries?" Mountjoy asked as he poured the wine. "Have those settled, have you?"

"Hughes is the problem," Lewrie said, almost spitting the name. "First, he over-rode my Midshipmen, Hillhouse and Britton, ordering them to land short of the battery, where it was darker, 'cause he didn't wish to alert the sentries. I put 'em on notice that *they* were in charge on the water, and they'd land the troops where we *planned* t'land 'em, in future. Hughes . . . he acted as if he was in charge of a regiment, confronted by an equal number, and he acted like he was trained," Lewrie griped with a shake of his head. "Open fire with rollin' volleys, kill, or daunt, the foe, and only go in with the bayonet once the enemy's been sufficiently whittled down. God!"

"You've spoken with him since you all returned?" Mountjoy asked with a quizzical expression. "How did that go?"

"*Decidedly* . . . not . . . well," Lewrie barked in sour humour, and grimacing.

Lewrie had invited all officers to a celebratory "drunk" aboard HMS *Sapphire*, including Midshipmen Hillhouse and Britton to join them, along with the two Ensigns of the detachment of the 77th Foot, Gilliam and Litchfield. His first intent was to congratulate them all on an operation that had gone off rather well, then had waited 'til everyone was "cherry merry" in wine, following the old adage that *in vino veritas;* in wine there is truth. It was only then that he had suggested that an informal review of the raid might prove helpful to the conduct of future operations; what worked, what might be improved or done differently.

As Pettus and Jessop circulated among them to top off their wineglasses with a sprightly, effervescent Spanish white, they all had sat dumbfounded for a minute or two, Who in the world *cared* what a junior officer thought? They hesitated, slack-jawed—and "half seas over" it must be confessed—waiting for Lewrie or Major Hughes to speak and *tell* them what to make of their recent experience.

"Well, sir," Midshipman Hillhouse at last spoke up, "we *could* have landed the 77th closer to the objective."

"It was a long dash at the double-quick, yes," Ensign Gilliam had said with a titter of remembrance, and at his daring to say anything. Major Hughes almost snapped his neck, whipping about to glare slit-eyed at Hillhouse, then in tooth-grinding affrontery as Ensign Gilliam spoke, as if he'd just been addressed by a talking tit-mouse.

Marine Lieutenant Keane, who had still appeared at least partially sobre, added that, in retrospect, the battery could have been taken more quickly if a sweep by two companies round both sides of the place might have done the trick, and they could have caught *all* the Spanish officers and gunners in their underdrawers . . . assuming that Spaniards wore such.

"That would've saved us a fair parcel of ammunition, what?" Lt. Staggs had chortled over their wasted volleys, which had raised a loud and drunken laugh and a chorus of agreement from all but Major Hughes, and it had gone on from there, loosening up, with everyone contributing. Some of the suggestions, of course, were just too silly, given the age, and state of inebriation, of the participants, but all in all, the session had proved to be somewhat productive, trailing off in remembrances of how much outright *fun* it was to smash and burn things, and how humiliated the Spanish soldiers had been, after being ordered to strip to shirts, trousers, and stockings, and all their uniforms, accoutrements, boots, and weapons had been piled inside their barracks and burned along with it.

Major Hughes, it must be admitted, most pointedly did *not* contribute much to the session, signalling his displeasure and unease with stifled harumphs, re-crossings of his immaculately-booted legs, black scowls, and now-and-then astonishingly high, or low, flappings of his thick eyebrows, and Lewrie had been convinced that he had heard some faint, deep *growls* rumbling in Hughes's throat that rivalled a wakened bear or a large watchdog.

With the last ridiculous ideas shot down, it had been time for drinking games, "a glass with you, sir!", and song. They were, for the most part, young enough to still be students, well-pleased with themselves, and reckoning themselves bold and gallant warriors. Food was served from the sideboard cabinet in the dining-coach; fingers of toasted cheese rolled in bread crumbs; baked potatoes filled with bits of bacon, cheese, and shredded onion; thick-sliced "Tommy", fresh bread from shore, with sliced ham or roast beef and mustard for sandwich makings; and both sweet and dill pickles. Lewrie had been amazed by how they had managed to stagger to the sideboard, load their plates, and return to their seats after so much wine had been taken aboard. He'd shared despairing looks with Pettus, for his cabins would need a *real* cleaning in the morning, and had feared that his carpets would never be the same. Fortunately, all had managed to stagger to the larboard side quarter-gallery when caught short, and no one, thank the Lord, had puked.

It had wound down after another hour, with the wine replaced by hot tea or coffee, and the officers of the 77th had been seen to the entry-port and waiting boats, though more than a few had had need of a Bosun's chair, roped into the sling on a board for a seat, hoisted aloft suspended from the main course yardarm, and lowered into a boat, with the youngest and drunkest, Litchfield and Gilliam, delighting in it so much that they shrilled, "Whee!"

Lewrie thought that he had managed the whole affair most handily, and had used the junior officers' comments and suggestions to do the goading and prompting without a direct confrontation with Major Hughes, all but patting himself on the back . . . but he'd been wrong.

"A *word,* sir," Hughes had rasped in a threatening growl as the last of the 77th's officers had departed the deck. "What a disreputable show, Captain Lewrie, I've never seen in all my born days, I tell you! Is that the way you run your ship, by a bloody committee, with damnable *democracy,* and a vote for all?"

"I thought it would prove useful, sir, since, as you said, we are breaking ground with such operations," Lewrie had bristled up, "and celebrate their first success."

"Prejudicial to good order and discipline is what I term it, sir!" Hughes had gravelled back, his face flushed with more than wine, and his eyes red. "Children, and subalterns, should be seen, but not heard. Next thing you know, they'll begin second-guessing my orders, and questioning me *why!* Damme, they're to obey my *every* order, else it all turns to utter chaos! You undermine my authority, sir, and I won't *have* it!"

"I've done nothing of the kind, sir!" Lewrie had shot back.

"General Dalrymple appointed *me* to command the landing forces, sir, *me!*" Hughes had insisted, getting louder and drawing the attention of the people in the harbour watch. "If you find my conduct lacking, do you think me incapable, say so to my face, here and now, and ask the General for another officer!"

"I do not think you incapable, Major Hughes," Lewrie had had to respond in kind, "but I do think you drunk. I have no intention of asking for you to be replaced."

"You just handle your part, Captain Lewrie," Hughes had fumed, "just get us where we're supposed to go, and leave the *military* part to those who know what the Devil they're doing, with no interference from . . . *amateurs!* Damme, I've spent twenty *years* at a soldier's trade, sir, Ensign to Major, and I know what I'm about more than a *sailor,* or a tailor's dummy of a *Marine,* and I'll show you, I'll show *all* of you, how to handle troops and win victories, damme if I won't!"

He had been almost chest-to-chest with Lewrie, and had seemed ready to make his points with jabs of a stiffened finger, before stepping back, wheeling to stomp to the entry-port, and start to descend with no help. As he'd doffed his plumed bicorne in a departing salute, Hughes had flung his last shot.

"I will show you all!" he had barked.

"No, that doesn't sound as if it went at all well," Mountjoy agreed, looking gloomy. "Do you think he's not really up to scratch?"

"At this moment, I haven't a bloody clue," Lewrie confessed. "He's efficient, has all the nigglin' little details seen to, and has his men trained, well-behaved, and . . . frisky. He takes good care of 'em. He's just so . . . rigid. Hopefully, I've lit a fire under his arse, or rowed him enough t'change his ways. We'll just have to see how he behaves on the next operation."

"How soon can you sail, then?" Mountjoy asked.

"Hmm . . . end of the week?" Lewrie loosely estimated. "I spoke with the Captain of a frigate that'd just come in, and he said that there'd been some vicious gales from Sardinia to the Balearics, and I expect 'em here before they blow themselves out. Might get some precious rain at the Rock by tomorrow."

"My gutters and rain-barrels are ready for it," Mountjoy said, all but clapping his hands in expectation, "and the house has a good, deep cistern. My hydrangeas could do with a good rain."

"Which're those?" Lewrie, who had not a single clue about botany beyond recognising the difference 'twixt flowers and weeds, asked.

"Those in the pots, there," Mountjoy told him as if amazed by his lack of knowledge.

"Ah," Lewrie said. "Heard from that fool, Romney Marsh, yet?"

"Just the one note," Mountjoy said, shaking his head in wonder. "Cryptic as all Hell . . . 'Have arrived, met Goya'."

"Who's Goya?" Lewrie asked, befuddled once more.

"A famous Spanish painter," Mountjoy said, snickering. "So . . . end of the week, you say?"

"Weather permittin', aye," Lewrie told him. As he sipped at his wine, though, he wondered again just what Major Hughes had meant when he said that he would show everyone how good a soldier he was.

*What's he goin' t'do* t'prove *it?* Lewrie wondered.

# CHAPTER THIRTY-ONE

The planning session for the raids on the semaphore towers went well, with the junior officers of the 77th asking sensible questions, and showing some eagerness that they had lacked before, after having a taste of their strange, new tasks, and coming through them with success, which filled them with a certain *elan*.

Major Hughes was his usual brisk and efficient self, showing no sign that he and Lewrie had almost come to loggerheads. For the landing at Almerimar, he decided that the two companies of the 77th would form on the right and advance up to guard facing the village, whilst Keane, Roe, and their Marines would have the honour of assailing the tower, driving off the few Spaniards reported there, and burning the tower and small troop quarters.

Lewrie would place *Sapphire* directly opposite the tower, and the troop transport would fetch-to to starboard of her, allowing the 77th to land on the right, though within arm's reach of the boats from his ship. Both ships, he told them, would have to fetch-to about two thirds of a mile from shore, making for a longer row this time, but the tide would be ebbing and the beach would be broad, with what the reports said was good cover in the vegetation behind the deep sand and the overwash barrows for the boat crews to guard their boats.

Salobreña took longer to plan for, but Major Hughes saw little difficulty, showing that hoped-for flexibility as he gestured over the enlarged hand-drawn map of the area round the town, and the objective. They would all go for the wood lot, first, three companies abreast of each other, with the Marines on the right flank, this time, then advance by companies, Kimbrough's company from the left flank, first, to cover the town, as far as one of the farmhouses' buildings, then the company under Captain Bowden would get into the olive orchard, followed by the Marines advancing as far as the pastures on the other side.

"There is a garrison of infantry inland at Órjiva . . . see the printed map," Hughes gruffly instructed, "but we hope to be in and out before they can get word of our presence. If our raid at Almerimar *does* draw Spanish troops to the coast to guard their precious towers, I cannot imagine that there would be much more than a detachment of several files, possibly an entire company, but I expect that we can deal with them easily. Even with our diversion offshore to the East following Almerimar, we should be back on the coast off Salobreña in such a short time that the Dons' initial response would be more deliberate than hasty. We've done nothing to make them panic, *yet!* As we do depart Almerimar going East, it's more than likely that the Dons feel that re-enforcing their coast defences from Almeria up to Cartagena is more prudent. Questions, gentlemen?"

There were a few, some notes made on their copies of the maps, arrangements for gunpowder kegs, flints and tinder made, and after a few hours, everyone seemed wolfish to get going.

"Think that covers everything, Captain Lewrie?" Hughes asked.

"I do believe it does, Major Hughes," Lewrie replied, satisfied that even the most minor matters had been dealt with.

"Then let's board the transport tomorrow morning, gentlemen," Hughes confidently concluded. "Bright-eyed, and *relatively* sobre, at least, and be about it! Let's show the Spanish how *real* soldiers go about their business . . . let's show the world!"

Imbued with confidence from their first relatively successful raid at Puerto Banús, the landing at Almerimar went off like clockwork, the officers and men of the 77th's detachment boarding their boats with alacrity, the boat crews forming up in line-abreast formation as if they'd been doing it for years, and, once the boats grounded the soldiers and Marines advanced on the semaphore tower, and created a screen 'twixt the tower and the town, in a twinkling, going in at the double-quick and raising great, feral cheers.

As soon as it was evident that two "*Inglese*" ships were coming to the town, church bells in Almerimar had begun to peal madly, audible even two-thirds of a mile offshore. Spaniards could be seen dashing about the streets, loading carts, hitching up mules, horses, or donkeys, saddling up, and piling their most treasured possessions in the carts or waggons, even snatching the town's clotheslines bare to salvage any scrap of clothing or bedding. The townspeople fled East up the coast towards Roquetas de Mar, or inland towards El Ejido, raising clouds of dust from the roads or fields.

There was no opposition, and the landing could have been done by only one company of men. The few Spanish soldiers who manned the semaphore tower stayed at their posts 'til British troops began to swarm ashore from the boats, and the arms of the tower with the black balls at the ends finally stopped wig-wagging, sagging in a downward vee as the positioning ropes were left slack, at last. Seven or eight Spaniards dashed off-inland, their officer and sergeant flailing away with whips to spur their donkeys to a full run, leaving those on foot in their dusty wake.

A few minutes after *Sapphire*'s Marines surrounded the tower, it and the Spanish signalmen's tents began to smoke, then break out into a roaring fire, helped along with lanthorn oil and scattered gunpowder, sending dense, rising, spreading clouds of dark grey smoke rising high in the morning sky, letting the towers up and down the coast know that the one at Almerimar was silenced for a good, long time, and if they weren't watchful, the same thing might soon happen to them.

The Marines marched back to the beach in a column-of-twos, and as soon as they were under way, the two companies of the 77th retired from their guard upon the town and fell in behind them, the trailing company still spread out in pairs of skirmishers to form a rearguard. The boats were soon filled, and gotten off the beach, and, in looser, more casual order, returned to the ships to muzzle by the masts' channel platforms and the scrambling nets. They boarded both ships with laughs, cheers, and impromptu songs, at least an hour before the first rum issue was piped.

No one had been injured, and the worst complaint was that some had gotten their boots and trousers wet to the knees, and had to go change their stockings once weapons and accoutrements had been stored away.

As planned, *Sapphire* led *Harmony* up the coast to the East, in plain sight and only a mile or two offshore of Roquetas de Mar, and Agua-dulce, and a Midshipman in *Sapphire*'s mainmast cross-trees could glee-fully report that he could see semaphore towers as far off as the city of Almeria whirling away like so many dervishes. Satisfied with the morn-ing's work, Lewrie then ordered the course to be altered, out to sea and out of sight, gradually fading hull-down from watchers on the tip of Cabo de Gata, as if further raids might take place East of Almeria, threat-ening Mojacar, Garrucha, Palomares, or Aguilas. Once completely out of sight, though, about both ships went once more, to shape course for their second objective.

One lone stroke upon the forecastle bell rang out most eerily as the ship's boy who tended it opened a small hooded lanthorn just long enough to see the last of the sand in his half-hour glass run out.

"Boats are in place and manned, sir," Lt. Westcott reported to Lewrie on the blackened quarterdeck.

"Very well, Mister Westcott," Lewrie replied, shivering a bit to the cool night breeze. "Load the boats. Pass word to Lieutenant Keane, and send the Execute lanthorn flash to *Harmony*."

"Aye, sir."

HMS *Sapphire* was fetched-to just a little over half a mile off the shore, slowly rolling to the faint scend of the sea, hull timbers and mast steps making faint creaking noises. The breeze was light, and the sea, though black as a boot, barely rippled, reflecting tiny lights from Salobreña's waterfront, the lights which burned that late in the town of Amuñécar off a bit to the West, and from Motril, higher up and inland from Salobreña, casting amber winkings from the tops of what waves there were, as if the warship lay on the edge of a lawn aswarm with fireflys that flashed in their hundreds as they hummed about.

*Hope they're up to it,* Lewrie thought, worrying that the training in the complete dark, and the experience that the soldiers had gotten from the first two landings, might not be enough to put them onto the shore at 4:30 A.M., over a full hour before false dawn. There was a nagging thought that he might be asking a bit too much of them this night. He peered shoreward intently, searching for any sign of breaking surf on the black beaches, but could not discern any disturbances. At least the boats would have an easy row in over a blessedly calm sea and ground on a beach on which the waves rolled in lazily to roil in ripples, sweep cross the hard sands, seep in, then retreat as slowly and as gently as the breathing of a sleeping kitten.

He went up to the poop deck for a better view, taking along a night-glass, despite the skewed view it would provide in its ocular.

Streetlights, doorway lights . . . were some of them moving, he wondered? Small as Salobreña was, could the town afford nightwatchmen? Even at that hour, fishermen might already be awake and astir, their wives stoking hearth fires, and one waterfront tavern or two might be open that early to dish up hearty breakfasts for men who had to rise that early and put out in their boats by sun-up. And all it would take would be one shout of alarm, and the whole attack could go smash!

"Dammit, dammit, dammit!" Lewrie whispered to the night.

"Light, sir!" Lt. Westcott shouted up to him, startling him. "Two flashes from the boats. They're in contact with each other!"

He'd been so intent on the blackness of the land that he had missed seeing it. Both ships were darkened, revealing nothing to any casual watcher, but now came another risk, the signal to proceed with the landing, from seaward, which any fool might spot!

"Three flashes back, Mister Westcott," Lewrie called back.

He looked for the tiny splashes from the blades of the oars as they dug in, for the eery phosphorescence that arose from disturbances in night-time waters, but this time there was nothing to see, no sign of the boats' very existence.

*Pray God it* stays *so!* he thought. He felt as if he was waiting for the wee plop of a pebble tossed down a well, a well so deep and infinite that it would never come.

He lowered the telescope and pushed its tubes shut, and despite a lifetime of training not to, he leaned on the bulwarks, arms on top of the cap-rails and his chest pressed against the wood, facing that stygian shore. Something bumped the back of his right knee above his boot, once, then again, and he groped down to find a cold nose and a furry muzzle; Bisquit had come up to seek company, awakened by all of the clumping of sailors and Marines leaving the ship.

"And a good morning t'you, too, Bisquit," Lewrie cooed in a soft voice, turning to kneel down and greet the dog with ruffles of his fur, gentle strokes of his perked ears, and a hug or two. "Come t'calm me down, have ye? In need o' company yourself? Ah, but you're a fine dog, you are." He got his face licked as Two Bells rang out from the forecastle belfry; it was five in the morning.

*If I'm too senior t'go ashore with 'em,* he told himself; *And have t'stand and wait, at least he'll keep me occupied for a while . . . 'til the shit begins t'fly. There's a belly needs scratchin'. Wish that worked for me!*

After the requisite belly rubs, Lewrie paced aft to the taffrails, peered at the shore some more, and sat down on the flag lockers for a while. Bisquit hopped up to sit beside him, leaning in close as if for reassurance, then finally turned about and laid his paws and and his head in Lewrie's lap, to the amusement of the hands who stood watch in the After-Guard, as the skies began to lighten, making the mountains of Sierra de Almijara an erose black mass above the shore.

Lewrie gave the dog a last ruffle of his head fur and rose to go exchange his night-glass for a day-glass, at long last, and peered shoreward from the quarterdeck. It was barely enough of the pre-dawn to make out the boats strung along the beach, and ant-like sailors on shore, forming a defensive arc around them. Higher upslope, he got a hint now and then of red coats and white crossbelts filtering through the trees of the wood lot and the orchards.

Bells began ringing in Salobreña, and doors and windows were flung open, revealing candlelight or lamp light from early risers responding to the alarm. A quick scan of the town showed Lewrie a mass of dark figures along the waterfront and quays, in the seaside streets, who seemed frozen in place, and only slowly bunching together to confer as to what the bells' tolling might mean. They were not panicked into fleeing, yet, but that might soon come.

"Gunfire, sir!" Lt. Harcourt pointed out. "Uphill, somewhere near the semaphore tower!"

"Rather a lot of it," Lt. Westcott commented more calmly with his own telescope to one eye.

Lewrie could see bright amber spurts of explosions as priming powder went off, the gushes of more amber-yellow sparks from muzzles, and a quickly rising fog of spent powder, in four places; three groups a bit downslope he took for his soldiers and Marines firing upward at somebody, and a rippling line of returning fire from dozens of muskets up above his own, spaced out around and a little below the dark bulk of the semaphore tower, whose arms, tipped with lanthorns, were going like Billy-Oh! The pre-dawn wind was so light, now, that the sound of gunfire could be heard, a continual crackling like bundles of twigs tossed onto a good campfire.

*Calm, fool!* Lewrie chid himself; *Cool and calm does it!*, though his first instinct was to stamp his boots, wave his arms, and demand that somebody tell him what the bloody Hell was going on.

"It appears that the Dons are quicker off the mark t're-enforce their damned towers, sirs," Lewrie said, lowering his telescope. "One day after we went ashore at Almerimar? Let's just hope that Hughes's estimate of a single company come down from Órjiva is right, and that we out-number them."

"It does look as if the enemy is in roughly company strength, sir," Lt. Westcott estimated. "Damn all the gunsmoke, though. Can't make out much anymore."

"There!" Lewrie said, pointing. "To the left. That would be Captain Kimbrough's company, going forward. They've marched ahead of their first smoke. You can almost make 'em out, now!"

A minute later, and the gunfire on the right flank moved up a bit closer to the semaphore tower, as Lt. Keane took his Marines out further, and re-opened fire into the Spanish left-hand of the line. As the volume of fire increased from the left, from Kimbrough's company, the centre of the British line moved up, as well.

"Am I imagining things, or are the Spanish falling back to the tower?" Lt. Harcourt wondered aloud. "Yes, I think they are!"

"Their gun flashes seem to be slackening, too," Lt. Elmes said. "Damme, a good, hard fight, and we're not in it!"

"Land fighting, sir?" Lewrie said with a shake of his head in dismissal. "Be careful what ye wish for, for it ain't pretty. Do pass word for Mister Snelling, and have him, his Surgeon's Mates, and the loblolly boys standing by, for we're sure t'have wounded comin' back."

Long before, in his Midshipman days, some wry fellow, he could not recall just who, had commented that glory and honour were won if battle happened over *yonder,* but when one was personally involved, it was only confusion and terror. Even so, Lewrie wished that he *could* be ashore, up with the 77th and his Marines, if only to see for himself how the fight was going, and if he could issue orders that saved the day, saved some lives, and won the field.

"I think our fellows are moving forward, again, sir," Lieutenant Westcott announced. "We may have gained the tower, and driven the Dons into the scrub behind it."

Four Bells rang out to mark six in the morning, and the sun was almost fully up, revealing more of the scene, the sailors and boats on the shore, the beach now sandy instead of grey, the light line of the gentle surf breaking ankle-high, and the details of the town off to the left. The details of the terrain pencilled upon Mountjoy's maps were more distinctive, the orchards and wood lot trees, the houses and barns of the scattered farmsteads, the long slope up to the semaphore tower and the tower itself. Upon that slope, Lewrie could espy tiny blotches of red and white scattered here and there, a sight that made him suck in a deep breath as his stomach went chill. British soldiers, some of his own Marines, lay on the ground where they had fallen, and they were too far away for him to see if they lay unmoving, or writhed in pain from wounds, wounds from which they might recover, pray God!

*God dammit, what a mess!* he thought, almost in pain; *No matter the care we took in plannin', we've thrown 'em in the quag.*

At long last, the gunfire dribbled off to scattered individual shots, and the groups of British troops were beyond the tower, swarming inside it, and starting the destruction. Uphill and around the tower there were a lot more wee blotches of men in blue and white uniforms on the ground. What remained of the Spanish infantry had run off, out-shot by troops that actually practiced live-fire on a regular basis, and as Lewrie made a quick count of the unmoving Spaniards, he felt a bit of relief that the numbers of enemy soldiers who had run might be too few to mount a counter-attack before the tower was set alight.

"Smoke, sir," Westcott said, with some delight. "They've lit it on fire. We'll have them back aboard the ships in the next hour."

*Sapphire*'s Marines came up the scrambling nets and the boarding battens in much quieter takings than their demeanours upon departure, and even the sailors who had manned their boats and had guarded the beach but had not been engaged in the fight seemed much more subdued. The Bosun's Mates and the Surgeon's loblolly boys saw to hoisting *Sapphire*'s wounded up the ship's sides by means of mess-table carrying boards for the seriously hurt, slung horizontal and lifted over the bulwarks with the main course yard, or in Bosuns' chairs for the others.

Through it all, Lewrie stood four-square and stoic amidships of the forward edge of the quarterdeck, hands clasped in the small of his back, 'til Lieutenant Keane reported to him.

"How bad?" Lewrie gruffly asked.

"Not *too* bad, all in all, sir," Lt. Keane said, doffing his hat. "Marine Private Pewitt slain, and five wounded, including Corporal Lester. He's the worst off. Lieutenant Roe got slightly nicked, and Sergeant Clapper twisted an ankle."

"It looked a lot worse from here," Lewrie said, allowing himself a quick sigh of relief. "The soldiers?"

"Captain Bowden's company, in the centre, got the worst of it, sir," Lt. Keane told him, looking weary and red-eyed. The right side of his face, right hand, and his mouth were stained with black powder from discharging and re-loading his own musket, from tearing the paper cartridges open with his teeth. "They were the first ones the Spanish saw in the gloom. I think he has three dead and ten wounded. Captain Kimbrough's lot suffered one dead and six hurt."

"How the Devil did the Dons come t'be there, I'm wonderin'," Lewrie groused. "It's only been a day and a night since we landed at Almerimar. Were they in strength?"

"About one company of foot, sir," Lt. Keane replied, pulling a calico cloth from his coat pocket to mop his face, spit on one corner, and scrub the bitter grains of powder from his lips. "Fifty or sixty, or thereabouts? We took one of their officers as prisoner, and I gathered, given my little Spanish, that they were quartered overnight in the town, *near* the tower, but weren't really there to guard the thing . . . they'd done a route march down from Órjiva just to keep their men fit, and had planned on marching back this morning, after a late breakfast. They'd been barracked overnight in a tavern, and I also gather that they'd had a good drunk.

"It was only our bad luck that some bloody farmer saw us when we were creeping through the wood lot and the orchards, and ran off to wake them, sir," Lt. Keane said, with a shrug.

"Well, if they weren't posted to protect that tower, then it's good odds that some troops from Órjiva *will* be, later," Lewrie decided. "If they're that dear to 'em, that means that one part of our plan is working . . . though it'll make future raids harder."

*Hell, impossible,* Lewrie gloomed to himself; *We're down nigh a half a company of troops, and when I get the lightly wounded back is anyone's guess. Would Dalrymple give me any re-enforcements if . . . ?*

"Major Hughes, sir?" Keane said.

"Hmm?" Lewrie asked, drawn back from his thoughts.

"Major Hughes, sir . . . we lost him," Keane repeated.

"Fallen? Damn," Lewrie spat, though without much sincerity.

"No, sir, I mean *lost* him," Keane insisted. "He just up and disappeared, as if the ground had swallowed him up. We searched, after we had driven the Dons off, but there was just no sign of him."

"How the Devil d'ye *lose* an officer?" Lewrie exclaimed.

"Don't know, sir," Keane replied, looking as if he took Lewrie's question as a personal reproach. "We were more spread out than usual, with Kimbrough out to the left to keep an eye on the town, Bowden in the centre, and our Marines on the right flank, perhaps fifty or more yards 'twixt companies. Major Hughes was with the centre. As soon as we all spotted the Spanish, he started yelling for us to close up and sent runners, just before the firing began. Well, sir, I saw no reason to, since our volleys into the Spanish left were knocking them down like ninepins, and I ordered rear ranks to advance, to get closer.

"The Major runs over to me, screaming, 'What the Hell do you think you're playing at?' and to shift left and form line," Keane went on. "A runner came from Captain Kimbrough, saying that he was advancing by ranks, the same as me, and Hughes . . . got even *louder* and said something like, 'Must I save all you fools from disaster?' and dashed off, leaving the runner with us.

"Captain Bowden says he saw him as he ran past behind his own line, and angling off uphill to where Kimbrough's men were closing, on the Spanish right," Keane continued. "Bowden says that the Major ordered him to stand fast and suppress the foe with fire, and that's the last *anyone* saw of him, for he never reached Kimbrough's company."

"Just damn my eyes," Lewrie exclaimed. "I never heard the like. D'ye think it's possible that the Dons captured him?"

"It's possible, I suppose, sir," Lt. Keane allowed, "but, neither Kimbrough nor Bowden recalls taking fire from any Spaniards *between* their companies, though he might have stumbled into a small party of shirkers or stragglers. The gunsmoke was getting pretty thick by then, so it was getting rather difficult for anyone to see damn-all."

"Damn, what a pity," Lewrie said.

*No, it ain't!* he thought; *I'm shot o' the bastard, either way. If God's just, Dalrymple might scrounge up a replacement. Perhaps he has another family friend's son on his staff who needs t'win himself some spurs?*

"We'll be returning to Gibraltar, soon as everyone's settled," Lewrie assured Keane. "See to your men, sir, and tell them that they did damned well . . . and that we'll 'Splice The Mainbrace' at Seven Bells of the Forenoon. I'll need your written account of the action for my report, along with Kimbrough's and Bowden's, as soon as I can collect them."

"Aye, sir," Keane replied, doffing his hat in departing salute, then trudging down the starboard ladderway to the waist, where most of his Marines were gathered, after turning in their arms and accoutrements. Their initial muted moods had livened, and a trade was springing up in Spanish shakoes, waistbelt and crossbelt plates, and some rank badges ripped from dead Spanish non-commissioned officers.

The dead Private and the wounded were on the orlop and the cockpit surgery, by then, out of sight, if not entirely out of mind.

Lewrie looked over at the transport. Her boats were being led for towing astern, and all her troops were back aboard. He would collect Kimbrough's and Bowden's reports, he thought sadly, when he went aboard *Harmony* in the afternoon, once safely out at sea.

He had four sea-burials to conduct over there.

He hoped those did not signify a dead end to operations, and his vaunting plans.

# CHAPTER THIRTY-TWO

"They *weren't* posted there to guard the semaphore tower?" Mr. Thomas Mountjoy asked, as if he needed further assurance after he had read Lewrie's report a second time.

"Not according to our prisoner, no," Lewrie told him, sprawled in one of Mountjoy's comfortable cushioned chairs on his rooftop gallery. He had a tall glass of Mountjoy's version of his patented cool tea in hand, and was savouring a rare, cool breeze that had arrived with an equally rare morning rain. The gurgle of rainwater sluicing down the tile gutters to catch-barrels and the house's deep cistern, was almost lulling him to a mild drowse. In all, he found it most pleasant to be away from the ship, on solid ground for a spell, and be cool, again. Autumn in the Mediterranean, on the coast of Spain, was still uncomfortably warm.

"They will, though," Mountjoy mused, looking disappointed even if the latest landings had been successful, if not costly. "And, if they do, we'd need a larger force, and at the moment, well . . ."

"Seven dead, aye," Lewrie said with a sigh, for Marine Corporal Lester had died of his wounds, and one of Captain Bowden's soldiers had succumbed, as well. "And nineteen ashore in the hospital, with two permanently lost to amputations. When I can get the others back will take weeks . . . twenty-four men short. Kimbrough and Bowden can shift men around, but that'd give us eighty-eight men, all ranks, and that's just not enough soldiers, and my Marines can't take up the slack."

"Dalrymple," Mountjoy gloomed. "He'll be loath to give us even a handful."

"One just can't take men from one of his regiments and splice 'em into another, among strangers, aye," Lewrie said, equally gloomy. "Assumin' he'd even consider it. Damme, Mountjoy, what we need is some more of your lot's money, another transport, another draught of men, and one more escortin' ship, maybe a frigate."

"And, a Brevet-Major," Mountjoy said with a wry expression.

"Damme, *I* didn't lose him," Lewrie hooted, "the bloody fool lost himself! We didn't even find a single one of his damned egret plumes. It's good odds the Spanish have him, and good riddance."

"If they have him, we'll hear of it, sooner or later," Mountjoy said, rising from his settee to go stand under the edge of the awning to savour the breeze that ruffled his loose shirt. "The Spanish are rather good at doing the honourable thing. They'll report Hughes as an officer on his parole, available to be exchanged for one of their own of equal rank. Aah, that feels hellish-good!" he said, holding both arms out to let the wind have its way.

"Assumin' we have one, of course," Lewrie owlishly commented.

"Haven't heard what Dalrymple's made of it, yet," Mountjoy went on, turning to face Lewrie. "Though I can imagine. Too bad you didn't come ashore in your best-dress uniform, for we've an appointment with the old cove after dinner, today."

"What a grand day for it, then," Lewrie groused, "rain, gloom, and dark clouds. Sounds just *too* bloody jolly. If he has a bad meal, he may shut us down completely."

"Or, tell us to limit our activities to easier objectives, in future," Mountjoy replied, looking sly.

"You have some in mind, something easier to hit?" Lewrie asked.

"A bit more far afield, this time," Mountjoy said, pointing to a slim leather folder which put Lewrie in mind of the pale tan ones that solicitors and barristers used, termed "law calf". It looked a little fatter than usual, as if Mountjoy had gotten a slew of reports, sketches from informers, and locally-made maps and coastal sea charts. "I'll take it along, if he's still amenable."

⚓

Sir Hew Dalrymple must have had a lacklustre dinner, or the weather had put him in a bout of the "Blue Devils", for their reception was very cool, and his appreciation of Lewrie's report was chary.

"A good show, but a most costly one," Dalrymple said, with one of his heavier sighs. "You note that you only have fourty-three Marine Privates at present, and that there are only eighty-eight effectives from the 77th, Captain Lewrie."

"Aye, sir," Lewrie replied, noting that Dalrymple did not address him with the chummier "Sir Alan" this time. "Though, I've yet to use my armed sailors, the ones who row the troops ashore and stand guard over the boats and the landing place."

From the corner of his eyes, he could see Mountjoy almost giving him a congratulary grin.

"Drilled in musketry, are they?" Sir Hew asked, with a dubious brow up, doubting the fighting qualities of sailors.

"Not as efficient as soldiers or Marines, sir," Lewrie told him, "but they can manage controlled volleys. They're more used to firing at will."

"Like country militia," Sir Hew disparaged, waving a hand in the air as if to shoo off such irregular troops. "If, as it now appears, the Spanish have placed small guard units at their semaphore towers, and re-enforced their coastal batteries and fortifications, it may very well be that they will stay in place, whether any further landings are made . . . perhaps for a good, long while, what? Why, one could imagine that, did you trail your colours up and down the coast with your transport in company with you, they would *have* to remain in place, tying down a sizable part of the Spanish Army which might otherwise be available to my counterpart, General Castaños, even is the transport empty, and I may at last send the detachment of the 77th to Sicily to re-join their regiment."

Lewrie had not penned any conclusions about the Spanish response to the raids, and had written nothing about *why* the Dons had been at Salobreña, and both he and Mountjoy were happy that Dalrymple took it as gospel that their efforts had already drawn a portion of the Spanish Army in Andalusia to a wasted task.

"Well, one would hope that you would not, Sir Hew," Mountjoy interjected, "not until their wounded are fully recovered, and they may all go together."

"Which will be some weeks, sir," Lewrie stuck in quickly. "In the meantime, we *do* have sufficient strength for, uhm . . . several easier objectives. Mister Mountjoy has a few in mind . . ."

"Do you, sir?" Dalrymple demanded, wheeling to face the civilian. "Are you in possession of *reliable* information? It would not do to blunder into fights which further decimate your forces, as the recent landing at Salobreña did. Remember the Greek general Pyrrhus . . . he won his battles, but destroyed his army in the process."

"*Most* reliable information, sir," Mountjoy assured the old fellow, who seemed to be becoming more "duffer-ish" by the day. "I have enough to be able to sketch out at least two more landings, though we have not yet laid any plans. Captain Lewrie has only been back a day or two, and has been busy seeing to the needs of his ship, and victualling the troops aboard the transport."

"Yayss, those soldiers of the 77th," Dalrymple drawled, frowning heavily. "And your ship's sailors and Marines, sir. It is already bad enough for the Town Major and Provosts to deal with all the bored drunks of the garrison, and a deal worse to deal with all your *swaggering* drunks and brawlers!"

"All the more reason to re-enforce us and get us back out to sea, sir?" Lewrie said quickly, experimenting with a winning grin. That earned him a scowl, and a twitch of Sir Hew Dalrymple's eyebrows.

"If, Mister Mountjoy, London wishes you to continue this programme of harassment," Dalrymple said, turning to face him, "and you may guarantee me that your so-called easier objectives will show more success than failure, I shall allow you to proceed . . . for the nonce, mind, at your present strength, for, as I have expressed before, there is nothing in my . . . larder . . . to spare.

"Captain Lewrie," Sir Hew said, rounding upon him, again. "In your opinion, could either of the company officers of the 77th serve in overall command of the landing force?"

"What little military experience they have, sir, has been gained during our landings," Lewrie had to tell him. "They were fresh from the regiment's home barracks, and their tailors. Captain Kimbrough is nineteen, and Captain Bowden is a year younger . . . unless either's had a birthday I don't know about."

Dalrymple mused that'un over so long that Lewrie thought he'd fallen asleep, his eyes closed, his chin on his chest, and his breathing deep.

"So . . ." he said, at last, drawing out the word to a chant. "You have need of an older, experienced field officer . . . *another!*"

"Aye, sir," Lewrie replied. "My senior Marine officer is very experienced, older than the other two, but, he's only a First Lieutenant, and I don't know how . . ."

"Of course not," Sir Hew snapped. "Just isn't done. Even did Admiralty award your man a brevet promotion, he'd still be only a Captain of Marines. No, I suppose I must give up an officer seconded to my staff, costing me someone who's only *just* become adept at all the boresome work of headquarters, to the detriment of my offices' efficiency. I shall consider whom I may select, and shall inform you of my choice. Will that be all the under-handed secret agent tomfoolery we must discuss today, Mister Mountjoy?"

"I do believe it is, Sir Hew," Mountjoy said, rising.

"Then I bid you both good day, sirs," Dalrymple replied, shooting to his feet, eager to see the backs of them. Lewrie and Mountjoy almost made it to the tall double doors before Dalrymple got in his parting shot.

"By the by, Captain Lewrie!" Dalrymple called out.

"Sir?"

"When I *do* send you a replacement for the unfortunate Major Hughes, promise me you'll try hard not to lose another one, what?" Dalrymple barked.

"I'll do my best, sir," Lewrie vowed.

# CHAPTER THIRTY-THREE

Mister Deacon, Mountjoy's grim assistant and bodyguard, had been waiting near the exit for his employer to emerge from the meeting, and nodded Lewrie a silent greeting as Lewrie gathered up his hat and his sword belt. Mountjoy gave Lewrie a confident nod and a wink, and that pair set off for the dockside, and their false-front offices.

Lewrie pulled out his pocket watch to determine if it might be time for an early shore supper, and how much time he had to waste with shopping before it was. He looked skyward past the Convent to the stony heights of the Rock; he'd never climbed to the top to see the view, or the Barbary apes, either, and wondered if he should take time to do so, someday soon. Wonder of wonders, though; as he lowered his view to the Convent and its entrance again, who should he see exiting but Maddalena Covilhã!

"Mistress Covilhã!" he called out.

"Ah, Captain Lewrie," she replied, performing a sketchy curtsy as he doffed his hat. She wore the same pale yellow sheath gown with a white shawl as she had the time they'd all dined together, and the same bonnet, and, in Lewrie's opinion, was looking rather winsome and fetching, though her expression was hard, half-angry, half-sad.

"My regrets, about Major Hughes," Lewrie told her.

"All I hear are regrets, Captain Lewrie," Maddalena said, with an impatient shake of her head. "But no one tells me what happened to him. He lodges here, but no one who knew him will talk. I went to his regiment, and they say nothing, either. Do you know, Captain?"

"I do," Lewrie replied, nodding gravely. "I was there. Whyever do they not inform you of his loss? Do they treat it like some state secret?"

"To them, I was his hired woman," Maddalena countered, "so no one will take the *time!* If I am not a wife, of his family . . . see?"

"Let us go and find a place to talk, Mistress Covilhā, and I'll tell you all I know," Lewrie offered, stepping forward to give her his arm, and relishing in her scents of fresh-washed hair and a light, citrony-lemony perfume.

A short block or two away, there was a tavern with an awninged outdoor sitting area and tables and chairs. He seated her, then took a chair across from her at a two-place table, laying his hat aside as a blue-aproned waiter came out to take their orders.

"Is he dead?" Maddalena asked plaintively after they'd ordered light and cool white wine.

"We think the Spanish made him a prisoner," Lewrie said, explaining how the assault on the semaphore tower had occurred, drawing on the tablecloth with a finger. He told her of the gunsmoke and the earliness of the hour, of the confusion, and the last recollections from the junior officers that he'd gathered for his report, what were Hughes's last words, and . . .

" 'Must I be the one to save you fools from disaster?' he said?" Maddalena repeated, and to Lewrie's astonishment, a faint smile curled to life on her lips. "*Māe de Deus,* who was the fool? And did your officers say that he was red in the face? He always was the . . . how do you say . . . blusterer, hah hah!" She laughed right out loud. "English words, some sound so funny!"

"But descriptive," Lewrie drolly replied. " 'Blunder' is another. He *blundered* into a party of Spanish stragglers, most-like, and they took him prisoner. I expect we'll hear from the Spanish authorities, sooner or later, that he's been taken somewhere inland and placed on his parole 'til he can be exchanged for a Spanish officer of equal rank."

"That will take long, Captain Lewrie?" Maddalena asked in some worry, turning sobre again. "A week or so?"

"If we hold a Spanish infantry Captain, and I don't know much on that head, it could take months," Lewrie supposed. "If we don't, well . . . it could be a year or more."

Maddalena's face sagged from hopeful and anxious to a look of utter despair. She put her elbows on the tabletop and pressed fingers to her temples, looking as if she would begin to weep.

"Didn't know ye missed him that much," Lewrie said, reaching a hand out, which she took and squeezed, hard.

"Before he sailed away the last time, he left me two pounds," Maddalena said, "the rent on my lodgings are due next week, and I have thirteen shillings, five pence left. My landlord, he will throw me out, and I will have nowhere to go."

"And how much is the rent?" Lewrie asked.

"Two pounds," she told him, "two pounds a month." She gave his hand another squeeze and made a wee snuffling sound. "Pardon," she pled, letting go his hand to pull a laced handkerchief from a reticle and dab at her nose and eyes.

"Month-to-month, not long-term?" Lewrie wondered aloud, scowling. "Not t'speak ill of the absent, but . . . what a cheese-parer! He *had* money, surely, or his family did. His tailor's bills looked like he spent hundreds . . . egret feathers and all."

"I know he did, but . . ." Maddalena agreed, looking him in the eyes, making a wee pout and a distraught shrug. "I know he had a full purse, even if he was very careful with it."

"Cheap?" Lewrie scoffed, "Or guarded?"

"Both," Maddalena replied, laughing. "Hmm . . . now that he is gone, is it possible he left his money in his rooms at the Convent, or with his regiment? Is there some way someone could get it for me?"

"Unless he left some instructions, a will, or something, I've my doubts," Lewrie had to tell her. "His uniforms, arms, and such will be crated up and stored with his regiment, and what funds he had would be sent on to him, along with his Army pay, to wherever the Spanish are holdin' him. Once his family's told, they might even advance him some money for his upkeep, too, but . . . if you weren't his wife . . ."

"Then I am lost," Maddalena weakly said, hugging herself with her head down. "If I had some way to have some of his money, I would take ship back to Oporto, and start again, but . . ."

"Portugal may not be safe for you, much longer," Lewrie said. "Ehm . . . did Hughes speak to you of how the world's goin'? Did he mention the rumour that Napoleon's ready to invade Portugal t'shut down her trade with Great Britain?"

"I heard that in the markets," Maddalena said, looking up at him, again. "The Major . . . Hughes, he did not explain much to me, or why the French would do so. He boasted that he might have the chance to march with a proper army to *defeat* the French, and how he would liberate Lisbon, if they did. He did not think that I was able to understand important matters," she said, with a sad bitterness.

"Portugal and Sweden are the last hold-outs from his Continental System, and he can't get at Sweden, so . . ." Lewrie explained, laying it all out for her. "You're safe as houses here at Gibraltar, but not at home in Oporto, or your hometown of Covilhā."

He poured them both refills from the wine bottle, and she took a sip or two, looking towards the harbour, and the streets, looking pensive and thoughtful. At last, she turned her gaze to Lewrie, again, frankly and directly.

"To stay here and be safe from the French, Captain Lewrie, I am in need of a protector," she said in a soft tone, smiling a little. "The first time we saw each other at the *ristoran,*" she said, using the Spanish word, "and when you dined with us . . . I felt you wished to be . . . you flirted with your eyes? Yes?"

Her slim hands were in motion, inches above the tablecloth, in hesitant, embarrassed fiddling.

"Yes, I did," Lewrie confessed with a smile. "Yes, I do want to protect you, Maddalena. That, and a lot more, and what's taken us so long?" he joked, which drew forth a hearty laugh from her, and both her hands took hold of his, this time, as she gazed at him longingly. "And I dare say I'll do ye a great deal better than Hughes ever did."

"I knew from the first that you would be a much kinder, a much more . . . pleasant man," Maddalena replied, beaming. "I *wished* from the first, that . . . I day-dreamed?"

Lewrie knew that there was a mutual attraction between them, but he wasn't going to bet the bank on how sincere her protestations of affection were.

"First things first, then," Lewrie said, letting go her hands and reaching for his glass to clink against hers to seal the bargain. "There's a branch of my London bank here, and I'll be needin' t'make a draught on my accounts. Then, we'll go settle with your landlord. After that, a grand supper, your choice of the chop-house!"

"Then let us go . . . how do I call you?" Maddalena asked with an impish expression, "Captain, or Lewrie, or . . . ?"

"My given name's Alan, Maddalena," he told her.

"Alan," she whispered as if it pleased her to her toes.

"Ye don't get *much* for two pounds a month," Lewrie commented, once they had climbed up the stairs to the second storey above the ground floor of her lodging house. There was one large, un-glazed window with inside shutters for night, with a rickety two-place dining table in front of it. Over to the left was a hard-seated, worn settee, a pair of wing-back chairs, and some end tables. Most of the right-hand wall was taken up with a waist-high stone hearth with an iron grill for cooking, the wood and kindling stored in buckets, and some pots, pans, kitchen tools, and a whisk and bucket to sweep out the embers. There was a doorway which led to the second room on the right-hand side, in which there was a decidedly ugly armoire and a couple of traveller's chests, a vanity table and stool with a large mirror, and an ancient wooden bed-stead with a high and garishly-carved headboard, and a mattress as thin as charity, held up by rope suspension. He gave the mattress a hard shove, and it emitted some alarming squeaks. To make matters even worse, Maddalena's windows overlooked a steep, narrow side street that led further uphill from the High Street, and he estimated that he could have spit and hit the narrow iron balconies on the other side!

" 'A poor thing, but mine own', hey?" Lewrie quoted.

"It is cool, most of the day," she told him. Indeed, the lodging house was in the permanent shadow of the mountainous Rock.

"Love what ye've done with it, even so," Lewrie allowed with a grin, for the coverlet on the bed was nice, the bed linens smelled as fresh as new-laundered and sun-dried. There were many candleholders, most black wrought iron, but some made of shiny pewter. In both of the rooms, there were rather good Turkey carpets, some colourful end table coverings, and the settee had been draped with a large, intricately-figured cloth to disguise its age. She'd hung some paintings she'd found in the used-goods markets that weren't all that bad, and of course there was a cross on one wall in the main room and a wood crucifix near the bedstead. Despite Hughes's parsimony, she had made the best of it, with planters and flowers on the outer window sills, some potted plants inside to brighten things up, and . . . there was a large wire cage in which a reddish warbler flitted and cheeped.

"So many need lodgings, so the prices are high, and you find what you can find," Maddalena said by way of apologising, going to the bird cage to whisper and coo to the warbler, which came to her inviting fingers and began to sing its song.

"Down the hallway, in front," Lewrie said, sticking his head out the front, door. "It's open."

"Ah, *sim*, a grain trader rented it, a man who had the temporary license?" Maddalena said, joining him at the door. "But, he lost the right for some reason, and gave it up yesterday."

"Let's go look," Lewrie prompted, leading her down the hall. "Now, this is much better!" he declared, after a quick look about.

The corner unit's two windows were glazed double doors which led to a wide iron balcony, and both of its rooms were much larger, to boot. The planked floors admittedly creaked, here and there, but it was much nicer, and they had been polished. Like Maddalena's it came furnished, but the appointments were newer and showed much less wear.

"How much did he pay for it, I wonder?" Lewrie mused aloud.

"Oh, I think I heard that it was three pounds a month," she said with a rueful look, as if that was simply too extravagant.

"Let's see your landlord," Lewrie announced.

A quarter-hour later, and Lewrie had taken the better lodgings for her, laying out £18 for the next six months, with another pound to see that all her own things would be moved for her, immediately. That lit a fire under her landlord, another of those English expatriates who'd served at Gibraltar and taken their retirement there. He whistled up some porters idling at a nearby tavern, and within the next hour, all her chests and household goods, her plants and linens, all her decorations, and the bird cage had been shifted. She and Lewrie had seen to her wardrobe, and it had proved to be a thin selection of clothing, which he swore that he would improve, at once.

"*Deus,* I cannot believe it!" Maddalena exclaimed after the last porter had gone and the door had been closed. She clutched her new key to her chest for a moment, then flung out her arms and whirled about in delight, dancing round the much larger main room.

"Done good, did I?" Lewrie teased.

She laughed, and came to him to give him a hug in gratitude, a hug which turned into a long, closely pressed embrace.

*Damme, but does she feel promisin'!* Lewrie thought in a delight of his own. He considered it too early on to grope her, but she felt slim and lean, and the press of her breasts against his waist-coat and shirt front bespoke firmness, and perhaps more to her than what her gown had hidden. The hoped-for revelation made his crutch tighten.

"Alan, I knew that you would be a kind man, but this! A very kind man you are," she said, almost purring with her cheek against his, and giving him a squeeze. "And one so generous!"

"D'ye think you'll be happier here?" he asked with a wide grin.

"Immensely happy!" she declared, breaking away at last, and leading him to sit with her on the settee.

"What else d'ye need? A cook? A maidservant?" he prompted to show her even more generosity.

"I have always cooked for myself, or my family," she shrugged the idea off. "Living alone, I do not need a maid, like the *grand* ladies. What would I do with myself if there was someone else to do all the work?" She found the concept amusing. "Even if this is much larger, where would I *keep* a maid? Maybe . . . oh, once a week, I may need a woman to come in and help with the cleaning, but only for a few hours. There is a laundry-woman nearby, and the markets, when I need something, and I do it by myself."

"How much did Hughes give you to maintain yourself when he was not around, then?" Lewrie offered.

"Two or three pounds," she told him. "It was more than enough. He called me . . . another of your odd English words . . . frugal? I need little. Bread, jam for breakfast, perhaps an egg. Cheese, bread, and fruit at mid-day, and I cook a soup with some vegetables for my supper, with a little something sweet for after. I live simply."

"With more, cheese, bread, and wine," Lewrie joshed.

"But, of course, Alan!" Maddalena said, flinging back her head to laugh. "When I wish something finer, I expect that *you* will take me out to a nice *ristoran*, or, how you say, a chop-house?"

"I noted you don't have a locking caddy," he said, craning his head round to peer towards the cooking facilities. "You'll need one, for coffee, tea, cocoa beans, and sugar."

"You British and your tea!" she teased. "I love coffee in the morning, and cocoa at night, but . . . !"

"If we don't find one before I sail, I'll leave you some extra, so you can buy what you need," Lewrie promised, describing the way he'd have his cool tea prepared, with lemon and sugar. "Why, with a little more, you could dine yourself out, when ye wish a better supper, like the lobster at Pescadore's."

That made her look away and down, and when she looked back up at him, she was frowning, and had turned serious.

"I have been under a man's protection before, Alan, but I have never been a whore," she solemnly explained. "I pray to all the saints that I never must be. A woman in Portugal, Spain, or here at Gibraltar especially, where there are so many soldiers . . . unless she is old, a woman who dines alone is mistaken for a whore, and that I will never do. When you are away, I live alone . . . frugally," she swore, her seriousness dissolved by amusement over that English word, again. "Your women in England, they dine out alone, or do they only do so escorted by a man? And what would you think of a woman who goes out alone?"

"Well, they can shop during the day alone, or with a maid or a friend," Lewrie flummoxed, "another girl, their mother, or a member of her family? At night, that's another proposition, 'cause there's the risk of criminals prowlin' about, then they *would* need a man's protection. T'be considered 'respectable' and all."

"But, what you think of a woman by herself at night?" Maddalena pressed, halfway 'twixt dead-serious, but with the air of someone who was eager to win a point.

"Well, is she pretty . . . ?" Lewrie teased, tongue-in-cheek.

"Aha! You see? Even *you* would think her a whore!" Maddalena crowed with delight to prove her assertion, playfully shoving on his chest. "Without a *Senhora Dona* or man of her family, it is not done!"

"Bit lonely, though, just sittin' round by yourself?" Lewrie posed, cocking his head to one side. "Mean t'say . . ."

"Ah, there is the newspaper, books to rent," Maddalena explained, "in Spanish, Portuguese, and English, there is sewing, my bird to talk to . . . I would *like* to get a kitten, but the Major did not like cats. Perhaps if you do not mind . . ."

"Get one!" Lewrie exclaimed, "get a pair! I've had cats aboard in my cabins for ages!" He quickly described Chalky, and what splendid company he made at sea.

Maddalena rewarded him with another close, long hug, and a kiss on his cheek. "*Por Deus,* but you are *wonderful* man!"

⚓

He found a runner to carry a note out to his ship, saying that he would be back aboard by the start of the Forenoon, then helped Maddalena finish stowing away all her things where she wanted them. They went out to the nearby markets for her staples; wine, cheese, bread, fruits and jams, olive oil for cooking, some spices, and coffee, cocoa beans, and coned sugar. She also needed flour, rice, and some of that Moroccan pasta, *cous cous*. Lewrie learned that it was one word, and was *not* pronounced "cows cows". He had to pay a street urchin to help get their "haul" up to her new lodgings.

They dined after sunset at a nearby establishment, lingering to talk and sip wine long after their spicy omelets, cured ham, sliced tomatoes, and rice puddings were finished.

Then . . . back at Maddalena's lodgings, with the heavy oak door locked and barred, Lewrie was invited to get comfortable, taking off his coat, waist-coat, neck-stock, and sword while she hummed to herself at her vanity in the bed-chamber. When she returned, she was barefoot, padding to join him on the settee in a dressing robe which she held close at the throat, as if hesitant to fulfill her part of the "bargain" she'd made with him for a time.

Only a few candles were lit, there was another bottle of that effervescent Spanish wine to share, and after some time spent talking and laughing softly, she leaned closer, then closer, 'til they shared a first, timid kiss. Lewrie did not wish to maul her, to begin their arrangement brutishly, but it was a damned hard thing to deny his rising excitement. Their embraces and kisses began gently, worshipping her fine neck, her ears, her eyes and cheeks, and it was Maddalena who responded with pleased moans, loosening her dressing robe to bare her shoulders, her throat, to his kisses, chuckling low and drawing him onward. Teasingly, tantalisingly, at last she took hold of his right hand, kissed his wrist and his palm, then placed his hand on her breast.

She slipped away from him, rose, snuffed all but one candle, and padded to the door of her bed-chamber, beckoning him to follow.

What fantacies Lewrie had envisioned of her form did not hold a candle to the reality of her. Her arms, back, and torso were lean and firm, sweetly tapering to the swell of her hips, a firm, flat belly, and long, slim legs. Her breasts were firm and warm, with large, dark *areoli* and puckery nipples, which Lewrie worshipped as he held her so very cuppable lean bottom.

Once completely nude, they stood by the side of the bed-stead, with her thighs slightly parted, and his hard manhood between, pressing together, their hips moving as Lewrie gently ran his hands over her smooth flesh, feeling as if he might explode that instant, and she loosed her long, dark hair to swish across her back and over his eager hands.

At last, she stepped back, looked him in the eyes with that same frank and open expression, smiling mysteriously as she got into bed and reached out to draw him down to join her, and her body, in the light of a single candle, was golden.

It had been so long, Lewrie wanted to roar, seize her hips, and thrust in at once, but instead, he kissed her all over, from her neck to her belly, which made her groan and writhe, and he could feel her belly quiver a little. With his senses alive beyond imagining, Lewrie slid up and eased into her, slowly, 'til he was sheathed in her warm wetness, so deep that there was no depth left to plumb, and Maddalena lifted her knees, reached down to his bottom, and urged him on to the last, and gave out a cry. He released at last, mindless minutes later, in a burst of immense, searing pleasure, thrusting away to salvage and savour the last waves of it, and Maddalena clawed at his back, panting and whimpering, then gave out a gasping, "*Sim*, yes, ahh!" and arched her back with her thighs about him, clinging as if she was drowning in her own joy, and snatching at anything that might keep her afloat.

Lewrie put the intensity of the experience down to how long it had been since he had lain with a woman, but he was wrong. Maddalena tantalised him to a second go, he kissed her all over to begin a third, and each time his delight was just as shattering, if not better. And, as they at last fell into an exhausted, entwined sleep, she bestowed one last, lingering kiss, and whispered, "I *felt* that you might be a wonderful man, Alan, but now I *know* . . . so wonderful in *all* things."

He looked back one last time before making his way to the quays the next morning, and Maddalena was standing on her balcony in her dressing gown, sipping coffee. He waved, feeling like a schoolboy, and she blew him a kiss, her smile as wide as his. Waking to snuggle and kiss, tease and chuckle, whispering tentative sweet nothings to each other, well . . . it had been all that he could do to rise, dress, and depart, wishing that he could take the whole day off, just once.

*Damme, I've "bought" me a woman!* Lewrie marvelled to himself; *And it may be the best bargain I've made in ages! So passionate and pleasin'! Just some long delays, so I can stay in port a few more days, please Jesus.*

His steps were jaunty, even as he realised that the arrangement could not last; such things rarely did. He would be at sea three weeks out of four, so long as they continued raiding the Spanish coast, and seeing to his ship's needs, and *Sapphire*'s people's needs, would take up most of his time in port, leaving little for Maddalena, who would, after a time, surely wish to seek a "cozier" keeper, who would be around more often. Men got bored after a while, which was why they ran out to seek mistresses, after their wives whelped littl'uns, and gave all their affections to the babes, or got porcine in the process. He knew of only one man of his acquaintance, his old school chum, Peter Rushton, now Viscount Draywick, who was still with his mistress, after six years, and that was most-likely due to the nearness of the lodgings he gave her to Parliament, and Peter's seat in the House of Lords.

Well, Tess *was* a charming, darling, and lovely creature, passionate—when Lewrie had bedded her—and Peter *had* told him that she was a "raree", one of the few young women he knew who had little desire for fripperies, luxuries, or costly things, and was more than happy to be snug, secure, and cared for.

*Christ!* Lewrie thought; *Maddalena's beginnin' t'sound like Tess! One from Portuguese peasantry, t'other Bog-Irish poor! I could never take her* t'London, *but . . . maybe she* is *a good, long-term bargain!*

# BOOK FOUR

And in regions far,
  Such heroes bring ye forth
    As those from whence we came,
Under that star
  Not known unto our North.

"To the Virginian Voyage"
Michael Drayton (1563-1631)

# CHAPTER THIRTY-FOUR

Minor repairs, re-tarring and slushing, re-roving with fresh rope, some touch-up paint, then re-victualling both ships took three days before the *Sapphire*'s people were given shore liberty, watch by watch, keeping Lewrie aboard most of the time, with only a few hours ashore from the start of the First Dog Watch 'til midnight. It might have been guilt that he might be abandoning his duties that tore him from Maddalena's fervent embraces before dawn, and "All Night In" which he really desired. His officers and crew could speculate, but no one knew for sure what drew him ashore so often. Japes were made that he *was* known in the Fleet as "Ram-Cat" Lewrie, and not for his choice of pets, or his fierceness in battle, either.

"Your note said you've a new objective in mind, Mountjoy?" he asked as he entered that worthy's lodgings, handing his sword and hat to Deacon, who gave him a knowing nod.

"Ah, Captain Lewrie!" Mountjoy said, springing to his feet in good cheer. "I do, sir, and may I name to you a replacement officer just seconded to us . . . Captain Richard Pomfret, late of the 16th Regiment of

Foot. Captain Pomfret, I name to you Captain Sir Alan Lewrie, Baronet, of HMS *Sapphire*."

"Honoured to make your acquaintance, Sir Alan," Captain Pomfret said, offering his hand, and a quick jerk of his head.

"As am I t'make yours, Captain Pomfret," Lewrie replied in kind, sizing him up. Pomfret was tall, nearly six feet, wide-shouldered and slim-waisted, with a hawk's beak nose, thick dark-blond hair, and pale green eyes, a fellow in his late twenties, Lewrie judged. He looked to be experienced, if the puckered scar on his right cheek meant anything.

"Captain Pomfret was in command of the 16th's Light Company, d'ye see, Captain Lewrie," Mountjoy went on, "and is more used to the skirmish than was Major Hughes." He said that with a wink.

"Mountjoy's told you of our past operations, and how irregular our tactics have been, then, sir?" Lewrie asked.

"He has, sir, as has General Dalrymple," Pomfret said with a confident grin. "It'd seem that rapid, assault, and aggressiveness, are your boys in such endeavours, after a stealthy landing and a quiet creep to the objective, of course. Sounds champion! I'm looking forward to the job. Met the other officers, and had a look-in at the 77th's barracks to introduce myself to the troops. They seem a fine lot."

"They've proven to be, aye," Lewrie agreed.

"And, here's Deacon with the wine," Mountjoy cheerfully said, playing the merry host. "Sit you down, sirs, and I will explain all."

After one glass of a crisp Portuguese white wine, and several minutes of chitchat by way of introductions, Mountjoy rose and went to fetch his charts and hand-drawn maps, along with the pertinent agents' reports.

"There are no towns or wee seaports near the objective that I have in mind, sirs," Mountjoy began, rolling out the chart. "There, at the tip of Cabo de Gata, on some high ground, the Spanish have begun a battery on this out-jutting spur of headland. Further inland, and above it, there already is a semaphore tower, manned by the usual handful of soldiers. The battery, so my reports say, will mount six twenty-four-pounders when completed. As you can see in this sketch, they've finished the foundations, and are erecting the stone walls, with a long section with four guns, and two shorter sections either end, angled back and will mount the other two cannon. The ramparts are up level with the flagged floor, now, and work is just started to raise the parapets to the planned height.

"Wooden barracks for the garrison are back here, up the slope," Mountjoy continued, using a stub of pencil to indicate the details, "and the powder magazine is being dug out here, 'twixt the works and the barracks, very deep . . . earthen, under a mound of excavated earth. They may flag its floor, just to keep damp out of the powder barrels, but that's not been done yet."

Mountjoy went on to explain that the masons and the labourers were drawn from several farming villages that lay inland, the stone brought in from quarries near Almeria by ox-drawn waggons, and the labourers fed and sheltered in a tent camp near the foot of the slope that led up to the semaphore tower.

"They ain't happy workers, mind," Mountjoy told them. "Here it is almost harvest season, and most of them have been conscripted for the work, dragooned from their fields, orchards, and flocks, and the pay is very low, and, at the moment, considerably in arrears."

"Slave labour, you mean," Captain Pomfret said, with a snort of derision, sitting more erect.

"Pretty much, yes," Mountjoy agreed, "and dragged away from their women and children, to boot. Oh, there are whores a'plenty at the tent camps, but I doubt if the workers have two *centavos* to rub together for that, much less enough for a skin of very rough wine, so they've little to do after dark beyond grumbling, and trying to run off, so I doubt if the workers will present your men much resistance, Captain Pomfret, when you land. They may *help* you tear the bloody place down!"

"It's not so far along that hitting it will delay them much," Lewrie pointed out, "we could kill the oxen, burn the waggons, burn the semaphore tower, but . . . if the magazine isn't finished, there'd be no powder to blow up, and no explosives we could use to destroy the ramparts, unless we haul our own up, and that'd take hundreds of kegs, and hours t'put in place. And, two questions . . . are the bloody guns already there, and where's the nearest beach?"

The headland of Cabo de Gata was too rocky for a landing, and the beach below it was much too narrow, according to the sea chart, and the sketches. The nearest beach was two hundred yards East of the headland, broader and sandier, but *Sapphire* and the transport could not fetch-to any closer than a mile from shore. It would be a long row, both ways.

"How large a garrison is there?" Pomfret asked, his forehead creased in worry. "The Spanish must have *some* force to keep the workers from running off, I should think, else the whole project falls apart for lack of diggers."

"There is at least a company of Spanish troops," Mountjoy had to admit, with a touch of worry in his own face. "A mixed bag, really. Cooks, infantry, some engineer officers and their aides, and about a dozen cavalry. My informants say that they're used to patrol round the site to prevent workers from deserting, and running down those of them who make off."

"Mountjoy, is this like Salobrena?" Lewrie asked, scowling. "The only target you know the most about?" He shared a quick look with Captain Pomfret, who had evidently been filled in on Salobrena by the officers of the 77th; neither man looked that confident. "It seems t'me that ye might let this'un hatch, first, or let the Dons lay their egg *before* we go smash it, when the workers are gone, and the powder's there, so there's more for the Spanish t'lose, and their garrison'd be about seventy-five or eighty artillerymen . . . about ten or twelve men per gun, maybe fifteen?"

"Rather a steep climb up from that beach to the battery, up a draw that could get us enfiladed from either side, what?" Pomfret pointed out. "Not to be a croaker . . . just saying."

"You *do* have other objectives in mind, don't you?" Lewrie demanded. "Something easier t'get at? It seems t'me that we'd be better off cruisin' up and down the shore, shellin' the place from a mile off with quoins out, at maximum elevation. *That'd* stir 'em up, and cause bags of chaos and mayhem.

"That's our brief, don't ye know, Captain Pomfret," Lewrie said to the Army officer with a wink and a grin, "creatin' chaos and mayhem in job-lots."

Mountjoy did not take that at all well; he sat back with his arms crossed upon his chest, scowling with his lips pursed and brows furrowed. "It is my best . . . our best . . . option at the moment, yes," he grudgingly confessed. "The others are too strongly defended, or too hard to get at, at present. Hmm." He drummed his right-hand fingers on his left arm. "How about this, sirs. *Sapphire* will close the coast and take it under fire, up and down, 'til the battery's damaged and the garrison and the workers have been run off. Then, if the two of you deem it practical, land the troops and scandalise the works and the semaphore tower. No pre-dawn surprises, do it in broad daylight."

"Well . . ." Lewrie tentatively responded, after taking a deep breath and slowly exhaling. "How do *I* judge if the battery's damaged sufficiently from a mile off, by telescope? How would Captain Pomfret judge that the defenders've been driven away from *his* transport, which will be fetched-to even *further* off? Whose responsibility is it to committ the troops into God knows what? Just a simple sailor, me."

"Good point, sir," Pomfret agreed, breaking out a wee smile. "The responsibility and assessment of the risk . . . not the 'simple sailor' part."

"Aye, I can hammer the place," Lewrie allowed, though still in some doubt as to the value of the attack. "Though it's more the work of howitzers or sea-mortars, with fused explosive shells. I'll take *Harmony* along, just in case, but I doubt if the troops, or my Marines, will have much of a chance t'get their feet wet. Perhaps you should take passage aboard *Sapphire*, Captain Pomfret," Lewrie suggested. "If a decision to land the troops must be made, it'd be best if we were face-to-face. Signal hoists are for *orders*, not discussion, and the best I could send would be 'yes', 'no', or, 'maybe'."

"I'd hoped to be with my troops, sir," Pomfret said, "but in this case, I agree that I should be in the same ship as you. My officers are practised enough in dis-embarking their companies, by now, and if we do decide to land the men, I could go in with your Marines."

"We're settled, then?" Mountjoy perkily said. "Everyone satisfied? Good!" he bulled on, not waiting for them to respond. "Deacon and I will prepare copies of the maps, sketches, and the chart, and we'll consider the battery at Cabo de Gata our next objective."

They shared a final glass of wine and some more idle chatter, in which, to Lewrie's shock, Pomfret casually revealed that he had been with his regiment on Sicily, but had been brought to Gibraltar and the naval hospital after being wounded in action, along with some men of the 16th Foot, and had only been on staff duties at the Convent for a fortnight after being released!

"Good God, d'ye think he's physically up to it?" Lewrie asked, with a queasy feeling, after Pomfret had taken his leave. "I doubt if Dalrymple'd appreciate it if he keeled over."

"He looks fit as a fiddle to me, and I've been assured that he is cleared for duty," Mountjoy replied with a faint grin. "An officer experienced at skirmishing is the best we could have hoped for, as you said yourself in the beginning."

"I'll have t'take your word for him, then," Lewrie said, with a shrug. "He doesn't seem *half* the tight-arse that Hughes was. Heard anything of what happened to him, yet?"

"No, the Spanish haven't sent Dalrymple any word," Mountjoy told him, then got a crafty look oh his phyz. "Speaking of Hughes . . . Mister Deacon told me you've adopted his mistress. If the lady that he saw you with is not Hughes's girl, then she's the spitting image."

"I have," Lewrie replied, grinning. "She is."

"Shore lodgings? Removing from one to another? Shopping?"

"Dammit, Mountjoy, have ye set him t'spy on *me?*" Lewrie barked.

"Nothing of the sort," Mountjoy replied, with a wave of his hand. "Just idle happenstance that he saw you. Christian *charity,* is it?"

"The stupid fool left her nothing, and made no arrangements for her upkeep should anything happen to him," Lewrie objected. "I asked about with his fellow officers, but he hadn't a thought for her. His loss. More like pagan lust, if you must categorise it. I was quite taken with Mistress Maddalena Covilhã from the first time I saw her and Hughes dining, as you well know, and as you cautioned me to shun, so Hughes wouldn't go pettish on us. Utterly *wasted* on a swine like Hughes. She's Portuguese . . ."

"From a mountain town named Covilhã, thence from Oporto, where she took up with a young man in the wine trade," Mountjoy interrupted, ticking off what he knew, "and followed him to Gibraltar in 1803. He perished in the last bout of Gibraltar Fever in 1804, and she's been 'under the protection' of a series of British officers since. She's fluent in English as well as Spanish and her native tongue, is well-read in all three languages, and is much brighter than one would imagine of a young woman from such a background, with a fine mind."

"You've spied on *her?*" Lewrie gawped.

"As soon as Hughes was chosen to command our troops, we looked into her," Mountjoy said, with that sort of "I know something that you don't know" superiority that was rife in the espionage trade, and which had always gotten right up Lewrie's nose. "I told you early on that Gibraltar's simply teeming with suspect foreigners, and the last thing we needed was a tempting young woman in contact with the enemy, who might beguile a braggart like Hughes into revealing too much of our plans, or my sources, and *how* we gathered information on potential targets. I have to protect my network."

"Mine arse on a band-box!" Lewrie barked.

"For your information, Mistress Covilhã is guileless and safe," Mountjoy assured him, slyly amused. "Though it wouldn't do to reveal too much of our doings to her, even so. Second-hand blabbing in the markets *could* be overheard by *real* enemy agents. For a time, I had a thought to recruit *her*, don't ye know, if only to see if Hughes could be trusted to keep mum, and, she's a clever girl, and could listen to what talk there is in the markets, and assist Deacon in shadowing any people we suspect. Who'd suspect a girl of twenty-three, out on her shopping, what?"

*Twenty-three?* Lewrie wolfishly thought; *Yum, yum!*

"So, take what joy you may, for as long as you can," Mountjoy suggested with a twinkle, "and I'm sure you'll treat her better than Hughes ever would."

"And make arrangements, should . . ." Lewrie agreed, stopping short of the thought of his own demise, and rapping the nearest wood surface for luck, and to ward off the very idea.

"Quite," Mountjoy said, beaming.

"Well, if that's all, I'm off," Lewrie said, tossing back the last of his wine and rising. "Time for my dinner . . . *our* dinner."

"*Bon appétit*!" Mountjoy cheerfully wished, with a wry wink. "Oh, by the by, before you go, I think I should pass along one bit of information that's reached me *via* Cummings and his damned boat. He's been into Cartagena, and says that there's some activity round the navy yards . . . a couple of large frigates now have their yards crossed and are victualling?"

"The Dons, preparing t'go to sea?" Lewrie said, frowning. "If that's so, perhaps I should leave the transport behind, this time. It ain't *all* the warships in Cartagena gettin' ready, is it? Their Navy hasn't ventured out since Trafalgar, and I can't think of a good reason for them t'start, unless our raids've pricked 'em too sore."

"Cummings said that it was only the two frigates," Mountjoy assured him as he rose to see him out, "but, he was in no position to nose about too closely. Do you think they *might* sail out against us?"

"Hmm . . . not unless they knew exactly where we'd be goin' this time," Lewrie replied, slowly mulling over the possibilities. "Else, they'd have to cruise the whole coast from Málaga to Alicante, lookin' for us, and that'd require that they manage t'slip past the blockadin' squadrons, first. To cruise in search of us would put them at risk of bein' spotted by our other ships, brought to action, and taken before they discover *us*."

"Well, keep a sharp eye peeled, no matter," Mountjoy cautioned.

"Aye, I shall," Lewrie promised, though he was quickly coming to see the odds of the Spanish sailing, and finding him, quite low.

*For now, I'll eat, drink, and be* hellish-*merry with Maddalena,* he told himself on the way down the stairs, past Mister Deacon's faint leer as if *he* knew exactly where he was going, and who he would be with. *Damn all sneakin' spies,* he thought; *And what they must think o' me. And the Dons? Tomorrow's another day!*

# CHAPTER THIRTY-FIVE

"*Mãe de Deus,*" Maddalena cooed with her head resting against his shoulder, still a little breathless from their last bout of lovemaking, with one slim leg cross his. "*Maravilhoso.*"

"My stars," Lewrie said with a chuckle of delight, sprawled on his back with his arms loosely embracing her. "Damned *right,* it was! Ye deserve a reward for *that,* me girl." Which statement made her laugh deep in her throat, snuggle closer, and make purring sounds. She had slipped atop him and had ridden "St. George", this time, abandoning her earlier reticence and modesty, spitted upon his lance, pierced to the heart and dying the "little death" as the mythic dragon had, hair swishing, strong fingers clutching his shoulders, rocking, thrusting mindlessly, and crying out 'til the moment she'd broken. He had not reached his release, and after a long moment, had thrust upwards and had driven her to a second effort, even more frantic than the first. Lewrie had taken hold of her wrists and had leaned her back, feeling how she'd grown snugger and snugger, savouring her wee yelps and gasps 'til the moment he'd exploded as hot and as fiercely as a great gun, and she had quivered and cried out as she'd found a second, searing wave of utter bliss, almost at the same instant as his, which had left them gasping and completely spent.

"That *was* my reward, Alan," Maddalena whispered close to his ear, a pleased-beyond-measure smile curling her lips. "I please you?"

"God, yes! You please me right down to me toes, Maddalena," he assured her, turning to share a long soul kiss, eliciting a long, happy groan from her before they snuggled up, again, eyes closed in exhaustion, and sighing. "Every time, in fact," he murmured.

"*Sim,* me too," she vowed, reaching up one hand to stroke at his cheek. "Such a wonder I never know . . .'til you," she said with a wee giggle. "Uhm . . . pardon, but I have to . . ."

She rose, slipping away from him, trailing her hand down his outstretched arm as she left the bed to go behind a Chinese-looking folding screen to use the chamber pot. "Play with Precious," she said.

Lewrie rolled over to her side of the bed and lifted the waiting kitten up to the sheets. "Spyin' on us, are ye, kitty?" he said.

Precious was Maddalena's latest acquisition, found in one of the local markets, though paying even six pence for him, when Gibraltar Town teemed with strays, Lewrie thought silly. He was a ram-cat, only three months or so old, wide-eyed and white-furred, with random splotches of ginger. As soon as he had all four paws down, he gave out a wee *Mew* and pounced on Lewrie's wiggled fingers, and his tiny fangs and claws were sharp! Before Lewrie could pull the sheets up to cover his groin, Precious discovered the ribbons which bound his cundum on, and the kitten made a pounce in that direction!

"Oh no, ye don't!" Lewrie cried, scooping him up.

Maddalena returned from behind the screen, her dressing gown on but unbound, and the sight of her marvellously pleasing and delightful body made Lewrie beam at her. "Here, you manage this wee beast whilst I take my turn before he claws me 'wedding tackle'."

"Oh, never do that, Precious," Maddalena cooed at her kitten, picking him up and cuddling it to her breast. "Some things are precious to me besides you," she added, looking teasingly at Lewrie.

*Here, that sounds damned promising,* Lewrie thought as he took off his cundum and stowed it in a linen draw-string bag, then let go a stream of pee into the chamber pot, quickly putting the lid back on, regretting that fetchingly good-looking young women's shite smelled as disagreeable as normal people's. "Whew!" he whispered, wrinkling his nose, before returning to the bed-chamber.

Maddalena had tied the sash of her dressing gown, so he felt that he should don his long-tailed shirt, at least, which might protect his groin should the kitten go exploring, again. He stretched out beside her on the bed, propped up on one elbow, gave her a short kiss, and accepted a glass of wine that she'd poured for him in his absence. A neutral American merchant ship, still allowed to trade with France, had come in with lashings of luxury goods including champagne, and he had purchased a case of twelve, and had brought two of them along for their evening together. Even warm, it still tasted very good.

"You must leave before midnight?" Maddalena asked with a little pout.

"Not tonight, no," Lewrie told her, with a gladsome sigh and a laugh. "Thought I'd take an 'All Night In', and go back aboard round sun-up." He grinned again, recalling what had passed last year when he'd had the *Reliant* frigate, when his ever-randy First Lieutenant, Geoffrey Westcott, had wished for an "All Night In" ashore in Buenos Aires, and their Sailing Master at the time had quipped, "All Night In in *what?*" *Should've asked "In* Whom!" he thought.

"*Bom*, good!" Maddalena said, leaning close to brush her cheek upon his. "I do not like when you leave me in the middle of the night. I like sleeping with you, the waking up, and seeing you off with coffee and some bread and jam."

"That pleases me, too," Lewrie muttered fondly. "It's hellish-hard t'leave your bed for me . . . your warmth, your sweet aroma?"

"You like my perfume?" she teased in a soft, promising voice.

"All of you *and* your perfume," he cooed back.

Maddalena scooted up the bed, plumped up the thick feather pillows, and lolled against the headboard, giving out a glad sigh.

"Ah," she said, cocking her head to one side to listen. Far off, there was a rumble of thunder. A breeze stirred the chintz drapes by the open doors to the balcony, and a patter of rain could be heard as a late autumn storm blew up. "Good!" she declared. "You cannot go to sea tomorrow. I pray it rains all week!"

"Won't last that long, more's the pity," Lewrie said, getting up to pad to the balcony for a look, then returning. "We'll be back at sea in a day or two. Gone for a fortnight, perhaps. About that," he added, getting back in bed, up by the headboard near her. "When I do sail, on the rare off-chance, I've made arrangements for you if . . . something happens to me. Don't look so distressed, Maddalena! It is only prudent. The branch offices of Coutts' Bank is holding a sum for you, and a letter of instructions. *If* I don't return, your rent will be paid for a full year beyond the six months. I already paid, and you're t'have ten pounds a month to live on. If ye wish to take passage somewhere else, you can exchange the year's rent for . . ."

She set aside her glass of wine and threw herself upon him to clutch him close and squeeze. "Do not say that, Alan! Do not tempt Fate! *Por Deus,* you give me more happiness than I know in years, so kind and generous, so gentle with me, so funny you are, so merry with me . . . !" She broke off in a choked sob, and he felt tears wetting her close-pressed cheek.

"Dear girl, dear girl!" he muttered, stroking her to try and ease her sudden fears. "I'll *not* leave you in the lurch like that un-thinking, uncaring fool Hughes did. I'd do the same for you even if I suddenly got orders sendin' me halfway round the world. I'd not sail off and just abandon you, in any case. You're dear to me."

He heard a quick, in-drawn breath, and knew that he'd erred badly. *Fool! Should've said* "becoming", *not* already *dear!* Lewrie chid himself: *God knows what she'll make of it, and . . .*

"You are dear to me, too, Alan," Maddalena whispered against his neck, then leaned back to look him in the eyes, sobrely for a moment, then began to beam as she took another shuddery breath. "So very dear!"

*Too late!* he thought; *I'm in the quag up t'my neck!*

Maddalena put her arms round his neck and kissed him, a writhing and long soul kiss with her breath growing musky again, and almost giggling deep in her throat in sheer delight of his declaration.

*Oh, Hell,* Lewrie thought; *In for the penny, in for the pound . . . and if I get her drunk enough, maybe she won't remember in the mornin'.*

She pulled him down over her, impatiently tugged the sash of her gown and parted it, then reached under the tails of his shirt to draw it upward, light fingers brushing against his re-awakening erection.

For a *very* brief moment, Lewrie considered qualifying his slip of the tongue, but decided to go with it, wondering if Maddalena's passion could be any greater than that she'd evinced before.

"Just . . . let me get a, ah, umm . . . cundum," he rasped.

# CHAPTER THIRTY-SIX

"Lastly," Lewrie said to the assembled officers and Mids gathered aboard the transport for a final planning session, "we've gotten a report that there are two Spanish frigates with their yards crossed and taking provisions aboard in Cartagena. How they expect to elude our blockade's beyond me, but one never knows, so we should be prepared for 'em, should they manage t'come out. Captain Hedgepeth?"

"Aye?" the ugly old bugger responded as if wakened from utter boredom. The most he'd done in the meeting was scratch his whiskers.

"Do we spot any strange sail whilst the troops are ashore, I'll fire two guns for a General Signal, and hoist Discontinue The Action," Lewrie told him. "Captain Pomfret, do I make the signal, drop whatever you're doing and get your troops back to the beach, instanter, for recovery. As soon as the troops are back aboard, Captain Hedgepeth, get under way and run Westerly as fast as you can. I will cover your withdrawal as best I can, even if you get back to Gibralter all alone."

"Ehm, what if the Dons are upon us before my Marines, and your boat crews, are back aboard *Sapphire*, sir?" Lieutenant Keane asked in a worried tone. "Mean t'say, sir, our ship would be short-handed, and Roe and I would miss out on a good fight."

"Hmm, little chance o' that, I think," Lewrie replied after a moment of thought. "With decent weather . . . else we'd not land . . . we should be able t'see their tops'ls over twelve miles away, and would have enough time to get everyone off the beach, at least an hour and a half before they were up within gun range. As I said, it's only a remote possibility, but, it's best if we didn't leave anything to mere chance. Questions? Answers? Anybody want a sweet?" he japed.

There were a few niggling details, mostly answered by Captain Pomfret since they dealt with operations ashore, and a meek gripe from Midshipmen Hillhouse and Britton that, if there *was* a possibility of a sea-fight in the offing, was there any way for them to get back aboard *Sapphire* before it happened, the answer to which was "no"; they had a responsibility to speed the men of the 77th back aboard *Harmony,* then aid Captain Hedgepeth in driving his ship out of harm's way as rapidly as she could, and if she was overtaken, organise the boat crews into as stout a resistance as possible.

The meeting broke up soon after that, and Lewrie and his two Marine officers took a boat back to *Sapphire*.

"Beg pardon, sor, but, we'll be goin' out on another'un soon?" his Cox'n Liam Desmond asked as he handled the boat's tiller.

"Good possibility, Desmond," Lewrie cryptically muttered back.

"Wish we was goin' ashore with th' solgers, sor," Furfy said. "I got me a taste for them cured Spanish hams, and sure, th' Spanish must have better wine than wot we can buy here."

"You go foraging, Furfy, and ye just might get taken by the Dons, like Major Hughes," Lewrie said with a grin. "No ham or wine, in a Spanish prison hulk, not for the likes of us."

"You'd be surprised by how raw and bad is the wine that we've run across," Marine Lieutenant Roe told Furfy. "Just peasant swill."

"Ah, well . . . someday," Furfy said, with a disappointed sigh.

"Mister Keane, might you join me in my cabins once we're back aboard?" Lewrie invited.

"Of course, sir," Keane replied.

"What do you make of Captain Pomfret?" Lewrie asked once they were seated, and had glasses of cool tea in hand.

"Oh, he's *miles* better than Major Hughes, sir!" Keane replied, with a smile on his face. "I gather he's had far more experience in combat, too.

And, having led a light company of skirmishers, he's much more . . . flexible," Keane related, searching for the right word for a second or so. "More . . . enthusiastic, too. In our latest exercises on the parade ground, he's not only worked us in separate companies, one covering the advance or retirement of the next, but broke the companies down into platoons of eight or ten men so that part of each company can advance whilst the rest are firing. In our case, he's drilled us as five files of ten men each, three delivering fire and two in motion, then two firing while three move. He said that he wished that he had a chance to get the troops used to skirmishing in pairs, too, sir . . . the rear-rank man covering his mate, and taking turns shooting, but, he thought it might be too much, too soon."

"Sounds . . . ambitious," Lewrie said, nodding. "Not that I know all that much about land-fighting, but it may be so novel an approach that the enemy would be confused, and overwhelmed by the speed with which it's done. So, you're satisfied, Mister Keane, in the tactics, and with Captain Pomfret?"

"Completely, so, sir," Keane enthusiastically told him, and that was saying something from a man as stern and sobre as Keane.

"Very good, then," Lewrie said, glad that the land side of any future landing seemed to be in good hands. "Weather allowing, we will embark the troops tomorrow afternoon, and sail at first light the day after. Thank you, Mister Keane, for your opinions."

"Aye, sir," Keane said, finishing his glass of tea and rising.

"More tea, sir?" Pettus asked once Keane had departed.

"No, not for now, Pettus," Lewrie told him, moving over to the settee where he could sprawl and prop his feet on the tray table. He still had his doubts about striking at the incomplete battery at Cabo de Gata, worried that Mountjoy might be too eager to show his superiors in London that they were getting a good return on the money they'd advanced him, and that he'd chosen Cabo de Gata for lack of actionable information on a better one. Lewrie hoped that Mountjoy hadn't opted for it out of quiet desperation! If *he'd* been in charge of selecting targets, he would have waited 'til that battery was complete, but . . . he wasn't in charge; he was *still* a gun-dog to Secret Branch, even after all these years.

"Sit up, beg, sic 'em," he sourly muttered. "*Good* boy!"

That drew Chalky from his contemplations of devouring the gulls that alit on the stern gallery's rails. He came trotting with his tail up, mewing for attention and leapt into Lewrie's lap for a minute or two of pets, before settling down for a slit-eyed nap, sprawled across Lewrie's legs.

Lewrie considered going to his desk to pore over the operational details one more time, closely scan the best coastal chart that could be found with a magnifying glass looking for the unforseen reef, shoal, or obstruction, but he'd already done that a dozen times. He yawned, and considered a nap might be of better use. The next day, the weather allowing, he'd be busy with the last-minute preparations and the loading of troops, and at getting his ship to sea the next. Tonight was his last opportunity for a run ashore, and a man would need to be well-rested for a night with Maddalena.

*Damme, I keep with her much longer, and I'll have t'send to London for another two dozen o' the Green Lantern's very best cundums,* he mused, not trusting the cheaper ones smuggled cross The Lines from Catholic Spain, where the prevention of babies was harshly dis-approved, if not the risk of catching the Pox from a diseased doxy. Lewrie thought that the Spanish might even accept that risk as a scare tactic to keep their benighted people chaste!

Since that blabbed "dear to me", and Maddalena's declaration in kind, she had not *said* anything more upon that head, but she had become fonder, more affectionate, and even more passionate for a certainty, walking closer to him when they went about the town, reaching across restaurant tables to touch hands when they dined, and rewarded him with bright, adoring smiles. In her lodgings, she even *hummed* to herself, and her bird and her kitten, as if pleased with the entire world, and when in bed . . . frantically and often!

*A nap, definitely,* Lewrie told himself; *Else a hot kiss and a cold breakfast'd like t'kill me!*

# CHAPTER THIRTY-SEVEN

"It seems we've created quite a scramble already, sir," Captain Pomfret said as he peered ashore with his pocket telescope. "Might I borrow your glass, Captain Lewrie?"

"Certainly," Lewrie said, handing over the much longer and much stronger day-glass as *Sapphire* and the transport closed the coast off Cabo de Gata under reduced sail.

"Oh, yes!" Pomfret said, with a laugh. "The semaphore tower is whirling away like a Turk Dervish, and the tent camp looks like an ant hill that some boys have kicked . . . all the workers are hitching or saddling up, and running inland."

"*El diablo negro*," Lt. Westcott said with a laugh, baring his teeth in a brief, harsh grin. "That's what the Dons called us when we were taking and burning anything that would float, before all of the pieces of our force were assembled."

"Their troops . . . they're standing fast," Pomfret pointed out, lowering the heavier telescope for a moment. "They're forming before the battery walls, those dozen cavalry on their left. Lancers, by God! How useless!" he scoffed.

"They won't be there long, after we open upon 'em," Westcott said.

"Those lancers might be better placed above the beach," Pomfret said, handing the day-glass back. "To disrupt our landing, though once we're ashore in strength they'd have no choice but to retreat up the draw, and it's too rough ground for them to re-form and charge us . . . their infantry would be more a threat to us."

"You only see the one company reported to us?" Lewrie asked.

"So far, yes, sir," Captain Pomfret replied, "and what passes as roads leading to the Cape are empty. We could see any re-enforcement coming for a long way off, the land's so open."

"Tell us when, Mister Yelland," Lewrie called out to the Sailing Master, who, with a syndicate of older and more mathematically-inclined Midshipmen, had been taking the known heights of the headland to determine when *Sapphire* was roughly a mile off.

"Almost, sir," Yelland called back.

"Seven fathom!" a leadsman in the fore chains shouted. "Seven fathom t'this line!"

"Almost, indeed," Lt. Westcott muttered under his breath.

The *Harmony* transport stood at least half a mile off *Sapphire*'s starboard quarters, already beginning to fetch-to into the wind, with her six landing boats already being drawn up from towing to the chain platforms on either beam.

"Six fathom! Six fathom t'this line!"

"Now, sir!" Yelland called out.

"Alter course to Due East, Mister Westcott, and run out the larboard guns," Lewrie ordered. "I'll have the upper-deck twelves as the first broadside, and the lower-deck twenty-fours the second."

"Aye, sir!"

*Sapphire*'s bows had been pointed at the headland, their view from the quarterdeck partially obscured by the jibs. As the helm was put over, the up-thrust jib boom and bowsprit swung clear, the jibs sweeping right like the parting of a stage curtain to reveal the headland and the battery to one and all. The ship rumbled and thundered as gun-ports were swung up and away, and the great guns were hauled to the port sills, already loaded with solid iron shot. Sailing Due East, their target lay four points off the larboard bows, slowly inching to abeam. A couple of minutes more, and fire could be opened.

"Have 'em prime, Mister Westcott," Lewrie snapped, eager to be about it, even if he thought it could be a waste of gunpowder at that range.

Below, gun-captains would be directing the crews to open the pans of their flintlock strikers to fill them with powder, then cock their locks, making sure that their trigger lines were slack. In the swab-water tubs between each gun, coils of slow-match sizzled, waiting to be wrapped round linstocks that would be applied to the touch-holes of the guns should the flintlock strikers fail, or a flint break at the wrong moment.

"Cast of the log!" Lewrie shouted, and a long minute later, Midshipman Fywell snatched the log line as it paid out and read the knots which had slipped through his fingers.

"Five and one-half knots, sir!" he piped back.

Lewrie looked aloft at the set of the sails, the direction at which the commissioning pendant lazily fluttered, and decided that it could be possible to get off three or four broadsides before the battery was too far aft of abeam for the guns to point in their narrow ports.

"As I told Mister Mountjoy, Captain Pomfret," Lewrie said, "it would be better to anchor a bomb vessel and pound the place with sea-mortars, with thirteen-inch explosive shells. We can only elevate our guns so high, and shootin' at an incomplete battery wall is too iffy. Go high and over by yards, strike short and tear up the ground under the battery, and the chance of solid hits is damned poor. We might as well shoot at a thin ribbon at a mile's range."

"You believe the best we'll accomplish will be to drive the enemy away, sir?" Pomfret said with a frown. "Hmm, I wonder what Mister Congreve's rockets could do to the place."

"Rockets, my God!" Lewrie hooted in sour mirth. "We tried 'em at Boulogne three years ago, and they weaved all over the place, and a couple of 'em came damned close t'hittin' my ship!"

"They will need a lot more experimenting with before they are useful," Lt. Westcott said with a shake of his head. "Our experience with them *did* put the wind up. Seared me out of a year's growth!"

"Time, I think, Mister Westcott," Lewrie decided at last, feeling a rising excitement even so. "You may open fire."

"Aye, sir. By broadsides, fire!" Westcott shouted.

All eleven of the upper gun deck's 12-pounders lashed out as one in a titanic crash and roar, and the larboard side was swathed in a sudden cloud of sour-reeking smoke.

"My word!" Pomfret gasped. "Impressive, even so!"

"Hope ye remembered t'stuff some candle wax in yer ears," Lewrie snickered. A moment later and the heavier 24-pounders bellowed even louder, and the concussion was strong enough to make his lungs flutter. Despite his own precautions, Lewrie's ears rang.

The ship rumbled and trembled as the guns of the larboard battery ran in to the stops of their breeching ropes, were re-loaded, and run out again, trundling tons of metal and gun carriages over the oak decks, with the squeal of wooden truck wheels added.

"Sounds like gastric distress," Captain Pomfret japed with his smaller pocket telescope to his eye, again. "Egad, Captain Lewrie, I don't think those soldiers are there any longer!"

Just before the guns delivered their second broadsides, Lewrie snatched a quick view of the headland and the battery, and saw that Pomfret was right; he could not see any Spanish casualties, but could espy a whole host of them running away, up towards the semaphore tower, in hopes that it might be out of range, or haring off along the rutted and dusty tracks to the East or West of the headland. Those lancers on their fine horses were galloping straight North into the foothills of the Sierra Alhamilla and the main road that led to Almeria, bent over their mounts' necks and looking back in terror.

The upper-deck 12-pounders roared again, followed long seconds later by the massive 24-pounders, and the view was blotted out, again. By the time *Sapphire* had sailed past the battery and the guns could no longer bear, they fell silent, and the ship was put about for another run, after a full three broadsides.

"Mister Westcott, bowse the larboard guns to the sills, and be ready with the starboard battery," Lewrie ordered in a too-loud shout in the sudden relative silence. "Stations for stays, and prepare to tack."

Steering Due West and following the six-fathom line, *Sapphire* pounded the Spanish battery with another three broadsides, turned out to sea to tack, then went Due East, again, hammering the place with yet another three salvoes. They repeated the manouevre for the better part of an hour. On the next Due East run, before the battery came abeam, Lewrie went up to the poop deck for a better view, joined by Captain Pomfret.

"Those soldiers are back," Pomfret, said. "Look to the right and above the semaphore tower. They're on a high knoll, just standing and watching. They *seem* to be in the same numbers as before."

"Now they've changed their breeches, aye," Lewrie said with a chuckle. "Too far off to interfere when you land your troops?"

"I imagine that once they see the boats going in, they'll find their courage and *try* to defend the place," Pomfret shrugged off, "but they'll also realise that they're out-numbered, and won't do much more than pestering us. I don't think they'll get too close, either, else we might direct all our cannonfire on *them*, hah hah!"

"Well, it looks as if we've done all we can to damage the battery," Lewrie said, leaning his elbows on the cap-rails of the bulwarks to steady his heavy day-glass. "And, as I feared, that ain't much."

The slope up to the parapets was so gouged with heavy iron shot that it appeared as if many tribes of badgers had dug their lairs, replete with several openings to each. The wooden barracks behind the battery had been turned to kindling, and the rooves had fallen in on the shattered walls. Several wild shots had even reached the semaphore tower, severed one long timber leg, and lopped off the platform at the top. The stone battery itself, though . . . the thick base wall *had* been undermined, and several of the massive stone blocks had been shifted. One upper section between openings for gun-ports was chipped and downed. All that expenditure of powder and shot, with little to show for it.

"We've accomplished nothing that the Spanish couldn't repair in a month," Lewrie sourly gravelled, lowering his telescope. "With no store of powder in their magazine, your men might have to take all our mauls and crow-levers and try *t'tear* the bloody thing down!"

"Iron mauls?" Captain Pomfret asked in sarcasm.

"Wood," Lewrie told him.

"Hah!" Pomfret barked in mirthless humour.

"Do you think it's worthwhile t'land the troops?" Lewrie asked.

"Well . . . we might set fire to what's left of the tower and the barracks," Pomfret allowed with a grimace, lifting his telescope for a another look. "There are some heavy waggons to haul the stone blocks left behind, and there are the hoisting frames. They'd burn well, too."

"Mister Westcott?" Lewrie called down to the quarterdeck. "Do you secure the guns. We've no more need of 'em. Hands to the braces and sheets, and prepare to fetch-to."

"Aye aye, sir!" Westcott replied.

"Fetching-to," Pomfret asked. "Is that like anchoring?"

"No, we cock up into the wind with the fore-and-aft sails trying t'keep us moving, and the forecourse laid a'back so she can't," Lewrie explained. "We'll slowly drift alee, but won't go anywhere all that fast.

Of course, I'll want more sea-room 'fore we do, 'fore we drift into the shallows."

"Deck, there!" one of the lookouts in the mainmast cross-trees shouted. "Two . . . strange . . . sail! Two points off th' larb'd bows!"

"Mine arse on a band-box!" Lewrie barked in astonishment. "They managed t'get out?"

"The Spanish frigates your mentioned before we left Gibraltar?" Captain Pomfret asked.

"They very might be," Lewrie said, lifting his head and cupping hand round his mouth to shout aloft. "How far away?"

"Hull-down, sir! T'gallants an' royals is all I kin make out!" was the reply.

"Mister Westcott," Lewrie said from the top of the poop deck's larboard ladderway, "we will *not* fetch-to. Nor will we land the soldiers. Alter course to Sou'east and make more sail."

"Aye, sir!" Westcott replied, looking wolfish at the prospect of a sea-fight.

"Mister Fywell?" Lewrie instructed the Midshipman aft by the flag lockers and log line. "Fetch out and hoist 'Discontinue The Action'. Mister Westcott? Load and fire two of the six-pounders of the starboard battery for the General Signal."

He looked aloft at the commissioning pendant, noting that the winds had altered during the course of the morning, and it was now more from the South; *Sapphire* could not steer Sou'east, and even driving at the closest "beat" to weather, could only make East-Sou'east. She'd clear Cabo de Gata easily, and *might* gain enough sea-room to get to windward of the two approaching strangers and hold the weather gage against them should they turn out to be Spanish.

"East-Sou'east is the closest she'll bear, sir," Lt. Westcott told him.

"Good enough, then. Lay her close-hauled on that course, and let's get the old scow *plodding* into action," Lewrie said, japing at his ship's slowness.

"To glory we steer, sir!" Westcott replied, quoting a snippet from Arne's famous song.

# CHAPTER THIRTY-EIGHT

Captain Hedgepeth aboard *Harmony* had gotten his ship under way as soon as the signal guns were fired off, and the flag hoist soared up *Sapphire*'s halliards. The six heavy 36-foot landing boats were led astern to be towed, but, if they proved too much of a drag, he could cast them loose. Lewrie suspected that Hedgepeth would, and that Captain Middleton would never get them for his desired gunboats. With all to the t'gallants and all jibs and stays'ls set, *Harmony* galloped off West, slightly canted over to starboard on larboard tack and an easy beam reach, spreading an impressive and broad white bridal train wake. She, the soldiers of the 77th detachment, and the sailors from *Sapphire*'s crew, would be safely out of it.

"Eight and a quarter knots, sir!" Midshipman Fywell reported.

"Damn' near enough t'take your breath away," Lewrie scoffed at that news, recalling how swift his *Reliant* frigate had been, hard on the wind. His Fourth Rate *trundled,* her larboard shoulders set to the sea, canted over from horizontal only about fifteen degrees, stiffer than he expected since the winds were not all that strong this late morning. He reckoned that if *Sapphire* could be gotten far enough up to windward of the two strange sail, and he had time to come about to larboard tack to engage them, she'd only be pressed over from level by about ten degrees or less, once the large main course was brailed up against the risk of fire from the discharge of her guns, and that would turn her into a very steady gun platform.

From his perch on the poop deck, Lewrie could make out two sets of sails from the deck, by now; t'gallants and royals, perhaps a hint of their tops'ls when the scend of the sea lifted them a few feet more. Whoever they were, they were bows-on to *Sapphire,* on larboard tack, a bit of separation between them as if sailing abreast of each other. By the slight cant of their sails, he suspected that they were also going close-hauled. If he managed to get to windward, they could not swing up any closer to him, but would have to stay on larboard tack, ceding him the right to fall down to them when *he* willed.

"Not exactly how I expected this morning to turn out, what?" Captain Pomfret commented as he paced up near Lewrie's shoulder.

"Not how I thought it would go, either, sir," Lewrie said with a rueful grin. "If they do turn out to be Spanish, you can write home to tell your people that you've been in your first sea-fight."

"What do you call it, 'yardarm to yardarm'?" Pomfret asked.

"I'd prefer not to," Lewrie admitted, laughing briefly. "That sort of battle's costly. You see how they've slipped to about three points off our larboard bows? We're close-hauled on one tack, they're doin' the same on opposite tack. Unless something goes smash aloft, I hope to get seaward or them," he said, explaining what that meant as an advantage, and how he would come about and match tacks to engage, and how he hoped to fall down upon them in his own good time.

"But, how do you expect to fight two of them?" Pomfret went on. "You said they might be two big frigates. How big?"

"They're most-like what we call Fifth Rates, mounting the Spanish equivalent of our eighteen-pounders," Lewrie said. "Does it come to about two cables' range, our lower-deck twenty-four-pounders should prove the difference . . . unless the Dons've developed carronades . . . those fat, stubby barrelled ones there? . . . there's more twenty-fours, though they're short-ranged. About four hundred yards is the most one can expect. But that gives us sixteen heavy guns to each beam.

"See the Dons yonder?" Lewrie pointed out, gesturing towards the pair of sails on the horizon. "They're hard on the wind and they can't steer any higher . . . like a coach on a narrow country lane with a rock wall on one side which it can't go through. Those frigates can't come near us, so long as I stand aloof to windward. They could tack or wear about to the same heading we're on now, but that'd make no sense. When a ship tacks, or alters course that drastically, it slows down and it takes a while t'get back up to speed, so even if they do tack, we end up chasin' *them*. They could split up, but that'd put 'em miles apart, and the idea is t'stay and support your consort. Strength, and comfort, in numbers, hey?"

"I think I see, but still . . ." Pomfret said with a frown, and a hapless shrug, for half of what Lewrie had said was Greek to him.

"If they're Spanish, they could be the finest frigates in their entire navy," Lewrie continued, lifting his telescope for another look at them. "The Dons, and the French for that matter, build grand ships, but, it's seamanship, gunnery, and experience at sea that matter, and according to Mountjoy's reports, they've only had their yards crossed for a fortnight or so . . . sittin' idle, swingin' at their anchorages, and their crews goin' stale and bored, and, I hope, dis-spirited by our blockade. All make-work and 'river discipline'?"

He lowered his day-glass and turned to Pomfret. "Much like the garrison at Gibraltar. Would you march 'em out against the French or the Dons right off, without a lick of re-trainin'? Then, there's gunnery. Anchored in harbour, ye *can't* stage live-fire. How many houses and docks do the Dons have t'spare if shot goes wild? We've had live-fire once or twice a week since I took command, *hang* the cost in shot and powder, and my crew can get off three rounds every two minutes. I doubt the Spanish can match that, after their initial broadsides, and that I think will be the edge. Well, hallo, Bisquit! Got a new bone, have ye? Tasty? Good and crunchy? Good fellow!"

Lewrie knelt down to ruffle the dog's head and neck ruff.

"Your dog is he, Captain Lewrie?" Pomfret enquired as he made "come hither" noises, offering his fingers to be smelled. Bisquit went to him, tail fluttering madly, and whining, with a grin on his face.

"Ship's dog," Lewrie said, explaining how the *Reliant* frigate had acquired him. "He's made a new friend."

"Eight and a half knots!" Midshipman Fywell reported.

Lewrie stood and looked aloft; the wind was picking up force, and looked to be coming more from the South by East than from Due South.

"Damn," Lewrie groused. "Mister Westcott, ease her to East by South, and I'll have the main t'gallant, middle, and topmast stays'ls hoisted. Drive her, hard."

Five Bells of the Forenoon were struck at the foc's'le belfry marking half-past ten of the morning. Lewrie went down to the quarterdeck, leaving Captain Pomfret on the poop deck to play with the dog.

"They're almost hull-up, now, Geoffrey," he muttered closely to the First Officer. "We may be engaged by Seven Bells. Let's advance the rum issue to eleven A.M."

"Six Bells it'll be, sir," Westcott agreed, nodding. "Do you intend to 'Splice The Mainbrace'? That'd encourage them."

"No, I don't want 'em *too* groggy when handlin' powder," Lewrie said. "We'll save that for after we've beaten those sons of bitches. I'll be aft for a bit. Carry on, sir."

"Aye, sir," Lt. Westcott said.

After a time, Captain Pomfret came down from the poop deck to the quarterdeck and looked round for Lewrie, still full of questions. He settled for Westcott. "Captain Lewrie seems confident, sir. Pardons if I intrude on your duties."

"No intrusion, Captain Pomfret," Westcott said with a laugh and a quick, savage grin. "Watch standing mostly involves standing about, looking attentive. It will be some time before we tack and beat to Quarters. The captain? Captain Lewrie takes nothing for granted, I assure you, but in this case he has grounds for confidence. In the Navy he's known as the 'Ram-Cat', ye know. Not for that cat he keeps in his cabins, but for his way of going after the foe . . . he earned that early on. I've served as his First for four years in two ships, and if anyone can surpass him, I'll eat my hat. He's probably been in more actions than most of us have had hot suppers, the Glorious First of June, Saint Vincent, Camperdown . . . Copenhagen? And many single ship fights in between. He fights clever, though he'll never believe it of himself. We're in very good hands, the *best* of hands."

"Something for me to write home about, then," Pomfret decided. "Am I properly equipped for it?"

"Hmm . . . sword, two pistols, silk shirt and stockings, just in case," Westcott said, looking him over from head to toe. "Wax in your ears? Good. I think that'll do quite nicely."

Lewrie came out of his cabins, after having a quick sponge-off, and loading and priming his weapons. He had changed to a silk shirt and stockings inside his boots, too, though the boots would unravel them something horrid. He wore his Gills' hanger on his left hip and had clipped his two new over-under double-barrelled pistols to his waistband, and had shoved his side-by-side double-barrelled Mantons in the deep side pockets of his uniform coat.

"You look perfectly piratical, sir," Lt. Westcott quipped.

"*Aarr,* and belike," Lewrie replied in a raspy growl, astonishing Pomfret, who was more used to the grave and sombre command style of senior Army officers. "All I'm lacking are half a dozen more pistols hung round my neck like Blackbeard, and slow-match fuses burnin' in my hair, hah! Let's see what the Dons've been up to in my absence."

He snatched his telescope from the binnacle cabinet and went to the poop deck on the leeward side to raise it and peer at them.

"Deck, there!" a lookout bawled. "They're showin' *Spanish* colours!" Lewrie also could make out the bright red-gold-red banners with the crowned coats of arms in the centre.

The leading frigate had hauled her wind slightly, falling off 'til she was in line-ahead of her consort, blending their sails into a single mass in Lewrie's ocular. Both were well above the horizon, tops'ls and courses towering above the dark hulls, their inner, outer, jibs and foremast stays'ls stretched wind-full and their bowsprits and jib booms thrust up aggressively, bobbing like lance tips of cantering armoured knights. He reckoned that they were no more than five miles off, making at least ten or eleven knots, he judged by the frothing mustachios under their forefeet, and closing the range rapidly.

He lowered his telescope and collapsed the tubes, tapping it on his left palm in thought. The Spanish warships looked to be about more than three points off *Sapphire*'s larboard bows, perhaps closer to three and a half points; they had lost some ground due to the shift of the winds, and now steered Sou'west by South. He sketched with a fingertip on the cap-rail, their course, his course, and where and when their opposing tracks would intersect.

*I've got* bags *of room to tack!* he thought with a feral smile.

Six Bells were struck, and a fiddler, a fifer, and a Marine drummer struck up "Molly Dawson", surprising the crew, who had only partially begun to gather. Bosun Terrell piped Clear Decks And Up Spirits, and the rum keg was fetched up to the belfry. Doling out the rum to all hands and ship's boys usually took about twenty minutes or so, with men milling round to find those who owed them "sippers" or "gulpers" for past favours, stretching the process out a few minutes more.

He would wait 'til the keg was borne below, and all the brass cups were gathered up before tacking, before sending them all to their guns, again. He returned to the quarterdeck.

"Mister Westcott, pass word to the galley for the fires to be staunched. Dinner'll have to wait today," he said. "We'll come about at Seven Bells, then go to Quarters. As soon as we're on course to the Sou'west by South, let's fetch out the anti-boarding nets and rig chain slings aloft on all the yards."

"Aye, sir," Westcott replied.

"I wonder . . ." Lewrie mused aloud. "Our gunnery this morning, it didn't achieve much, but it *was* closely grouped round the target, didn't you think?"

"It was, sir," Westcott agreed, "with very little left or right of the battery, and we hit the slope just underneath so many times we almost dug down to the foundations."

"The Spanish'll fire high, and open at long range, hopin' that they'll carry top-masts and spars away t'cripple us. Well, perhaps we can play that game, too, at say, two-thirds of a mile?"

"They won't be expecting that from a British warship, sir," Lt. Westcott said, and his grin was positively evil.

"We'll get to close quarters and hull 'em 'twixt wind and water later on, but in the beginning? Hmm!" Lewrie said, with a smile of his own.

"Wear, sir, not tack," Westcott suggested. "There's less of a chance for something aloft to carry away and put us 'in irons' at the worst moment. If we miss stays . . ."

"You're right, as usual, Geoffrey," Lewrie agreed. "Aye, we'll wear instead. That'll shorten the range a little bit, too."

He waited, pacing round the quarterdeck from his traditional post at the windward bulwarks to the lee side, forcing himself to be patient, to appear outwardly calm. He petted Bisquit when the dog quit the poop deck and his bone, heading for the lower decks and handouts of food in anticipation of dinner being served. He watched as the rum keg was closed and escorted below by armed Marines, as the Jack In The Breadroom gathered up the cups.

"Pipe All Hands," Lewrie commanded at last, standing squared on his feet amidships of the quarterdeck by the hammock stanchions, hands in the small of his back and looking down into the crowded waist.

"Ship's company, face aft and hark to the Captain!" Westcott shouted.

"Lads, recall when I read myself in at the Nore," Lewrie began in his best quarterdeck voice, "I told you that I would do my best to find a way to turn *Sapphire* from a boresome escort to a *fighting* ship. We've made a decent start on that, you and I, but today. . . . *Here* is your time, *here* is your morning to win fame for yourselves and this ship, and show those motherless Dons over yonder who really rules the oceans! Are you ready?"

A great, enthusiastic cheer greeted his words. When he raised a hand, and it subsided, he continued.

"In a few minutes, we'll wear about, and then we'll beat to Quarters," he said, "and we will engage the Spanish. You showed me earlier today that you've become some of the finest naval gunners in the world, even at a full mile's range. Do ye think you can do that again? Can ye aim small and hit hard?"

His crew's response was a hearty growl.

"We'll take 'em on one at a time, first at long range, then at close quarters, and *hammer* the bastards 'til they curse the day they thought they could try *us* on, and curse the moment they clapped eyes on *Sapphire*! God bless every one of you Sapphires, and our good ship. Now, let's be about it!"

"Ship's company, dismiss," Lt. Westcott ordered, his cry lost in the great, savage din of shouts and huzzahs.

Lewrie looked at the Spanish frigates from the lee bulwarks; they were now a little more than two miles off. It was time.

"Bosun Terrell, pipe Stations To Wear!" he shouted.

# CHAPTER THIRTY-NINE

As the helm was put over, HMS *Sapphire* slowly hauled her wind, falling off from "full and by" with taut canvas eased and loosed, the yards slowly being angled to the opposite tack to the squealing of the wooden balls in the parrels that bound the yards to the masts, amid a rustling thunder of sailcloth, and groans of the masts and the hull timbers, her stern crossing the eye of the wind at last, and her yards re-braced in the proper spiral set from courses to t'gallants. She came back to the edge of the winds, all her sails bellied out, again filled with drive and power.

"Now, Mister Westcott," Lewrie ordered, "beat to Quarters."

The young Marine drummer began the Long Roll, the fiddler and fifer struck up one of Lewrie's favourite tunes, "The Bowld Soldier Boy", and *Sapphire* thundered again as deal-and-canvas partitions were struck, furniture was folded or struck below, and the gun decks were turned into long, open alleyways full of men, guns, truck carriages, and gun tools. Ship's boys serving as powder monkeys dashed to the magazine for their first pre-made charges of propellant, fetching them back in flash-proof leather tubes to kneel behind their assigned guns.

"The ship is at Quarters, sir, and steady on Sou'west by South," Lieutenant Westcott reported, formally doffing his hat in salute, and of a much graver manner than earlier.

"Very well, Mister Westcott," Lewrie said with a nod, graver himself, now that they were on the cusp of battle. He went to the starboard side, the lee side now, to peer at the Spanish frigates. The turn-about had slowed *Sapphire* considerably, and she was now only slowly gaining back what speed she'd had. The Spanish ships were now on their starboard quarters, about a mile and a half off, having lost none of their speed and gaining on *Sapphire*.

"A matched pair, sir," the Sailing Master, Mr. Yelland, said. "Both sport bright red gunwale stripes, alike as peas in a pod."

"Sister ships?" Westcott wondered aloud. "The best that they could order out, once Madrid heard of our raids?"

"Damme, I'll bet they think they're *special*," Lewrie drawled.

*Damn, what if they are?* he had to ask himself, though.

He felt a tiny flicker of doubt, worried that the Spanish had picked among the officers of their navy blockaded in Cartagena, among their best gunners and most experienced seamen, had supplanted the two frigates' complements for one special mission . . . to rid their coast of one particular British pest, *el diablo negro*.

*Oh, goat shit*, he thought with a scowl; *There's not a navy in the* world *that'd do that! Certainly not the Spanish! Too many prides t'be hurt. It makes more sense that they were sneaked out to deliver supplies to Ceuta, or sneak their way into Cádiz, t'concentrate what's left of their fleet.*

He reckoned that they *might* be special, chosen to make that sort of effort, their captains the boldest available, but *Sapphire*'s very presence had scotched those plans, and they'd stumbled upon them by mistake, by a fluke of bad luck.

He pursed his lips and heaved a silent snort, deriding himself, then looked out to starboard to see what the Spanish were doing, and how they were placed. They had worked their way up to within three points abaft of abeam, and would be up even with *Sapphire* in another quarter-hour. And, they were just a little over a mile off.

"Mister Westcott? Take two reefs in the main course," Lewrie snapped, back to business. "We'll not brail up all the way 'til we're closely engaged. And, alter course . . . give us a point free."

"Aye aye, sir!"

As topmen scrambled out the main course yard, bare feet juddering on the foot-ropes for balance with arms over the yard for their lives to haul the heavy, taut sail to the first reef line, the helm was put up one point, and other hands on deck and sail-tending gangways tailed onto braces and sheets to ease the set of the sails. The angle of the deck eased a few degrees more upright as *Sapphire* sagged off from full-and-by to more of a close reach as she began her slow descent upon the Spanish. With the huge main course reefed, she lost speed, too; the quick cast of the log-line showed only seven and one half knots.

"Hmm, they're not brailing up their main courses, sir," Mister Yelland commented. "Do you think they wish to get beyond us, first?"

"No tactical advantage in that, Mister Yelland," Lewrie said, "unless . . . they have somewhere else they need to be. They're under a mile off, d'ye make 'em? Mister Westcott, I'll have another point free. Once we're steady, we'll open upon them. Whether they wish a fight or not, we're going t'give 'em one!"

*Sapphire* fell off the wind even further, to West by South, and angling more acutely towards the Spanish frigates which were still on a course of Sou'west by West. If all ships continued on, *Sapphire* would eventually cross the lead frigate's bows.

"Steady on West by South, sir," Westcott reported.

"Pass word to Mister Harcourt and Mister Elmes," Lewrie said, "my compliments to both, and they are to open gun-ports and concentrate their broadsides upon the lead ship."

"Am I in the way?" Captain Pomfret whispered to the Sailing Master.

"You could stand by the door to Captain Lewrie's cabins, sir," Yelland told him, "aft of the helm, and under the poop overhang, but you couldn't see much. For a good view, you could go up and aft by taffrail lanthorns. The signalmen have nothing to do, and you could sit on the flag lockers. Though, it may get a bit 'windy' up there, mind," he suggested with a wink.

"Windy?" Pomfret asked, wondering what he meant.

"With the odd enemy roundshot, sir," Yelland said, chuckling.

HMS *Sapphire* rumbled and thudded as the ports were swung up and the great guns wheeled up to the port sills. Gun-captains crouched behind the breeches, hand-signalling for crewmen with crow-levers to lift the truck carriages to shift aim left of right, and drawing the wood-block quoins from beneath the breeches to lift the muzzles to their maximum elevation.

"Ready, sir!" Midshipman Ward breathlessly shrilled as he dashed up from the waist to the quarterdeck and knuckling the brim of his hat.

"Open fire, Mister Westcott," Lewrie ordered.

"By broadside . . . fire!" Westcott shouted.

Gun-captains waited for the scend of the sea, to the point of the up-roll when the ship was at her steadiest, before jerking their taut trigger lines. The starboard side of the ship erupted in smoke, jutting flame, and swirls of sparks amid the sudden, thick bank of powder smoke. Frustrated, Lewrie trotted up the starboard ladderway to the poop deck for a slightly clearer view.

*That's just bloody* magnificent*!* he thought in joy.

It was one of the prettiest sights he ever hoped to see. The sea was a most marvellous and striking blue, the sky mostly clear with only a few wispy white clouds. The leading Spanish frigate's ebony hull with that broad red gunwale paint, and her relatively new white sails was a lovely bit of perfection of the shipbuilders' art, and she stood out starkly against the high mountains of the Andalusian coast.

And she was surrounded by a sleet-storm of iron roundshot that raised great, and rather pretty, feathers and pillars of spray where shot hit the sea short and caromed up from First Graze, skipping into her hull the last few hundred yards to thud into her planking. Some shot bracketed her bow and stern, wide of the mark but not all that much mis-directed. He even thought that he could see her courses and tops'ls twitch, collapse, then re-fill with wind.

"That's *damned* good shooting!" he yelled to encourage his crew. "Now, serve her another!"

"By broadside, on the up-roll . . . fire!" Lt. Westcott roared.

An instant later, and *Sapphire*'s starboard guns bellowed once more, hurling solid iron shot at 1,200 feet per second, wreathing herself in yellow-tinged, dingy smoke reeking of sulfur.

"Yes, by God!" Lewrie said with a laugh. As that smoke wafted alee, he avidly sought signs of damage through his telescope as gouts of disturbed water near her waterline leapt upward, as sails twitched again as they were holed, and bits of the Spanish frigate's bulwarks and hammock-filled stanchions were smashed away. "Best gunners in the entire Navy, the best in the world, indeed!"

As he watched, the frigate's large main course was clewed up, and enemy topmen scooted out the yard to brail it up. She was readying to return fire. A signal hoist went up her after halliards, and the trailing frigate began to take in her main course, as well. They would fight. "Now, it gets int'resting," Lewrie muttered.

The lead frigate endured two more broadsides from *Sapphire* before her side erupted in smoke and jets of flame. The range had been closing all along, and she was only half a mile off when she opened upon the British ship. Heeled over to the press of wind and still on a beat to weather, her guns would reach further, their maximum elevation aided by the cant of her decks. Shot moaned overhead as Lewrie fought the natural inclination to duck, crouch, or cringe. One ball hummed over the poop, between the bulwarks and the lower spanker boom, creating a sudden gust of air that shoved him against the bulwarks, and came near to sending his hat overboard. There were several loud thuds and crashes as enemy shot hit home. Lewrie peered over the side and saw the hazes and swirls of splinters rising where some shot had hit, flinging engrained dust and paint or tar from the wounds.

"On the up-roll, by broadside . . . fire!" Lt. Westcott yelled, his voice gone raspy from the effort, and the ever-present smoke.

In the heat of the moment, some of Lewrie's gun-captains had forgotten to re-insert the quoin blocks under their guns' breeches, too intent on reloading, priming, over-hauling tackle, and running out as the range shortened. While most of *Sapphire*'s broadsides were aimed at the Spaniard's hull, some shots went high. Unwittingly they emulated French or Spanish practice, which was to cripple an enemy's speed and manouevrability by taking down masts and rigging before closing for a slug-fest at musket-shot.

"By broadside, fire!" and *Sapphire* roared out her fury once more. Her guns were hot, now, and when they discharged, they did not slam back in recoil, but leapt clear of the deck by several inches, slewing off-centre and straining breeching ropes, making the stout iron ring-bolts groan, and making gunners dodge aside to keep from being hit, or their feet caught in the tackles.

When the smoke cleared from that broadside, Lewrie whooped in glee, pointing to the Spaniard and yelling, "Just look at that!" Those shots from the guns with the quoin blocks fully out had pummeled the frigate's rigging. Her fore royal mast and yard, her fore t'gallant mast and yard above the cross-trees, had been shot away, falling like a hewn pine-tree to leeward, and dragging her outer flying jib with it. A moment later and her main t'gallant stays'l parted from the foremast to swirl back against the main mast. All that wreckage hung for a long moment as Spanish sailors scrambled up from the foremast fighting top to chop or slash it away, but it all broke free and fell, the yards of her topmasts spearing into the frigate's fore tops'l to rip it open like a gutted fish before finally falling clear into the sea!

"Another point free, Mister Westcott!" Lewrie ordered. "Close the range on her!"

*And make the angle too great for the trailin' frigate t'shoot at us*, he grimly told himself; *Just take 'em on one at a time!*

With her foremast sails ravaged and short a jib, the Spanish frigate slowed, though she still was at least two knots faster than the two-decker, still steering Sou'west by South while *Sapphire* was now sailing Due West, the angle of approach greater, and drawing together. Gamely, her side lit up with a broadside of her own. Roundshot moaned or shrieked past the bows, past the stern, above the decks, punching holes in *Sapphire*'s sails, and slamming into her side, making her planking squawk parrot-like as thick, seasoned oak was stove in.

"By broadside . . . fire!" and *Sapphire* gave as good as she got, crushingly so. Her lower-deck 24-pounders hulled the Spanish frigate, and Lewrie could see fresh, star-shaped shot holes blasted into that former loveliness, could see her masts sway and quiver from the force of the blows. Something had shattered the frigate's main tops'l yard and the windward half collapsed onto the brailed-up main course yard, jerking the brace-line for the main t'gallant apart, and both sails winged out alee, the tops'l fluttering like a shirt on a clothesline, and the upper t'gallant angling out almost fore-and-aft, flattened by the winds and making the frigate heel leeward.

"We're almost close enough, now, to employ the carronades and six-pounders, sir!" Westcott shouted up to Lewrie.

Lewrie looked forward and found his cabin-servant, Jessop, at one of the quarterdeck carronades, promoted from powder monkey to a gunner. Jessop was hopping from one bare foot to the other in impatience. He looked aft at Lewrie as if pleading.

"Aye, Mister Westcott, serve 'em with ev'rything!" Lewrie called back.

"Woo-hoo!" Jessop could be heard yelling.

"*All* guns, by broadside . . . fire!" Westcott shouted.

With the addition of the 24-pounder carronades, it was an avalanche that struck the Spaniard, even as she got off a ragged broadside of her own. Both ships blanketed themselves in powder smoke and blotted out any chance of a view for long moments before being blown alee. The damaged tops'l, the un-controllable flatted-out t'gallant, had drawn the frigate over several more degrees of heel, forcing her fire to dash high above *Sapphire*'s decks, but the two-decker's fire, aimed "'Twixt Wind And Water", smashed into her side, gun-ports, bulwarks, and her waterline. Lewrie could see the frigate's underwater coppering, tinged and streaked algae-green, exposed for a foot or more, as several heavy round-shot punched ragged, dark holes through it. If she rolled upright, the frigate surely would begin to flood!

Spanish sailors were high aloft in her rigging trying to control her t'gallant, slashing and hacking at any line that held the sail taut to the wind. At last, it was freed to flutter leeward, horizontal to the sea, and the frigate righted herself, those shot holes now smothered in foamy, disturbed seawater. She lost more speed due to all her damage aloft, and finally fell a point off the wind to bring her guns to point abeam at *Sapphire*, but she was limping, by then.

"By broadside, *fire!*"

That was the stroke that did her in. When the smoke cleared, all could take delight in seeing her entire foremast above the fighting top falling, taking her fore tops'l and the last of her jibs and stays'l over her starboard side, pressed by the wind. The sudden drag in the sea jerked the frigate's head downwind, reducing her to a crawling cripple. *Sapphire*'s sailors erupted in taunts, jeers, and loud cheering, and the fifer and fiddler struck up a lively jig in celebration.

"Oh, the poor bastard!" Westcott shouted, pointing off at the trailing frigate. She had been following in her leader's wake, about one cable astern, and was turning leeward abruptly to avoid collision!

"Cease fire, Mister Westcott!" Lewrie ordered over the loud din of his crew. "Pipe the Still. We'll let 'em celebrate when the work's finished. A water break for the gun crews, but put the hands to the sheets and braces, and get us back on the eye of the wind 'til we see what this'un intends to do."

"Aye, sir," Lt. Westcott replied. "Bosun, pipe the Still, then hands to sheets and braces!"

That call, the Still, was rarely heard aboard *Sapphire*, though there were some severe disciplinarians in the Royal Navy who ran their men and their ships in silence by day and night, with all orders passed by Bosun's calls.

"I thought you'd finish her, sir," Captain Pomfret said as the crew's cheers fell away, and sailors fell to their required duties.

"She is finished, for now," Lewrie told him, intently peering leeward at the trailing frigate, which was now masked by her crippled leader. "Her foremast's gone by the board, and without jibs, she can't keep anywhere close to the wind. They might rig something up sooner or later, but, she's out of the fight, with her fore tops'l and her fore course gone. If her captain has any sense, he'll turn and sail into Almeria for shelter, with 'both sheets aft'. That's what's called a 'soldier's wind'," he added with a wry expression. "No slur intended."

"You're turning away from the second?" Pomfret asked.

"Aye," Lewrie cheerfully admitted, "we're gettin' back hard on the wind, so we stay above her, same as we did the first. Once she's clear of her consort, and comes back on the wind herself, she'll never be able t'claw out a yard closer to us. She'll be about half a mile to loo'rd, or thereabouts, in easy gun range. Her captain might consider takin' shelter in Almeria, too, goin' about and runnin' back to Cartagena, or continuin' the fight, beatin' his way West and hopin' to out-run us. We'll have to see what his intentions are before committing."

"Her captain might hope that his greater speed will allow him to get ahead before taking too much damage," Lt. Westcott chimed in, "though what a lone frigate hopes to do to the Westward is anybody's guess."

"So, they didn't come out after us, specifically?" Pomfret enquired, shaking his head in wonder. "Curiouser and curiouser."

"Once we take the second, we'll have t'ask him, sir," Lewrie said. "How's your Spanish? Mine's abysmal."

"There she is, sir," Lt. Westcott said in rising excitement at the prospect of further action. "Just getting clear of the first one."

"Hard on the wind, again, hmm," Lewrie speculated. "For now, that is. Fire one six-pounder from the foc's'le, Mister Westcott. We might goad a proud Spanish *hidalgo* into a fight, after all. Challenge him!"

The traditional shot was fired, a mild yelp compared to heavy guns' roars, and a lone cloud of spent powder smoke drifted quickly alee. A long minute later and a flat bang came from the Spaniard. He *would* fight!

# CHAPTER FORTY

"Give us a point free, Mister Westcott," Lewrie ordered after a look aloft at the commissioning pendant. The wind was holding from the Sou'east, and the Spanish frigate was sailing Sou'west by West, as she and her sister ship had from the first. The range was about half a sea-mile, but that would slowly close as *Sapphire* fell down upon her.

"She's opened," Westcott pointed out as the frigate's side lit up in jets of fire and a dense cloud of smoke.

"Quoins fully out, remind the gun-captains," Lewrie demanded, "and have 'em load chain-shot and expanding bar-shot for the next broadside. You may open, Mister Westcott."

"On the up-roll, by broadside . . . fire!" and HMS *Sapphire* shook, trembled, and groaned to the recoil of her guns once more.

"Captain Pomfret?" Lewrie called out, looking round the quarter-deck for the Army officer. "You've a watch with a second hand? Excellent! I'd admire did you time the Spanish broadsides and let me know how long it takes 'em t're-load and run back out. The longer, the better for us."

"By broadside . . . fire!"

A second salvo from the Spanish frigate was headed their way, moaning and keening louder and shriller as the roundshot approached, then turning *basso* as balls passed over and beyond. The frigate aimed high, hoping to cripple *Sapphire*'s sails and rigging, and taut canvas was puckered and holed aloft. Several lines parted, and some blocks came raining down onto the weather deck. One ball plucked a topman and a Marine from the mizen mast's fighting top, flinging them down to the poop deck. The Surgeon's loblolly boys were called for to tend to them, but what was left of them was beyond any care.

"By broadside . . . fire!"

The Spanish frigate had begun two points abaft of abeam to the two-decker, but she was coming up quickly. Within a few minutes, she might even fetch up directly abeam, then slowly work her way ahead of *Sapphire,* making an escape.

*We can't keep on like this,* Lewrie thought; *Else she'll get away. Damned if I'll let her, but . . .*

"Alter course one more point to loo'rd, Mister Westcott. We'll have to engage her more closely. Pass word to the gun decks to mind their elevation," Lewrie snapped. "Cast of the log!"

It took a long, infuriating minute for the report to come back that *Sapphire* was only making a bit over seven knots.

"Damme!" he spat, sure that the Spaniard was still making ten or better!

"By broadside, fire!" and the sea round the Spanish frigate was frothed by the impacts of roundshot, and several holes appeared on her, just before the view was blotted out by a return broadside. The enemy shot moaned, keened, and thrummed about *Sapphire,* raising great splashes alongside, smashing into her thick oak sides, making her hull drum and screech. There was a louder bang, a metallic clang as if a church bell had fallen from a high belfry, and people were shouting below. Midshipman Ward came to the quarterdeck, his uniform askew, and it and his face smudged with spent powder. "We've a twenty-four-pounder dis-mounted, sir!" he shouted, "struck right on the muzzle, and off its carriage! Two men *under* it, sir!"

"Calmly, Mister Ward," Lewrie sternly chid him. "The men are looking to us for steadiness. My compliments to Mister Elmes, and he's t'see to it."

"Ehm, aye, sir," Ward said with a gulp, then dashed below.

"Pardons, sir, but their timing?" Captain Pomfret said, waving his pocket watch. "It's taking them just about one minute 'twixt their broadsides, and the last one appeared rather ragged, taking about ten seconds from the first shot to the last. Almost 'fire at will', hey?"

"Now, that's what I hoped to hear, sir!" Lewrie crowed, quite pleased. "They're gettin' tired and dis-organised."

"By broadside, fire!"

Crash-bang-tinkle! A Spanish shot smashed into the starboard quarter gallery of the officer's wardroom and carried straight through the other side. Another crashed into the starboard bulwarks, scattering stowed hammocks, ripping a chunk from the bulwark in a cloud of splinters, and cutting a brace-tender in two!

"You may not have that spare cabin you've been using, Captain Pomfret," Lewrie said, leaning far out over the starboard bulwarks to survey the damage, "or the 'necessaries', either."

"Lord, what was that?" Lt. Westcott cried, pointing at their foe. "I could have sworn I saw a flash of flame and smoke aboard her!"

There *was* a sooty cloud of smoke forward of amidships, a rising cloud that lingered long after her last gush of powder smoke drifted alee. Lewrie raised a telescope and saw ant-like Spanish sailors with water buckets, dipping them overside into the sea and hauling them up. A longer perusal showed that the frigate's side had been chewed up, two gun-ports had been turned into one, her larboard side best bower anchor was gone, and the long, out-jutting cat-head beam was amputated, and aloft. "Hah!" he cheered. Both her fore and main masts were missing her royal and t'gallant upperworks! "*That'll* slow her down! She won't get beyond us! Mister Westcott, steer one more point alee!"

"Helmsmen, make her head Due West. Bosun Terrell, ease braces and sheets," Westcott called out through a brass speaking-trumpet.

"Damme, but I do believe she's sheeting home her main course!" the Sailing Master, Mr. Yelland, shouted. "She is!"

"Hell of a risk, that," Lewrie commented with a scowl.

"Why, sir?" Pomfret asked.

"There's always a risk that it'd catch fire from the discharge of the guns, sir," Lewrie told him, "That's why ours is reefed out of danger, and if this scow was any faster, it'd be brailed all the way up."

"Steady on Due West, thus!" Westcott shouted. "By broadside, fire!"

The Spanish frigate still insisted on sailing close-hauled to the winds, and was spreading her main course to make up for the loss of her fore and main mast upperworks, but their course, and *Sapphire*'s course, would eventually result in an intersection.

*Question is, who crosses whose bows first?* Lewrie wondered.

"Carronades and six-pounders in the next broadside, Mister Westcott!" Lewrie snapped. "Shoot her to wood scraps! Pass word to aim to hull her!"

The Spanish frigate was swimming up to only one point abaft of abeam, out-footing *Sapphire,* and firing yet another broadside of her own, yet this one was very ragged; a pair of guns, several single discharges, another pair, then some more seconds apart. Lewrie reckoned that if Pomfret was right, it would be at least another full minute or longer before she could fire again.

"All guns, on the up-roll, by broadside . . . fire!" and their ship rocked as if gut-punched by the recoil. A vast fogbank of smoke blossomed into being, swept downwind by the breeze, smothering their view of the enemy, and rolling down onto the frigate.

"Make our head West by North, Mister Westcott!" Lewrie yelled. "Close the range!" He knew that he was getting "gun-drunk", caught up in the fight to the point that fine tactics were abandoned, but Lewrie didn't care, by then. The evil reek of spent powder and the titanic roar of his guns were too intoxicating for cool, detached thinking any longer.

"By broadside, fire!" and when the pall of gunsmoke drifted alee, there was the enemy frigate, with her bowsprit shot away and her jibs flagging to leeward, with her larboard-side main course yard a shattered stub that had ripped that great sail in half as it had fallen. There were more holes in her bulwarks, along her row of gun-ports. At last, she was beginning to haul her wind and bear away towards the coast, but that was many miles off, by then. She had come up fully abeam to *Sapphire* but she would not out-foot her any longer, and it was the two-decker which would do the over-taking, still holding the wind gage.

"By broadside, fire!" this time at about one cable's range and above the smoke, everyone on deck could see her masts shiver and shake at the impact. The frigate's return fire was no more a broadside but a feeble stutter. At such close range, Lewrie was surprised by how many roundshot moaned overhead, not into the hull, wondering if the Spanish gunners were even trying to aim any longer.

"Hit her again!" Lewrie demanded, pounding a fist on the caprails. "Cut her bloody *guts* out! *Skin* the bastards!"

"By broadside . . . fire!"

"Steer North-Nor'west, Mister Westcott," he ordered, his ears ringing despite the wax he'd crammed into them. "Fetch her up close!"

The Spanish captain must have realised that he could no longer fight an equal fight against those heavy 24-pounders and the "Smashers", the heavy carronades. The frigate was suddenly swinging away to Due North with the range down to two hundred yards or less, appearing as if she'd put completely about, wearing to the opposite tack to flee for Almeria and the safety of its harbour and shore batteries.

"Put the wind fine on the larboard quarters, Mister Westcott!" Lewrie shouted. "Hands to the sheets and braces and ease her! If she keeps on turnin', we might get a chance to rake her!"

*Sapphire* hauled her wind, sagging off the wind and plodding at her slow, sedate pace to follow the Spanish frigate, which was starting to wear, and show her stern!

"Make it count! Slow and steady . . . on the up-roll, as you *bear* . . . fire!"

No, it would not be a perfect right-angled rake, the sort that tore through the transom and stern windows and concentrated roundshot down the full length of an enemy's decks like a blast from a fowling piece, over-turning guns and slaughtering sailors by the dozens.

*Sapphire*'s gunfire took the frigate on her larboard quarters, shattering the lighter wood of her quarter-galleries, grazing through the stern transom, shattering and tearing away glass and window sashes, destroying her taffrails and both night lanthorns, punching into her captain's and her officers' quarters, and dis-mounting or over-turning guns and carriages. The frigate's mizen mast swayed to the impact of heavy shot that hit its thicker lower section below the quarterdeck. A section of the quarterdeck's larboard bulwarks was turned into a cloud of arm-length splinters, scything away men of her After-Guard, helmsmen, and her officers. She ceased her turn and sagged to leeward, as if no longer under control, The spanker, boomed out over the quarterdeck, was shot full of holes, but her proud flag still flew from its after-most lift line, as did another from a signal halliard.

"Lay us alongside, Mister Westcott!" Lewrie shouted. "Ready a boarding party!"

"Sir! Sir!" Midshipman Fywell called from the poop deck. "The first frigate is back under way, and is coming up astern of us!"

Lewrie dashed up the ladderway to the poop deck for a look-see, and was astounded to see that the Spanish had managed to get her back into action, with jury-rigged jibs stretched from her foremast fighting top to her forecastle, jib boom, and her figurehead. She barely crawled, her gripe and cut-water parting the sea with hardly a ripple of a foam mustachio. She heeled to larboard a few degrees, even with the wind pressing her from the Sou'east. Her un-damaged starboard gun battery was run out, though.

"Still a mile off, and it'll take her a quarter-hour 'til she comes up with us," Lewrie decided aloud. "If her captain had any sense, he'd make off for repairs, or strike his colours."

*But, he won't,* Lewrie thought; *He's going to atone for Trafalgar and win some glory for the Spanish Navy, even if it kills him!*

" 'Vast the boarding party, Mister Westcott," Lewrie called down to his quarterdeck. "That first frigate's back in action, and is makin' for us. Lay us abeam of this 'un," he said, pointing to the nearest frigate, "and continue firing."

He stayed on the poop deck to make some quick calculations and decisions. The nearest Spaniard was headed North by West, driven by the wind and most-likely with her steering tackle damaged or shot away and unable to change course 'til it was re-roved, which might take a few minutes. *Sapphire* was steering North-Nor'west with the wind fine on her larboard quarters, slowly separating from her unless she wore to take the wind fine on her starboard quarters, and sailing at about the same pace as the Spaniard, going no faster than the wind blew.

A mile or so off to the Sou'east, that first Spanish frigate was limping back into the fight, bound Nor'west as if she hoped to get onto *Sapphire*'s stern for at least one rake.

"By broadside . . . fire!"

The range to their opponent, though slowly opening, was about a hundred yards, and it was simply devastating. They were close enough to hear the frigate's hull scream in parroty squawks as her scantlings were shot clean through. Her gun deck was so ravaged that it was impossible to count her original number of gun-ports. Her response, when it came, was a meagre six or seven guns before her damaged mizen mast gave way to another hit or two, and it slowly toppled forward, swivelling, wrenching up deck timbers and planking through which it pierced, crashing against her main mast and taking down sails, yards, and running rigging, and spilling sailors and naval infantry from the tops to the decks. Both of the flags were dragged down with it, and it was a long minute before Lewrie could see an officer digging through her smashed-open flag lockers for another. At the same time, another officer came up from below with a bed sheet, and the two men began to argue as to which should be displayed! They tugged each others' flags, swung fists, and one of them pulled a pistol on his fellow!

"Speaking-trumpet, Mister Westcott!" Lewrie demanded, and one of the Mids stationed on the quarterdeck ran it up to him.

"Hey!" Lewrie shouted across. "*Hola!* Make up your bloody minds what you're going t'do! Strike, or fight? Uh, *rendición*, or . . . *combato*?" he yelled, not knowing if those were even Spanish words. "What is 'broadside' in Spanish? Anybody?" he called down his officers.

"Try *andanada,* sir," Captain Pomfret offered, looking as if he found amusement in Lewrie's flummoxing in a foreign language.

"*Andanada, muchos andanada, comprend?*" Lewrie shouted over to the Spanish frigate, wondering if "comprend" was French. He pointed at the side of his ship and the two re-loaded and run-out gun batteries.

The two Spaniards had themselves a short palaver, then the one with the large national flag went to the stern and draped it over the shattered stern. The one with the bed sheet gave his to a sailor who went up the mainmast shrouds to the ravaged fighting top to bind it to the after-most stay.

"We . . . yield to you, *señor*!" a young *Aspirante,* the Spanish equivalent of a Midshipman, shouted back. "We strike!"

"*Now,* you can form a boarding party, Mister Westcott, and take possession of her," Lewrie said, whooping in triumph. He looked aft to see how close the other Spanish frigate was, and caught sight of her as she began a slow turn alee. She was breaking off, now that her consort had surrendered. Whatever her captain had intended in bringing his ship back into action despite her parlous condition, it was evident that he'd seen the light, and recognised the futility of the gesture. She continued turning, performing a sloppy wear cross the eye of the wind, and began to limp Nor'east, possibly for Almeria.

"Should we go after her, too, sir?" Westcott asked from the foot of the starboard poop deck ladderway.

"Wish we could, but . . ." Lewrie said with a grimace. "Better we deal with the bird in hand. Fetch-to, sir, and fetch up the boats from astern.

Somebody who knows the language tell our Spaniards to fetch-to, as well."

Captain Pomfret shouted that over to the frigate, then frowned over the reply. "They say their steering's gone, Captain Lewrie, and are unable. They . . ." He paused to listen to further shouts. "They say they will take in all sail, but they will need assistance to set things back in order."

"Very well," Lewrie said with a weary sigh, "I'll have the Carpenter and his crew, the Bosun and his Mate, the Sailmaker and his Mate, and a working-party of topmen, with some strong-backed Landsmen, board her, along with two files of Marines."

"Aye, sir," Westcott said, "I'll see it organised, directly."

"Best include Mister Snelling and his Surgeon's Mates, too, if they can be spared from tending our own wounded," Lewrie added. "How many of ours are down?"

"Ehm, seven dead and nineteen wounded, sir," Westcott grimly toted up. "Amazing, really."

Lewrie leaned far out over the poop deck bulwarks to survey the engaged side of his ship, noting the shot holes, the places where enemy roundshot had lodged when they failed to penetrate, and the dents in the stout oak scantlings where balls had struck but bounced off. The order for Secure From Quarters had been piped, and the muzzles of the guns were jerking back inboard, and those ports that had survived were being lowered. He was amazed, and grateful, that all those hits that should have filled his gun decks with swarms of splinters had not scythed down dozens more of his men!

"Put Mister Harcourt and Mister Elmes to our own repairs, Mister Westcott," Lewrie ordered, then shambled loose-hipped down the ladderway to the quarterdeck, strongly desiring a sit-down, perhaps even a lie-down, and a pint of small-beer. His throat was parched and raspy from shouting orders, his leg, which he had thought completely healed, was faintly aching, and he was suddenly bone-weary and drooping in the lassitude which always seemed to overtake him after a long, hard fight. His head was nodding, and it was hard for him to keep his eyes open.

"A splendid victory, if I may say so, Captain Lewrie," Pomfret congratulated. "Not that I know much of naval battles. Even taking a spectator's part in one still leaves me full of questions."

"Splendid?" Lewrie responded, shrugging. "I'll have t'take your word for that, Captain Pomfret."

# CHAPTER FORTY-ONE

Lewrie had ordered his collapsible wood-and-canvas deck chair fetched up to the poop deck, and had taken himself a long, restoring nap, oblivious for the better part of an hour to the thuds, bangs, and screechings of saws as *Sapphire*'s damage was seen to sufficient for a safe return to Gibraltar. He was wakened by a wet nose, then a wet tongue, and some wee, tentative "wakey-wakey" woofs from Bisquit, who had gotten over his terror of loud gunfire and was seeking comfort and attention to acknowledge him, and give him pets.

He cossetted the dog for a few minutes, then got to his feet, a bit stiff and sore, but well-rested, had several dips of water from the nearest scuttlebutt, and returned to duty.

"Mister Snelling and the Spanish Surgeon and their Mates have had their hands full, sir," Lt. Westcott reported, shuffling through a sheaf of notes he'd made. "There were nigh three hundred men in *San Pedro*'s crew, and we've found nearly ninety of them dead, with over an hundred men wounded." That drew an amazed whistle from Lewrie. "Her captain and two of her other officers are among the slain. Half her larboard guns are dis-mounted, carriages shattered, and one burst. That explains the flash and smoke we saw, sir. We've rigged a spare spanker to the stump of her mizen, and cut away and jettisoned everything that got shot off . . . they had plenty of spare spars, so we can get tops'ls up, and we can replace her fore course and main course. All in all, she can be got under way by dusk. Her jib boom's dicey-looking, but it'll take a foresail or two, for balance on the helm, which we've re-roved, so she'll steer . . . after a fashion."

"Want her, Geoffrey?" Lewrie asked. "If only for a time?"

"They don't award Fifth Rates to Lieutenants, or Commanders," Westcott laughed off. "Better you assign Harcourt the chore, again. If the Gibraltar dockyards can set her right, and she's off for home, let him take the chance of re-assignment."

"But, if Admiralty makes *him* a Commander, not you . . . sooner or later, you *must* be promoted," Lewrie protested. "You've more than earned it."

"Still trying to get rid of me?" Westcott scoffed. "That hurts!"

"You'd rather stay and be amused by my foolishness?" Lewrie asked with a brow up.

"Oh, something like that," Westcott replied, with a grin and a shrug. "By the by, the other frigate is the *San Pablo,* and they *were* sister ships, and have always worked together since they were put in commission two years ago, sir. Saints Peter and Paul? She's still in sight, off to the Nor'east, about six or seven miles away, barely making steerage way."

"Hmm, let's go after her, and make it a clean sweep," Lewrie decided of a sudden. "God knows we could use the prize money, whenever *that* comes due. Our prisoners aboard the *San Pedro* are well in hand?"

"All Spanish arms, even personal knives, are secured, and the spirits stores are well-guarded," Westcott told him. "Those still on their feet we've herded round the mainmast, now the heavy work's done, so I should assume so. We've three files of Marines aboard her, to boot, under Lieutenant Roe."

"We'll gamble, then, and go after the other," Lewrie ordered. "Get us under way to the Nor'east, Mister Westcott."

"Aye aye, sir!" was the eager, hungry reply.

HMS *Sapphire* had hardly begun to sail after the *San Pablo* when urgent cries came from the lookouts aloft. "Th' Chase is rollin' on her beam ends! Deck, there! Th' Chase looks t'be sinkin'!"

"Clap on sail, Mister Westcott," Lewrie snapped.

Lewrie went up to the poop deck and raised his telescope. It was a much better vantage point than his old practice of scaling the mainmast shrouds almost to the cat-harpings, and even suited his lazy nature!

"Damme, she's goin'!" he muttered.

The frigate's masts were canted far over to larboard, and she looked very low in the water, with the sea breaking mildly just under her line of gun-ports though he could see the coppering tacked to her stern, as if she was also down by the head with her stern cocked up. Looking closer, he could make out weak streams of water gushing from her, as if her sailors were flailing away madly at her pumps, but it seemed a losing fight.

"Cast of the log!" he demanded.

"Seven and a half knots, sir!" Midshipman Griffin shouted back after a long minute to let the log-line run and be pinched after the sand ran out of a minute glass.

*We'll be too late*, Lewrie thought; *Those poor buggers*.

Time out of mind, since Tudor days, England and Spain had detested each other, and it was natural to loathe the Dons. When engaged at war with them, in the heat of battle at close broadsides or teeth-to-teeth with crossed blades, killing them any way possible without a thought and exulting in their slaughter bothered good Englishmen no more than piling up dead rabbits, or a terrier's kills in a rat pit.

Helpless sailors of any nation, though . . . men who risked the sea and its perils, and who were suffering a fate that could befall any British sailor, if his luck ran out, that was another matter.

It would take *Sapphire* the better part of an hour to reach the stricken frigate, and she would slip beneath the waves long before, no matter what frantic efforts the Spanish could do to prolong the inevitable.

Six miles off, and Lewrie could see what was left of her upperworks falling free over her larboard side as her sailors chopped, cut, and axed away everything standing above her fighting tops to ease the weight that was dragging her over. For a short, hopeful moment, she did come a bit more upright, but those shot holes that had been blown into her a little below the waterline continued to flood her innards.

Four miles off, and quarterdeck and forecastle guns were cast overside, but that made little difference. The *San Pablo* had borne her ship's boats on the boat-tier beams that spanned the waist, and they had been turned to scrap wood, but they were freed and shoved by human force to the larboard side, where great sections of the bulwarks that remained were hacked down, and the boats put over, though not a one of them floated.

Three miles off, and Lewrie could see the tangle of ropes that bound spare sails that had been fothered over the shot holes, and the fothering patches seeming to *breathe* as air compressed in her orlop and bilges pressed out, and the sea dimpled them inward.

Two miles off, and the *San Pablo*'s bows were submerged up to the forecastle, and she suddenly roiled onto her larboard side and began to go down in a foaming welter of great air bubbles and flying spray shot out of her hull.

"Damme, damme, damme!" Lewrie muttered, closing the tubes of his telescope, thinking that he could hear the mortal groaning noises of a proud ship beginning to drown, and the faint screams and prayers for salvation from her crew!

Her masts slid under, 'til only the mizen stood above the sea, and a hint of her taffrails and her captain's cabin windows, the red-gold-red flag of Spain still flying, and then even that was gone in a boiling froth of foam as she gave up her last exhale and headed for the bottom.

"Fetch-to, close as you can, Mister Westcott, and man all the boats," Lewrie ordered, chiding himself for not going after her sooner. Even with aid so close, the long minutes required to bring up to the winds and bring the boats up from astern, then man them and get them off, was too long for many of the Spanish sailors. Some survivors clung to broken yards or the shattered ship's boats, some hung on to floating hatch gratings, and some of the frigate's walking wounded lay atop them. But Lewrie could see many bodies floating face-down and drowned, and what had become of her badly wounded who could not be moved from her belowdecks surgery did not bear thinking about. Many men who'd managed to escape her had gotten entangled in the confused masses of standing and running rigging and had drowned, unable to claw their way to the surface, and . . . it appeared that it was not only the majority of British sailors that could not swim, but it was the same case with the Spanish. Spanish sailors were thrashing in panic, flailing the water and slipping under even as he watched!

All he could do was pace the poop deck, head down so he didn't have to watch any longer, with his hands clasped in the small of his back, trying to shut out the terrified shouts, screams, and prayers and play stern and stoic, and wait for the final report.

"Ah, Mister Westcott," Lewrie said at last as his First Officer came to the poop deck after the last boat had been recovered. "What's the count?"

"We only managed to save fifty-nine of them, sir," Westcott said, lifting his hat in formal salute. "None of her officers or her Mids. Her captain . . . he was determined to go down with his ship, and those in command who'd survived the fight swore they'd do the same. Damned if they didn't gather in his cabins for a last drink before she went. I've never *heard* the like!"

"Perhaps the Spanish treasury is so empty, he thought it likely they'd ask him t'pay t'replace her," Lewrie said with a brief snort of the blackest of gallows humour. "Poor devils. Rig out boats for towing, and get us under way to rejoin our prize, Mister Westcott."

"Aye, sir," Westcott said, looking grim and disappointed with his best efforts to save more. "Shape course for Gibraltar?"

"Aye, Gibraltar," Lewrie said, nodding gravely. He lingered on the poop deck for several minutes to savour the airs. It was getting on for November, and even the Mediterranean was turning brisk. The sun was lowering in the West, getting on towards dusk, and the skies in that direction were almost glowing amber, yellow, and red.

*Red skies at night, sailor's delight,* he glumly thought, though far from delighted by then. At last, he descended to the quarterdeck, hoping that his cabins, which he had not seen since the ship had gone to Quarters that morning, might have been put back in some semblance of decent order, though he dreaded the idea that he would have to dine in his officers who remained aboard, along with Captain Pomfret and a few Mids; they'd be cock-a-whoop boisterous, too ready to celebrate, and he would have much preferred to dine alone, just him and Chalky.

"Too bad about the other Spanish frigate, ain't it, sir?" Captain Pomfret commented. "All those poor, drowned men! Still, defeating two enemy ships in one day is quite a rare feat, I should think. Make all the papers and cheer folks back home something wondrous! My congratulations, Captain Lewrie . . . even if, as I understand the process of 'to the victor go the spoils', your ship will only reap prize money on the one, what?"

"You shall share in it, too, Captain Pomfret," Lewrie assured him with a faint grin. "You were present upon our decks. Take joy o' that. Dine with me tonight. With any luck, my cook, Yeovill, will prepare us something special."

"Delighted to hear that I should prosper, even in a small way, and I would also be delighted to dine, and celebrate your victory," Pomfret eagerly said.

"Yes, it was a victory, wasn't it?" Lewrie mused, wanting no more than to go aft and get off his feet. "Not completely mine, though. If a grand victory it was, it's *Sapphire*'s victory, *their* victory," he said, pointing forward to the many sailors on deck. "It's *always* theirs."

# EPILOGUE

I begin by taking. I shall find scholars afterwards to demonstrate my perfect right.

FREDERICK II, THE GREAT
KING OF PRUSSIA (1712-1786)

# CHAPTER FORTY-TWO

Captain Sir Alan Lewrie, Bart., was having one of the worst mornings of his life. To say that he felt rowed beyond all temperance, to describe his mood of being betrayed, and as ill-used as if assailed by so many bears, would be an understatement.

He could not return aboard HMS *Sapphire* and indulge in a roaring, satisfying rage in the privacy of his great-cabins; that would result in a terrorised cat, a howling ship's dog, and cringing cabin-servants, and possibly the abuse of his furniture, and stubbed toes. Quite possibly his officers, Mids, and sailors who could not help over-hearing a long, curse-laden tirade, and the gay tinkle of flung glassware, might imagine that he'd taken complete leave of his senses.

Lewrie *could* relate the wrenching circumstances to Lieutenant Geoffrey Westcott later, after he had drained off all his bile, but it was not yet time for that; he had to *see* straight, first, and, at the moment, he felt that if he looked in a mirror, his eyes would be red, like a Viking Berserker warrior of old!

*I* may *laugh about this in future . . . but I rather doubt it,* he fumed to himself.

Naturally, he would not go to his mistress's, Maddalena Covilhã's lodgings and burden *her* with it. She'd think him demented, and fear that she'd made a bad bargain with a raving lunatick, one she'd never know when he might go off, again, perhaps on her. Maddalena *seemed* intelligent enough a woman to understand, but it might be more than an hour, and three bottles of wine, before he completely vented.

No, the only person upon whom he could empty his spleen was Mr. Thomas Mountjoy, for part of his bad news affected that worthy's operations, and if he hadn't heard about it yet, Mountjoy would surely be as shocked as he was, and just as angry.

"Deacon," Lewrie growled at the dangerous fellow as he entered Mountjoy's lodgings, not caring how he took the curtness. "Is he in?"

"Yes, Captain Lewrie, I'll announce . . ." Deacon offered, but Lewrie brushed past him and thundered up the stairs to the top-floor set of rooms, burst through the door into the sitting room, and bawled, "Damn 'em, Mountjoy, those two bloody fools, Dalrymple and Middleton, have taken away my boats! How the Devil am I t'land troops? They're going t'be turned into harbour gunboats!"

He caught Mountjoy at his small dining table in his shirtsleeves, with a napkin tucked into his collar, carefully picking away the shell of a cupped, boiled egg, the perfect picture of domestic bliss.

"I know," Mountjoy said, so calmly that Lewrie felt the sudden urge to leap over the table, take him by the throat, and throttle him.

"You *know?* Bloody Hell!" Lewrie roared. "What the . . . ?"

"Given the sudden change in circumstances, 'the Dowager' don't think we should be antagonising the Spanish any longer," Mountjoy said as he dug into his soft-boiled egg with a tiny spoon and took a dainty bite. "As London has long wished, Dalrymple now wishes that the Dons direct their outrage 'gainst the French, not us. He made a strong request . . . well, call it an order sugared with a veiled threat . . . that we, you and I, suspend offensive operations 'til the situation sorts itself out."

"Shut down?" Lewrie gawped, feeling as if his head would pop. "When were *you* goin' t'tell me? And, *what* bloody circumstances?"

"Marshal Junot's Army of Observation has crossed the Pyrenees, and is marching on Portugal," Mountjoy matter-of-factly told him, as if it was no more vital a matter than the morning's temperature. "We got word of it last evening, so it's days late, and Junot is probably already near Salamanca, and making good time, so our ambassador in Lisbon, Lord Strangford, relates. Oddest damned thing . . ."

Mountjoy paused to smear butter and jam on a slice of toast, take a bite, and chew.

"Odd? Yayss?" Lewrie prompted, his sarcasm dripping.

"Just round midnight last night, I received a covert despatch from Romney Marsh, from Madrid, announcing the very same news," Mountjoy said. "A poulterer came to the door with two chickens I did not order, with Marsh's note. 'Contract signed, goods on way to Lisbon, Madrid merchants out-bid and upset', it said. Meaning, I take it, that there was some formal, written pact or treaty arranged by Godoy and his arse-licking Francophiles, and that news of a French Army on Spanish soil has outraged your common Spaniard to no end. Better for Godoy had he *not* put it down on paper, and let it happen with little notice, but, that's *his* problem."

"Marsh? That fool?" Lewrie spat.

"Oh, as mad as a hatter, is Romney Marsh," Mountjoy heartily agreed, laughing, "but if he's a fool, he's a most useful one."

"Mine arse on a band-box," Lewrie said, all his pent-up, eager to be spilled rage quite flown his head, leaving him feeling deflated and weak in the knees. He pulled out a chair and sat down.

"Tea?" Mountjoy offered. "And, there's a basket of toast."

"We're t'make nice with the Spanish now, are we?" Lewrie asked. "Just let bygones be bygones, and hope they come t'love us?"

"That may take some doing on their part, since you've done such a grand job of making their lives miserable, of late," Mountjoy told him with a snicker. "I've word that that battery you bombarded has been abandoned, the one you blew up won't be re-built, and even the semaphore towers you burned have been left in ruins. I *told* you that Spain is completely broke. With so much of Spain's treasury going to the French, there's little left to spend on their own needs. Spain's less a French ally than one of her impoverished colonies.

"To add insult to injury, here you just up and bested two of the best frigates left to the Spanish Navy," Mountjoy went on, imparting Lewrie with a cheery wink. "Congratulations on that. 'The Dowager' is of the same mind, and thought it a fine feat, but . . . Dalrymple also believes that, now the French have violated Spanish sovereignty, we've done more than enough to rub their proud noses in the muck, and shame them. Do have a cup of tea while it's still hot."

"Have some brandy t'go with it?" Lewrie grumpily demanded.

"But of course I do, good fellow!" Mountjoy said, springing to his feet to fetch a bottle.

*Good fellow?* Lewrie thought, scowling; *Please, mine arse! I'll not be cossetted like a dog who does tricks!*

"The troops, the transport?" Lewrie asked as Mountjoy returned with the brandy. "What happens to them?"

"Surplus to requirements, I'm afraid," Mountjoy said, sighing as if in sympathy. "Captain Pomfret, and the detachment of the 77th, will be off to Sicily to re-join their regiments in the field, with an host of good stories to tell, I should imagine. Captain Hedgepeth is most likely taking the transport to Lisbon."

Halfway through stirring sugar and lemon into his brandy-laced cup of tea, Lewrie raised a questioning brow. "Lisbon?"

"Our ambassador, Lord Strangford, and his retinue, must be evacuated, along with all British subjects," Mountjoy replied. "So many engaged in the wine, port, and sherry trade, so many merchants, and so many debtors hiding out in Portugal from their creditors in England? Hedgepeth and his *Harmony* might even be hired on to evacuate the royal family. A fellow in my line of work at the embassy sent me a letter in the same packet with the ambassador's, stating that he has it on good assurance that the Regent, Prince João, is determined to leave nothing to the French, and he'll not leave a single member of his courtiers or ministers behind to head a puppet government, so dozens and dozens of ships will be necessary. Prince João intends to move everything to the Vice-Royalty of Brazil."

"Hope the courtiers enjoy all the mosquitos," Lewrie gloomed.

As he poured himself another cup of tea, admittedly one more a tea-flavoured brandy, Mountjoy went on to praise the sagacity of the Regent of Portugal, who had seen the handwriting on the wall when Emperor Napoleon Bonaparte had initiated his Continental System to deny Britain any European trade, certain that he'd be threatened to join or else face invasion and conquest. Prince João had pretended to agree, but had strung out the negotiations so long that Bonaparte had lost patience, realising that he had been played the fool.

"My counterpart wrote that João is also determined to ship the crown jewels, the treasury, the royal libraries, and even the gilded coaches to Brazil," Mountjoy said with another wink, leaning closer and lowering his voice as if French grenadiers had their ears pressed to the doors. "He's been packing up and preparing for months, can you imagine?"

"What's in the jam pot?" Lewrie asked. "Orange marmalade?"

"Hmm?" Mountjoy replied, looking dis-appointed that Lewrie was not gushingly impressed. "Lemon marmalade."

"Give it a shove in my direction, if ye please," Lewrie asked. As long as he had to listen to Mountjoy jawing on, he decided that he could have a wee bite, as well. With nothing more for *Sapphire* to do and offensive operations scotched, he thought that he might even take up whist, or chess! Or try to learn Spanish.

"D'ye think I might be useful at Lisbon?" Lewrie wondered.

"I believe we've a squadron there already, under Sir Sydney Smith," Mountjoy told him, furrowing his brow to recall correctly. "For now, I'm sure that Dalrymple and Captain Middleton would prefer that there's a naval presence at Gibraltar . . . some sailors to man the new gunboats? For now, there's no more call for any further chaos or mayhem along the Spanish coast. I've Cummings and his boat to keep me in touch with agents and their informers, so I can get a sense of how the Spanish are taking their government's surrender to Bonparte's whim. Who knows, sir? That one request we got for British arms for a rebellion 'gainst Madrid might be repeated, and become widespread! Imagine your ship sailing into some major port in Andalusia, with arms to land, and being cheered in the streets!"

"That'd take some *fanciful* imagining," Lewrie groused.

"Well, think on this," Mountjoy posed, leaning closer, again, lest he'd be overheard by French pigeons on the gallery outside. "We know that Dalrymple has good relations with his opposite number, General Castaños. If he and his officers are disgusted enough that they rebel against Madrid, that could ignite the whole country, and open a door for a British army to land, then, in hand with the Spanish, head for Cádiz and take it from behind!

"Then, there's an earlier despatch that Marsh sent me, anent internal divisions in Madrid which may bubble over to our advantage," Mountjoy went on in that insufferable "I know something you don't" way that had always irked Lewrie, "King Carlos of Spain's been reduced to a figurehead, under Godoy and his set of French-lovers, and the Spanish people blame *him* for all their troubles. They'd rather have Ferdinand, his heir, on the throne, even if he is a dim-witted, lantern-jawed fool. King Carlos distrusts Ferdinand, Ferdinand's plotting to take the throne and get rid of Godoy, and Godoy is plotting against Ferdinand, so some sort of coup is *bound* to happen which could turn all Spain topsy-turvy, and against the French, at last."

"I'll believe it when I see it happen," Lewrie grumped, going for another slice of toast, the butter plate, and the jam pot.

"It means nothing to you?" Mountjoy exclaimed, unable to grasp that Lewrie was not as enthusiastic over the prospects as he. "But of course, the suspension of operations, losing the troops, transport, and those boats has been an appalling wrench, just when you were getting so good at these new-fangled 'amphibious' landings."

"It ain't just that," Lewrie grumbled. "It's the Prize-Court."

# CHAPTER FORTY-THREE

"The Prize-Court?" Mountjoy asked, puzzled.

"The bastards," Lewrie said, getting his "fume" back, nigh as hot as before. "Oh, there's no problem with the *San Pedro,* that's as clear as day. No, it's that French *corvette* I brought in months ago, *Le Cerf.* Comes of me tryin' t'be just too clever by half! Remember that I had all four transports fly Navy ensigns, and pretend t'be a squadron? Well, the transports' masters, and the shipowners, got an idea in their greedy little civilian heads that if they *pretended* t'be frigates, and sailed into battle 'stead of runnin' off like they were supposed to do, then they were 'in sight' at the moment the *corvette* struck her colours, and it's Navy custom for all ships of the Fleet 'in sight' when that happens get t'share in the prize money! They've put together a suit t'get their cut, and sent a lawyer down from London to argue for 'em!"

"My word!" Mountjoy exclaimed. "Can they really do that?"

"Whether they can or not, they've laid the suit, and it'll be *years* 'fore a final ruling," Lewrie gravelled. "The local Court'll rule, but it'll have to go to Admiralty, maybe as high as the Privy Council, to sort it all out. To make things worse, Colonel Fry, of the Kent Fusiliers, learned of it, and since they were play-actin' as Marines at the bulwarks of the transports, damned if the *regiment's* not laid a separate suit t'get their share, too, 'cause Army regiments have been seconded to serve as Marines in the past, and there's a precedent! If the Prize-Court rules in their favour, and the transports', it'd be the year 1900 before it's settled, as bad as a contested will in Chancery Court! If any o' my crew is still livin' when it's settled, they *might* get enough t'buy a bottle of Gibraltar 'Blackstrap' wine! Christ!"

"Hmm . . . well, look on the bright side, sir," Mountjoy urged, striving for a sympathetic note to his voice, though Lewrie could see that he was having a hard time stifling his amusement. "You have the Spanish frigate to make up for it, and isn't there some monetary reward for the other, even if she sank? What do they call it, Head and Gun Money, depending on how many cannon and men were aboard her? You have that straightforward, and . . . there *is* the credit you have won for the doing. I shall write Mister Peel in London to make sure that your victory is properly appreciated by Admiralty, by the Secretary of State at War, and by the Crown. The involvement of Army detachments will receive proper praise at Horse Guards, as well. I guarantee it."

"Well . . ." Lewrie grumped, allowing himself to be cossetted out of his pet, after all.

"Not much I can do about your problem with the Prize-Court," Mountjoy added with a shrug, "but, perhaps Mister Peel may be able to portray the Army's suit, and the transport owners' suit, as grasping and greedy in the London papers. One never knows, public sentiment can be quite powerful, now and then. A description of how clever your ruse was when confronted with two French warships might sway opinion to your side."

"Well, there is that," Lewrie grudgingly allowed. "The tracts that the abolitionists circulated saved my bacon when I got tried for stealin' slaves, even if I'll *never* live down 'Saint Alan' or 'Black Alan the Liberator'. Gawd!"

"That's the spirit, Captain Lewrie!" Mountjoy said, all but giving him an encouraging pat on the back. "In the meantime, there's the gunboats that Captain Middleton is getting. They'll need to be armed and manned, and that'll keep you and your crew busy here in the harbour. I know, you don't want them to go too stale, so you could leave some behind and cruise the coast, as you did before, while the men left in harbour staff the gunboats. In rotation, perhaps? Cruise, and make a *minor* nuisance of yourself 'gainst Spanish shipping. Can't guarantee how long that may last, mind. As far as Admiralty is concerned, you are still on Independent Orders, seconded to me, but that could change, depending on how London reacts to the invasion of Portugal. More tea, Captain Lewrie?"

"After I return," Lewrie said, getting up. "Where do ye keep your 'necessary'?" He needed a good, long pee.

"In the bed-chamber, yonder," Mountjoy said, rising to see him in the right direction, then sat and poured himself another cup.

In mid-pee, Mountjoy had a second thought, and shouted from the dining table to the bed-chamber. "By the way, Dalrymple told me that the Spanish authorities have sent word about Major Hughes!"

"Alive, is he?" Lewrie shouted back.

"Alive and well, and free on his parole at Málaga!" Mountjoy informed him. "And may be for some time, the damned fool."

Lewrie returned from the bed-chamber and came to the table to pour, sweeten, and add lemon to a fresh cup. Mountjoy waved him to take the air on the rooftop gallery.

"How long?" Lewrie asked.

"When asked to declare his name and rank, Hughes said that he was a Major," Mountjoy happily explained, leaning on the balustrade and sipping his tea. "Not a Brevet-Major, or his substantive rank of Captain, but plain Major. So, unless we've a Spanish officer of the same rank in custody, or several lower-ranked officers to exchange for him, I fear he's doomed to languish. Dalrymple and the officers of his regimental mess are putting together a package for him, his ready cash, and his back-pay, so Hughes can afford decent lodgings and keep himself well-fed, well-liquoured, and amused. Now, on the off-chance that Spain becomes our ally anytime soon, they might send him back, with no exchange necessary, but . . ." Mountjoy said with a wry shrug. "The Spanish allowed him to send some letters to his family, and to his regimental mess, to make arrangements about his camp gear and his kit, what debts to clear with Gibraltar merchants, and such."

"Did Hughes write to Maddalena?" Lewrie asked, "Was there anything for her up-keep?"

"Not a word, and not a farthing," Mountjoy told him, screwing up his face in dislike for the man. "Will you tell her of his fate?"

"In passing, perhaps," Lewrie told him, "though I doubt that she'd care overly much. He treated her callously, the damned swine."

"In that regard, Captain Lewrie, as you are in a great many things, you are a very fortunate man," Mountjoy gravely praised him. "Take joy for as long as orders, and circumstances, let you."

"Thankee for the sentiment, Mountjoy, and I intend to," Lewrie told him. "Well, now I've shed my anger, I'll be off. Let me know if there's anything in the works along your line I could help with."

*Harbour-guard work? Work my men up t'man gunboats? Lord!* he thought as he strolled the quayside. He wondered how long that training would take, before he could get his ship back to sea for some of those nuisance cruises, how would he man his ship short-handed if he had to leave a sizable portion in port while he was away, and where could the men left behind be lodged without a ship? He *could* use the prison hulk, the old *Guerrier,* for a temporary barracks, but she was arsehole to elbow with Spanish and French prisoners, already, and the sicknesses that arose so readily in the hulks could kill half of them in a fortnight!

*Christ, I'll have t'be* nice *to Captain Middleton!* he thought; *All co-operative and full o' suggestions about armin' the damned gunboats! I'll have t'be* helpful*!*

That picture was just too dreadful to be contemplated. He had lost, and it irked him sorely; lost his boats, lost the transport, lost the troops, and lost his mission, reduced to being a temporary Senior Naval Officer Present, again.

*Has its compensations, though,* he realised, feeling a burst of whimsy; *There's Maddalena, for as long as the Navy lets* that *last.*

He spun about from approaching the quays to take a boat out to *Sapphire* and set off with a purposeful stride for her lodgings, trotted up the stairs, and knocked on the door. A long minute later, and the lock was opened, and the door swung open.

"Alan! *Meu querido!*" Maddalena said with a surprised but instantly happy smile on her face. "So early! Come in! I was washing my hair, so excuse the way I . . . !"

She was clad in her dressing gown, her long, dark hair up in a towel wrap, damp underneath all from a sponge bath, and wisps of her hair wetly clinging to him as he swept her into his arms and kissed her, lifted her off her feet, and danced her round the room.

"Uhmm, what is this for, Alan?" she breathlessly asked, laughing in delight.

"Thought I'd take you out to dine, Maddalena," Lewrie told her, leaning back a bit to savour the joy in her eyes. "Catch you before you started cooking anything, and enjoy a long, delicious dinner with you. Sound good to you?"

"Oh, yes! I would love it! I will wear my new gown, it's the pale blue one," Maddalena happily agreed. "I hope you will like it."

"I'd like you in anything, Maddalena," Lewrie vowed.

"Let me dry my hair and change," she said, slipping away, with her hands trailing down his coat sleeves to his fingers as if loath to be separated, then almost danced behind her screen to complete her preparations. "There is wine in the cooling bucket," she offered.

Lewrie lifted the bottle from the water bucket and poured himself a glass, then wandered round the lodgings, a grin on his face.

"Hallo, bird," he said to the warbler in its cage, waggling fingers to lure it to the bars. "Hallo, Precious," he said to the kitten, and tossed the cork for a toy, which got pounced and footballed in a twinkling.

"Honey, I'm *home!*" he whispered, immensely pleased with Life, for as long as the good parts lasted, at least.